WOLFVILLE NIGHTS

"HE HEAVES THIS SILVER PHIL ON HIGH TO THE LENGTH OF HIS LONG ARM."—*Page 37.*

Wolfville Nights

by

Alfred Henry Lewis

Author of "Wolfville", "Wolfville Days", "Peggy O'Nea", &c.

WILDSIDE PRESS

CONTENTS.

To

William Greene Sterett,

this volume is

inscribed.

NEW YORK CITY,

August 1, 1902

MY DEAR STERETT:—

In offering this book to you I might
have advantage of the occasion to express my
friendship and declare how high I hold you as a
journalist and a man. Or I might speak of those
years at Washington when in the gallery we worked
shoulder to shoulder; I might recall to you the wit
of Hannum, or remind you of the darkling Barrett,
the mighty Decker, the excellent Cohen, the
vivid Brown, the imaginative Miller, the volatile
Angus, the epigrammatic Merrick, the quietly
satirical Splain, Rouzer the earnest, Boynton the
energetic, Carson the eminent, and Dunnell, famous
for a bitter, frank integrity. I might remember
that day when the gifted Fanciulli, with no more
delicate inspiration than crackers, onions, and
cheese, and no more splendid conservatory than
Shoemaker's, wrote, played and consecrated to you
his famous "Lone Star March" wherewith he so
disquieted the public present of the next concert in

the White House grounds. Or I might hark back
to the campaign of '92, when together we struggled
against national politics as evinced in the city of
New York; I might repaint that election night
when, with one hundred thousand whirling dervishes
of democracy in Madison Square, dancing dances,
and singing songs of victory, we undertook through
the hubbub to send from the "Twenty-third street
telegraph office" half-hourly bulletins to our papers
in the West; how you, accompanied of the dignified Richard Bright, went often to the Fifth
Avenue Hotel; and how at last you dictated your
bulletins—a sort of triumphant blank verse, they
were—as Homeric of spirit as lofty of phrase—to
me, who caught them as they came from your lips,
losing none of their fire, and so flashed them all
burning into Texas, far away. But of what avail
would be such recount? Distance separates us
and time has come between. Those are the old
years, these are the new, with newer years beyond.
Life like a sea is filling from rivers of experience.
Forgetfulness rises as a tide and creeps upward to
drown within us those stories of the days that were.
And because this is true, it comes to me that you
as a memory must stand tallest in the midst of my
regard. For of you I find within me no forgetfulness. I have met others; they came, they tarried,
they departed. They came again; and on this
second encounter the recollection of their existences
smote upon me as a surprise. I had forgotten
them as though they had not been. But such is

not your tale. Drawn on the plates of memory, as with a tool of diamond, I carry you both in broadest outline and in each least of shade ; and there hangs no picture in the gallery of hours gone, to which I turn with more of pleasure and of good. Nor am I alone in my recollection. Do I pass through the Fifth Avenue Hotel on my way to the Hoffman, that vandyked dispenser leans pleasantly across his counter, to ask with deepest interest: "Do you hear from the Old Man now?" Or am I belated in Shanley's, a beaming ring of waiters—if it be not an hour overrun of custom—will half-circle my table, and the boldest, "Pat," will question timidly, yet with a kindly Galway warmth : "How's the Old Man?" Old Man! That is your title : at once dignified and affectionate ; and by it you come often to be referred to along Broadway these ten years after its conference. And when the latest word is uttered what is there more to fame! I shall hold myself fortunate, indeed, if, departing, I'm remembered by half so many half so long. But wherefore extend ourselves regretfully? We may meet again ; the game is not played out. Pending such bright chance, I dedicate this book to you. It is the most of honour that lies in my lean power. And in so doing, I am almost moved to say, as said Goldsmith of Johnson in his offering of *She Stoops to Conquer :* "By inscribing this slight performance to you, I do not mean to so much compliment you as myself. It may do me some honour to inform the public that I have lived many

years in intimacy with you. It may serve the interests of mankind also to inform them that the
greatest wit may be found in a character without
impairing the most unaffected piety." I repeat, I
am all but moved to write these lines of you. It
would tell my case at least ; and while description
might limp in so far as you lack somewhat of that
snuffle of " true piety " so often engaging the John-
sonian nose, you make up the defect with possession of a wider philosophy, a better humour and a
brighter, quicker wit than visited or dwelt beneath
the candle-scorched wig of our old bully lexico-
grapher.

ALFRED HENRY LEWIS.

Some Cowboy Facts.

THERE are certain truths of a botanical character that are not generally known. Each year the trees in their occupation creep further west. There are regions in Missouri — not bottom lands — which sixty years ago were bald and bare of trees. To-day they are heavy with timber. Westward, beyond the trees, lie the prairies, and beyond the prairies, the plains; the first are green with long grasses, the latter bare, brown and with a crisp, scorched, sparse vesture of vegetation scarce worth the name. As the trees march slowly westward in conquest of the prairies, so also do the prairies, in their verdant turn, become aggressors and push westward upon the plains. These last stretches, extending to the base of that bluff and sudden bulwark, the Rocky Mountains, can go no further. The Rockies hold the plains at bay and break, as it were, the teeth of the desert. As a result of this warfare of vegetations, the plains are to first disappear in favour of the prairies; and the prairies to give way before the trees. These mutations all wait on rain; and as the rain belt goes ever and ever westward, a strip of plains each year surrenders its aridity, and the prairies and then the trees press on and take new ground.

These facts should contain some virtue of interest ; the more since with the changes chronicled, come also changes in the character of both the inhabitants and the employments of these regions. With a civilised people extending themselves over new lands, cattle form ever the advance guard. Then come the farms. This is the procession of a civilised, peaceful invasion; thus is the column marshalled. First, the pastoral; next, the agricultural; third and last, the manufacturing;—and per consequence, the big cities, where the treasure chests of a race are kept. Blood and bone and muscle and heart are to the front; and the money that steadies and stays and protects and repays them and their efforts, to the rear.

Forty years ago about all that took place west of the Mississipi of a money-making character was born of cattle. The cattle were worked in huge herds and, like the buffalo supplanted by them, roamed in unnumbered thousands. In a pre-railroad period, cattle were killed for their hides and tallow, and smart Yankee coasters went constantly to such ports as Galveston for these cargoes. The beef was left to the coyotes.

Cattle find a natural theatre of existence on the plains. There, likewise, flourishes the pastoral man. But cattle herding, confined to the plains, gives way before the westward creep of agriculture. Each year beholds more western acres broken by the plough ; each year witnesses a diminution of the cattle ranges and cattle herding. This need ring no bell of alarm concerning a future barren of a beef

supply. More cattle are the product of the farm-
regions than of the ranges. That ground, once
range and now farm, raises more cattle now than
then. Texas is a great cattle State. Ohio, Indiana,
Illinois, Iowa, and Missouri are first States of agriculture. The area of Texas is about even with
the collected area of the other five. Yet one finds
double the number of cattle in Ohio, Indiana, Illinois, Iowa, and Missouri than in Texas, to say
nothing of tenfold the sheep and hogs. No; one
may be calm; one is not to fall a prey to any hunger
of beef.

While the farms in their westward pushing do
not diminish the cattle, they reduce the cattleman and pinch off much that is romantic and
picturesque. Between the farm and the wire
fence, the cowboy, as once he flourished, has been
modified, subdued, and made partially to disappear.
In the good old days of the Jones and Plummer
trail there were no wire fences, and the sullen farmer
had not yet arrived. Your cowboy at that time
was a person of thrill and consequence. He wore
a broad-brimmed Stetson hat, and all about it a
rattlesnake skin by way of band, retaining head
and rattles. This was to be potent against head-
aches—a malady, by the way, which swept down
no cowboy save in hours emergent of a spree. In
such case the snake cure didn't cure. The hat was
retained in defiance of winds, by a leathern cord
caught about the back of the head, not under the
chin. This cord was beautiful with a garniture of

three or four perforated poker chips, red, yellow, and blue.

There are sundry angles of costume where the dandyism of a cowboy of spirit and conceit may acquit itself; these are hatband, spurs, saddle, and leggins. I've seen hatbands made of braided gold and silver filigree; they were from Santa Fe, and always in the form of a rattlesnake, with rubies or emeralds or diamonds for eyes. Such gauds would cost from four hundred to two thousand dollars. Also, I've encountered a saddle which depleted its proud owner a round twenty-five hundred dollars. It was of finest Spanish leather, stamped and spattered with gold bosses. There was gold-capping on the saddle horn, and again on the circle of the cantle. It was a dream of a saddle, made at Paso del Norte; and the owner had it cinched upon a bronco dear at twenty dollars. One couldn't have sold the pony for a stack of white chips in any faro game of that neighbourhood (Las Vegas) and they were all crooked games at that.

Your cowboy dandy frequently wears wrought steel spurs, inlaid with silver and gold; price, anything you please. If he flourish a true Brummel of the plains his leggins will be fronted from instep to belt with the thick pelt, hair outside, of a Newfoundland dog. These "chapps," are meant to protect the cowboy from rain and cold, as well as plum bushes, wire fences and other obstacles inimical, and against which he may lunge while riding headlong in the dark. The hair of the Newfoundland, thick and

long and laid the right way, defies the rains; and
your cowboy loathes water.

Save in those four cardinals of vanity enumerated,
your cowboy wears nothing from weakness; the rest
of his outfit is legitimate. The long sharp heels of
his boots are there to dig into the ground and hold
fast to his mother earth while roping on foot. His
gay pony when "roped" of a frosty morning would
skate him all across and about the plains if it were
not for these heels. The buckskin gloves tied in one
of the saddle strings are used when roping, and to
keep the half-inch manila lariat—or mayhap it's horse-
hair or rawhide pleated—from burning his hands.
The red silken sash one was wont aforetime to see
knotted about his waist, was used to hogtie and hold
down the big cattle when roped and thrown. The
sash—strong, soft and close—could be tied more
tightly, quickly, surely than anything besides. In
these days, with wire pastures and branding pens and
the fine certainty of modern round-ups and a
consequent paucity of mavericks, big cattle are
seldom roped; wherefor the sash has been much
cast aside.

The saddle-bags or "war-bags,"—also covered of
dogskin to match the leggins, and worn behind, not
forward of the rider—are the cowboy's official
wardrobe wherein he carries his second suit of
underclothes, and his other shirt. His handkerchief, red cotton, is loosely knotted about the cowboy's neck, knot to the rear. He wipes the sweat
from his brow therewith on those hot Texas days

when in a branding pen he "flanks" calves or
feeds the fires or handles the irons or stands off the
horned indignation of the cows, resentful because of
burned and bawling offspring.

It would take two hundred thousand words to
tell in half fashion the story of the cowboy. His
religion of fatalism, his courage, his rides at full
swing in midnight darkness to head and turn and
hold a herd stampeded, when a slip on the storm-
soaked grass by his unshod pony, or a misplaced
prairie-dog hole, means a tumble, and a tumble
means that a hundred and fifty thousand dollars
worth of cattle, with hoofs like chopping knives,
will run over him and make him look and feel and
become as dead as a cancelled postage stamp; his
troubles, his joys, his soberness in camp, his
drunkenness in town, and his feuds and occasional
"gun plays" are not to be disposed of in a preface.
One cannot in such cramped space so much as hit
the high places in a cowboy career.

At work on the range and about his camp—for,
bar accidents, wherever you find a cowboy you will
find a camp—the cowboy is a youth of sober quiet
dignity. There is a deal of deep politeness and
nothing of epithet, insult or horseplay where everybody wears a gun.

There are no folk inquisitive on the ranges. No
one asks your name. If driven by stress of conversation to something akin to it the cowboy will say:
"What may I call you, sir?" And he's as careful
to add the "sir," as he is to expect it in return.

You are at liberty to select what name you prefer. Where you hail from? where going? why? are queries never put. To look at the brand on your pony—you, a stranger—is a dangerous vulgarity to which no gentleman of the Panhandle or any other region of pure southwestern politeness would stoop. And if you wish to arouse an instant combination of hate, suspicion and contempt in the bosom of a cowboy you have but to stretch forth your artless Eastern hand and ask: " Let me look at your gun."

Cowboys on the range or in the town are exces-sively clannish. They never desert each other, but stay and fight and die and storm a jail and shoot a sheriff if needs press, to rescue a comrade made cap-tive in their company. Also they care for each other when sick or injured, and set one another's bones when broken in the falls and tumbles of their craft. On the range the cowboy is quiet, just and peaceable. There are neither women nor cards nor rum about the cow camps. The ranches and the boys themselves banish the two latter; and the first won't come. Women, cards and whiskey, the three war causes of the West, are confined to the towns.

Those occasions when cattle are shipped and the beef-herds, per consequence, driven to the shipping point become the only times when the cowboy sees the town. In such hours he blooms and lives fully up to his opportunity. He has travelled perhaps two hundred miles and has been twenty days on the trail, for cattle may only be driven about ten miles a day; he has been up day and night and slept half the

time in the saddle; he has made himself hoarse
singing "Sam Bass" and "The Dying Ranger"
to keep the cattle quiet and stave off stampedes; he
has ridden ten ponies to shadows in his twenty days
of driving, wherefore, and naturally, your cowboy
feels like relaxing.

There would be as many as ten men with each beef-
herd; and the herd would include about five thousand head. There would be six "riders," divided
into three watches to stand night guard over the
herd and drive it through the day; there would be
two "hoss hustlers," to hold the eighty or ninety
ponies, turn and turn about, and carry them along
with the herd; there would be the cook, with four
mules and the chuck wagon; and lastly there would
be the herd-boss, a cow expert he, and at the head
of the business.

Once the herd is off his hands and his mind at the
end of the drive, the cowboy unbuckles and reposes
himself from his labours. He becomes deeply and
famously drunk. Hungering for the excitement of
play he collides amiably with faro and monte and
what other deadfalls are rife of the place. Never
does he win; for the games aren't arranged that
way. But he enjoys himself; and his losses do not
prey on him.

Sated with faro bank and monte—they can't be
called games of chance, the only games of chance
occurring when cowboys engage with each other
at billiards or pool—sated, I say, with faro and
Mexican monte, and exuberant of rum, which last

has regular quick renewal, our cowboy will stagger to his pony, swing into the saddle, and with gladsome whoops and an occasional outburst from his six shooter directed toward the heavens, charge up and down the street. This last amusement appeals mightily to cowboys too drunk to walk. For, be it known, a gentleman may ride long after he may not walk.

If a theatre be in action and mayhap a troop of "Red Stocking Blondes," elevating the drama therein, the cowboy is sure to attend. Also he will arrive with his lariat wound about his body under his coat ; and his place will be the front row. At some engaging crisis, such as the "March of the Amazons," having first privily unwound and organised his lariat to that end, he will arise and "rope" an Amazon. This will produce bad language from the manager of the show, and compel the lady to sit upon the stage to the detriment of her wardrobe if no worse, and all to keep from being pulled across the footlights. Yet the exercise gives the cowboy deepest pleasure. Having thus distinguished the lady of his admiration, later he will meet her and escort her to the local dancehall. There, mingling with their frank companions, the two will drink, and loosen the boards of the floor with the strenuous dances of our frontier till daylight does appear.

For the matter of a week, or perchance two—it depends on how fast his money melts—in these fashions will our gentleman of cows engage his hours and expand himself. He will make a deal of noise, drink a deal of whiskey, acquire a deal of what he terms "action"; but he harms nobody, and, in a town toughened to his racket and which needs and gets his money, disturbs nobody.

"Let him whoop it up; he's paying for it, ain't he?" will be the prompt local retort to any inquiry as to why he is thus permitted to disport.

So long as the cowboy observes the etiquette of the town, he will not be molested or "called down" by marshal or sheriff or citizen. There are four things your cowboy must not do. He must not insult a woman; he must not shoot his pistol in a store or bar-room; he must not ride his pony into those places of resort; and as a last proposal he must not ride his pony on the sidewalks. Shooting or riding into bar-rooms is reckoned as dangerous; riding on the sidewalk comes more under the head of insult, and is popularly regarded as a taunting defiance of the town marshal. On such occasions the marshal never fails to respond, and the cowboy is called upon to surrender. If he complies, which to the credit of his horse-sense he commonly does, he is led into brief captivity to be made loose when cooled. Does he resist arrest, there is an explosive rattle of six shooters, a mad scattering of the careful citizenry out of lines of fire, and a cowboy or marshal is added to the host beyond. At the close of the festival, if the marshal still lives he is congratulated; if the cowboy survives he is lynched; if both fall, they are buried with the honours of frontier war; while whatever the event, the communal ripple is but slight and only of the moment, following which the currents of Western existence sweep easily and calmly onward as before.

A. H. L.

WOLFVILLE NIGHTS

CHAPTER I.

The Dismissal of Silver Phil.

"His name, complete, is 'Silver City Philip.' In them social observances of the Southwest wherein haste is a feacher an' brev'ty the bull's eye aimed at, said cognomen gets shortened to 'Silver Phil.'"

The Old Cattleman looked thoughtfully into his glass, as if by that method he collected the scattered elements of a story. There was a pause; then he lifted the glass to his lips as one who being now evenly equipped of information, proposed that it arrive hand in hand with the inspiration which should build a tale from it.

"Shore, this Silver Phil is dead now; an' I never yet crosses up with the gent who's that sooperfluous as to express regrets. It's Dan Boggs who dismisses Silver Phil; Dan does it in efforts he puts forth to faithfully represent the right.

"Doc Peets allers allows this Silver Phil is a 'degen'rate;' leastwise that's the word Peets uses. An' while I freely concedes I ain't none too cl'ar as to jest what a degen'rate is, I stands ready to back Peets' deescription to win. Peets is, bar Colonel William Greene Sterett, the best eddicated sharp in

Arizona; also the wariest as to expressin' views.
Tharfore when Peets puts it up, onflinchin', that
this yere Silver Phil's a degen'rate, you-all can
spread your blankets an' go to sleep on it that a
degen'rate he is.

"Silver Phil is a little, dark, ignorant, tousled-
ha'red party, none too neat in costume. He's as
black an' small an' evil-seemin' as a Mexican; still,
you sees at a glance he ain't no Greaser neither.
An' with all this yere surface wickedness, Silver
Phil has a quick, hyster'cal way like a woman or a
bird; an' thar's ever a grin on his face. You can
smell 'bad' off Silver Phil, like smoke in a house,
an' folks who's on the level—an' most folks is—
conceives a notion ag'in him the moment him an'
they meets up.

"The first time I observes Silver Phil, he's walkin' down the licker room of the Red Light. As he
goes by the bar, Black Jack—who's rearrangin' the
nosepaint on the shelf so it shows to advantage—
gets careless an' drops a bottle.

"'Crash!' it goes onto the floor.

"With the sound, an' the onexpected suddenness
of it stampedin' his nerves, that a-way, Silver Phil
leaps into the air like a cat; an' when he 'lights, he's
frontin' Black Jack an' a gun in each hand.

"'Which I won't be took!' says Silver Phil, all
flustered.

"His eyes is gleamin' an' his face is palin' an' his
ugly grin gets even uglier than before. But like a
flash, he sees thar's nothin' to go in the air about—

nothin' that means him; an' he puts up his hardware an' composes himse'f.

"'You-all conducts yourse'f like a sport who has something on his mind,' says Texas Thompson, who's thar present at the time, an' can't refrain from commentin' on the start that bottle-smashin' gives Silver Phil.

"This Silver Phil makes no response, but sort o' grins plenty ghastly, while his breath comes quick.

"Still, while you-all notes easy that this person's scared, it's plain he's a killer jest the same. It's frequent that a-way. I'm never much afraid of one of your cold game gents like Cherokee Hall; you can gamble the limit they'll never put a six-shooter in play till it's shorely come their turn. But timid, feverish, locoed people, whose jedgment is bad an' who's prone to feel themse'fs in peril; they're the kind who kills. For myse'f I shuns all sech. I won't say them erratic, quick-to-kill sports don't have courage; only it strikes me—an' I've rode up on a heap of 'em—it's more like a fear-bit f'rocity than sand.

"Take Enright or Peets or Cherokee or Tutt or Jack Moore or Boggs or Texas Thompson; you're plumb safe with sech gents—all or any. An' yet thar ain't the first glimmer of bein' gun-shy about one of 'em; they're as clean strain as the eternal granite, an' no more likely to hide out from danger than a hill. An' while they differs from each other, yet they're all different from sech folks as Silver Phil. Boggs, goin' to war, is full of good-humoured grandeur, gala and confident, ready to start or stop like a good hoss. Cherokee Hall is quiet an' wordless; he gets pale, but sharp an' deadly; an' his notion is to fight for a finish. Peets is haughty an' sooperior on the few o'casions when he onbends in battle, an' comports himse'f like a gent who fights downhill; the same, ondoubted, bein' doo to them book advantages of Peets which elevates him an' lifts him above the common herd a whole lot. Enright who's oldest is of course slowest to embark in blood, an' pulls his weepons—when he does pull 'em—with sorrowful resignation.

" 'Which I'm shorely saddest when I shoots,' says Enright to me, as he reloads his gun one time.

" These yere humane sentiments, however, don't deter him from shootin' soon an' aimin' low, which latter habits makes Wolfville's honoured chief a highly desp'rate game to get ag'inst.

" Jack Moore, bein' as I explains former, the ex-ecyootive of the Stranglers, an' responsible for law an' order, has a heap of shootin' shoved onto him from time to time. Jack allers transacts these fireworks with a ca'm, offishul front, the same bein' devoid, equal, of anger or regrets. Tutt, partic'lar after he weds Tucson Jennie, an' more partic'lar still when he reaps new honours as the originator of that blessed infant Enright Peets Tutt, carries on what shootin' comes his way in a manner a lot dignified an' lofty; while Texas Thompson—who's mebby morbid about his wife down in Laredo demandin' she be divorced that time—although he picks up his hand in a fracas, ready an' irritable an' with no delays, after all is that well-balanced he's bound to be each time plumb right.

"Which, you observes, son, from these yere settin's forth, that thar's a mighty sight of difference between gents like them pards of mine an' degen'-rates of the tribe of Silver Phil. It's the difference between right an' wrong; one works from a impulse of pure jestice, the other is moved of a sperit of crime; an' thar you be.

"Silver Phil, we learns later—an' it shore jestifies Peets in his theeries about him bein' a degen'rate— has been in plenty of blood. But allers like a cat; savage, gore-thirsty, yet shy, prideless, an' ready to fly. It seems he begins to be homicidal in a humble way by downin' a trooper over near Fort Cummings. That's four years before he visits us. He's been blazin' away intermittent ever since, and allers crooel, crafty an' safe. It's got to be a shore thing or Silver Phil quits an' goes into the water like a mink.

"This yere ondersized miscreant ain't ha'nted about Wolfville more'n four days before he shows how onnecessary he is to our success. Which he works a ha'r copper on Cherokee Hall. What's a ha'r copper? I'll onfold, short and terse, what Silver Phil does, an' then you saveys. Cherokee's dealin' his game—farobank she is; an' if all them national banks conducts themse'fs as squar' as that enterprise of Cherokee's, the fields of finance would be as safely honest as a church. Cherokee's turnin' his game one evenin'; Faro Nell on the lookout stool where she belongs. Silver Phil drifts up to the lay-out, an' camps over back of the king-end. He gets chips, an' goes to takin' chances alternate on the king, queen, jack, ten ; all side an' side they be. Cherokee bein' squar' himse'f ain't over-prone to expect a devious play in others. He don't notice this Silver Phil none speshul, an' shoves the kyards.

" Silver Phil wins three or four bets ; it's Nell that catches on to his racket, an' signs up to Cherokee onder the table with her little foot. One glance an' Cherokee is loaded with information. This Silver Phil, it seems, in a sperit of avarice, equips himse'f with a copper—little wooden checker, is what this copper is—one he's done filched from Cherokee the day prior. He's fastened a long black hoss-ha'r to it, an' he ties the other end of the hoss-ha'r to his belt in front. This ha'r is long enough as he's planted at the table that a-way, so it reaches nice to them four nearest kyards,—the king, queen, jack, ten. An' said ha'r is plumb invisible except to eyes as sharp as Faro Nell's. The deceitful Silver Phil will have a stack on one of 'em, coppered with this yere ha'r copper. He watches the box. As the turns is made, if the kyards come his way, well an' good. Silver Phil does nothin' but garners in results. When the kyards start to show ag'in him, however, that's different. In sech events Silver Phil draws in his breath, sort o' takin' in on the hoss-ha'r, an' the copper comes off the bet.

When the turn is made, thar's Silver Phil's bet—by virchoo of said fraud—open an' triumphant an' waitin' to be paid.

"Cherokee gets posted quick an' with a look. As sharp as winkin' Cherokee has a nine-inch bowie in his hand an' with one slash cuts the hoss-ha'r clost up by Silver Phil's belt.

"'That's a yoonique invention!' observes Cherokee, an' he's sarcastic while he menaces with the knife at Silver Phil; 'that contraption is shorely plenty sagacious! But it don't go here. Shove in your chips.' Silver Phil obeys: an' he shows furtive, ugly, an' alarmed, an' all of 'em at once. He don't say a word. 'Now pull your freight,' concloods Cherokee. 'If you ever drifts within ten foot of a game of mine ag'in I'll throw this knife plumb through you—through an' through.' An' Cherokee, by way of lustration lets fly the knife across the bar-room. It comes like a flash.

"'Chuck!'

"Thar's a picture paper pasted onto the wooden wall of the Red Light, displayin' the liniaments of some party. That bowie pierces the picture—a shot in the cross it is—an' all with sech fervour that the p'int of the blade shows a inch an' a half on the other side of that individyool board.

"'The next time I throws a knife in your presence,' remarks Cherokee to Silver Phil, an' Cherokee's as cold an' p'isonous as a rattlesnake, 'it'll be la'nched at you.'

"Silver Phil don't say nothin' in retort. He's

aware by the lib'ral way Cherokee sep'rates himse'f
from the bowie that said weepon can't constitoote
Cherokee's entire armament. An' as Silver Phil
don't pack the sperit to face no sech flashlight warrior, he acts on Cherokee's hint to *vamos*, an fades
into the street. Shore, Cherokee don't cash the
felon's chips none ; he confiscates 'em. Cherokee
ain't quite so tenderly romantic as to make good to
a detected robber. Moreover, he lets this Silver
Phil go onharmed when by every roole his skelp is
forfeit. It turns out good for the camp, however,
as this yere experience proves so depressin' to Silver
Phil he removes his blankets to Red Dog. Thar
among them purblind tarrapins, its inhabitants, it's
likely he gets prosperous an' ondetected action on
that little old ha'r copper of his.

" It's not only my beliefs, but likewise the opinions of sech joodicial sports as Enright, Peets, an'
Colonel Sterett, that this maverick, Silver Phil, is
all sorts of a crim'nal. An' I wouldn't wonder if
he's a pure rustler that a-way ; as ready to stand up
a stage as snake a play at farobank. This idee
settles down on the Wolfville intell'gence on the
heels of a vicissitoode wherein Dan Boggs performs,
an' which gets pulled off over in the Bird Cage
Op'ry House. Jack Moore ain't thar none that
time. Usual, Jack is a constant deevotee of the
dramy. Jack's not only a first-nighter, he comes
mighty clost to bein' a every-nighter. But this
partic'lar evenin' when Boggs performs, Jack's rummagin' about some'ers else.

"If Jack's thar, it's even money he'd a-had that second shot instead of Boggs; in which event, the results might have been something graver than this yere minoote wound which Boggs confers. I'm confident Jack would have cut in with the second shot for sech is his offishul system. Jack more'n once proclaims his position.

"'By every roole of law,' says Jack at epocks when he declar's himse'f, 'an' on all o'casions, I, as kettle-tender to the Stranglers, is entitled to the first shot. When I uses the term "o'casion," I would be onderstood as alloodin' to affairs of a simply social kind, an' not to robberies, hold-ups, hoss-larcenies, an' other an' sim'lar transactions in spec'latif crime when every gent defends his own. Speakin' social, however, I reasserts that by every roole of guidance, I'm entitled to the first shot. Which a doo regyard for these plain rights of mine would go far to freein' Wolfville upper circles of the bullets which occurs from time to time, an' which even the most onconventional admits is shore a draw-back. All I can add as a closer,' concloods Jack, 'is that I'll make haste to open on any sport who transgresses these fiats an' goes to shootin' first. Moreover, it's likely that said offender finds that when I'm started once, what I misses in the orig'nal deal I'll make up in the draw, an' I tharfore trusts that none will prove so sooicidal as to put me to the test.'

"This Bird Cage Op'ry House evenin', however, Jack is absent a heap. Dan Boggs is present, an' is leanin' back appreciatin' the show an' the Val-

ley Tan plenty impartial. Dan likes both an' is doin'
'em even jestice. Over opp'site to Dan is a drunken
passel of sports from Red Dog, said wretched hamlet bein' behind Wolfville in that as in all things
else an' not ownin' no op'ry house.

"As the evenin' proceeds—it's about sixth drink
time—a casyooal gun goes off over among the Red
Dog outfit, an' the lead tharfrom bores a hole in the
wall clost to Dan's y'ear. Nacherally Dan don't
like it. The show sort o' comes to a balk, an' takin' advantages of the lull Dan arises in a listless way
an' addresses the Red Dogs.

"'I merely desires to inquire,' says Dan 'whether
that shot is inadvertent; or is it a mark of innocent
joobilation an' approval of the show; or is it meant
personal to me?'

"'You can bet your moccasins!' shouts one of
the Red Dog delegation, 'thar's no good fellowship
with that gun-play. That shot's formal an' serious
an' goes as it lays.'

"'My mind bein' now cl'ar on the subject of
motive,' says Dan; 'the proper course is plain.

With this retort Dan slams away gen'ral—shoots
into the flock like—at the picnickers from Red
Dog, an' a party who's plenty drunk an' has his
feet piled up on a table goes shy his off big toe.

"As I remarks yeretofore it's as well Jack Moore
ain't thar. Jack would have corralled something
more momentous than a toe. Which Jack would
have been shootin' in his capac'ty as marshal, an'
couldn't onder sech circumstances have stooped to

toes. But it's different with Dan. He is present
private an' only idlin' 'round; an' he ain't driven to
take high ground. More partic'lar since Dan's playin' a return game in the nacher of reproofs an'
merely to resent the onlicensed liberties which Red
Dog takes with him, Dan, as I says, is free to accept
toes if he so decides.

" When Dan busts this yere inebriate, the victim
lams loose a yell ag'inst which a coyote would pro-
test. That sot thinks he's shore killed. What with
the scare an' the pain an' the nosepaint, an' regyardin' of himse'f as right then flutterin' about the
rim of eternity, he gets seized with remorse an'
allows he's out to confess his sins before he quits.
As thar's no sky pilot to confide in, this drunkard
figgers that Peets 'll do, an' with that he onloads on
Peets how, bein' as he is a stage book-keep over in
Red Dog, he's in cahoots with a outfit of route
agents an' gives 'em the word when its worth while
to stand-up the stage. An' among other crim'nal
pards of his this terrified person names that outlaw
Silver Phil. Shore, when he rounds to an' learns
it ain't nothin' but a toe, this party's chagrined to
death.

"This yere confidin' sport's arrested an' taken
some'ers—Prescott mebby—to be tried in a shore-
enough co't for the robberies; the Red Dog Stranglers not bein' game to butt in an' hang him a lot
themse'fs. They surrenders him to the marshal
who rides over for him; an' they would have turned
out Silver Phil, too, only that small black outcast

don't wait, but goes squanderin' off to onknown climes the moment he hears the news. He's vamoosed Red Dog before this penitent bookkeep ceases yelpin' an' sobbin' over his absent toe.

"It ain't no time, however, before we hears further of Silver Phil; that is, by way of roomer. It looks like a couple of big cow outfits some'ers in the San Simon country—they're the 'Three-D' an' the 'K-in-a-box' brands—takes first to stealin' each other's cattle, an', final, goes to war. Each side retains bands of murderers an' proceeds buoyantly to lay for one another. Which Silver Phil enlists with the 'Three-D' an' sneaks an' prowls an' bushwhacks an' shoots himse'f into more or less bloody an' ignoble prom'nence. At last the main war-chiefs of the Territory declar's themse'fs in on the riot an' chases both sides into the hills; an' among other excellent deeds they makes captive Silver Phil.

"It's a great error they don't string this Silver Phil instanter. But no; after the procrastinatin' fashion of real law, they permits the villain—who's no more use on the surface of Arizona that a-way than one of them hydrophoby polecats whose bite is death—to get a law sharp to plead an' call for a show-down before a jedge an' jury. It takes days to try Silver Phil, an' marshals an' sheriff gents is two weeks squanderin' about gettin' witnesses; an' all to as much trouble an' loss of time an' *dinero* as would suffice to round-up the cattle of Cochise county. Enright an' the Stranglers would have turned the trick in twenty minutes an' never left the New York Store ontil with Silver Phil an' a lariat they reepairs to the windmill to put the fin- ishin' touches on their lucoobrations.

"Still, dooms slow an' shiftless as they shore be, at the wind-up Silver Phil's found guilty, an' is put in nom'nation by the presidin' alcade to be hanged; the time bein' set in a crazy-hoss fashion for a month away. As Silver Phil—which he's that bad an' hard he comes mighty clost to bein' game—is leavin' the co't-room with the marshal who's ridin' herd on him, he says:

"'I ain't payin' much attention at the time,'— Silver Phil's talkin' to that marshal gent,—'bein' I'm thinkin' of something else, but do I onderstand that old grey sport on the bench to say you-all is to hang me next month?'

"'That's whatever!' assents this marshal gent, 'an' you can gamble a bloo stack that hangin' you is a bet we ain't none likely to overlook. Which we're out to put our whole grateful souls into the dooty.'

"'Now I thinks of it,' observes Silver Phil, 'I'm some averse to bein' hanged. I reckons, speakin' free an' free as between fellow sports, that in order for that execootion to be a blindin' success I'll have to be thar personal?'

"'It's one of the mighty few o'casions,' responds the marshal, 'when your absence would shorely dash an' damp the gen'ral joy. As you says, you'll have to be thar a heap personal when said hangin' occurs.'

" ' I'm mighty sorry,' says Silver Phil, 'that you-
all lays out your game in a fashion that so much
depends on me. The more so, since the longer I
considers this racket, the less likely it is I'll be
thar. It's almost a cinch, with the plans I has,
that I'll shore be some'ers else.'

" They corrals Silver Phil in the one big upper
room of a two-story 'doby, an' counts off a couple of
dep'ty marshals to gyard him. These gyards, comin' squar' down to cases, ain't no improvement,
moral, on Silver Phil himse'f ; an' since they're
twice his age—Silver Phil not bein' more'n twenty—
it's safe as a play to say that both of 'em oughter
have been hanged a heap before ever Silver Phil is
born. These two hold-ups, however, turns dep'ty
marshals in their old age, an' is put in to stand
watch an' watch an' see that Silver Phil don't work
loose from his hobbles an' go pirootin' off ag'in into
parts onknown. Silver Phil is loaded with fetters,
—handcuffs an' laig-locks both—an' these hold-up
sentries is armed to the limit.

" It's the idee of Doc Peets later, when he hears
the details, that if the gyards that time treats Silver
Phil with kindness, the little felon most likely would
have remained to be hanged. But they don't : they
abooses Silver Phil ; cussin' him out an' herdin' him
about like he's cattle. They're a evil-tempered
couple, them dep'ties, an' they don't give Silver Phil
no sort o' peace.

" ' As I su'gests yeretofore,' says Doc Peets, when
he considers the case, 'this Silver Phil is a degen'.

rate. He's like a anamile. He don't entertain no reg'lar scheme to work free when he waxes sardonic with the marshal; that's only a bluff. Later, when them gyards takes to maltreatin' him an' battin' him about, it wakes up the venom in him, an' his cunnin' gets aroused along with his appetite for revenge.'

" This Silver Phil, who's lean an' slim like I explains at the jump, has hands no bigger than a cat's paws. It ain't no time when he discovers that by cuttin' himse'f a bit on the irons, he can shuck the handcuffs whenever he's disposed. Even then, he don't outline no campaign for liberty; jest sort o' roominates an' waits.

" It's one partic'lar mornin', some two weeks after Silver Phil's sentenced that a-way. The marshal gent himse'f ain't about, bein' on some dooty over to Tucson. Silver Phil is upsta'rs on the top floor of the 'doby with his gyards. Which he's hotter than a wildcat; the gyards an' him has been havin' a cussin' match, an' as Silver Phil outplays 'em talkin', one of 'em's done whacked him over the skelp with his gun. The blood's tricklin' down Silver Phil's fore'erd as he sits glowerin'.

" One of the gyards is loadin' a ten-gauge Greener —a whole mouthful of buckshot in each shell. He's grinnin' at Silver Phil as he shoves the shells in the gun an' slams her shet.

" 'Which I'm loadin' that weepon for you,' says the gyard, contemplatin' Silver Phil derisive.

" 'You be, be you!' replies Silver Phil, his eyes

burnin' with rage. 'Which you better look out a whole lot ; you-all may get it yourse'f.'

"The gyard laughs ugly an' exasperatin' an' puts the ten-gauge in a locker along with two or three Winchesters. Then he turns the key on the fire-arms an' goes caperin' off to his feed.

"The other gyard, his *compadre*, is settin' on a stool lookin' out a window. Mebby he's considerin' of his sins. It would be more in his hand at this time if he thinks of Silver Phil.

"Silver Phil, who's full of wrath at the taunts of the departed gyard, slips his hands free of the irons. Most of the hide on his wrists comes with 'em, but Silver Phil don't care. The gyard's back is to him as that gent sits gazin' out an' off along the dusty trail where it winds gray an' hot toward Tucson. Silver Phil organises, stealthy an' cat-cautious ; he's out for the gyard's gun as it hangs from his belt, the butt all temptin' an' su'gestive.

"As Silver Phil makes his first move the laig-locks clanks. It ain't louder than the jingle of a brace of copper *centouse* knockin' together. It's enough, however; it strikes on the y'ear of that thoughtful gyard like the roar of a '44. He em-erges from his reverie with a start ; the play comes cl'ar as noonday to him in a moment.

"The gyard leaps, without even lookin' 'round, to free himse'f from the clutch of Silver Phil. Which he's the splinter of a second too late. Silver Phil makes a spring like a mountain lion, laig-locks an' all, an' grabs the gun. As the gyard goes clat-

terin' down sta'rs, Silver Phil pumps two loads into
him an' curls him up at the foot. Then Silver Phil
hurls the six-shooter at him with a volley of mal'dic-
tions.

"Without pausin' a moment, Silver Phil grabs
the stool an' smashes to flinders the locker that
holds the 10-gauge Greener. He ain't forgot none;
an' he's fair locoed to get that partic'lar weepon
for the other gyard. He rips it from the rack an'
shows at the window as his prey comes runnin' to
the rescoo of his pard:

"'Oh, you! Virg Sanders!' yells Silver Phil.

"The second gyard looks up; an' as he does,
Silver Phil gives him both bar'ls. Forty-two buckshot; an' that gyard's so clost he stops 'em all! As
he lays dead, Silver Phil breaks the Greener in two,
an' throws, one after the other, stock an' bar'l at
him.

"'Which I'll show you-all what happens when
folks loads a gun for me!' says Silver Phil.

"Nacherally, this artillery practice turns out
the entire plaza. The folks is standin' about the
'doby which confines Silver Phil, wonderin' whatever that enthoosiast's goin' to do next. No, they
don't come after him, an' I'll tell you why. Shore,
thar's twenty gents lookin' on, any one of whom, so
far as personal apprehensions is involved, would
trail Silver Phil single-handed into a wolf's den.
Which he'd feel plumb confident he gets away with
Silver Phil an' the wolves thrown in to even up the
odds. Still, no one stretches forth to capture Sil-

ver Phil on this yere voylent o'casion. An' these
is the reasons. Thar's no reg'lar offishul present
whose dooty it is to rope up this Silver Phil. If
sech had chanced to be thar, you can put down a
stack he'd come a-runnin', an' him or Silver Phil
would have caught up with the two gyards on their
journey into the beyond. But when it gets down to
private people volunteerin' for dooty as marshals,
folks in the Southwest goes some slothful to work.
Thar's the friends of the accoosed—an' as a roole
he ain't none friendless—who would mighty likely
resent sech zeal. Also, in the case of Silver Phil,
his captivity grows out of a cattle war. One third
the public so far as it stands about the 'doby where
Silver Phil is hived that time is 'Three-D' ad-
herents, mebby another third is ' K-in-a-box ' folks,
while the last third is mighty likely nootral.
Whichever way it breaks, however, thar's a tacit
stand-off, an' never a sport of 'em lifts a finger or
voice to head off Silver Phil.

"'Which she's the inalien'ble right of Americans
onder the constitootion to escape with every chance
they gets,' says one.

"'That's whatever!' coincides his pard; 'an'
moreover this ain't our round-up nohow.'

" It's in that fashion these private citizens adjusts
their dooty to the state while pausin' to look on, in a
sperit of cur'osity while Silver Phil makes his next
play.

"They don't wait long. Silver Phil comes out
on the roof of a stoop in front. He's got a Win-

chester by now, an' promptly throws the muzzle tharof on a leadin' citizen. Silver Phil allows he'll plug this dignitary if they don't send up a sport with a file to cut loose the laig-locks. Tharupon the pop'lace, full of a warm interest by this time, does better. They gropes about in the war-bags of the Virg Sanders sharp who stops the buckshot an' gets his keys ; a moment after, Silver Phil is free.

"Still, this ontirin' hold-up goes on menacin' the leadin' citizen as former. Which now Silver Phil demands a bronco, bridled an' saddled. He gives the public ten minutes ; if the bronco is absent at the end of ten minutes Silver Phil allows he'll introdooce about a pound of lead into where that village father does his cogitatin'. The bronco appears with six minutes to spar'. As it arrives, the vivacious Silver Phil jumps off the roof of the stoop—the same bein' low—an' is in the saddle an' out o' sight while as practised a hand as Huggins is pourin' out a drink. Where the trail bends 'round a *mesa* Silver Phil pulls up.

"'Whoop! whoop! whoopee! for Silver Phil,' he shouts.

"Then he waves the Winchester, an' as he spurs 'round the corner of the hill it's the last that spellbound outfit ever sees of Silver Phil.

"Nacherally now," remarked my old friend, as he refreshed himself with a mouthful of scotch, "you-all is waitin' an' tryin' to guess wherever does Dan Boggs get in on this yere deal. An' it won't take no time to post you ; the same bein' a comfort.

" Not one word do we-all wolves of Wolfville hear of the divertin' adventures of Silver Phil—shootin' up his gyards an' fetchin' himse'f free—ontil days after.   No one in camp has got Silver Phil on his mind at all ; at least if he has he deems him safe an' shore in hock, a-waitin' to be stretched.   Considerin' what follows, I never experiences trouble in adoptin' Doc Peets' argyments that the eepisodes wherein this 'onhappy Silver Phil figgers sort o' aggravates his intellects ontil he's locoed.

" ' Bein' this Silver Phil's a degen'rate,' declar's Peets, explanatory, ' he's easy an' soon to loco. His mind as well as his moral nacher is onbalanced congenital.   Any triflin' jolt, much less than what that Silver Phil runs up on, an' his fretful wits is shore to leave the saddle.

" Now that Silver Phil's free, but loonatic like Peets says, an' doubly vicious by them tantalisin' gyards, it looks like he thinks of nothin' but wreckin' reprisals on all who's crossed his trail.   An' so with vengeance eatin' at his crim'nal heart he p'ints that bronco's muzzle straight as a bird flies for Wolfville.   Whoever do you-all reckon now he wants ?   Cherokee Hall ?   Son, you've followed off the wrong waggon track.   Silver Phil—imagine the turpitoode of sech a ornery wretch !—is out for the lovely skelp of Faro Nell who detects him in his ha'r-copper frauds that time.

" Which the first intimations we has of Silver Phil after that escape, is one evenin' about fifth drink time—or as you-all says ' four o'clock.'   The

sun's still hot an' high over in the west.   Thar's no
game goin'; but bein' it's as convenient thar as
elsewhere an' some cooler, Cherokee's settin' back
of his layout with Faro Nell as usual on her lookout perch.   Dan Boggs is across the street in the
dancehall door, an' his pet best bronco is waitin'
saddled in front.   Hot an' drowsy; the street save
for these is deserted.

"It all takes place in a moment.   Thar's a clatter-
ing rush; an' then, pony a-muck with sweat an'
alkali dust, Silver Phil shows in the portals of the
Red Light.   Thar's a flash an' a spit of white smoke
as he fires his six-shooter straight at Faro Nell.

"Silver Phil is quick, but Cherokee is quicker.
Cherokee sweeps Faro Nell from her stool with
one motion of his arm an' the bullet that's searchin'
for her lifts Cherokee's ha'r a trifle where he 'most
gets his head in its way.

"Ondoubted, this Silver Phil allows he c'llects
on Faro Nell as planned.   He don't shoot twice, an'
he don't tarry none, but wheels his wearied pony,
gives a yell, an' goes surgin' off.

"But Silver Phil's got down to the turn of that
evil deal of his existence.   He ain't two hundred
yards when Dan Boggs is in the saddle an' ridin'
hard.   Dan's bronco runs three foot for every one
of the pony of Silver Phil's; which that beaten an'
broken cayouse is eighty miles from his last mouthful of grass.

"As Dan begins to crowd him, Silver Phil turns
in the saddle an' shoots.   The lead goes 'way off

yonder—wild.   Dan, grim an' silent, rides on without returnin' the fire.

" 'Which I wouldn't dishonour them guns of
mine,' says Dan, explainin' later the pheenomenon
of him not shootin' none, ' which I wouldn't dishonour them guns by usin' 'em on varmints like
this yere Silver Phil.'

" As Silver Phil reorganises for a second shot his
bronco stumbles.   Silver Phil pitches from the saddle an' strikes the grass to one side.   As he half
rises, Dan lowers on him like the swoop of a hawk.
It's as though Dan's goin' to snatch a handkerchief
from the ground.

"As Dan flashes by, he swings low from the saddle
an' his right hand takes a troo full grip on that outlaw's shoulder.   Dan has the thews an' muscles of
a cinnamon b'ar, an' Silver Phil is only a scrap of a
man.   As Dan straightens up in the stirrups, he
heaves this Silver Phil on high to the length of his
long arm ; an' then he dashes him ag'inst the flint-
hard earth ; which the manoover—we-all witnesses
it from mebby a quarter of a mile—which the manoover that a-way is shore remorseless !   This Silver
Phil is nothin' but shattered bones an' bleedin'
pulp.   He strikes the plains like he's come from
the clouds an' is dead without a quiver.

" ' Bury him ?   No ! ' says Old Man Enright to
Dave Tutt who asks the question.   ' Let him find
his bed where he falls.

" While Enright speaks, an' as Dan rides up to us
at the Red Light, a prompt raven drops down over

where this Silver Phil is layin'.   Then another
raven an' another—black an' wide of wing—comes
floatin' down.   A coyote yells—first with the short,
sharp yelp, an' then with that multiplied patter of
laughter like forty wolves at once.   That daylight
howl of the coyote allers tells of a death.   Shore
raven an' wolf is gatherin'.   As Enright says : ' This
yere Silver Phil ain't likely to be lonesome none
to-night.'

" ' Did you kill him, Dan ? ' asks Faro Nell.

" ' Why, no, Nellie,' replies Dan, as he steps
outen the stirrups an' beams on Faro Nell.   She's
still a bit onstrung, bein' only a little girl when all is
said.   ' Why, no, Nellie ; I don't kill him speecific
as Wolfville onderstands the word ; but I dismisses
him so effectual the kyard shore falls the same for
Silver Phil.' "

CHAPTER II.

Colonel Sterett's Panther Hunt,

" PANTHERS, what we-all calls ' mountain lions,' "
observed the Old Cattleman, wearing meanwhile
the sapient air of him who feels equipped of his subject, " is plenty furtive, not to say mighty sedyoo-
lous to skulk. That's why a gent don't meet up
with more of 'em while pirootin' about in the hills.
Them cats hears him, or they sees him, an' him still
ignorant tharof; an' with that they bashfully withdraws. Which it's to be urged in favour of mountain
lions that they never forces themse'fs on no gent;
they're shore considerate, that a-way, an' speshul of
themse'fs. If one's ever hurt, you can bet it won't
be a accident. However, it ain't for me to go 'round
impugnin' the motives of no mountain lion; partic'lar when the entire tribe is strangers to me complete. But still a love of trooth compels me to
concede that if mountain lions ain't cowardly, they're
shore cautious a lot. Cattle an' calves they passes
up as too bellicose, an' none of 'em ever faces any
anamile more warlike than a baby colt or mebby
a half-grown deer. I'm ridin' along the Caliente
once when I hears a crashin' in the bushes on the
bluff above—two hundred foot high, she is, an' as

sheer as the walls of this yere tavern. As I lifts my eyes, a fear-frenzied mare an' colt comes chargin' up an' projects themse'fs over the precipice an' lands in the valley below. They're dead as Joolius Cæsar when I rides onto 'em, while a brace of mountain lions is skirtin' up an' down the aige of the bluff they leaps from, mewin' an' lashin' their long tails in hot enthoosiasm. Shore, the cats has been chasin' the mare an' foal, an' they locoes 'em to that extent they don't know where they're headin' an' makes the death jump I relates. I bangs away with my six-shooter, but beyond givin' the mountain lions a convulsive start I can't say I does any execootion. They turns an' goes streakin' it through the pine woods like a drunkard to a barn raisin'.

"Timid? Shore! They're that timid seminary girls compared to 'em is as sternly courageous as a passel of buccaneers. Out in Mitchell's canyon a couple of the Lee-Scott riders cuts the trail of a mountain lion and her two kittens. Now whatever do you-all reckon this old tabby does? Basely deserts her offsprings without even barin' a tooth, an' the cow-punchers takes 'em gently by their tails an' beats out their joovenile brains. That's straight; that mother lion goes swarmin' up the canyon like she ain't got a minute to live. An' you can gamble the limit that where a anamile sees its children perish without frontin' up for war, it don't possess the commonest roodiments of sand. Sech, son, is mountain lions.

" It's one evenin' in the Red Light when Colonel
Sterett, who's got through his day's toil on that
Coyote paper he's editor of, onfolds concernin' a pan-
ther round-up which he pulls off in his yooth.

" ' This panther hunt,' says Colonel Sterett, as
he fills his third tumbler, ' occurs when mighty
likely I'm goin' on seventeen winters.   I'm a leader
among my young companions at the time ; in fact,
I allers is.   An' I'm proud to say that my soopre-
macy that a-way is doo to the dom'nant character
of my intellects.   I'm ever bright an' sparklin' as a
child, an' I recalls how my aptitoode for learnin'
promotes me to be regyarded as the smartest lad in
my set.   If thar's visitors, to the school, or if the
selectmen invades that academy to sort o' size us
up, the teacher allers plays me on 'em.   I'd go to
the front for the outfit.   Which I'm wont on sech
harrowin' o'casions to recite a ode—the teacher's
done wrote it himse'f—an' which is entitled *Napoleon's Mad Career*.   Thar's twenty-four stanzas to it ;
an' while these interlopin' selectmen sets thar lookin' owley an' sagacious, I'd wallop loose with the
twenty-four verses, stampin' up and down, an' ac-
companyin' said recitations with sech a multitood
of reckless gestures, it comes plenty clost to backin'
everybody plumb outen the room.   Yere's the first
verse :

> I'd drink an' sw'ar an' r'ar an' t'ar
>   An' fall down in the mud,
> While the y'earth for forty miles about
>   Is kivered with my blood.

" ' You-all can see from that speciment that our
schoolmaster ain't simply flirtin' with the muses
when he originates that epic ; no sir, he means business ; an' whenever I throws it into the selectmen, I
does it jestice. The trustees used to silently line
out for home when I finishes, an' never a yeep. It
stuns 'em ; it shore fills 'em to the brim !

" ' As I gazes r'arward,' goes on the Colonel, as
by one rapt impulse he uplifts both his eyes an' his
nosepaint, ' as I gazes r'arward, I says, on them sun-
filled days, an' speshul if ever I gets betrayed into
talkin' about 'em, I can hardly t'ar myse'f from the
subject. I explains yeretofore, that not only by
inclination but by birth, I'm a shore-enough 'risto-
crat. This captaincy of local fashion I assoomes
at a tender age. I wears the record as the first
child to don shoes throughout the entire summer
in that neighbourhood ; an' many a time an' oft
does my yoothful but envy-eaten compeers lambaste
me for the insultin' innovation. But I sticks to my
moccasins ; an' to-day shoes in the Bloo Grass
is almost as yooniversal as the licker habit.

" ' Thar dawns a hour, however, when my p'sition
in the van of Kaintucky *ton* comes within a ace of
bein' ser'ously shook. It's on my way to school one
dewey mornin' when I gets involved all inadvertent
in a onhappy rupture with a polecat. I never does
know how the misonderstandin' starts. After all,
the seeds of said dispoote is by no means important ;
it's enough to say that polecat finally has me thoroughly convinced.

Followin' the difference an' my defeat, I'm witless enough to keep goin' on to school, whereas
I should have returned homeward an' cast myse'f
upon my parents as a sacred trust. Of course,
when I'm in school I don't go impartin' my troubles
to the other chil'en; I emyoolates the heroism of
the Spartan boy who stands to be eat by a fox, an'
keeps 'em to myself. But the views of my late
enemy is not to be smothered; they appeals to my
young companions; who tharupon puts up a most
onneedful riot of coughin's an' sneezin's. But nobody knows me as the party who's so pungent.

"'It's a tryin' moment. I can see that, once I'm
located, I'm goin' to be as onpop'lar as a b'ar in a
hawg pen; I'll come tumblin' from my pinnacle in
that proud commoonity as the glass of fashion an'
the mold of form. You can go your bottom *peso*,
the thought causes me to feel plenty perturbed.

"'At this peril I has a inspiration; as good, too,
as I ever entertains without the aid of rum. I determines to cast the opprobrium on some other boy
an' send the hunt of gen'ral indignation sweepin'
along his trail.

"'Thar's a innocent infant who's a stoodent at
this temple of childish learnin' an' his name is Riley
Bark. This Riley is one of them giant children
who's only twelve an' weighs three hundred pounds.
An' in proportions as Riley is a son of Anak,
physical, he's dwarfed mental; he ain't half as well
upholstered with brains as a shepherd dog. That's
right; Riley's intellects, is like a fly in a saucer of

syrup, they struggles 'round plumb slow. I decides to uplift Riley to the public eye as the felon who's disturbin' that seminary's sereenity. Comin' to this decision, I p'ints at him where he's planted four seats ahead, all tangled up in a spellin' book, an' says in a loud whisper to a child who's sittin' next :

" ' Throw him out ! '

" ' That's enough. No gent will ever realise how easy it is to direct a people's sentiment ontil he take a whirl at the game. In two minutes by the teacher's bull's-eye copper watch, every soul knows it's pore Riley ; an' in three, the teacher's done drug Riley out doors by the ha'r of his head an' chased him home. Gents, I look back on that yoothful feat as a triumph of diplomacy ; it shore saves my standin' as the Beau Brummel of the Bloo Grass.

" ' Good old days, them ! ' observes the Colonel mournfully, 'an' ones never to come ag'in ! My sternest studies is romances, an' the peroosals of old tales as I tells you-all prior fills me full of moss an' mockin' birds in equal parts. I reads deep of *Walter Scott* an' waxes to be a sharp on Moslems speshul. I dreams of the Siege of Acre, an' Richard the Lion Heart; an' I simply can't sleep nights for honin' to hold a tournament an' joust a whole lot for some fair lady's love.

" ' Once I commits the error of my career by joustin' with my brother Jeff. This yere Jeff is settin' on the bank of the Branch fishin' for bullpouts at the time, an' Jeff don't know I'm hoverin' near at all. Jeff's reedic'lous fond of fishin'; which he'd

sooner fish than read *Paradise Lost.* I'm romancin'
along, sim'larly bent, when I notes Jeff perched on
the bank. To my boyish imagination Jeff at once
turns to be a Paynim. I drops my bait box, couches
my fishpole, an' emittin' a impromptoo warcry,
charges him. It's the work of a moment ; Jeff's onhossed an' falls into the Branch.

"' But thar's bitterness to follow vict'ry. Jeff
emerges like Diana from the bath an' frales the
wamus off me with a club. Talk of puttin' a crimp
in folks ! Gents when Jeff's wrath is assuaged I'm
all on one side like the leanin' tower of Pisa. Jeff
actooally confers a skew-gee to my spinal column.

"' A week later my folks takes me to a doctor.
That practitioner puts on his specs an' looks me
over with jealous care.

"' " Whatever's wrong with him, Doc ? " says my
father.

"' " Nothin'," says the physician, " only your son
Willyum's five inches out o' plumb."

"' Then he rigs a contraption made up of guy-
ropes an' stay-laths, an' I has to wear it; an'
mebby in three or four weeks he's got me warped
back into the perpendic'lar.'

"' But how about this cat hunt?" asks Dan
Boggs. ' Which I don't aim to be introosive none,
but I'm camped yere through the second drink
waitin' for it, an' these procrastinations is makin'
me kind o' batty.'

"' That panther hunt is like this,' says the Colonel,
turnin' to Dan. ' At the age of seventeen, me an'

eight or nine of my intimate brave comrades founds what we-all denom'nates as the "Chevy Chase Huntin' Club." Each of us maintains a passel of odds an' ends of dogs, an' at stated intervals we convenes on hosses, an' with these fourscore curs at our tails goes yellin' an' skally-hootin' up an' down the countryside allowin' we're shore a band of Nimrods.

"'The Chevy Chasers ain't been in bein' as a institootion over long when chance opens a gate to ser'ous work. The deep snows in the Eastern mountains it looks like has done drove a panther into our neighbourhood. You could hear of him on all sides. Folks glimpses him now an' then. They allows he's about the size of a yearlin' calf; an' the way he pulls down sech feeble people as sheep or lays desolate some he'pless henroost don't bother him a bit. This panther spreads a horror over the county. Dances, pra'er meetin's, an' even poker parties is broken up, an' the social life of that region begins to bog down. Even a weddin' suffers; the bridesmaids stayin' away lest this ferocious monster should show up in the road an' chaw one of 'em while she's *en route* for the scene of trouble. That's gospel trooth! the pore deserted bride has to heel an' handle herse'f an' never a friend to yoonite her sobs with hers doorin' that weddin' ordeal. The old ladies present shakes their heads a heap solemn.

"'"It's a worse augoory," says one, "than the hoots of a score of squinch owls."

" 'When this reign of terror is at its height, the
local eye is rolled appealin'ly towards us Chevy
Chasers. We rises to the opportoonity. Day after
day we're ridin' the hills an' vales, readin' the milk
white snow for tracks. An' we has success. One
mornin' I comes up on two of the Brackenridge
boys an' five more of the Chevy Chasers settin' on
their hosses at the Skinner cross roads. Bob Crittenden's gone to turn me out, they says. Then
they p'ints down to a handful of close-wove bresh
an' stunted timber an' allows that this maraudin'
cat-o-mount is hidin' thar ; they sees him go skulk-
in' in.

" 'Gents, I ain't above admittin' that the news
puts my heart to a canter. I'm brave ; but conflicts
with wild an' savage beasts is to me a novelty an'
while I faces my fate without a flutter, I'm yere to
say I'd sooner been in pursoot of minks or raccoons
or some varmint whose grievous cap'bilities I can
more ackerately stack up an' in whose merry ways
I'm better versed. However, the dauntless blood
of my grandsire mounts in my cheek ; an' as if the
shade of that old Trojan is thar personal to su'gest
it, I searches forth a flask an' renoos my sperit ; thus
qualified for perils, come in what form they may, I
resolootely stands my hand.

" 'Thar's forty dogs if thar's one in our company
as we pauses at the Skinner cross roads. An' when
the Crittenden yooth returns, he brings with him
the Rickett boys an' forty added dogs. Which
it's worth a ten-mile ride to get a glimpse of that out-

fit of canines ! Thar's every sort onder the canopy :
thar's the stolid hound, the alert fice, the sapient
collie ; that is thar's individyool beasts wherein the
hound, or fice, or collie seems to preedominate as a
strain. The trooth is thar's not that dog a-whinin'
about our hosses' fetlocks who ain't proudly de-
scended from fifteen different tribes, an' they
shorely makes a motley mass meetin'. Still, they're
good, zealous dogs ; an' as they're going to go for'-
ard an' take most of the resks of that panther, it
seems invidious to criticise 'em.

' " One of the Twitty boys rides down an' puts
the eighty or more dogs into the bresh. The rest
of us lays back an' strains our eyes. Thar he is !
A shout goes up as we descries the panther stealin'
off by a far corner. He's headin' along a hollow
that's full of bresh an' baby timber an' runs parallel
with the pike. Big an' yaller he is ; we can tell
from the slight flash we gets of him as he darts
into a second clump of bushes. With a cry—what
young Crittenden calls a " view halloo,"—we goes
stampedin' down the pike in pursoot.

" ' Our dogs is sta'nch ; they shore does themse'fs
proud. Singin' in twenty keys, reachin, from growls
to yelps an' from yelps to shrillest screams, they
pushes dauntlessly on the fresh trail of their terrified quarry. Now an' then we gets a squint of the
panther as he skulks from one copse to another jest
ahead. Which he's goin' like a arrow ; no mistake ! As for us Chevy Chasers, we parallels the
hunt, an' continyoos poundin' the Skinner turn-

pike abreast of the pack, ever an' anon givin' a en-
couragin' shout as we briefly sights our game.

"'Gents,' says Colonel Sterett, as he ag'in
refreshes himse'f,' its needless to go over that hunt
in detail. We hustles the flyin' demon full eighteen
miles, our faithful dogs crowdin' close an' breathless
at his coward heels. Still, they don't catch up with
him ; he streaks it like some saffron meteor.

"'Only once does we approach within strikin'
distance ; that's when he crosses at old Stafford's
whiskey still. As he glides into view, Crittenden
shouts :

"'"Thar he goes!"

"'For myse'f I'm prepared. I've got one of
these misguided cap-an'-ball six-shooters that's built
doorin' the war; an' I cuts that hardware loose !
This weepon seems a born profligate of lead, for
the six chambers goes off together. Which you
should have seen the Chevy Chasers dodge! An'
well they may ; that broadside ain't in vain ! My
aim is so troo that one of the r'armost dogs evolves
a howl an' rolls over ; then he sets up gnawin' an'
lickin' his off hind laig in frantic alternations. That
hunt is done for him. We leaves him doctorin'
himse'f an' picks him up two hours later on our
triumphant return.

"'As I states, we harries that foogitive panther
for eighteen miles an' in our hot ardour founders two
hosses. Fatigue an' weariness begins to overpower
us ; also our prey weakens along with the rest. In
the half glimpses we now an' ag'in gets of him its

plain that both pace an' distance is tellin' fast.
Still, he presses on; an' as thar's no spur like fear,
that panther holds his distance.

"'But the end comes. We've done run him into
a rough, wild stretch of country where settlements
is few an' cabins roode. Of a sudden, the panther
emerges onto the road an' goes rackin' along the
trail. We pushes our spent steeds to the utmost.

"'Thar's a log house ahead; out in the stump-
filled lot in front is a frowsy woman an' five small
children. The panther leaps the rickety worm-fence
an' heads straight as a bullet for the cl'arin'!
Horrors! the sight freezes our marrows! Mad an'
savage, he's doo to bite a hunk outen that devoted
household! Mutooally callin' to each other, we
goads our hosses to the utmost. We gain on the
panther! He may wound but he won't have time
to slay that fam'ly.

"'Gents, it's a soopreme moment! The panther
makes for the female squatter an' her litter, we
pantin' an' pressin' clost behind. The panther is
among 'em; the woman an' the children seems
transfixed by the awful spectacle an' stands rooted
with open eyes an' mouths. Our emotions shore
beggars deescriptions.

"'Now ensooes a scene to smite the hardiest of
us with dismay. No sooner does the panther find
himse'f in the midst of that he'pless bevy of little
ones, than he stops, turns round abrupt, an' sets
down on his tail; an' then upliftin' his muzzle he
busts into shrieks an' yells an' howls an' cries, a

complete case of dog hysterics! That's what he
is, a great yeller dog; his reason is now a wrack
because we harasses him the eighteen miles.

"'Thar's a ugly outcast of a squatter, mattock in
hand, comes tumblin' down the hillside from some-
'ers out back of the shanty where he's been grub-
bin':

"'"What be you-all eediots chasin' my dog for?"
demands this onkempt party. Then he menaces us
with the implement.

"'We makes no retort but stands passive. The
great orange brute whose nerves has been torn to
rags creeps to the squatter an' with mournful howls
explains what we've made him suffer.

"'No, thar's nothin' further to do an' less to be
said. That cavalcade, erstwhile so gala an' buoyant,
drags itself wearily homeward, the exhausted dogs
in the r'ar walkin' stiff an' sore like their laigs is
wood. For more'n a mile the complainin' howls of
the hysterical yeller dog is wafted to our y'ears.
Then they ceases; an' we figgers his sympathizin'
master has done took him into the shanty an' shet
the door.

"'No one comments on this adventure, not a
word is heard. Each is silent ontil we mounts the
Big Murray hill. As we collects ourse'fs on this
eminence one of the Brackenridge boys holds up his
hand for a halt. "Gents," he says, as—hosses,
hunters an' dogs—we-all gathers 'round, "gents, I
moves you the Chevy Chase Huntin' Club yereby
stands adjourned *sine die*." Thar's a moment's

pause, an' then as by one impulse every gent, hoss an' dog, says "Ay!" It's yoonanimous, an' from that hour till now the Chevy Chase Huntin' Club ain't been nothin' save tradition. But that panther shore disappears; it's the end of his vandalage; an' ag'in does quadrilles, pra'rs, an poker resoom their wonted sway. That's the end; an' now, gents, if Black Jack will caper to his dooties we'll uplift our drooped energies with the usual forty drops."

CHAPTER III.

How Faro Nell Dealt Bank.

"RICHES," remarked the Old Cattleman, "riches says you! Neither you-all nor any other gent is competent to state whether in the footure he amasses wealth or not. The question is far beyond the throw of your rope."

My friend's tone breathed a note of strong contradiction while his glance was the glance of experience. I had said that I carried no hope of becoming rich; that the members of my tribe were born with their hands open and had such hold of money as a riddle has of water. It was this which moved him to expostulatory denial.

"This matter of wealth, that a-way," he continued, "is a mighty sight a question of luck. Shore, a gent has to have capacity to grasp a chance an' savey sufficient to get his chips down right. But this chance, an' whether it offers itse'f to any specific sport, is frequent accident an' its comin' or failure to come depends on conditions over which the party about to be enriched ain't got no control. That's straight, son! You backtrack any fortune to its beginnin', an some'ers along the trail or at the farthest end you'll come up with the fact that it took a accident or two, what we-all darkened

mortals calls 'luck,' to make good the play. It's
like gettin' shot gettin' rich is ; all you has to do is
be present personal at the time, an' the bullet does
the rest.

"You distrusts these doctrines. You shore won't
if you sets down hard an thinks. Suppose twenty
gents has made a surround an' is huntin' a b'ar.
Only one is goin' to down him. An' in his clumsy
blunderin' the b'ar is goin' to select his execootioner
himse'f. That's a fact ; the party who downs the
b'ar, final, ain't goin' to pick the b'ar out ; the b'ar's
goin' to pick him out. An' it's the same about
wealth ; one gent gets the b'ar an' the other nine-
teen—an' they're as cunnin' an' industr'ous as the
lucky party—don't get nothing—don't even get a
shot. I repeats tharfore, that you-all settin' yere
this evenin', firin' off aimless observations, don't
know whether you'll quit rich or not."

At the close of his dissertation, my talkative
companion puffed a cloud which seemed to hang
above his venerable head in a fashion of heavy blue
approval. I paused as one impressed by the utter
wisdom of the old gentleman. Then I took another
tack.

"Speaking of wealth," I said, "tell me concerning the largest money you ever knew to be won or
lost at faro—tell me a gambling story."

"Tell you-all a gamblin' tale," he repeated, and
then mused as if lost in retrospection. "If I hesitates it's because of a multitoode of incidents from
which to draw. I've beheld some mighty cur'ous

doin's at the gamblin' tables. Once I knows a party
who sinks his hopeless head on the layout an' dies
as he loses his last chip. This don't happen in
Wolfville none. No, I don't say folks ain't cashed
in at farobank in that excellent hamlet an' gone
singin' to their home above ; but it ain't heart disease. Usual it's guns ; the same bein' invoked by
sech inadvertencies as pickin' up some other gent's
bet.

"Tell you-all a story about gamblin'! Now I
reckons the time Faro Nell rescoos Cherokee Hall
from rooin is when I sees the most *dinero* changed
in at one play. You can gamble that's a thrillin'
eepisode when Faro Nell steps in between Cherokee
an' the destroyer. It's the gossip of the camp for
days, an' when Wolfville discusses anything for days
that outfit's plumb moved.

" This gent who crowds Cherokee to the wall
performs the feat deliberate. He organises a sort
o' campaign ag'in Cherokee ; what you might
term a fiscal dooel, an' at the finish he has Cherokee corralled for his last *peso*. It's at that p'int
Nell cuts in an' redeems the sityooation a heap.
It's all on the squar'; this invadin' sport simply
outlucks the bank. That, an' the egreegious limit
Cherokee gives him, is what does the trick.

" In Wolfville, we-all allers recalls that sharp-set
gent who comes after Cherokee with respect. In
fact he wins our encomiums before he sets in ag'in
Cherokee—before ever he gets his second drink at
the Red Light bar. He comes ramblin' over with

Old Monte from Tucson one evenin'; that's the first
glimpse we has of him. An' for a hour, mebby,
followin' his advent, seein' the gen'ral herd is busy
with the mail, he has the Red Light to himse'f.

"On this yere o'casion, thar's likewise present in
Wolfville—he's been infringin' 'round some three
days—a onsettled an' migratory miscreant who's
name is Ugly Collins. He's in a heap of ill repoote
in the territories, this Ugly Collins is; an' only he
contreebutes the information when he arrives in
camp that his visit is to be mighty temp'rary,
Enright would have signed up Jack Moore to take
his guns an' stampede him a lot.

"At the time I'm talkin' of, as thar's no one
who's that abandoned as to go writin' letters to
Ugly Collins, it befalls he's plenty footloose. This
leesure on the part of Ugly Collins turns out some
disast'rous for that party. Not havin' no missives
to read leaves him free to go weavin' about permiscus an' it's while he's strayin' here an' thar that
he tracks up on this stranger who's come after Cherokee.

"Ugly Collins sees our pilgrim in the Red Light
an', except Black Jack,—who of course is present
offishul—the stranger's alone. He's weak an' meek
an' shook by a cough that sounds like the overture
to a fooneral. Ugly Collins, who's a tyrannizin'
cowardly form of outcast, sizes him up as a easy
prey. He figgers he'll have a heap of evil fun with
him, Ugly Collins does. Tharupon he approaches
the consumptive stranger:

" ' You-all seems plenty ailin', pard,' says Ugly Collins.

" ' Which I shore ain't over peart none,' retorts the stranger.

" ' An' you-all can put down a bet,' returns Ugly Collins, ' I learns of your ill-health with regrets. It's this a-way: I ain't had no exercise yet this evenin' ; an' as I tracks in yere, I registers a vow to wallop the first gent I meets up with to whom I've not been introdooced ;—merely by way of stretchin' my muscles. Now I must say—an' I admits it with sorrow—that you-all is that onhappy sport. It's no use ; I knows I'll loathe myse'f for crawlin' the hump of a gent who's totterin' on the brink of the grave ; but whatever else can I do ? Vows is vows an' must be kept, so you might as well prepare yourse'f for a cloud of sudden an' painful vicissitoodes.'

" As Ugly Collins says this he kind o' reaches for the invalid gent where he's camped in a cha'r. It's a onfortunate gesture ; the invalid—as quick as a rattlesnake,—prodooces a derringer, same as Doc Peets allers packs, from his surtoot an' the bullet carries away most of Ugly Collins' lower jaw.

" ' You-all is goin' to be a heap sight more of a audience than a orator yereafter, Collins,' says Doc Peets, as he ties up the villain's visage that a-way. ' Also, you oughter be less reckless an' get the address of your victims before embarkin' on them skelp-collectin' enterprises of yours. That gent you goes ag'inst is Doc Holliday ; as hard a game as lurks anywhere between the Slope an' the Big Muddy.'

"Does the Stranglers do anything to this Holli day? Why, no, not much; all they does is present him with a Colt's-44 along with the compliments of the camp.

"'An' it's to be deplored,' says Enright, when he makes the presentation speech to Holliday, 'that you-all don't have this weepon when you cuts loose at Collins instead of said jimcrow derringer. In sech events, that hoss-thief's death would have been assured. Shore! shootin' off Collins' jaw is good as far as it goes, but it can't be regyarded as no sech boon as downin' him complete.

"It's after supper when this Holliday encounters Cherokee; the two has a conference. This Holliday lays bar' his purpose.

"'Which I'm yere,' says this Holliday, 'not only for your money, but I wants the camp.' Then he goes for'ard an' proposes that they plays till one is broke; an, if it's Cherokee who goes down, he is to *vamos* the outfit while Holliday succeeds to his game. 'An' the winner is to stake his defeated adversary to one thousand dollars wherewith to begin life anew,' concloodes this Holliday.

"'Which what you states seems like agreeable offers,' says Cherokee, an' he smiles clever an' gentlemanly. 'How strong be you-all, may I ask?'

"'Thirty thousand dollars in thirty bills,' replies this Holliday. 'An' now may I enquire how strong

be you? I also likes to know how long a trail I've
got to travel.'

"'My roll is about forty thousand big,' says
Cherokee. Then he goes on: 'It's all right; I'll
open a game for you at second drink time sharp.'

"'That's comfortin' to hear,' retorts this Holliday. 'The chances,—what with splits an' what with
the ten thousand you oversizes me,—is nacherally
with you; but I takes 'em. If I lose, I goes back
with a even thousand; if I win, you-all hits the
trail with a thousand, while I'm owner of your roll
an' bank. Does that onderstandin' go?'

"'It goes!' says Cherokee. Then he turns off
for a brief powwow with Faro Nell.

"'But thar's one thing you-all forgets, Cherokee,'
says Nell. 'If he breaks you, he's got to go on an'
break me. I've a bundle of three thousand; he's
got to get it all before ever the play is closed.
Tell this yere Holliday party that.'

"Cherokee argues ag'in it; but Nell stamps
'round an' starts to weep some, an' at that, like every
other troo gent, he gives in abject.

"'Thar's a bet I overlooks,' observes Cherokee,
when he resoomes his talk with this Holliday;
'it's my partner. It's only a little matter of three
thousand, but the way the scheme frames itse'f up,
after I'm down an' out, you'll have to break my
partner before Wolfville's all your own.'

"'That's eminent satisfactory,' returns this Holliday. 'An' I freely adds that your partner is a dead
game sport to take so brief a fortune an'—win

all, lose all—go after more'n twenty times as
much. Your partner's a shore enough optimist that
a-way.'

"Cherokee don't make no retort. This Holliday
ain't posted none that the partner Cherokee's mentionin' is Faro Nell, an' Cherokee allows he won't
onbosom himse'f on that p'int onless his hand is
forced.

"When the time arrives to open the game, the
heft of Wolfville's public is gathered at the Red
Light. The word goes 'round as to the enterprisin' Holliday bein' out for Cherokee's entire game;
an' the prospect of seein' a limit higher than a
cat's back, an' a dooel to the death, proves mighty
pop'lar. The play opens to a full house, shore!

"'What limit do you give me?' says this Holliday, with a sort o' cough, at the same time settin'
in opposite to Cherokee. 'Be lib'ral; I ain't more'n
a year to live, an' I've got to play 'em high an' hard
to get average action. If I'm in robust health now,
with a long, useful life before me, the usual figgers
would do. Considerin' my wasted health, however,
I shore hopes you'll say something like the even
thousand.'

"'Which I'll do better than that,' returns Cherokee, as he snaps the deck in the box, 'I'll let you
fix the limit to suit yourse'f. Make it the ceilin' if
the sperit moves you.'

"'That's gen'rous!' says Holliday. 'An' to
mark my appreciation tharof, I'll jest nacherally
take every resk of splits an' put ten thousand in the

pot, coppered; ten thousand in the big squar'; an'
ten thousand, coppered, on the high kyard.'

"Son, we-all sports standin' lookin' on draws a
deep breath. Thirty thousand in three ten thousand dollar bets, an' all on the layout at once,
marks a epock in Wolfville business life wherefrom
folks can onblushin'ly date time! Thar it lays,
however, an' the two sharps most onmoved tharby
is Cherokee an' Holliday themse'fs.

"'Turn your game!' says this Holliday, when
his money is down, an' leanin' back to light a
seegyar.

"Cherokee makes the turn. Never does I witness
action so sudden an' complete! It's shore the
sharpest! The top kyard as the deck lays in the
box is a ten-spot. An' as the papers is shoved
forth, how do you-all reckon they falls! I'm a
Mexican! if they don't come seven-king! This
Holliday wins all along; Cherokee is out thirty
thousand an' only three kyards showed! How's
that for perishin' flesh an' blood!

"I looks at Cherokee; his face is as ca'm as a
Injun's; he's too finely fibred a sport to so much
as let a eyelash quiver. This Holliday is equally
onemotional. Cherokee shoves over three yaller
chips.

"'Call 'em ten thousand each,' says Cherokee.
Then he waits for this Holliday to place his next
bets.

"'Since you-all has exackly that sum left in your
treasury,' observes this Holliday, puffin' his seegyar,

' I reckons I'll let one of these yaller tokens go, coppered, on the high kyard ag'in. You-all doubles or breaks right yere.'

" The turn falls trey-eight. Cherokee takes in that ten thousand dollar chip.

" ' Bein's that I'm still playin' on velvet,' remarks this Holliday, an' his tone is listless an' languid like he's only half interested, ' I'll go twenty thousand on the high kyard, open. This trip we omits the copper.'

" The first kyard to show is a deuce. It's better than ten to one Cherokee will win. But disapp'intment chokes the camp ; the next kyard is a ace, an' Cherokee's swept off his moccasins. The bank is broke ; and to signify as much, Cherokee turns his box on its side, counts over forty thousand dollars to this Holliday an' gets up from the dealer's cha'r.

" As Cherokee rises, Faro Nell slides off the lookout's stool an' into the vacated cha'r. When Cherokee loses the last bet I hears Nell's teeth come together with a click. I don't dare look towards her at the time ; but now, when she turns the box back, takes out the deck, riffles an' returns it to its place I gives her a glance. Nell's as game as Cherokee. As she sets over ag'inst this lucky invalid her colour is high an' her eyes like two stars.

" ' An' now you've got to break me,' says Nell to this Holliday. ' Also, we restores the *statu quo*, as Colonel Sterett says in that *Coyote* paper, an' the limit retreats to a even hundred dollars.'

" ' Be you-all the partner Mister Hall mentions ? ' asks this Holliday, at the same time takin' off his sombrero an' throwin' away his seegyar.

" Nell says she is.

" ' Miss,' says this Holliday, ' I feels honoured to find myse'f across the layout from so much sperit an' beauty. A limit of one hundred, says you ; an' your word is law! As a first step then, give me three thousand dollars worth of chips an' make 'em fifty dollars each. I'll take the same chance with you on that question of splits I does former, an' I wants a hundred on every kyard, middle to win ag'in the ends.'

" The deal begins ; Nell is winner from the jump ; she takes in three bets to lose one plumb down to the turn. This Holliday calls the turn for the limit ; an' loses. The kyards go into the box ag'in an' a next deal ensooes. So it continyoos ; an' Nell beats this Holliday hard for half a hour. Nell sees she's in luck ; an' she feels that strong she conclooods to press it some.

" ' The limit's five hundred ! ' says Nell to this Holliday. ' Come after me ! '

" Holliday bows like he's complimented. ' I'm after you ; an' I comes a-runnin',' he says.

" Down goes his money all over the lay-out ; only now its five hundred instead of one hundred.

" It's no avail, this Holliday still loses. At the end of a hour Nell sizes up her roll ; she's a leetle over forty thousand strong ; jest where Cherokee stands at the start.

"Nell pauses as she's about to put the deck in the box for a deal. She looks at this Holliday a heap thoughtful. That look excites Dan Boggs who's been on the brink of fits since ever the play begins, he's that 'motional.

"'Don't raise the limit, Nell!' says Dan in a awful whisper. 'That's where Cherokee's weak at the go-off. He ought never to have thrown away the limit.'

"Nell casts her eyes—they're burnin' like coals! —on Dan. I can see his bluff about Cherokee bein' weak has done decided her mind.

"'Cherokee does right,' says Nell to Dan, 'like Cherokee allers does. An' I'll do the same as Cherokee. Stranger,' goes on Nell, turnin' from Dan to this Holliday; 'go as far as you likes. The bridle's off the hoss.'

"'An' much obleeged to you, Miss!' says this Holliday, with another of them p'lite bows. 'As the kyards goes in the box, I makes you the same three bets I makes first to Mister Hall. Ten thousand, coppered, in the pot; ten thousand, open, in the big squar'; an' ten thousand on the high kyard, coppered.'

"'An' now as then,' says Nell, sort o' catchin' her breath, 'the ten-spot's the soda kyard!'

"Son, it won't happen ag'in in a billion years! Nell's right hand shakes a trifle—she's only a child, mind, an' ain't got the nerves that goes with case-hardened sports—as she shoves the ten-spot forth. But it's comin' her way; her luck holds; as certain as we all sets yere drinkin' toddy, the same two kyards shows for her as for Cherokee, but this time they falls 'king-seven'; the bank wins, an' pore Holliday is cleaned out.

"'Thar, Cherokee,' says Nell, an' thar's a soft smile an' a sigh of deep content goes with the observation, 'thar's your bank ag'in; only it's thirty thousand stronger than it is four hours ago.'

"'Your bank, ladybird, you means!' says Cherokee.

"'Well, our bank, then,' retorts Nell. 'What's the difference? Don't you-all tell me we're partners?' Then Nell motions to Black Jack. 'The drinks is on me, Jack,' she says; 'see what the house will have.'

CHAPTER IV.

How The Raven Died.

" WHICH if you-all is out to hear of Injuns, son,"
observed the Old Cattleman, doubtfully, "the best
I can do is shet my eyes an' push along regyardless,
like a cayouse in a storm of snow. But I don't
guarantee no facts; none whatever! I never does
bend myse'f to severe study of savages an' what
notions I packs concernin' 'em is the casual frootes
of what I accidental hears an' what I sees. It's
only now an' then, as I observes former, that Injuns invades Wolfville; an' when they does, we-
all scowls 'em outen camp—sort o' makes a sour
front, so as to break 'em early of habits of visitin'
us. We shore don't hone none to have 'em hankerin'
'round.

" Nacherally, I makes no doubt that if you goes
clost to Injuns an' studies their little game you finds
some of 'em good an' some bad, some gaudy an'
some sedate, some cu'rous an' some indifferent,
same as you finds among shore-enough folks. It's
so with mules an' broncos; wherefore, then, may not
these differences exist among Injuns? Come squar'
to the turn, you-all finds white folks separated the
same. Some gents follows off one waggon track an'
some another; some even makes a new trail.

" Speakin' of what's opposite in folks, I one time an' ag'in sees two white chiefs of scouts who frequent comes pirootin' into Wolfville from the Fort. Each has mebby a score of Injuns at his heels who pertains to him personal. One of these scout chiefs is all buck-skins, fringes, beads an' feathers from y'ears to hocks, while t'other goes garbed in a stiff hat with a little jim crow rim—one of them kind you deenom'nates as a darby—an' a diag'nal overcoat ; one chief looks like a dime novel on a spree an' t'other as much like the far East as he saveys how. An' yet, son, this voylent person in buckskins is a Second Lootenent—a mere boy, he is—from West P'int ; while that outcast in the reedic'lous hat is foaled on the plains an' never does go that clost to the risin' sun as to glimpse the old Missouri. The last form of maverick bursts frequent into Western bloom ; it's their ambition, that a-way, to deloode you into deemin' 'em as fresh from the States as one of them tomatter airtights.

" Thar's old gent Jeffords ; he's that sort. Old Jeffords lives for long with the Apaches ; he's found among 'em when Gen'ral Crook—the old 'Grey Fox'—an' civilisation and gatlin' guns comes into Arizona arm in arm. I used to note old Jeffords hibernatin' about the Oriental over in Tucson. I shore reckons he's procrastinatin' about thar yet, if the Great Sperit ain't done called him in. As I says, old Jeffords is that long among the Apaches back in Cochise's time that the mem'ry of man don't run

none to the contrary. An' yet no gent ever sees
old Jeffords wearin' anything more savage than a
long-tail black surtoot an' one of them stove pipe
hats. Is Jeffords dangerous? No, you-all couldn't
call him a distinct peril ; still, folks who goes devotin'
themse'fs to stirrin' Jeffords up jest to see if he's
alive gets disasterous action.   He has long grey ha'r
an' a tangled white beard half-way down his front ;
an' with that old plug hat an' black coat he's
a sight to frighten children or sour milk!   Still,
Jeffords is all right.   As long as towerists an' other
inquisitive people don't go pesterin' Jeffords, he
shore lets 'em alone.   Otherwise, you might as well
be up the same saplin' with a cinnamon b'ar ; which
you'd most likely hear something drop a lot !

   " For myse'f, I likes old Jeffords, an' considers
him a pleasin' conundrum.   About tenth drink time
he'd take a cha'r an' go camp by himse'f in a far
corner, an' thar he'd warble hymns.   Many a time
as I files away my nosepaint in the Oriental have
I been regaled with,

> Jesus, Lover of my soul,
>   Let me to Thy bosom fly,
> While the nearer waters roll,
>   While the tempest still is high,

as emanatin' from Jeffords where he's r'ared back
conductin' some personal services.   Folks never
goes buttin' in interferin' with these concerts ;
which it's cheaper to let him sing.

   " Speakin' of Injuns, as I su'gests, I never does
see over-much of 'em in Wolfville.   An' my earlier

experiences ain't thronged with 'em neither, though
while I'm workin' cattle along the Red River I
does carom on Injuns more or less. Thar's one
old hostile I recalls speshul; he's a fool Injun
called Black Feather;—Choctaw, he is. This Black
Feather's weakness is fire-water; he thinks more
of it than some folks does of children.

"Black Feather used to cross over to where Dick
Stocton maintains a store an' licker house on the
Upper Hawgthief. Of course, no gent sells these
Injuns licker. It's ag'in the law; an' onless you-all
is onusual eager to make a trip to Fort Smith with
a marshal ridin' herd on you doorin' said visit, impartin' of nosepaint to aborigines is a good thing
not to do. But Black Feather, he'd come over to
Dick Stocton's an' linger 'round the bar'ls of Valley
Tan, an' take a chance on stealin' a snifter or two
while Stocton's busy.

"At last Stocton gets tired an' allows he'll lay for
Black Feather. This yere Stocton is a mighty
reckless sport; he ain't carin' much whatever he
does do; he hates Injuns an' shot guns, an' loves
licker, seven-up, an' sin in any form; them's Stocton's prime characteristics. An' he gets mighty
weary of the whiskey-thievin' Black Feather, an' lays
for him.

"One evenin' this aggravatin' Black Feather
crosses over an' takes to ha'ntin' about Dick Stocton's licker room as is his wont. It looks like Black
Feather has already been buyin' whiskey of one of
them boot-laig parties who takes every chance an'

goes among the Injuns an' sells 'em nosepaint on the sly. 'Fore ever he shows up on the Upper Hawg-thief that time, this Black Feather gets nosepaint some'ers an' puts a whole quart of it away in the shade; an' he shore exhibits symptoms. Which for one thing he feels about four stories tall!

"Stocton sets a trap for Black Feather. He fills up the tin cup into which he draws that Valley Tan with coal-oil—karoseen you-all calls it—an' leaves it, temptin' like, settin' on top a whiskey bar'l. Shore! it's the first thing Black Feather notes. He sees his chance an' grabs an' downs the karoseen; an' Stocton sort o' startin' for him, this Black Feather gulps her down plump swift. The next second he cuts loose the yell of that year, burns up about ten acres of land, and starts for Red River. No, I don't know whether the karoseen hurts him none or not; but he certainly goes squatterin' across the old Red River like a wounded wild-duck, an' he never does come back no more.

"But, son, as you sees, I don't know nothin' speshul or much touchin' Injuns, an' if I'm to dodge the disgrace of ramblin' along in this desultory way, I might better shift to a tale I hears Sioux Sam relate to Doc Peets one time in the Red Light. This Sam is a Sioux, an a mighty decent buck, considerin' he's Injun; Sam is servin' the Great Father as a scout with the diag'nal-coat, darby-hat sharp I mentions. Peets gives this saddle-tinted longhorn a 4-bit piece, an' he tells this yarn. It sounds plenty childish; but you oughter b'ar in mind that savages, mental, ain't no bigger nor older than ten year old young-ones among the palefaces.

" ' This is the story my mother tells me,' says Sioux Sam, 'to show me the evils of cur'osity. " The Great Sperit allows to every one the right to ask only so many questions," says my mother, " an' when they ask one more than is their right, they die."

" ' This is the story of the fate of *Kaw-kaw-chee*, the Raven, a Sioux Chief who died long ago exackly as my mother told me. The Raven died because he asked too many questions an' was too cur'ous. It began when Sublette, who was a trader, came up the *Mitchi-zoor-rah*, the Big-Muddy, an' was robbed by the Raven's people. Sublette was mad at this, an' said next time he would bring the Sioux a present so they would not rob him. So he brought a little cask of fire-water an' left it on the bank of the Big-Muddy, Then Sublette went away, an' twenty of the Raven's young men found the little cask. An' they were greedy an' did not tell the camp ; they drank the fire-water where it was found.

" ' The Raven missed his twenty young men an' when he went to spy for them, behold ! they were dead with their teeth locked tight an' their faces an' bodies writhen an' twisted as the whirlwind twists the cottonwoods. Then the Raven thought an' thought ; an' he got very cur'ous to know why his young men died so writhen an' twisted. The fire-water had a whirlwind in it, an' the Raven was eager to hear. So he sent for Sublette.

"'Then the Raven an' Sublette had a big talk. They agreed not to hurt each other; an' Sublette was to come an' go an' trade with the Sioux; an' they would never rob him.

"'At this, Sublette gave the Raven some of the whirlwind that so killed an' twisted the twenty young men. It was a powder, white; an' it had no smell. Sublette said its taste was bitter; but the Raven must not taste it or it would lock up his teeth an' twist an' kill him. For to swallow the white powder loosed the whirlwind on the man's heart an' it bent him an' twisted him like the storms among the willows.

"'But the Raven could give the powder to others. So the Raven gave it in some deer's meat to his two squaws; an' they were twisted till they died; an' when they would speak they couldn't, for their teeth were held tight together an' no words came out of their mouths,—only a great foam. Then the Raven gave it to others that he did not love; they were twisted an' died. At last there was no more of the powder of the whirlwind; the Raven must wait till Sublette came up the Big-Muddy again an' brought him more.

"'There was a man, the Gray Elk, who was of the Raven's people. The Gray Elk was a *Choo-ayk-eed*, a great prophet. And the Gray Elk had a wife; she was wise an' beautiful, an' her name was Squaw-who-has-dreams. But Gray Elk called her *Kee-nee-moo-sha*, the Sweetheart.

"'While the Raven waited for Sublette to bring

him more powder of the whirlwind, a star with a long tail came into the sky. This star with the tail made the Raven heap cur'ous. He asked Gray Elk to tell him about it, for he was a prophet. The Raven asked many questions; they fell from him like leaves from a tree in the month of the first ice. So the Gray Elk called *Chee-bee*, the Spirit; an' the Spirit told the Gray Elk. Then the Gray Elk told the Raven.'

" ' It was not a tail, it was blood—star blood; an' the star had been bit an' was wounded, but would get well. The Sun was the father of the stars, an' the Moon was their mother. The Sun, *Gheezis*, tried ever to pursue an' capture an' eat his children, the stars. So the stars all ran an' hid when the Sun was about. But the stars loved their mother who was good an' never hurt them; an' when the Sun went to sleep at night an' *Coush-ee-wan*, the Darkness, shut his eyes, the Moon an' her children came together to see each other. But the star that bled had been caught by the Sun; it got out of his mouth but was wounded. Now it was frightened, so it always kept its face to where the Sun was sleeping over in the west. The bleeding star, *Sch-coo-dah*, would get well an' its wound would heal.

" ' Then the Raven wanted to know how the Gray Elk knew all this. An' the Gray Elk had the Raven into the medicine lodge that night; an' the Raven heard the spirits come about an' heard their voices; but he could not understand. Also, the Raven saw a wolf all fire, with wings like the eagle which flew

overhead. Also he heard the Thunder, *Boom-wa·
wa*, talking with the Gray Elk; but the Raven
couldn't understand. The Gray Elk told the Raven
to draw his knife an' stab with it in the air outside
the medicine lodge. An' when he did, the Raven's
blade an' hand came back covered with blood.
Still, the Raven was cur'ous an' kept askin' to be
told how the Gray Elk knew these things. An' the
Gray Elk at last took the Raven to the Great Bachelor Sycamore that lived alone, an' asked the Raven
if the Bachelor Sycamore was growing. An' the
Raven said it was. Then Gray Elk asked him how
he knew it was growing. An' the Raven said he
didn't know. Then Gray Elk said he did not know
how he knew about *Sch-coo-dah*, the star that was
bit. This made the Raven angry, for he was very
cur'ous; an' he thought the Gray Elk had two
tongues.

"'Then it came the month of the first young
grass an' Sublette was back for furs. Also he
brought many goods; an' he gave to the Raven
more of the powder of the whirlwind in a little box.
At once the Raven made a feast of ducks for the
Gray Elk; an' he gave him of the whirlwind powder; an' at once his teeth came together an' the
Gray Elk was twisted till he died.

"'Now no one knew that the Raven had the
powder of the whirlwind, so they could not tell why
all these people were twisted and went to the Great
Spirit. But the Squaw-who-has-dreams saw that it
was the Raven who killed her husband, the Gray

Elk, in a vision. Then the Squaw-who-has-dreams went into the mountains four days an' talked with *Moh-kwa*, the Bear who is the wisest of the beasts. The Bear said it was the Raven who killed the Gray Elk an' told the Squaw-who-has-dreams of the powder of the whirlwind.

"'Then the Bear an' the Squaw-who-has-dreams made a fire an' smoked an' laid a plot. The Bear did not know where to find the powder of the whirlwind which the Raven kept always in a secret place. But the Bear told the Squaw-who-has-dreams that she should marry the Raven an' watch until she found where the powder of the whirlwind was kept in its secret place; an' then she was to give some to the Raven, an' he, too, would be twisted an' die. There was a great danger, though; the Raven would, after the one day when they were wedded, want to kill the Squaw-who-has-dreams. So to protect her, the Bear told her she must begin to tell the Raven the moment she was married to him the Story-that-never-ends. Then, because the Raven was more cur'ous than even he was cruel, he would put off an' put off giving the powder of the whirlwind to the Squaw-who-has-dreams, hoping to hear the end of the Story-that-never-ends. Meanwhile the Squaw-who-has-dreams was to watch the Raven until she found the powder of the whirlwind in its secret place.

"'Then the wise Bear gave the Squaw-who-has-dreams a bowlful of words as seed, so she might plant them an' raise a crop of talk to tell the Story-that-never-ends. An' the Squaw-who-has-dreams planted the seed-words, an' they grew an' grew an' she gathered sixteen bundles of talk an' brought them to her wigwam. After that she put beads in her hair, an' dyed her lips red, an' rubbed red on her cheeks, an' put on a new blanket; an' when the Raven saw her, he asked her to marry him. So they were wedded ; an' the Squaw-who-has-dreams went to the teepee of the Raven an' was his wife.

"'But the Raven was old an' cunning like *Yah. mee-kee*, the Beaver, an' he said, "He is not wise who keeps a squaw too long!" An' with that he thought he would kill the Squaw-who-has-dreams the next day with the powder of the whirlwind. But the Squaw-who-has-dreams first told the Raven that she hated *When-dee-goo*, the Giant ; an' that she should not love the Raven until he had killed *When-dee-goo*. She knew the Giant was too big an' strong for the Raven to kill with his lance, an' that he must get his powder of the whirlwind; she would watch him an' learn its secret place. The Raven said he would kill the Giant as the sun went down next day.

"'Then the Squaw-who-has-dreams told the Raven the first of the Story-that-never-ends an' used up one bundle of talk; an' when the story ended for that night, the Squaw-who-has-dreams was saying: "An' so, out of the lake that was red as the sun came a great fish that was green, with yellow wings, an' it walked also with feet, an' it came up to me an' said :" But then she would tell no more that night ; nor could the Raven, who was crazy with cur'osity, prevail on her. " I must now sleep an' dream what the green fish with the yellow wings said," was the reply of the Squaw-who-has-dreams, an' she pretended to slumber. So the Raven, because he was cur'ous, put off her death.

" ' All night she watched, but the Raven did not go to the secret place where he had hidden the powder of the whirlwind. Nor the next day, when the sun went down, did the Raven kill the Giant. But the Squaw-who-has-dreams took up again the Story-that-never-ends an' told what the green fish with the yellow wings said ; an' she used up the second bundle of talk. When she ceased for that time,the Squaw-who-has-dreams was saying : " An' as night fell, *Moh-kwa*, the Bear, called to me from his canyon, an' said for me to come an' he would show me where the great treasure of fire-water was buried for you who are the Raven. So I went into the canyon, an' *Moh-kwa*, the Bear, took me by the hand an' led me to the treasure of fire-water which was greater an' richer than was ever seen by any Sioux."

" ' Then the Squaw-who-has-dreams would tell no more that night, while the Raven eat his fingers with cur'osity. But he made up a new plan not to twist the Squaw-who-has-dreams until she showed him the treasure of fire-water an' told him the end of the Story-that-never-ends. On her part, however, the Squaw-who-has-dreams, as she went to sleep, wept an' tore the beads from her hair an' said the

Raven did not love her; for he had not killed the Giant as he promised. She said she would tell no more of the Story-that-never-ends until the Giant was dead; nor would she show to a husband who did not love her the great treasure of fire-water which *Moh-kwa*, the Bear, had found. At this, the Raven who was hot to have the treasure of fire-water an' whose ears rang with cur'osity to hear the end of the Story-that-never-ends saw that he must kill the Giant. Therefore, when the Squaw-who-has-dreams had ceased to sob and revile him, an' was gone as he thought asleep, the Raven went to his secret place where he kept the powder of the whirlwind an' took a little an' wrapped it in a leaf an' hid the leaf in the braids of his long hair. Then the Raven went to sleep.

"'When the Raven was asleep the Squaw-who-has-dreams went also herself to the secret place an' got also a little of the powder of the whirlwind. An' the next morning she arose early an' gave the powder of the whirlwind to the Raven on the roast buffalo, the *Pez-hee-kee*, which was his food.

"'When the Raven had eaten, the Squaw-who-has-dreams went out of the teepee among the people an' called all the Sioux to come an' see the Raven die. So the Sioux came gladly, and the Raven was twisted an' writhen with the power of the whirlwind wrenching at his heart; an' his teeth were tight like a trap; an' no words, but only foam, came from his mouth; an' at last the Spirit, the *Chee-bee*, was twisted out of the Raven; an' the

Squaw-who-has-dreams was revenged for the death of the Gray Elk whom she loved an' who always called her *Kee-nee-moo-sha*, the Sweetheart, because it made her laugh.

"'When the Raven was dead, the Squaw-who-has-dreams went to the secret place an' threw the powder of the whirlwind into the Big-Muddy; an' after that she distributed her fourteen bundles of talk that were left among all the Sioux so that everybody could tell how glad he felt because the Raven was twisted and died. An' for a week there was nothing but happiness an' big talk among the Sioux; an' *Moh-kwa*, the Bear, came laughing out of his canyon with the wonder of listening to it; while the Squaw-who-has-dreams now, when her revenge was done, went with *When-dee-goo*, the Giant, to his teepee and became his squaw. So now everything was ended save the Story-that-never-ends.'

"When Sioux Sam gets this far," concluded the Old Cattleman, " he says, ' an' my mother's words at the end were: " An' boys who ask too many questions will die, as did the Raven whose cur'osity was even greater than his cruelty." ' "

CHAPTER V.

The Queerness of Dave Tutt.

"WHICH these queernesses of Dave's," observed the Old Cattleman, "has already been harrowin' an' harassin' up the camp for mighty likely she's two months, when his myster'ous actions one evenin' in the Red Light brings things to a climax, an' a over-strained public, feelin' like it can b'ar no more, begins to talk.

"It's plumb easy to remember this Red Light o'casion, for jest prior to Dave alarmin' us by becomin' melodious, furtive—melody bein' wholly onnacheral to Dave, that a-way—thar's a callow pin-feather party comes caperin' in an' takin' Old Man Enright one side, asks can he yootilise Wolfville as a strategic p'int in a elopement he's goin' to pull off.

"'Which I'm out to elope a whole lot from Tucson,' explains this pin-feather party to Enright, 'an' I aims to cinch the play. I'm a mighty cautious sport, an' before ever I hooks up for actooal freightin' over any trail, I rides her once or twice to locate wood and water, an' pick out my camps. Said system may seem timorous, but it's shore safer a heap. So I asks ag'in whether you-all folks

has any objections to me elopin' into Wolfville with
my beloved, like I su'gests. I ain't out to spring
no bridals on a onprotected outfit, wherefore I pre-
cedes the play with these queries.'

"'But whatever's the call for you to elope at
all?' remonstrates Enright. 'The simple way now
would be to round up this lady's paternal gent, an'
get his consent.'

"'Seein' the old gent,' says the pin-feather party,
''speshully when you lays it smoothly off like that,
shore does seem simplicity itse'f. But if you was
to prance out an' try it some, it would be found
plenty complex. See yere!' goes on the pin-feather
party, beginnin' to roll up his sleeve, 'you-all impresses me as more or less a jedge of casyooalities.
Whatever now do you think of this?' An' the pinfeather party exhibits a bullet wound in his left
fore-arm, the same bein' about half healed.

"'Colt's six-shooter,' says Enright.

"'That's straight,' says the pin-feather party,
buttonin' up his sleeve; 'you calls the turn. I wins
out that abrasion pleadin' with the old gent. Which
I tackles him twice. The first time he opens on
me with his 44-gun before ever I ends the sentence. But he misses. Nacherally, I abandons them
marital intentions for what you-all might call the
"nonce" to sort o' look over my hand ag'in an' see
be I right. Do my best I can't on earth discern no
reasons ag'in the nuptials. Moreover, the lady—
who takes after her old gent a heap—cuts in on the
play with a bluff that while she don't aim none to

crowd my hand, she's doo to begin shootin' me up herse'f if I don't show more passionate anxiety about leadin' her to the altar. It's then, not seein' why the old gent should go entertainin' notions ag'in me, an' deemin' mebby that when he blazes away that time he's merely pettish and don't really mean said bullet none, that I fronts up ag'in.'

"'An' then,' asks Enright, 'whatever does this locoed parent do?'

"'Which I jest shows you what,' says the pin-feather party. 'He gets the range before ever I opens my mouth, an' plugs me. At that I begins to half despair of winnin' his indorsements. I leaves it to you-all; be I right?'

"'Why,' says Enright, rubbin' his fore'erd some doobious, 'it would look like the old gent is a leetle set ag'in you. Still, as the responsible chief of this camp, I would like to hear why you reckons Wolfville is a good place to elope to. I don't s'ppose it's on account of them drunkards over in Tucson makin' free with our good repoote an' lettin' on we're light an' immoral that a-way?'

"'None whatever!' says the pin-feather party. 'It's on account of you wolves bein' regyarded as peaceful, staid, an' law abidin' that I first considers you. Then ag'in, thar ain't a multitood of places clost about Tucson to elope to nohow; an' I can't elope far on account of my roll.'

"The replies of this pin-feather party soothes Enright an' engages him on that side, so he ups an' tells the 'swain,' as Colonel Sterett calls him later in the *Coyote*, to grab off his inamorata an' come a-runnin'.

"'Which, givin' my consent,' says Enright when explainin' about it later, 'is needed to protect this tempest-tossed lover in the possession of his skelp. The old gent an' that maiden fa'r has got him between 'em, an' onless we opens up Wolfville as a refooge, it looks like they'll cross-lift him into the promised land.'

"But to go back to Dave."

Here my old friend paused and called for refreshments. I seized the advantage of his silence over a glass of peach and honey, to suggest an eagerness for the finale of the Tucson love match.

"No," responded my frosty friend, setting down his glass, "we'll pursoo the queernesses of Dave. That Tucson elopement 'is another story a heap,' as some wise maverick says some'ers, an' I'll onload it on you on some other day.

"When Dave evolves the cadencies in the Red Light that evenin', thar's Enright, Moore an' me along with Dan Boggs, bein' entertained by hearin' Cherokee Hall tell us about a brace game he gets ag'inst in Las Vegas one time.

"'This deadfall — this brace I'm mentionin',' says Cherokee, 'is over on the Plaza. Of course, I calls this crooked game a "brace" in speakin' tharof to you-all sports who ain't really gamblers none. That's to be p'lite. But between us, among a'credited kyard sharps, a brace game is allers allooded to as "the old thing." If you refers to a game of chance as "the old thing," they knows at once that every chance is 'liminated an' said deevice rigged for murder.'

"'That's splendid, Cherokee,' says Faro Nell, from her lookout's roost by his shoulder; 'give 'em a lecture on the perils of gamblin' with strangers.'

"Thar's no game goin' at this epock an' Cherokee signifies his willin'ness to become instructive.

"'Not that I'm no beacon, neither,' says Cherokee, ' on the rocky wreck-sown shores of sport; an' not that I ever resorts to onderhand an' doobious deals myse'f; still, I'm cap'ble of p'intin' out the dangers. Scientists of my sort, no matter how troo an' faithful to the p'int of honour, is bound to savey all kyard dooplicities in their uttermost depths, or get left dead on the field of finance. Every gent should be honest. But more than honest—speshully if he's out to buck faro-bank or set in on casyooal games of short-kyards—every gent should be wise. In the amoosements I mentions to be merely honest can't be considered a complete equipment. Wherefore, while I never makes a crooked play an' don't pack the par'fernalia so to do, I'm plenty astoote as to how said tricks is turned.

"'Which sports has speshulties same as other folks. Thar's Texas Thompson, his speshulty is ridin' a hoss; while Peets's speshulty is shootin' a derringer, Colonel Sterett's is pol'tics, Enright's is jestice, Dave's is bein' married, Jack Moore's is upholdin' law an' order, Boggs's is bein' sooperstitious, Missis Rucker's is composin' bakin' powder biscuits, an' Huggins's is strong drink.'

" ' Whatever is my speshulty, Cherokee?' asks
Faro Nell, who's as immersed as the rest in these
settin's forth ; 'what do you-all reckon now is my
speshulty ? '

" ' Bein' the loveliest of your sex,' says Cherokee,
a heap emphatic, an' on that p'int we-all strings our
game with his.

" ' That puts the ambrosia on me,' says Faro
Nell, blushin' with pleasure, an' she calls to Black
Jack.

" ' As I observes,' goes on Cherokee, ' every sport
has his speshulty.   Thar's Casino Joe ; his is that
he can " tell the last four."   Nacherally, bein' thus
gifted, a game of casino is like so much money in
the bank for Joe.   Still, his gifts ain't crooked,
they're genius ; Joe's simply born able to " tell the
last four."

" ' Which, you gents is familiar by repoote at
least with the several plans for redoocin' draw-poker
to the prosaic level of shore-things.   Thar's the
" bug " an' the " foot-move " an' the " sleeve holdout " an' dozens of kindred schemes for playin' a
cold hand.   An' thar's optimists, when the game is
easy, who depends wholly on a handkerchief in
their laps to cover their nefariousness.   If I'm
driven to counsel a gent concernin' poker it would
be to never play with strangers ; an' partic'lar to
never spec'late with a gent who sneezes a lot, or
turns his head an' talks of draughts of cold air in-
vading' the place, or says his foot's asleep an' gets
up to stampede about the room after a hand is

dealt an' prior to the same bein' played. It's four to one this afflicted sharp is workin' a holdout. Then thar's the "punch" to mark a deck, an' the "lookin' glass" to catch the kyards as they're dealt. Then thar's sech manoovers as stockin' a deck, an' shiftin' a cut, an' dealin' double. Thar's gents who does their work from the bottom of a deck—puts up a hand on the bottom, an' confers it on a pard or on themse'fs as dovetails with their moods. He's a one-arm party—shy his right arm, he is—who deals a hand from the bottom the best I ever beholds.

"'No, I don't regyard crooked folks as dangerous at poker, only you've got to watch 'em. So long as your eye is on 'em a heap attentive they're powerless to perform their partic'lar miracle, an' as a result, since that's the one end an' aim of their efforts, they becomes mighty inocuous. As a roole, crooked people ain't good players on the squar', an' as long as you makes 'em play squar', they're yours.

"'But speakin' of this devious person on the Las Vegas Plaza that time: The outfit is onknown to me—I'm only a pilgrim an' a stranger an' don't intend to tarry none—when I sets up to the lay-out. I ain't got a bet down, however, before I sees the gent who's dealin', sign-up the seven to the case-keep, an' instanter I feels like I'd known that bevy of bandits since long before the war. Also, I real-ises their methods after I takes a good hard look. That dealer's got what post gradyooates in faro-bank robbery calls a "end squeeze" box ; the deck is trimmed—"wedges" is the name—to put the odds ag'in the evens, an' sanded so as to let two kyards come at a clatter whenever said pheenom-enon is demanded by the exigencies of their crimes; an' thar you be. No, it's a fifty-two-kyard deck all right, an' the dealer depends on "puttin' back" to keep all straight. An' I'm driven to concede that the put-back work of said party is like a romance; puttin' back's his speshulty. His left hand would sort o' settle as light as a dead leaf over the kyard he's after that a-way—not a tenth part of a second—an' that pasteboard would come along, palmed, an' as his hand floats over the box as he's goin' to make the next turn the kyard would reassoome its cunnin' place inside. An' all as smoothly serene as pray'r meetin's.'

"'An', nacherally, you denounces this felon,' says Colonel Sterett, who's come in an' who's in-tegrity is of the active sort.

"'Nacherally, I don't say a word,' retorts Chero-kee. 'I ain't for years inhabited these roode an' sand-blown regions, remote as they be from best ideals an' high examples of the East, not to long before have learned the excellence of that maxim about lettin' every man kill his own snakes. I says nothin'; I merely looks about to locate the victim of them machinations with a view of goin' ag'inst his play.'

"It's when Cherokee arrives at this place in his recitals that Dave evolves his interruptions. He's camped by himse'f in a reemote corner of the room, an' he ain't been noticin' nobody an' nobody's been noticin' him. All at once, in tones which is low but a heap discordant, Dave hums to himse'f something that sounds like :

> ' Bye O babe, lie still in slumber,
> Holy angels gyard thy bed.'

"At this, Cherokee in a horrified way stops, an' we-all looks at each other. Enright makes a dispar'-in' gesture towards Dave an' says :

" 'Gents, first callin' your attention to the fact that Dave ain't over-drinkt an' that no nosepaint theery is possible in accountin' for his acts, I asks you for your opinions. As you knows, this thing's been goin' for'ard for some time, an' I desires to hear if from any standp'int of public interest do you-all figger that steps should be took ? '

"In order to fully onderstand Enright in all he means, I oughter lay bar' that Dave's been con-ductin' himse'f in a manner not to be explained for mighty likely she's eight weeks. Yeretofore, thar's no more sociable sport an' none whose system is easier to follow in all Wolfville than Dave. While holdin' himse'f at what you might call ' par ' on all o'casions, Dave is still plenty minglesome an' fra-ternal with the balance of the herd, an' would no more think of donnin' airs or puttin' on dog than he'd think of blastin' away at one of us with his gun. Yet eight weeks prior thar shorely dawns a change.

"Which the first symptom—the advance gyard as it were of Dave's gettin' queer—is when Dave's standin' in front of the post-office. Thar's a far-away look to Dave at the time, like he's tryin' to settle whether he's behind or ahead on some deal. While thus wropped in this fit of abstraction Dan Boggs comes hybernatin' along an' asks Dave to p'int into the Red Light for a smell of Valley Tan. Dave sort o' rouses up at this an' fastens on Dan with his eyes, half truculent an' half amazed, same as if he's shocked at Dan's familiarity. Then he shakes his head decisive.

" ' Don't try to braid this mule's tail none ! ' says Dave, an' at that he strides off with his muzzle in the air. Boggs is abashed.

" ' Which these insultin' bluffs of Dave's,' says Boggs, as we canvasses the play a bit later, ' would cut me to the quick, but I knows it ain't on the level. Dave ain't himse'f when he declines said nosepaint—his intellects ain't in camp.'

" This ontoward an' onmerited rebuke to Boggs is followed by further breaks as hard to savey. Dave ain't no two days alike. One time he's that haughty he actooally passes Enright himse'f in the street an' no more heed or recognition than if Wolfville's chief is the last Mexican to come no'th of the line. Then later Dave is effoosive an' goes about riotin' in the s'ciety of every gent whereof he cuts the trail. One day he won't drink ; an' the next he's tippin' the canteen from sun-up till he's claimed by sleep. Which he gets us mighty near distracted ; no one can keep a tab on him. What with them silences an' volyoobilities, sobrieties an' days of drink, an' all in bewilderin' alternations, he's shore got us goin' four ways at once.

"'In spite of the fact,' continyooes Dan Boggs when we're turnin' Dave's conduct over in our minds an' rummagin' about for reasons; 'in spite of the fact, I says, that I'm plenty posted in advance that I'm up ag'inst a gen'ral shout of derision on account of me bein' sooperstitious, I'm yere to offer two to one Dave's hoodooed. Moreover, I can name the hoodoo.'

"'Whatever is it then?' asks Texas Thompson; 'cut her freely loose an' be shore of our solemn consid'ration.'

"'It's opals,' says Boggs. 'Them gems as every well-instructed gent is aware is the very sperit of bad luck. Dave's wearin' one in his shirt right now. It's that opal pin wherewith he decks himse'f recent while he's relaxin' with nosepaint in Tucson. I'm with him at the time an' I says to him: "Dave, I wouldn't mount that opal none. Which all opals is implacable hoodoos, an' it'll likely conjure up your rooin." But I might as well have addressed that counsel to a buffalo bull for all the respectful heed I gains. Dave gives me a grin, shets one eye plenty cunnin', an' retorts: "Dan, you're envious; you wants that ornament yourse'f an' you're out to try an make me diskyard it in your favour. Sech schemes, Dan, can't make the landin'. Opals that a-way is as harmless as bull snakes. Also, I knows what becomes my looks; an' while I ain't vain,

still, bein' married as you're aware, it's wisdom in
me to seize every openin' for enhancin' my pulcri-
toode. The better I looks, the longer Tucson
Jennie loves me ; an' I'm out to reetain that lady's
heart at any cost." No, I don't onbend in no
response,' goes on Boggs. ' Them accoosations of
Dave about me honin' for said bauble is oncalled for.
I'd no more pack a opal than I'd cut for deal an'
embark on a game of seven-up with a ghost. As I
states, the luck of opals is black.'

" ' I was wont to think so,' says Enright, ' but thar
once chances a play, the same comin' off onder my
personal notice, that shakes my convictions on that
p'int. Thar's a broke-down sport—this yere's long
ago while I'm briefly sojournin' in Socorro—who's
got a opal, an' he one day puts it in hock with a
kyard sharp for a small stake. The kyard gent says
he ain't alarmed none by these charges made of
opals bein' bad luck. It's a ring, an' he sticks it
on his little finger. Two days later he goes broke
ag'in four jacks.

" ' This terrifies him ; he begins to believe in the
evil inflooences of opals. He presents the jewelry
to a bar-keep, who puts it up, since his game limits
itse'f to sellin' licker an', him bein' plenty careful
not to drink none himse'f, his contracted destinies
don't offer no field for opals an' their malign effects. In less time than a week, however, his wife
leaves him ; an' also that drink-shop wherein he
officiates is blown down by a high wind.

" ' That bar-keep emerges from the rooins of his

domestic hopes an' the desolation of that gin mill,
an' endows a lady of his acquaintance with this
opal ornament. It ain't twenty-four hours when
she cuts loose an' weds a Mexican.

"'Which by this time, excitement is runnin' high,
an' you-all couldn't have found that citizen in Socorro with a search warrant who declines to believe
in opals bein' bad luck. On the hocks of these
catastrophes it's the common notion that nobody
better own that opal; an' said malev'lent stone in
the dooal capac'ty of a cur'osity an' a warnin' is
put in the seegyar case at the Early Rose s'loon.
The first day it's thar, a jeweller sharp come in for
his daily drinks—he runs the jewelry store of that
meetropolis an' knows about diamonds an' sim'lar
jimcracks same as Peets does about drugs—an'
he considers this talisman, scrootinisin' it a heap
clost. "Do you-all believe in the bad luck of
opals?" asks a pard who's with him. "This thing
ain't no opal," says the jeweller sharp, lookin' up;
"it's glass."

"'An' so it is: that baleful gewgaw has been
sailin' onder a alias; it ain't no opal more'n a Colt's
cartridge is a poker chip. An', of course, it's plain
the divers an' several disasters, from the loss of
that kyard gent's bank-roll down to the Mexican
nuptials of the ill-advised lady to whom I alloodes,
can't be laid to its charge. The whole racket
shocks an' shakes me to that degree,' concloods
Enright, 'that to-day I ain't got no settled views on
opals', none whatever.'

"'Jest the same, I thinks it's opals that's the trouble with Dave,' declar's Boggs, plenty stubborn, an' while the rest of us don't yoonite with him, we receives his view serious an' respectful so's not to jolt Boggs's feelin's.

"Goin' back, however, to when Dave sets up the warble of 'Bye O baby!' that a-way, we-all, follow-in' Enright's s'licitation for our thoughts, abides a heap still an' makes no response. Enright asks ag'in: 'What do you-all think?'

"At last Boggs, who as I sets forth frequent is a nervous gent, an' one on whom silence soon begins to prey, ag'in speaks up. Bein' doubtful an' mindful of Enright's argyment ag'in his opal bluff, however, Boggs don't advance his concloosions this time at all emphatic. In a tone like he's out ridin' for in-formation himse'f, Boggs says:

"'Mebby, if it ain't opals, it's a case of straight loco.'

"'While I wouldn't want to readily think Dave locoed,' says Enright, 'seein' he's oncommon firm on his mental feet, still he's shore got something on his mind. An' bein' it is something, it's possible as you says that Dave's intellects is onhossed.'

"'Whatever for a play would it be,' says Chero-kee, 'to go an' ask Dave himse'f right now?'

"'I'd be some slow about propoundin' sech sur-mises to Dave,' says Boggs. 'He might get hostile; you can put a wager on it, he'd turn out disagree-'ble to a degree, if he did. No, you-all has got to har.dle a loonatic with gloves. I knows a gent who entangles himse'f with a loonatic, askin' questions, an' he gets all shot up.'

" ' I reckons, however,' says Cherokee, ' that I'll assoome the resk. Dave an' me's friends; an' I allows if I goes after him in ways both soft an' care-less, so as not to call forth no suspicions, he'll take it good-humoured even if he is locoed.'

" We-all sets breathless while Cherokee sa'nters down to where Dave's still wropped in them melo-dies.

" ' Whatever be you hummin' toones for, Dave?' asks Cherokee all accidental like.

" ' Which I'm rehearsin',' says Dave, an' he shows he's made impatient. ' Don't come infringin' about me with no questions,' goes on Dave. ' I'm like the ancient Romans, I've got troubles of my own ; an' no sport who calls himse'f my friend will go ag-gravatin' me with ontimely inquis'tiveness.' Then Dave gets up an' pulls his freight an' leaves us more onsettled than at first.

" For a full hour, we does nothin' but canvass this yere question of Dave's aberrations. At last a idee seizes us. Thar's times when Dave's been seen caucusin' with Missis Rucker an' Doc Peets. Most likely one of 'em would be able to shed a ray on Dave. By a excellent coincidence, an' as if to he'p us out, Peets comes in as Texas Thompson su'gests that mebby the Doc's qualified to onravel the myst'ry.

" ' Tell you-all folks what's the matter with Dave?' says Peets. ' Pards, it's simply not in the deck. Meanin' no disrespects—for you gents knows me too well to dream of me harborin' anything but feelin's of the highest regyards for one an' all—I'll have to leave you camped in original darkness. It would be breakin' professional confidences. Shore, I saveys Dave's troubles an' the causes of these vagaries of his; jest the same the traditions of the medical game forces me to hold 'em sacred an' secret.'

" ' Tell us at least, Doc,' says Enright, ' whether Dave's likely to grow voylent. If he is, it's only proper that we arranges to tie him down.'

" ' Dave may be boisterous later,' says Peets, an' his reply comes slow an' thoughtful, like he's con- siderin'; 'he may make a joyful uproar, but he won't wax dangerous.' This yere's as far as Peets'll go; he declines to talk longer, on professional grounds.

" ' Which suspense, this a-way,' says Boggs, after Peets is gone, ' an' us no wiser than when he shows in the door, makes me desp'rate. I'll offer the mo- tion: Let's prance over in a bunch, an demand a explanation of Missis Rucker. Dave's been talkin' to her as much as ever he has to Peets, an' thar's no professional hobbles on the lady; she's footloose, an' free to speak.'

" ' We waits on you, Marm,' says Enright, when ten minutes later Boggs, Cherokee, Texas Thompson an' he is in the kitchen of the O. K. Restauraw where Missis Rucker is slicin' salt hoss an' layin' the fragrant foundations of supper; ' we waits on

you- all to ask your advice. Dave Tutt's been carryin' on in a manner an' form at once doobious
an' threatenin'. It ain't too much to say that we-
all fears the worst. We comes now to invite you to
tell us all you knows of Dave an' whatever it is
that so onsettles him. Our idee is that you onderstands a heap about it.'

" ' See yere, Sam Enright,' retorts Missis Rucker,
pausin' over the salt hoss, 'you ain't doin' yourse'f
proud. You better round up this herd of inebriates
an' get 'em back to the Red Light. Thar's nothin'
the matter with Dave; leastwise if it was the matter
with you, you'd be some improved. Dave Tutt's a
credit to this camp; never more so than now; the
same bein' a mighty sight more'n I could say of any
of you-all an' stick to the trooth.'

" 'Then you does know, Missis Rucker,' says
Enright, 'the secret that's gnawin' at Dave.'

" ' Know it,' replies Misses Rucker, ' of course, I
knows it. But I don't propose to discuss it none
with you tarrapins. I ain't got no patience with
sech dolts! Now that you-all is yere, however,
I'll give you notice that to-morry you can begin to
do your own cookin' till you hears further word
from me. I'm goin' to be otherwise an' more con-
genially engaged. Most likely I'll be back in my
kitchen ag'in in a day or two; but I makes no
promises. An' ontil sech time as I shows up, you-
all can go scuffle for yourse'fs. I've got more
important dooties jest now on my hands than cookin' chuck for sots.'

"As Missis Rucker speaks up mighty vigorous, an' as none of us has the nerve to ask her further an' take the resk of turnin' loose her temper, we lines out ag'in for the Red Light no cl'arer than what we was.

"'I could ask her more questions,' says Enright, 'but, gents, I didn't deem it wise. Missis Rucker is a most admirable character; but I'm sooperstitious about crowdin' her too clost. Like Boggs says about opals, thar's plenty of bad luck lurkin' about Missis Rucker's environs if you only goes about it's deevelopment the right way.'

"'The sityooation is too many for me,' says Boggs, goin' up to the bar for a drink, 'I gives it up. I ain't got a notion left, onless it is that Dave's runnin' for office; that is, I might entertain sech a thought only thar ain't no office.'

"'The next day Missis Rucker abandons her post; an' we tharupon finds that feedin' ourse'fs keeps us busy an' we don't have much time to discuss Dave. Also, Dave disappears;—in fact, both Dave an' Missis Rucker fades from view.

"It's about fo'rth drink time the evenin' of the third day, an' most of us is in the Red Light. Thar's a gloom overhangs us like a fog. Mebby it's the oncertainties which envelops Dave, mebby it's because Missis Rucker's done deserted an' left us to rustle for ourse'fs or starve. Most of us is full of present'ments that something's due to happen.

"All at once, an' onexpected, Dave walks in. A sigh of relief goes up, for the glance we gives him shows he's all right—sane as Enright—clothed an' in his right mind as set fo'th in holy writ. Also, his countenance is a wrinkle of glee.

" 'Gents,' says Dave, an' his air is that patronisin' it would have been exasperatin' only we're so relieved, 'gents, I'm come to seek congratyoolations an' set 'em up. Peets an' that motherly angel, Missis Rucker, allows I'll be of more use yere than in my own house, whereat I nacherally floats over. Coupled with a su'gestion that we drinks, I wants to say that he's a boy, an' that I brands him "Enright Peets Tutt." ' "

CHAPTER VI.

With the Apache's Compliments.

"ONDOUBTED," observed the Old Cattleman, during one of our long excursive talks, "ondoubted, the ways an' the motives of Injuns is past the white man's findin' out. He's shore a myst'ry, the Injun is! an' where the paleface forever fails of his s'loo-tion is that the latter ropes at this problem in copper-colour from the standp'int of the Caucasian. Can a dog onderstand a wolf? Which I should re-mark not!

"It's a heap likely that with Injuns, the white man in his turn is jest as difficult to solve. An' without the Injun findin' onusual fault with 'em, thar's a triangle of things whereof the savage accooses the paleface. The Western Injuns at least—for I ain't posted none on Eastern savages, the same bein' happily killed off prior to my time—the Western Injuns lays the bee, the wild turkey, an' that weed folks calls the 'plantain,' at the white man's door. They-all descends upon the Injun hand in hand. No, the Injun don't call the last-named veg'table a 'plantain;' he alloodes to it as 'the White Man's Foot.'

"Thar's traits dominant among Injuns which it wouldn't lower the standin' of a white man if he

ups an' imitates a whole lot. I once encounters a
savage—one of these blanket Injuns with feathers
in his ha'r—an' bein' idle an' careless of what I'm
about, I staggers into casyooal talk with him.
This buck's been East for the first time in his
darkened c'reer an' visited the Great Father in
Washin'ton. I asks him what he regyards as the
deepest game he in his travels goes ag'inst. At
first he allows that pie, that a-way, makes the most
profound impression. But I bars pie, an' tells him
to su'gest the biggest thing he strikes, not on no
bill of fare. Tharupon, abandonin' menoos an'
wonders of the table, he roominates a moment an'
declar's that the steamboat—now that pie is ex-
clooded—ought to get the nom'nation.

"'The choo-choo boat,' observes this intelligent
savage, 'is the paleface's big medicine.'

"'You'll have a list of marvels,' I says, 'to ava-
lanche upon the people when you cuts the trail of
your ancestral tribe ag'in?'

"'No,' retorts the savage, shakin' his head ontil
the skelp-lock whips his y'ears, an' all mighty
decisive; 'no; won't tell Injun nothin'.'

"'Why not?' I demands.

"'If I tell,' he says, 'they no believe. They
think it all heap lie.'

"Son, consider what a example to travellers is
set by that ontootered savage? That's what makes
me say thar be traits possessed of Injuns, personal, which a paleface might improve himse'f by
copyin'.

" Bein' white myse'f, I'm born with notions ag'in
Injuns.   I learns of their deestruction with relief, an' never sees one pirootin' about, full of life
an' vivacity, but the spectacle fills me with vain
regrets.   All the same thar's a load o' lies told East
concernin' the Injun.   I was wont from time to time
to discuss these red folks with Gen'ral Stanton, who
for years is stationed about in Arizona, an'—merely
for the love he b'ars to fightin'—performs as chief
of scouts for Gen'ral Crook.

" ' Our divers wars with the Apaches,' says Gen'-
ral Stanton, ' comes more as the frootes of a misdeal
by a locoed marshal than anything else besides.
When Crook first shows up in Arizona—this is
in the long ago—an' starts to inculcate peace among
the Apaches, he gets old Jeffords to bring Cochise
to him to have a pow-wow.   Jeffords rounds up
Cochise an' herds him with soft words an' big promises into the presence of Crook.   The Grey Fox—
which was the Injun name for Crook—makes
Cochise a talk.   Likewise he p'ints out to the chief
the landmarks an' mountain peaks that indicates
the Mexican line.   An' the Grey Fox explains to
Cochise that what cattle is killed an' what skelps
is took to the south'ard of the line ain't goin' to
bother him a bit.   But no'th'ard it's different ; thar
in that sacred region cattle killin' an' skelp collectin'
don't go.   The Grey Fox shoves the information
on Cochise that every trick turned on the American
side of the line has done got to partake of the
characteristics of a love affair, or the Grey Fox with

his young men in bloo—his walk-a-heaps an' his
hoss-warriors—noomerous as the grass, they be—
will come down on Cochise an' his Apaches like a
coyote on a sage hen or a pan of milk from a top
shelf an' make 'em powerful hard to find.

" ' Cochise smokes an' smokes, an' after considerin' the bluff of the Grey Fox plenty profound,
allows he won't call it. Thar shall be peace between
the Apache an' the paleface to the no'th'ard of
that line. Then the Grey Fox an' Cochise shakes
hands an' says " How ! " an' Cochise, with a bolt or
two of red calico wherewith to embellish his squaws,
goes squanderin' back to his people, permeated to
the toes with friendly intentions.

" ' Sech is Cochise's reverence for his word,
coupled with his fear of the Grey Fox, that years
float by an' every deefile an' canyon of the Southwest is as safe as the aisles of a church to the moccasins of the paleface. Thus it continyoos ontil
thar comes a evenin' when a jimcrow marshal, with
more six-shooters than hoss sense, allows he'll ap-
prehend Cochise's brother a whole lot for some
offense that ain't most likely deuce high in the
category of troo crime. This ediot offishul reaches
for the relative of Cochise ; an' as the latter—bein'
a savage an' tharfore plumb afraid of captivity—
leaps back'ard like he's met up with a rattlesnake,
the marshal puts his gun on him an' plugs him so
good that he cashes in right thar. The marshal says
later in explanation of his game that Cochise's
brother turns hostile an' drops his hand on his knife.

Most likely he does ; a gent's hands — even a Apache's—has done got to be some'ers.

"'But the killin' overturns the peaceful pro-grammes built up between the Grey Fox an' Cochise. When the old chief hears of his brother bein' downed, he paints himse'f black an' red an' sends a bundle of arrows tied with a rattlesnake skin to the Grey Fox with a message to count his people an' look out for himse'f. The Grey Fox, who realises that the day of peace has ended an' the sun gone down to rise on a mornin' of trouble, fills the rattle-snake skin with cartridges an' sends 'em back with a word to Cochise to turn himse'f loose. From that moment the war-jig which is to last for years is on. After Cochise comes Geronimo, an' after Geronimo comes Nana ; an' one an' all, they adds a heap of spice to life in Arizona. It's no exaggeration to put the number of palefaces who lose their ha'r as the direct result of that fool marshal layin' for Cochise's brother an' that Injun's consequent cut-tin' off, at a round ten thousand. Shore ! thar's scores an' scores who's been stood up an' killed in the hills whereof we never gets a whisper. I, myse'f, in goin' through the teepees of a Apache outfit, after we done wipes 'em off the footstool, sees the long ha'r of seven white women who couldn't have been no time dead.

"'Who be they? Folks onknown who's got shot into while romancin' along among the hills with schemes no doubt of settlement in Californy.

"'With what we saveys of the crooelties of the Apaches, thar's likewise a sperit of what book-sharps

calls chivalry goes with 'em ; an' albeit on one ha'r-
hung o'casion I profits mightily tharby, I'm onable
to give it a reason. You wouldn't track up on no
sim'lar weaknesses among the palefaces an' you-all
can put down a stack on that.

"'It's when I'm paymaster,' says the Gen'ral,
reachin' for the canteen, 'an' I starts fo'th from
Fort Apache on a expedition to pay off the nearby
troops. I've got six waggons an' a escort of twenty
men. For myse'f, at the r'ar of the procession, I
journeys proudly in a amb'lance. Our first camp is
goin' to be on top of the mesa out a handful of
miles from the Fort.

"' The word goes along the line to observe a heap
of caution an' not straggle or go rummagin' about
permiscus, for the mountains is alive with hostiles.
It's five for one that a frownin' cloud of 'em is hangin' on our flanks from the moment we breaks into
the foothills. No, they'd be afoot; the Apaches
ain't hoss-back Injuns an' only fond of steeds as
food. He never rides on one, a Apache don't, but
he'll camp an' build a fire an' eat a corral full of
ponies if you'll furnish 'em, an' lick his lips in thank-
fulness tharfore. But bein' afoot won't hinder 'em
from keepin' up with my caravan, for in the mountains the snow is to the waggon beds an' the best we
can do, is wriggle along the trail like a hurt snake at
a gait which wouldn't tire a papoose.

"' We've been pushin' on our windin' uphill way
for mighty likely half a day, an' I'm beginnin'—so
dooms slows is our progress—to despair of gettin'

out on top the mesa before dark, when to put a coat of paint on the gen'ral trouble the lead waggon breaks down. I turns out in the snow with the rest, an' we-all puts in a heated an' highly profane half-hour restorin' the waggon to health. At last we're onder headway ag'in, an' I wades back through the snow to my amb'lance.

"'As I arrives at the r'ar of my offishul waggon, it occurs to me that I'll fill a pipe an' smoke some by virchoo of my nerves, the same bein' torn and frayed with the many exasperations of the day. I gives my driver the word to wait a bit, an' searchin' forth my tobacco outfit loads an' lights my pipe. I'm planted waist deep in the mountain snows, but havin' on hossman boots the snow ain't no hardship.

"'While I'm fussin' with my pipe, the six waggons an' my twenty men curves 'round a bend in the trail an' is hid by a corner of the canyon. I reflects at the time—though I ain't really expectin' no perils—that I'd better catch up with my escort, if it's only to set the troops a example. As I exhales my first puff of smoke and is on the verge of tellin' my driver to pull out—this yere mule-skinner is settin' so that matters to the r'ar is cut off from his gaze by the canvas cover of my waggon—a slight noise attracts me, an' castin' my eye along the trail we've been climbin', I notes with feelin's of disgust a full dozen Apaches comin'. An' it ain't no hyperbole to say they're shore comin' all spraddled out.

"'In the lead for all the deep snow, an' racin' up on me like the wind, is a big befeathered buck, painted to the eyes; an' in his right fist, raised to hurl it, is a 12-foot lance. As I surveys this pageant, I realises how he'pless, utter, I be, an' with what ca'mness I may, adjusts my mind to the fact that I've come to the end of my trails. He'pless? Shore! I'm stuck as firm in the snow as one of the pines about me; my guns is in the waggon outen immediate reach; thar I stands as certain a prey to that Apache with the lance as he's likely to go up ag'inst doorin' the whole campaign. Why, I'm a pick-up! I remembers my wife an' babies, an' sort o' says "Goodbye!" to 'em, for I'm as certain of my finish as I be of the hills, or the snows beneath my feet. However, since it's all I can do, I continyoos to smoke an' watch my execootioners come on.

"'The big lance Injun is the dominatin' sperit of the bunch. As he draws up to me—he's fifty foot in advance of the others—he makes his lance shiver from p'int to butt. It fairly sings a death song! I can feel it go through an' through me a score of times. But I stands thar facin' him; for, of course, I wants it to go through from the front. I don't allow to be picked up later with anything so on-fashionable as a lance wound in my back. That would be mighty onprofessional!

"'You onderstands that what now requires minutes in the recital don't cover seconds as a play. The lance Injun runs up to within a rod of me an' halts. His arm goes back for a mighty cast of the lance; the weepon is vibrant with the very sperit of hate an' malice. His eyes, through a fringe of ha'r that has fallen over 'em, glows out like a cat's eyes in the dark.

"We stands thar—I still puffin my pipe, he with his lance raised—an' we looks on each other—I an' that paint-daubed buck! I can't say whatever is his notion of me, but on my side I never beholds a savage who appeals to me as a more evil an' forbiddin' picture!

"'As I looks him over a change takes place. The fire in his eyes dies out, his face relaxes its f'rocity, an' after standin' for a moment an' as the balance of the band arrives, he turns the lance over his arm an' with the butt presented, surrenders it into my hand. You can gamble I don't lose no time in arguin' the question, but accepts the lance with all that it implies. Bringin' the weepon to a 'Right Shoulder' an' with my mind relieved, I gives the word to my mule-skinner—who's onconscious of the transactions in life an' death goin' on behind his back—an' with that, we-all takes up our march an' soon comes up on the escort where it's ag'in fixed firm in the snow about a furlong to the fore. My savages follows along with me, an' each of 'em as grave as squinch owls an' tame as tabby cats.

"'Joke? no; them Apaches was as hostile as Gila monsters! But beholdin' me, as they regyards it —for they don't in their ontaught simplicity make allowance for me bein' implanted in the snow, gunless an' he'pless—so brave, awaitin' deestruction without a quiver, their admiration mounts to sech heights it drowns within 'em every thought of can-

cellin' me with that lance, an' tharupon they pays
me their savage compliments in manner an' form
deescribed. They don't regyard themse'fs as sur-
renderin' neither; they esteems passin' me the lance
as inauguratin' a armistice an' looks on themse'fs as
guests of honor an' onder my safegyard, free to say
" How!" an' *vamos* back to the warpath ag'in whenever the sperit of blood begins to stir within their
breasts. I knows enough of their ways to be posted
as to what they expects; an' bein', I hopes, a gent
of integrity, I accedes to 'em that exact status which
they believes they enjoys.

" ' They travels with me that day, eats with me
that evenin' when we makes our camp, has a drink
with me all 'round, sings savage hymns to me
throughout the night, loads up with chuck in the
mornin', offers me no end of flattery as a dead game
gent whom they respects, says *adios;* an' then they
scatters like a flock of quail. Also, havin' resoomed
business on old-time lines, they takes divers shots
at us with their Winchesters doorin' the next two
days, an' kills a hoss an' creases my sergeant. Why
don't I corral an' hold 'em when they're in my
clutch? It would have been breakin' the trooce as
Injuns an' I onderstands sech things; moreover,
they let me go free without conditions when I was
loser by every roole of the game.' "

CHAPTER VII.

The Mills of Savage Gods.

"THAR might, of course, be romances in the West," observed the Old Cattleman, reflectively, in response to my question, "but the folks ain't got no time. Romance that a-way demands leesure, an' a party has to be more or less idlin' about to get what you-all might style romantic action. Take that warjig whereof I recently relates an' wherein this yere Wild Bill Hickox wipes out the McCandlas gang—six to his Colt's, four to his bowie, an' one to his Hawkins rifle; eleven in all—I asks him myse'f later when he's able to talk, don't he regyard the eepisode as some romantic. An' Bill says, 'No, I don't notice no romance tharin; what impresses me most is that she's shore a zealous fight—also, mighty busy.'

"Injuns would be romantic, only they're so plumb ignorant they never once saveys. Thar's no Injun word for 'romantic'; them benighted savages never tumblin' to sech a thing as romance bein' possible. An' yet said aborigines engages in plays which a eddicated Eastern taste with leesure on its hands an' gropin' about for entertainment would pass on as romantic.

"When I'm pesterin' among the Osages on that one o'casion that I'm tryin' to make a round-up of

my health, the old buck Strike Axe relates to me a
tale which I allers looks on as possessin' elements.
Shore ; an' it's as simple an' straight as the sights
of a gun. It's about a squaw an' three bucks, an'
thar's enough blood in it to paint a waggon.
Which I reckons now I'll relate it plain an' easy an'
free of them frills wherewith a professional racon-
toor is so prone to overload his narratives.

"The Black Cloud is a Osage medicine man an'
has high repoote about Greyhoss where he's pitched
his teepee an' abides. He's got a squaw, Sunbright,
an' he's plenty jealous of this yere little Sunbright.
The Black Cloud has three squaws, an' Sunbright is
the youngest. The others is Sunbright's sisters,
for a Osage weds all the sisters of a fam'ly at once,
the oldest sister goin' to the front at the nuptials to
deal the weddin' game for the entire outfit.

"Now this Sunbright ain't over-enamoured of
Black Cloud ; he's only a half-blood Injun for one
thing, his father bein' a buffalo-man (negro) who's
j'ined the Osages, an' Sunbright don't take kindly
to his nose which is some flatter than the best
rools of Osage beauty demands ; an' likewise thar's
kinks in his ha'r. Still, Sunbright sort o' keeps her
aversions to herse'f, an' if it ain't for what follows
she most likely would have travelled to her death-
blankets an' been given a seat on a hill with a
house of rocks built 'round her—the same bein'
the usual burial play of a Osage—without Black
Cloud ever saveyin' that so far from interestin'
Sunbright, he only makes her tired.

" Over south from Black Cloud's Greyhoss camp
an' across the Arkansaw an' some'ers between the
Polecat an' the Cimmaron thar's livin' a young
Creek buck called the Lance. He's straight an' slim
an' strong as the weepon he's named for; an' he
like Black Cloud is a medicine sharp of cel'bration
an' stands' way up in the papers. The Creeks is
never weary of talkin' about the Lance an' what a
marvel as a medicine man he is ; also, by way of insultin' the Osages, they declar's onhesitatin' that
the Lance lays over Black Cloud like four tens, an'
offers to bet hosses an' blankets an' go as far as the
Osages likes that this is troo.

" By what Strike Axe informs me,—an' he ain't
none likely to overplay in his statements—by what
Strike Axe tells me, I says, the Lance must shore
have been the high kyard as a medicine man.   Let
it get dark with the night an' no moon in the skies,
an' the Lance could take you-all into his medicine
lodge, an' you'd hear the sperits flappin' their pin-
ions like some one flappin' a blanket, an' thar'd be
whisperin's an' goin's on outside the lodge an' in,
while fire-eyes would show an' burn an' glower up
in the peak of the teepee ; an' all plenty skeary an'
mystifiyin'. Besides these yere accomplishments
the Lance is one of them mesmerism sports who
can set anamiles to dreamin'. He could call a coyote or a fox, or even so fitful an' nervous a prop'sition as a antelope ; an' little by little, snuffin' an'
snortin', or if it's a coyote, whinin', them beasts
would approach the Lance ontil they're that clost

he'd tickle their heads with his fingers while they stands shiverin' an' sweatin' with apprehensions. You can put a bet on it, son, that accordin' to this onbiassed buck, Strike Axe, the Lance is ondoubted the big medicine throughout the Injun range.

"As might be assoomed, the Black Cloud is some heated ag'in the Lance an' looks on him with baleful eye as a rival. Still, Black Cloud has his nerve with him constant, an' tharfore one day when the Osages an' Creeks has been dispootin' touchin' the reespective powers of him an' the Lance, an' this latter Injun offers to come over to Greyhoss an' make medicine ag'in him, Black Cloud never hesitates or hangs back like a dog tied onder a wag- gon, but calls the bluff a heap prompt an' tells the Lance to come.

"Which the day is set an' the Lance shows in the door, as monte sharps would say. Black Cloud an' the Lance tharupon expands themse'fs an' delights the assembled Creeks an' Osages with their whole box of tricks, an' each side is braggin' an' boastin' an' puttin' it up that their gent is most likely the soonest medicine man who ever buys black paint. It's about hoss an' hoss between the two.

"Black Cloud accompanies himse'f to this con- test with a pure white pony which has eyes red as roobies—a kind o' albino pony— an' he gives it forth that this milk-coloured bronco is his 'big medicine' or familiar sperit. The Lance observes that the little red-eyed hoss is mighty impressive to

the savages, be they Creeks or Osages. At last he
says to Black Cloud :

"'To show how my medicine is stronger than
yours, to-morry I'll make your red-eyed big medicine bronco go lame in his off hind laig.'

" Black Cloud grins scornful at this; he allows
that no sport can make his white pony go lame.

" He's plumb wrong ; the next mornin' the
white pony is limpin' an' draggin' his off hind hoof,
an' when he's standin' still he p'ints the toe down
like something's fetched loose. Black Cloud is
sore ; but he can't find no cactus thorn nor nothin'
to bring about the lameness an' he don't know what
to make of the racket. Black Cloud's up ag'inst it,
an' the andience begins to figger that the Lance's
medicine is too strong for Black Cloud.

"What's the trouble with the red-eyed pony ?
That's simple enough, son. The Lance done creeps
over in the night an' ties a hossha'r tight about the
pony's laig jest above the fetlock. Black Cloud
ain't up to no sech move, the same bein' a trade
secret of the Lance's an' bein' the hossha'r is hid
in the ha'r on the pony's laig, no one notes its presence.

" After Black Cloud looks his red-eyed big medicine pony all over an' can't onderstand its lameness,
the Lance asks him will he cure it. Black Cloud,
who's scowlin' like midnight by now, retorts that he
will. So he gets his pipe an' fills it with medicine
tobacco an' blows a mouthful of smoke in the red-
eyed pony's nose. Sech remedies don't work; that

pony still limps on three laigs, draggin' the afflicted member mighty pensive.

"At last the Lance gives Black Cloud a patronisin' smile an' says that his medicine'll cure the pony sound an' well while you're crackin' off a gun. He walks up to the pony an' looks long in its red eyes; the pony's y'ears an' tail droops, its head hangs down, an' it goes mighty near to sleep. Then the Lance rubs his hand two or three times up an' down the lame laig above the fetlock an' elim'nates that hossha'r ligature an' no one the wiser. A moment after, he wakes up the red-eyed pony an' to the amazement of the Osages an' the onbounded delight of the Creeks, the pony is no longer lame, an' the laig so late afflicted is as solid an' healthy as a sod house. What's bigger medicine still, the red-eyed pony begins to follow the Lance about like a dog an' as if it's charmed; an' it likewise turns in to bite an' r'ar an' pitch an' jump sideways if Black Cloud seeks to put his paw on him. Then all the Injuns yell with one voice: 'The Lance has won the Black Cloud's big medicine red-eyed pony away from him.'

"The Lance is shore the fashion, an' Black Cloud discovers he ain't a four-spot by compar'son. His repootation is gone, an' the Lance is regyarded as the great medicine along the Arkansaw.

"Sunbright is lookin' on at these manoovers an' her heart goes out to the Lance; she falls more deeply in love with him than even the red-eyed bronco does. That evenin' as the Lance is goin' to his camp onder the cottonwoods, he meets up with Sunbright standin' still as a tree in his path with her head bowed like a flower that's gone to sleep. The Lance saveys; he knows Sunbright; likewise he knows what her plantin' herse'f in his way an' her droopin' attitoode explains. He looks at her, an' says:

"'I am a guest of the Osages, an' to-night is not the night. Wait ontil the Lance is in his own tee-pee on the Polecat; then come.'

"Sunbright never moves, never looks up; but she hears an' she knows this is right. No buck should steal a squaw while he's a guest. The Lance walks on an' leaves her standin', head bowed an' motion-less.

"Two days later the Lance is ag'in in his own teepee. Sunbright counts the time an' knows that he must be thar. She skulks from the camp of Black Cloud an' starts on her journey to be a new wife to a new husband.

"Sunbright is a mile from camp when she's inter-rupted. It's Black Cloud who heads her off. Black Cloud may not be the boss medicine man, but he's no fool, an' his eyes is like a wolf's eyes an' can see in the dark. He guesses the new love which has stampeded Sunbright.

"Injuns is a mighty cur'ous outfit. Now if Sun-bright had succeeded in gettin' to the lodge of her new husband, the divorce between her an' Black Cloud would have been complete. Moreover, if on the day followin' or at any time Black Cloud had

found her thar, he wouldn't so much as have wagged
a y'ear or batted a eye in recognition.   He wouldn't
have let on he ever hears of a squaw called ' Sunbright.'   This ca'mness would be born of two
causes.   It would be ag'in Injun etiquette to go
trackin' about makin' a onseemly uproar an' disturbin' the gen'ral peace for purely private causes.
Then ag'in it would be beneath the dignity of a
high grade savage an' a big medicine sharp to conduct himse'f like he'd miss so trivial a thing as a
squaw.

   " But ontil Sunbright fulfils her elopement projects an' establishes herse'f onder the protectin'
wing of her new love, she's runnin' resks.   She's
still the Black Cloud's squaw; an' after she pulls
her marital picket pin an' while she's gettin' away, if
the bereaved Black Cloud crosses up with her he's
free, onder the license permitted to Injun husbands,
to kill her an' skelp her an' dispose of her as con-
sists best with his moods.

   " Sunbright knows this; an' when she runs ag'in
the Black Cloud in her flight, she seats herse'f in the
long prairie grass an' covers her head with her blanket an' speaks never a word.

   " ' Does Sunbright so love me,' says Black Cloud,
turnin' a heap ugly, ' that she comes to meet me?
Is it for me she has combed her h'ar an' put on a
new feather an' beads?   Does she wear her new
blanket an' paint her face bright for Black Cloud?
Or does she dress herse'f like the sun for that Creek
coyote, the Lance ?'   Sunbright makes no reply.

Black Cloud looks at her a moment an' then goes on: "It's for the Lance! Good! I will fix the Sunbright so she will be a good squaw to my friend, the Lance, an' never run from his lodge as she does now from Black Cloud's.' With that he stoops down, an' a slash of his knife cuts the heel-tendons of Sunbright's right foot. She groans, and writhes about the prairie, while Black Cloud puts his knife back in his belt, gets into his saddle ag'in an' rides away.

"The next day a Creek boy finds the body of Sunbright where she rolls herse'f into the Greyhoss an' is drowned.

"When the Lance hears the story an' sees the knife slash on Sunbright's heel, he reads the trooth. It gives him a bad heart ; he paints his face red an' black an thinks how he'll be revenged. Next day he sends a runner to Black Cloud with word that Black Cloud has stole his hoss. This is to arrange a fight on virtuous grounds. The Lance says that in two days when the sun is overhead Black Cloud must come to the three cottonwoods near the mouth of the Cimmaron an' fight, or the Lance on the third day an' each day after will hunt for him as he'd hunt a wolf ontil Black Cloud is dead. The Black Cloud's game, an' sends word that on the second day he'll be thar by the three cottonwoods when the sun is overhead ; also, that he will fight with four arrows.

"Then Black Cloud goes at once, for he has no time to lose, an' kills a dog near his lodge. He

cuts out its heart an' carries it to the rocky canyon
where the rattlesnakes have a village. Black Cloud
throws the dog's heart among them an' teases them
with it; an' the rattlesnakes bite the dog's heart
ag'in an' ag'in ontil it's as full of p'isen as a bottle
is of rum. After that, Black Cloud puts the
p'isened heart in the hot sun an' lets it fret an'
fester ontil jest before he goes to his dooel with
the Lance. As he's about to start, Black Cloud
dips the four steel arrowheads over an' over in the
p'isened heart, bein' careful to dry the p'isen on the
arrowheads; an' now whoever is touched with
these arrows so that the blood comes is shore to
die. The biggest medicine in the nation couldn't
save him.

"Thar's forty Osage and forty Creek bucks at
the three cottonwoods to see that the dooelists get
a squar' deal. The Lance an' Black Cloud is thar;
each has a bow an' four arrows; each has made
medicine all night that he may kill his man.

"But the dooel strikes a obstacle.

"Thar's a sombre, sullen sport among the Osages
who's troo name is the 'Bob-cat,' but who's called
the 'Knife Thrower.' The Bob-cat is one of the
Osage forty. Onknown to the others, this yere
Bob-cat—who it looks like is a mighty impression-
able savage—is himse'f in love with the dead
Sunbright. An' he's hot an' cold because he's
fearful that in this battle of the bows the Lance'll
down Black Cloud an' cheat him, the Bob-cat, of
his own revenge. The chance is too much; the

Bob-cat can't stand it an' resolves to get his stack down first. An' so it happens that as Black Cloud an' the Lance, painted in their war colours, is walkin' to their places, a nine-inch knife flickers like a gleam of light from the hand of the Bob-cat, an' merely to show that he ain't called the 'Knife Thrower' for fun, catches Black Cloud flush in the throat, an' goes through an' up to the gyard at the knife-haft. Black Cloud dies standin', for the knife p'int bites his spine.

"No, son, no one gets arrested; Injuns don't have jails, for the mighty excellent reason that no In-jun culprit ever vamoses an' runs away. Injun crim'-nals, that a-way, allers stands their hands an' takes their hemlock. The Osages, who for Injuns is some shocked at the Bob-cat's interruption of the dooel—it bein' mighty onparliamentary from their standp'ints—tries the Bob-cat in their triboonals for killin' Black Cloud an' he's decided on as guilty accordin' to their law. They app'ints a day for the Bob-cat to be shot; an' as he ain't present at the trial none, leavin' his end of the game to be looked after by his reelatives, they orders a kettle-tender or tribe crier to notify the Bob-cat when an' where he's to come an' have said sentence execooted upon him. When he's notified, the Bob-cat don't say nothin'; which is satisfactory enough, as thar's nothin' to be said, an' every Osage knows the Bob-cat'll be thar at the drop of the handkerchief if he's alive.

"It so turns out; the Bob-cat's thar as cool as

wild plums. He's dressed in his best blankets an' leggin's; an' his feathers an' gay colours makes him a overwhelmin' match for peacocks. Thar's a white spot painted over his heart.

"The chief of the Osages, who's present to see jestice done, motions to the Bob-cat, an' that gent steps to a red blanket an' stands on its edge with all the blanket spread in front of him on the grass. The Bob-cat stands on the edge, as he saveys when he's plugged that he'll fall for'ard on his face. When a gent gets the gaff for shore, he falls for'ard. If a party is hit an' falls back'ards, you needn't get excited none; he's only creased an' 'll get over it.

"Wherefore, as I states, the Bob-cat stands on the edge of the blanket so it's spread out in front to catch him as he drops. Thar's not a word spoke by either the Bob-cat or the onlookers, the latter openin' out into a lane behind so the lead can go through. When the Bob-cat's ready, his cousin, a buck whose name is Little Feather, walks to the front of the blanket an' comes down careful with his Winchester on the white mark over the Bob-cat's heart. Thar's a moment's silence as the Bob-cat's cousin runs his eye through the sights; thar's a flash an' a hatful of gray smoke; the white spot turns red with blood; an' then the Bob-cat falls along on his face as soft as a sack of corn.

"What becomes of the Lance? It's two weeks later when that scientist is waited on by a delegation of Osages. They reminds him that Sunbright has two sisters, the same bein' now widows by vir-

choo of the demise of that egreegious Black Cloud.
Also, the Black Cloud was rich ; his teepee was
sumptuous, an' he's left a buckskin coat with ivory
elk teeth sewed onto it plenty as stars at night.
The coat is big medicine ; moreover thar's the milk-
white big medicine bronco with red eyes. The
Osage delegation puts forth these trooths while the
Lance sets cross-laiged on a b'arskin an' smokes
willow bark with much dignity. In the finish, the
Osage outfit p'ints up to the fact that their tribe is
shy a medicine man, an' a gent of the Lance's accomplishments who can charm anamiles an' lame
broncos will be a mighty welcome addition to the
Osage body politic. The Lance lays down his pipe
at this an' says, ' It is enough ! ' An' the next day
he sallies over an' weds them two relicts of Black
Cloud an' succeeds to that dead necromancer's
estate an' both at one fell swoop. The two widows
chuckles an' grins after the manner of ladies, to get
a new husband so swift ; an' abandonin' his lodge
on the Polecat the Lance sets up his game at
Greyhoss, an' onless he's petered, he's thar dealin'
it yet."

CHAPTER VIII.

Tom and Jerry; Wheelers.

"OBSTINACY or love, that a–way, when folks pushes 'em to excess, is shore bad medicine. Which I'd be a heap loath to count the numbers them two attribootes harries to the tomb. Why, son, it's them sentiments that kills off my two wheel mules, Tom an' Jerry."

The Old Cattleman appeared to be on the verge of abstract discussion, As a metaphysician, he was not to be borne with. There was one method of escape; I interfered to coax the currents of his volubility into other and what were to me, more interesting channels.

"Tell me of the trail; or a story about animals," I urged. "You were saying recently that perfect systems of oral if not verbal communication existed among mules, and that you had listened for hours to their gossip. Give me the history of one of your freighting trips and what befell along the trail; and don't forget the comment thereon—wise, doubtless, it was—of your long-eared servants of the rein and trace-chain."

"Tell you what chances along the trail? Son, you-all opens a wide-flung range for my mem'ry to graze over. I might tell you how I'm lost once,

freightin' from Vegas into the Panhandle, an' am
two days without water—blazin' Jooly days so hot
you couldn't touch tire, chain, or bolt-head without
fryin' your fingers. An' how at the close of the
second day when I hauls in at Cabra Springs, I
lays down by that cold an' blessed fountain an'
drinks till I aches. Which them two days of thirst
terrorises me to sech degrees that for one plumb
year tharafter, I never meets up with water when I
don't drink a quart, an' act like I'm layin' in ag'in
another parched spell.

"Or I might relate how I stops over one night
from Springer on my way to the Canadian at a
Triangle-dot camp called Kingman. This yere is a
one-room stone house, stark an' sullen an' alone on
the desolate plains, an' no scenery worth namin' but
a half-grown feeble spring. This Kingman ain't
got no windows; its door is four-inch thick of oak;
an' thar's loopholes for rifles in each side which
shows the sports who builds that edifice in the
stormy long-ago is lookin' for more trouble than comfort an' prepares themse'fs. The two cow-punchers
I finds in charge is scared to a standstill; they
allows this Kingman's ha'nted. They tells me how
two parties who once abides thar—father an' son
they be— gets downed by a hold-up whose aim is
pillage, an' who comes cavortin' along an' butchers
said fam'ly in their sleep. The cow-punchers
declar's they hears the spooks go scatterin' about
the room as late as the night before I trails in. I
ca'ms 'em—not bein' subject to nerve stampedes

myse'f, an' that same midnight when the sperits
comes ha'ntin' about ag'in, I turns outen my blankets an' lays said spectres with the butt of my mule
whip—the same when we strikes a light an' counts
'em up bein' a couple of kangaroo rats. This yere
would front up for a mighty thrillin' tale if I throws
myse'f loose with its reecital an' daubs in the colour
plenty vivid an' free.

" Then thar's the time I swings over to the K-bar-8
ranch for corn—bein' I'm out of said cereal—an' runs
up on a cow gent, spurs, gun-belt, big hat an' the
full regalia, hangin' to the limb of a cottonwood,
dead as George the Third, an' not a hundred foot
from the ranch door. An' how inside I finds a half-
dozen more cow folks, lookin' grave an' sayin'
nothin'; an' the ranch manager has a bloody bandage about his for'ead, an' another holdin' up his left
arm, half bandage an' half sling, the toot ensemble,
as Colonel Sterett calls it, showin' sech recent war
that the blood's still wet on the cloths an' drops on
the floor as we talks. An' how none of us says a
word about the dead gent in the cottonwood or
of the manager who's shot up; an' how that same
manager outfits me with ten sacks of mule-food an'
I goes p'intin' out for the Southeast an' forgets
all I sees an' never mentions it ag'in.

" Then thar's Sim Booth of the Fryin' Pan outfit, who's one evenin' camped with me at Antelope
Springs; an' who saddles up an' ropes onto the
laigs of a dead Injun where they're stickin' forth—
bein' washed free by the rains—an' pulls an' rolls

that copper-coloured departed outen his sepulchre a lot, an' then starts his pony off at a canter an' sort o' fritters the remains about the landscape. Sim does this on the argyment that the obsequies, former, takes place too near the spring. This yere Sim's pony two months later steps in a dog hole when him an' Sim's goin' along full swing with some cattle on a stampede, an' the cayouse falls on Sim an' breaks everything about him incloosive of his neck. The other cow-punchers allers allow it's because Sim turns out that aborigine over by Antelope Springs.   Now sech a eepisode, properly elab'rated, might feed your attention an' hold it spellbound some.

"Son, if I was to turn myse'f loose on, great an' little, the divers incidents of the trail, it would con-soome days in the relation. I could tell of cactus flowers, blazin' an' brilliant as a eye of red fire ag'in the brown dusk of the deserts ; or of mile-long fields of Spanish bayonet in bloom ; or of some Mexican's doby shinin' like a rooby in the sunlight a day's journey ahead, the same one onbroken mass from roof to ground of the peppers they calls *chili*, all reddenin' in the hot glare of the day.

"Or, if you has a fancy for stirrin' incident an' lively scenes, thar's a time when the rains has raised the old Canadian ontil that quicksand ford at Tas-cosa—which has done eat a hundred teams if ever it swallows one !—is torn up complete an' the bottom of the river nothin' save b'ilin' sand with a shallow yere an' a hole deep enough to drown a house scooped out jest beyond. An' how since I can't pause a week or two for the river to run down an' the ford to settle, I goes spraddlin' an' tumblin' an' swimmin' across on Tom, my nigh wheeler, opens negotiations with the LIT ranch, an' Bob Roberson, has his riders round-up the pasture, an' comes chargin' down to the ford with a bunch of one thousand ponies, all of 'em dancin' an' buckin' an' prancin' like chil'en outen school. Roberson an' the LIT boys throws the thousand broncos across an' across the ford for mighty likely it's fifty times. They'd flash 'em through—the whole band together —on the run; an' then round 'em up on the opp'- site bank, turn 'em an' jam 'em through ag'in. When they ceases, the bottom of the river is tramped an' beat out as hard an' as flat as a floor, an' I hooks up an' brings the waggons over like the ford—bottomless quicksand a hour prior—is one of these yere asphalt streets.

" Or I might relate about a cowboy tournament that's held over in the flat green bottom of Parker's arroya; an' how Jack Coombs throws a rope an' fastens at one hundred an' four foot, while Waco Simpson rides at the herd of cattle one hundred foot away, ropes, throws an' ties down a partic'lar steer, frees his lariat an' is back with the jedges ag'in in forty-eight seconds. Waco wins the prize, a Mexican saddle—stamp-leather an' solid gold she is—worth four hundred dollars, by them onpreece- dented alacrities.

" Or, I might impart about a Mexican fooneral

where the hearse is a blanket with two poles along the aige, the same as one of these battle litters ; of the awful songs the mournful Mexicans sings about departed ; of the candles they burns an' the dozens of baby white-pine crosses they sets up on little jim-crow stone-heaps along the trail to the tomb ; meanwhiles, howlin' dirges constant.

"Now I thinks of it I might bresh up the recollections of a mornin' when I rolls over, blankets an' all, onto something that feels as big as a boot-laig an' plenty squirmy ; an' how I shows zeal a-gettin' to my feet, knowin' I'm reposin' on a rattlesnake who's bunked in ag'in my back all sociable to warm himse'f. It's worth any gent's while to see how heated an' indignant that serpent takes it because of me turnin' out so early and so swift.

"Then thar's a mornin' when I finds myse'f not five miles down the wind from a prairie fire ; an' it crackin' an' roarin' in flame-sheets twenty foot high an' makin' for'ard jumps of fifty foot. What do I do? Go for'ard down the wind, set fire to the grass myse'f, an' let her burn ahead of me. In two minutes I'm over on a burned deestrict of my own, an' by the time the orig'nal flames works down to my fire line, my own speshul fire is three miles ahead an' I myse'f am ramblin' along cool an' saloobrious with a safe, shore area of burnt prairie to my r'ar.

"An' thar's a night on the Serrita la Cruz doorin' a storm, when the lightnin' melts the tire on the wheel of my trail-waggon, an' me layin' onder it at the time. An' it don't even wake me up, Thar's the time, too, when I crosses up at Chico Springs with eighty Injuns who's been buffalo huntin' over to the South Paloduro, an' has with 'em four hundred odd ponies loaded with hides an' buffalo beef an' all headed for their home-camps over back of Taos. The bucks is restin' up a day or two when I rides in ; later me an' a half dozen jumps a band of antelopes jest 'round a p'int of rocks. Son, you-all would have admired to see them savages shoot their arrows. I observes one young buck a heap clost. He holds the bow flat down with his left hand while his arrows in their cow-skin quiver sticks over his right shoulder. The way he would flash his right hand back, yank forth a arrow, slam it on his bow, pull it to the head an' cut it loose, is shore a heap earnest. Them missiles would go sailin' off for over three hundred yards, an' I sees him get seven started before ever the first one strikes the ground. The Injuns acquires four antelope by this archery an' shoots mebby some forty arrows ; all of which they carefully reclaims when the excitement subsides. She's trooly a sperited exhibition an' I finds it mighty entertainin'.

"I throws these hints loose to show what might be allooded to by way of stories, grave and gay, of sights pecooliar to the trail if only some gent of experience ups an' devotes himse'f to the relations. As it is, however, an' recurrin' to Tom an' Jerry—the same bein' as I informs you, my two wheel mules—I reckons now I might better set forth as to how they comes to die that time. It's his obstinacy that downs Jerry; while pore, tender Tom perishes the victim—volunteer at that—of the love he b'ars his contrary mate.

"Them mules, Tom an' Jerry, is obtained by me orig'nal in Vegas. They're the wheelers of a eight-mule team; an' I gives Frosty—who's a gambler an' wins 'em at monte of some locoed sport from Chaparita—twelve hundred dollars for the outfit. Which the same is cheap an' easy at double the *dinero*.

"These mules evident has been part an' passel of the estates of some Mexican, for I finds a cross marked on each harness an' likewise on both wag-gons. Mexicans employs this formal'ty to run a bluff on any evil sperit who may come projectin' round. Your American mule skinner never makes them tokens. As a roole he's defiant of sperits; an' even when he ain't he don't see no refooge in a cross. Mexicans, on the other hand, is plenty strong on said symbol. Every mornin' you beholds a Mexican with a dab of white on his fore'erd an' on each cheek bone, an' also on his chin where he crosses himse'f with flour; shore, the custom is yooniversal an' it takes a quart of flour to fully fortify a full-blown Greaser household ag'inst the antic'pated perils of the day.

"No sooner am I cl'ar of Vegas—I'm camped near the Plaza de la Concepcion at the time—when I rounds up the eight mules an' looks 'em over with reference to their characters. This is jest after I acquires 'em. It's allers well for a gent to know

what he's ag'inst; an' you can put down a stack the
disp'sitions of eight mules is a important problem.

"The review is plenty satisfactory. The nigh
leader is a steady practical person as a lead mule
oughter be, an' I notes by his ca'm jedgmatical eye
that he's goin' to give himse'f the benefit of every
doubt, an' ain't out to go stampedin' off none without knowin' the reason why. His mate at the other
end of the jockey-stick is nervous an' hysterical;
she never trys to solve no riddles of existence herse'f, this Jane mule don't, but relies on her mate
Peter an' plays Peter's system blind. The nigh
p'inter is a deecorous form of mule with no bad habits; while his mate over the chain is one of these
yere hard, se'fish, wary parties an' his little game
is to get as much of everything except work an'
trouble as the lay of the kyards permits. My nigh
swing mule is a wit like I tells you the other day.
Which this jocose anamile is the life of the team an'
allers lettin' fly some dry, quaint observation. This
mule wag is partic'lar excellent at a bad ford or a
hard crossin', an his gay remarks, full of p'int as a
bowie knife, shorely cheers an' uplifts the sperits of
the rest. The off swing is a heedless creature who
regyards his facetious mate as the very parent of
fun, an' he goes about with his y'ear cocked an'
his mouth ajar, ready to laugh them 'hah, hah!'
laughs of his'n at every word his pard turns loose.

"Tom an' Jerry is different from the others.
Bein' bigger an' havin' besides the respons'bilities
of the hour piled onto them as wheel mules must,

they cultivates a sooperior air an' is distant an' reserved in their attitoodes towards the other six. As to each other their pose needs more deescription. Tom, the nigh wheeler—the one I rides when drivin'—is infatyooated with Jerry. I hears a sky-sharp aforetime preach about Jonathan an' David. Yet I'm yere to assert, son, that them sacred people ain't on speakin' terms compared to the way that pore old lovin' Tom mule feels towards Jerry.

"This affection of Tom's is partic'lar amazin' when you-all recalls the fashion in which the sullen Jerry receives it. Doorin' the several years I spends in their s'ciety I never once detects Jerry in any look or word of kindness to Tom. Jerry bites him an' kicks him an' cusses him out constant; he never tol'rates Tom closter than twenty foot onless at times when he orders Tom to curry him. Shore, the imbecile Tom submits. On sech o'casions when Jerry issues a summons to go over him, usin' his upper teeth for a comb an' bresh, Tom is never so happy. Which he digs an' delves at Jerry's ribs that a-way like it's a honour; after a half hour, mebby, when Jerry feels refreshed s'fficient, he w'irls on Tom an' dismisses him with both heels.

"'I track up on folks who's jest the same,' says Dan Boggs, one time when I mentions this onaccountable infatyooation of Tom. 'This Jerry loves that Tom mule mate of his, only he ain't lettin' on. I knows a lady whose treatment of her husband is a dooplicate of Jerry's. She metes out the worst of it to that long-sufferin' shorthorn at every bend in the trail; it looks like he never wins a good word or a soft look from her once. An' yet when that party cashes in, whatever does the lady do? Takes a hooker of whiskey, puts in p'isen enough to down a dozen wolves, an' drinks off every drop. "Far'well, vain world, I'm goin' home," says the lady ; "which I prefers death to sep'ration, an' I'm out to jine my beloved husband in the promised land." I knows, for I attends the fooneral of that family—said fooneral is a double-header as the lady, bein' prompt, trails out after her husband before ever he's pitched his first camp—an' later assists old Chandler in deevisin' a epitaph, the same occurrin' in these yere familiar words :

> " She sort o got the drop on him,
> In the dooel of earthly love ;
> Let's hope he gets an even break
> When they meets in heaven above."

" ' Thar, 'concloods Dan, ' is what I regyards as a parallel experience to this Tom an' Jerry. The lady plays Jerry's system from soda to hock, an' yet you-all can see in the lights of that thar sooicide how deep she loves him.'

" ' That's all humbug, Dan,' says Enright ; ' the lady you relates of isn't lovin'. she's only locoed that a-way.'

" ' Whyever if she's locoed, then,' argues Dan, ' don't they up an' hive her in one of their madhouse

camps? She goes chargin' about as free an' fearless
as a cyclone.'

"'All the same,' says Texas Thompson, 'her
cashin' in don't prove no lovin' heart. Mebby she
does it so's to chase him up an' continyoo onbroken
them hectorin's of her's. I could onfold a fact or
two about that wife of mine who cuts out the
divorce from me in Laredo that would lead you to
concloosions sim'lar. But she wasn't your wife;
an' I don't aim to impose my domestic afflictions
on this innocent camp, which bein' troo I mootely
stands my hand.'

" This Jerry's got one weakness; however, I don't
never take advantage of it. He's scared to frenzy
if you pulls a gun. I reckons, with all them crimes
of his'n preyin' on his mind, that he allows you're
out, to shoot him up. Jerry is ca'm so long as your
gun's in the belt, deemin' it as so much onmeanin'
ornament. But the instant you pulls it like you're
goin' to put it in play, he onbuckles into piercin'
screams. I reaches for my six-shooter one evenin'
by virchoo of antelopes, an' that's the time I discovers this foible of Jerry's. I never gets a shot.
At the sight of the gun Jerry evolves a howl an'
the antelopes tharupon hits two or three high places
an' is miles away. Shore, they thinks Jerry is some
new breed of demon.

" When I turns to note the cause of Jerry's clamours he's loppin' his fore-laigs over Tom's back an'
sobbin' an' sheddin' tears into his mane. Tom
sympathises with Jerry an' says all he can to teach

him that the avenger ain't on his trail. Nothin'
can peacify Jerry, however, except jammin' that
awful six-shooter back into its holster. I goes over
Jerry that evenin' patiently explorin' for bullet
marks, but thar ain't none. No one's ever creased
him ; an' I figgers final by way of a s'lootion of his
fits that mighty likely Jerry's attended some killin'
between hoomans, inadvertent, an' has the teeth of
his apprehensions set on aige.

"Jerry is that high an' haughty he won't come up
for corn in the mornin' onless I petitions him partic'lar an' calls him by name. To jest whoop
'Mules!' he holds don't incloode him. Usual I humours Jerry an' shouts his title speshul, the others
bein' called in a bunch. When Jerry hears his name
he walks into camp, delib'rate an' dignified, an'
kicks every mule to pieces who tries to shove in
ahead.

"Once, feelin' some malignant myse'f, I tries
Jerry's patience out. I don't call ' Jerry,' merely
shouts ' Mules ' once or twice an' lets it go at that.
Jerry, when he notices I don't refer to him partic'-
lar lays his y'ears back ; an' although his r'ar elevation is towards me I can see he's hotter than a hor-
net. The faithful Tom abides with Jerry ; though
he tells him it's feed time an' that the others with a
nosebag on each of 'em is already at their repasts.
Jerry only gets madder an' lays for Tom an' tries to
bite him. After ten minutes, sullen an' sulky, hunger beats Jerry an' he comes bumpin' into camp
like a bar'l down hill an' eases his mind by wallopin'

both hind hoofs into them other blameless mules, peacefully munchin' their rations. Also, after Jerry's let me put the nosebag onto him he reeverses his p'sition an' swiftly lets fly at me. But I ain't in no trance an' Jerry misses. I don't frale him ; I saveys it's because he feels hoomiliated with me not callin' him by name.

"As a roole me an' Jerry gets through our dooties harmonious. He can pull like a lion an' never flinches or flickers at a pinch. It's shore a vict'ry to witness the heroic way Jerry goes into the collar at a hard steep hill or some swirlin', rushin' ford. Sech bein' Jerry's work habits I'm prepared to overlook a heap of moral deeficiencies an' never lays it up ag'in Jerry that he's morose an' repellant when I flings him any kindnesses.

" But while I don't resent 'em none by voylence, still Jerry has habits ag'inst which I has to gyard. You-all recalls how long ago I tells you of Jerry's bein' a thief. Shore, he can't he'p it ; he's a born kleptomaniac. Leastwise ' kleptomaniac ' is what Colonel Sterett calls it when he's tellin' me of a party who's afflicted sim'lar.

" ' Otherwise this gent's a heap respectable,' says the Colonel. ' Morally speakin' thar's plenty who's worse. Of course, seein' he's crowdin' forty years, he ain't so shamefully innocent neither. He ain't no debyootanty ; still, he ain't no crime-wrung debauchee. I should say he grades midway in between. But deep down in his system this person's a kleptomaniac, an' at last his weakness gets its hobbles off an' he turns himse'f loose, an' begins to jest nacherally take things right an' left. No, he don't get put away in Huntsville; they sees he's locoed an' he's corraled instead in one of the asylums where thar's nothin' loose an' little kickin' 'round, an' tharfore no temptations.'

" Takin' the word then from Colonel Sterett, Jerry is a kleptomaniac. I used former to hobble Jerry but one mornin' I'm astounded to see what looks like snow all about my camp. Bein' she's in Joone that snow theery don't go. An' it ain't snow, it's flour; this kleptomaniac Jerry creeps to the wag-gons while I sleeps an' gets away, one after the other, with fifteen fifty-pound sacks of flour. Then he entertains himse'f an' Tom by p'radin' about with the sacks in his teeth, shakin' an' tossin' his head an' powderin' my 'Pride of Denver' all over the plains. Which Jerry shore frosts that scenery plumb lib'ral.

" It's the next night an' I don't hobble Jerry; I pegs him out on a lariat. What do you-all reckon now that miscreant does? Corrupts pore Tom who you may be certain is sympathisin' 'round, an' makes Tom go to the waggons, steal the flour an' pack it out to him where he's pegged. The soopine Tom, who otherwise is the soul of integrity, abstracts six sacks for his mate an' at daybreak the wretched Jerry's standin' thar, white as milk himse'f, an' flour a foot deep in a cirkle whereof the radius is his rope Tom's gazin' on Jerry in a besotted way like he allows he's certainly the greatest sport on earth,

"Which this last is too much an' I ropes up Jerry for punishment. I throws an' hawgties Jerry, an' he's layin' thar on his side. His eye is obdoorate an' thar's neither shame nor repentance in his heart. Tom is sort o' sobbin' onder his breath ; Tom would have swapped places with Jerry too quick an' I sees he has it in his mind to make the offer, only he knows I'll turn it down."

"The other six mules comes up an' loafs about observant an' respectful. They jestifies my arrangements ; besides Jerry is mighty onpop'lar with 'em by reason of his heels. I can hear Peter the little lead mule sayin' to Jane, his mate: "The boss is goin' to lam Jerry a lot with a trace-chain. Which it's shore comin' to him ! ""

"I w'irls the chain on high an' lays it along Jerry's evil ribs, *kerwhillup*! Every other link bites through the hide an' the chain plows a most excellent an' wholesome furrow. As the chain descends, the sympathetic Tom jumps an' gives a groan. Tom feels a mighty sight worse than his *compañero*. At the sixth wallop Tom can't b'ar no more, but with tears an' protests comes an' stands over Jerry an' puts it up he'll take the rest himse'f. This evidence of brotherly love stands me off, an' for Tom's sake I desists an' throws Jerry loose. That old scoundrel—while I sees he's onforgivin' an' a-harbourin' of hatreds ag'in me—don't forget the trace-chain an' comports himse'f like a law-abidin' mule for months. He even quits bitin' an' kickin' Tom, an' that lovin' beast seems like he's goin' to break his heart over it, 'cause he looks on it as a sign that Jerry's gettin' cold.

"But thar comes a day when I loses both Tom an' Jerry. It's about second drink time one August mornin' an' me an' my eight mules goes scamperin' through a little Mexican plaza called Tramperos on our way to the Canadian. Over by a 'doby stands a old fleabitten gray mare ; she's shore hideous.

"Now if mules has one overmasterin' deloosion it's a gray mare ; she's the religion an' the goddess of the mules. This knowledge is common ; if you-all is ever out to create a upheaval in the bosom of a mule the handiest, quickest lever is a old gray mare. The gov'ment takes advantage of this aberration of the mules. Thar's trains of pack mules freightin' to the gov'ment posts in the Rockies. They figgers on three hundred pounds to the mule an' the freight is packed in panniers. The gov'-ment freighters not bein' equal to the manifold mysteries of a diamond-hitch, don't use no reg'lar shore-enough pack saddle but takes refooge with their ignorance in panniers.

"Speakin' gen'ral, thar's mebby two hundred mules in one of these gov'ment pack trains. An' in the lead, followed, waited on an' worshipped by the mules, is a aged gray mare. She don't pack nothin' but her virchoo an' a little bell, which last is hung 'round her neck. This old mare, with nothin' but her character an' that bell to encumber her, goes fa'rly flyin' light. But go as fast an' as far as she pleases, them long-y'eared locoed worshippers of her's won't let her outen their raptured sight. The last one of 'em, panniers, freight an' all, would go surgin' to the topmost pinnacle of the Rockies if she leads the way.

"An' at that this gray mare don't like mules none; she abhors their company an' kicks an' abooses 'em to a standstill whenever they draws near. But the fool mules don't care; it's ecstacy to simply know she's livin' an' that mule's cup of joy is runnin' over who finds himse'f permitted to crop grass within forty foot of his old, gray bell-bedecked idol.

" We travels all day, followin' glimpsin' that flea-bitten cayouse at Tramperos. But the mules can't think or talk of nothin' else. It arouses their religious enthoosiasm to highest pitch; even the cynic Jerry gets half-way keyed up over it. I looks for trouble that night; an' partic'lar I pegs out Jerry plenty deep and strong. The rest is hobbled, all except Tom. Gray mare or not, I'll gamble the outfit Tom wouldn't abandon Jerry, let the indoocement be ever so alloorin'.

" Every well-organised mule team that a-way allers carries along a bronco. This little steed, saddled an' bridled, trots throughout the day by the side of the off-wheeler, his bridle-rein caught over the wheeler's hame. The bronco is used to round up the mules in event they strays or declines in the mornin' to come when called. Sech bein' the idee, the cayous is allers kept strictly in camp.

" 'James' is my bronco's name ; an' the evenin',
followin' the vision of that Tramperos gray mare I
makes onusual shore that James stays with me.
Not that gray mares impresses James—him bein' a
hoss an' hosses havin' religious convictions different
from mules—or is doo to prove temptations to him ;
but he might conceal other plans an' get strayed
prosecootin' of 'em to a finish.   I ties James to the
trail-waggon, an' followin' bacon, biscuits, airtights
an' sech, the same bein' my froogal fare when on
the trail, I rolls in onder the lead-waggon an' gives
myse'f up to sleep.

" Exactly as I surmises, when I turns out at sun-
up thar's never a mule in sight.   Every one of them
idolaters goes poundin' back, as fast as ever he can
with hobbles on, to confess his sins an' say his pray'rs
at the shrine of that old gray mare.   Even Jerry,
whose cynicism should have saved him, pulls his
picket-pin with the rest an', takin' Tom along, goes
curvin'off.   It ain't more than ten minutes, you can
gamble! when James an' me is on their trails.

"One by one, I overtakes the team strung all
along between my camp an' Tramperos.   Peter, the
little lead mule, bein' plumb agile an' a sharp on
hobbles, gets cl'ar thar; an' I finds him devourin'
the goddess gray mare with heart an' soul an' eyes,
an' singin' to himse'f the while in low, satisfied
tones.

" As one after the other I passes the pilgrim
mules I turns an' lifts about a squar' inch of hide
off each with the blacksnake whip I'm carryin', by

way of p'intin' out their heresies an' arousin' in 'em a eagerness to get back to their waggons an' a upright, pure career. They takes the chastisement humble an' dootiful, an' relinquishes the thought of reachin' the goddess gray mare.

" When I overtakes old Jerry I pours the leather into him speshul, an' the way him an' his pard Tom goes scatterin' for camp refreshes me a heap. An' yet after I rescoos Peter from the demoralisin' inflooences of the gray mare, an' begins to pick up the other members of the team on the journey back, I'm some deepressed when I don't see Tom or Jerry. Nor is either of them mules by the waggons when I arrives.

" It's onadulterated cussedness! Jerry, with no hobbles an' merely draggin' a rope, can lope about free an' permiscus. Tom, with nothin' to hamper him but his love for Jerry, is even more lightsome an' loose. That Jerry mule, hatin' me an' allowin' to make me all the grief he can, sneakingly leaves the trail some'ers after I turns him an' touches him up with the lash. An' now Tom an' Jerry is shorely hid out an' lost a whole lot. It's nothin' but Jerry's notion of revenge on me.

" I camps two days where I'm at, an' rounds up the region for the trooants. I goes over it like a fine-tooth comb an' rides James to a show-down. That bronco never is so long onder the saddle since he's foaled; I don't reckon he knows before thar's so much hard work in the world as falls to him when we goes ransackin' in quest of Tom an' Jerry.

"It's no use; the ground is hard an' dry an' I can't even see their hoof-marks. The country's so rollin', too, it's no trouble for 'em to hide. At last I quits an' throws my hand in the diskyard. Tom an' Jerry is shore departed an' I'm deeficient my two best mules. I hooks up the others, an' seein' it's down hill an' a easy trail I makes Tascosa an' refits.

" I never crosses up on Tom an' Jerry in this yere life no more, but one day I learns their fate. It's a month later on my next trip back, an' I'm camped about a half day's drive of that same locoed plaza of Tramperos. As I'm settin' in camp with the sun still plenty high—I'm compilin' flapjacks at the time —I sees eight or ten ravens wheelin' an' cirklin' over beyond a swell about three miles to the left.

" ' Tom an' Jerry for a bloo stack ! ' I says to myse'f; an' with that I cinches the saddle onto James precip'tate.

" Shore enough ; I'm on the scene of the tragedy. Half way down a rocky slope where thar ain't grass enough to cover the brown nakedness of the ground lies the bones of Tom an' Jerry. This latter, who's that obstinate an' resentful he won't go back to camp when I wallops him on that gray mare mornin', allows he'll secrete himse'f an' Tom off to one side an' worrit me up. While he's manooverin' about he gets the half-inch rope he's draggin' tangled good an' fast in a mesquite bush. It shorely holds him ; that bush is old Jerry's last picket—his last camp. Which he'd a mighty sight better played his hand out with me, even if I does ring in a trace-chain on him at needed intervals. Jerry jest nacherally starves to death for grass an' water. An' what's doubly hard the lovin' Tom, troo to the last, starves with him. Thar's water within two miles; but Tom declines it, stays an' starves with Jerry, an' the ravens an' the coyotes picks their frames."

CHAPTER IX.

The Influence of Faro Nell.

" THAR'S no doubt about it," observed the Old
Cattleman, apropos of the fairer, better sex—for
woman was the gentle subject of our morning's
talk; " thar's no doubt about it, females is a refinin'
an' ennoblin' inflooence; you-all can hazard your
chips on that an' pile 'em higher than Cook's Peak!
An' when Faro Nell prefers them requests, she's
ondoubted moved of feelin's of mercy. They shore
does her credit, said motives does, an' if she had
asked Cherokee or Jack Moore, or even Texas
Thompson, things would have come off as effective
an' a mighty sight more discreet. But since he's
standin' thar handy, Nell ups an' recroots Dan
Boggs on the side of hoomanity, an' tharupon Dan
goes trackin' in without doo reflection, an' sets the
Mexicans examples which, to give 'em a best deescription, is shore some bad. It ain't Nell's fault,
but Dan is a gent of sech onusual impulses that
you-all don't know wherever Dan will land none,
once you goes pokin' up his ha'r-hung sensibil'ties
with su'gestions that is novel to his game. Still,
Nell can't he'p it; an' in view of what we knows to
be the female record since ever the world begins, I

re-asserts onhesitatin' that the effects of woman is good. She subdooes the reckless, subjoogates the rebellious, sobers the friv'lous, burns the ground from onder the indolent moccasins of that male she's roped up in holy wedlock's bonds, an' p'ints the way to a higher, happier life. That's whatever! an' this dramy of existence, as I once hears Colonel Sterett say, would be a frost an' a failure an' bog plumb down at that, if you was to cut out the leadin' lady roles an' ring up the curtain with nothin' but bucks in the cast.'

" Narrow an' contracted as you may deem said camp to be, Wolfville itse'f offers plenty proof on this head. Thar's Dave Tutt: Whatever is Dave, I'd like for to inquire, prior to Tucson Jennie runnin' her wifely brand on to him an' redoocin' him to domesticity? No, thar's nothin' so evil about Dave neither, an' yet he has his little ways. For one thing, Dave's about as extemporaneous a prop'sition as ever sets in a saddle, an' thar's times when you give Dave licker an' convince him it's a o'casion for joobilation, an' you-all won't have to leave no ' call ' with the clerk to insure your-se'f of bein' out early in the mornin.' Son, Dave would keep that camp settin' up all night.

" But once Dave comes onder the mitigatin' spells of Tucson Jennie, things is changed. Tucson Jennie knocks Dave's horns off doorin' the first two weeks ; he gets staid an' circumspect an' tharby plays better poker an' grows more urbane.

" Likewise does Benson Annie work mir'cles

sim'lar in the conduct of that maverick French which Enright an' the camp, to allay the burnin' excitement that's rendin' the outfit on account of the Laundry War, herds into her lovin' arms. Tenderfoot as he is, when we-all ups an' marries him off that time, this French already shows symptoms of becomin' one of the most abandoned sports in Arizona. Benson Annie seizes him, purifies him, an' makes him white as snow.

"An' thar's Missis Rucker;—as troo a lady as ever bakes a biscuit! Even with the burdens of the O. K. Restauraw upon her she still finds energy to improve old Rucker to that extent he ups an' rides off towards the hills one mornin' an' never does come back no more.

"'Doc,' he says to Doc Peets, while he's fillin' a canteen in the Red Light prior to his start; 'I won't tell you what I'm aimin' to accomplish, because the Stranglers might regyard it as their dooty to round me up. But thar's something comin' to the public, Doc; so I yereby leaves word that next week, or next month, or mebby later, if doubts is expressed of my fate, I'm still flutterin' about the scenery some'ers an' am a long ways short of dead. An' as I fades from sight, Doc, I'll take a chance an' say that the clause in the Constitootion which allows that all gents is free an' equal wasn't meant to incloode no married man.' An' with these croode bluffs Rucker chases forth for the Floridas.

"No, the camp don't do nothin'; the word gets passed 'round that old Rucker's gone prospectin'

an' that he will recur in our midst whenever thar's
a reg'lar roll-call. As for Missis Rucker, personal,
from all we can jedge by lookin' on—for thar's shore
none of us who's that locoed we ups an' asks—I
don't reckon now she ever notices that Rucker's
escaped.

"Yere's how it is the time when Faro Nell, her
heart bleedin' for the sufferin's of dumb an' he'pless
brutes, employs Dan Boggs in errants of mercy an'
Dan's efforts to do good gets ill-advised. Not that
Dan is easily brought so he regyards his play as erroneous; Enright has to rebooke Dan outright in
set terms an' assoome airs of severity before ever
Dan allows he entertains a doubt.

" ' Suppose I does retire that Greaser's hand from
cirk'lation?' says Dan, sort o' dispootatious with
Enright an' Doc Peets, who's both engaged in p'intin' out Dan's faults. 'Mexicans ain't got no more
need for hands than squinch owls has for hymn
books. They won't work; they never uses them
members except for dealin' monte or clawin' a
guitar. I regyards a Mexican's hands that a-way,
when considered as feachers in his makeup, as
sooperfluous.'

" ' Dan, you shore is the most perverse sport!'
says Enright, makin' a gesture of impatience an' at
the same time refillin' his glass in hopes of a ca'mer
frame. 'This ain't so much a question of hands as
it's a question of taste. Nell's requests is right, an'
you're bound to go about the rescoo of said chicken
as the victim of crooelties. Where you-all falls

down is on a system. The method you invokes is impertinent. Don't you say so, Doc?'

" ' Which I shore does,' says Peets. ' Dan's conduct is absolootely oncouth.'

" Dan lays the basis for these strictures in the followin' fashion: It's a *fieste* with the Mexicans— one of the noomerous saint's days they gives way to when every Greaser onbuckles an' devotes himse'f to merriments—an' over in Chihuahua, as the Mexican part of the camp is called, the sunburnt portion of Wolfville's pop'lation broadens into quite a time. Thar's hoss races an' monte an' mescal an' pulque, together with roode music sech as may be wrung from primitive instruments like the guitar, the fiddle, an' tin cans half filled with stones.

" Faro Nell, who is only a child as you-all might say, an' ready to be engaged an' entertained with childish things, goes trippin' over to size up the gala scene.

" Thar's a passel of young Mexicans who's Ridin' for the Chicken's Head. This yere is a sport something like a Gander Pullin', same as we-all engages in on Thanksgivin' days an' Christmas, back when I'm a boy in Tennessee. You saveys a Gander Pullin'? Son, you don't mean sech ignorance! Thar must have been mighty little sunshine in the life of a yooth in the morose regions where you was raised for you-all never to disport yourse'f, even as a spectator, at a Gander Pullin'! It wouldn't surprise me none after that if you ups an' informs me you never shakes a fetlock in that dance called money-musk.

"To the end that you be eddicated,—for it's bet-ter late than never,—I'll pause concernin' Boggs an' the Mexicans long enough to eloocidate of Gander Pullin's.

"As I su'gests, we onbends in this pastime at sech epocks as Christmas an' Thanksgivin.' I don't myse'f take actooal part in any Gander Pullin's. Not that I'm too delicate, but I ain't got no hoss. Bein' a pore yooth, I spends the mornin' of my c'reer on foot, an' as a hoss is a necessary ingreedi-ent to a Gander Pullin', I never does stand in per-sonal on the festival, but is redooced to become a envy-bitten looker-on.

"Gander Pullin's is conducted near a tavern or a still house so's the assembled gents won't want the inspiration befittin' both the season an' the scene, an' is commonly held onder the auspices of the pro-prietor tharof. Thar's a track marked out in a cir-kle like a little racecourse for the hosses to gallop on. This course runs between two poles pinned into the ground ; or mebby it's two trees. Thar's a rope stretched from pole to pole,—taut an' stiff she's stretched ; an' the gander who's the object of the meetin', with his neck an' head greased a heap lavish, is hung from the rope by his two hind laigs. As the gander hangs thar, what Colonel Sterett would style 'the cynosure of every eye,' you'll notice that a gent by standin' high in the stirrups can get a grip of the gander's head.

" As many as determines to distinguish themse'fs
in the amoosement throws a two-bit piece into a
hat. Most likely thar'll be forty partic'pants. They
then lines up, Injun file, an' goes caperin' round the
course, each in his place in the joyous procession.
As a gent goes onder the rope he grabs for the gander's head ; an' that party who's expert enough to
bring it away in his hand, wins the hat full of two-
bit pieces yeretofore deescribed.

" Which, of course, no gent succeeds the first ·
dash outen the box, as a gander's head is on some
good and strong ; an' many a saddle gets emptied
by virchoo of the back'ard yanks a party gets.
But it's on with the dance ! They keeps whoopin'
an' shoutin' an' ridin' the cirkle an' grabbin' at the
gander, each in his cheerful turn, ontil some strong
or lucky party sweeps away the prize, assoomes
title to the two-bit pieces, goes struttin' to the licker
room an' buys nosepaint for the pop'lace tharwith.

" Shore, doorin' a contest a gent's got to keep
ridin' ; he's not allowed to pause an' dally with the
gander an' delay the game. To see to this a brace
of brawny sharps is stationed by each pole with
clubs in their willin' hands to reemonstrate with any
hoss or gent who slows down or stops as he goes
onder the gander.

" Thar you have it, son ; a brief but lively picture
of a Gander Pullin' as pulled former in blithe old
Tennessee. An' you'll allow, if you sets down to a
ca'm, onja'ndiced study of the sport, that a half
hour of reasonable thrill might be expected to flow

from it. Gander Pullin's is popular a lot when I'm a yearlin'; I knows that for shore; though in a age which grows effete it's mighty likely if we-all goes back thar now, we'd find it fallen into disuse as a reelaxation.

"In Ridin' for the Chicken's Head, a Mexican don't hang up his prey none same as we-all does at Gander Pullin's. He buries it in the ground to sech degrees that nothin' but the head an' neck protroodes. An' as the Mexicans goes flashin' by on their broncos, each in turn swings down an' makes a reach for the chicken's head. The experiment calls for a shore-enough rider; as when a party is over on one side that a-way, an' nothin' to hold by but a left hand on the saddlehorn an' a left spur caught in the cantle, any little old pull will fetch him out on his head.

"This day when Faro Nell comes bulgin' up to amoose her young an' idle cur'osity with the gayeties of Chihuahua, the Ridin' for the Chicken's Head is about to commence. Which they're jest plantin' the chicken. At first Nell don't savey, as she ain't posted deep on Mexican pastimes. But Nell is plenty quick mental; as, actin' look-out for Cherokee's bank, she's bound to be. Wherefore Nell don't study the preeliminaries long before she gets onto the roodiments of some idee concernin' the jocund plans of the Greasers.

"At last the chicken is buried, an' thar's nothin' in sight but its anxious head. Except that it can turn an' twist its neck some, it's fixed in the ground as firm an' solid as the stumps of a mesquite bush.

"The first Greaser—he's a gaudy party with more colours than you could count in any rainbow —is organisin' for a rush. He's pickin' up his reins an' pushin' his moccasins deep into his tap-pedaries, when, as he gives his cayouse the spur, the beauty of Ridin' for the Chicken's Head bursts full on Faro Nell. Comin' on her onexpected, Nell don't see no pleasure in it. It don't present the attractions which so alloores the heart of a Greaser. Without pausin' to think, an' feelin' shocked over the fate that's ridin' down on the buried chicken, Nell grips her little paws convulsive an' snaps her teeth. It's then her eye catches Dan Boggs, who's contemplatin' details an' awaitin' the finish with vivid interest.

"'Oh, Dan!' says Nell, grabbin' Dan's arm, 'I don't want that chicken hurt none! Can't you-all make 'em stop?'

"'Shore!' says Dan, prompt to Nell's cry. 'I preevails on 'em to cease easy.'

"As Dan says this, that radiant cavalier is sweepin' upon the pore chicken like the breath of destiny. He's bendin' from the saddle to make a swoop as Dan speaks. Thar ain't a moment to lose an' Dan's hand goes to his gun.

"'Watch me stop him,' says Dan; an' as he does, his bullet makes rags of the Mexican's hand not a inch from the chicken's head.

"For what time you-all might need to slop out a

drink, the onlookin' Mexicans stands still. Then the stoopefyin' impressions made by Dan's pistol practice wears off an' a howl goes up like a hundred wolves. At this Dan gets his number-two gun to b'ar, an' with one in each hand, confronts the tan-coloured multitoode.

" 'That's shore a nice shot, Nell!' says Dan over his shoulder, ropin' for the congratoolations he thinks is comin.'

"But Nell don't hear him; she's one hundred yards away an' streakin' it for the Red Light like a shootin' star. She tumbles in on us with the brake off like a stage-coach downhill.

" 'Dan's treed Chihuahua!' gasps Nell, as she heads straight for Cherokee; 'you-all better rustle over thar plumb soon!'

"Cherokee jumps an' grabs his hardware where they're layin' onder the table. Bein' day-light an' no game goin', an' the day some warm besides, he ain't been wearin' 'em, bein' as you-all might say in negligee. Cherokee buckles on his belts in a second an' starts; the rest of us, however, since we're more ackerately garbed, don't lose no time an' is already half way to Dan.

" It ain't a two-minute run an' we arrives in time. Thar's no more blood, though thar might have been, for we finds Dan frontin' up to full two hundred Greasers, their numbers increasin' and excitement runnin' a heap high. We cuts in between Dan an' Mexican public opinion and extricates that over-vol'tile sport.

"But Dan won't return ontil he exhoomes the chicken, which is still bobbin' an' twistin' its onharmed head where the Mexican buries it. Dan digs it up an' takes it by the laigs; Enright meanwhile cussin' him out, fervent an' nervous, for he fears some locoed Greaser will cut loose every moment an' mebby crease a gent, an' so leave it incumbent on the rest of us to desolate Chihuahua.

"'It's for Nell,' expostulates Dan, replyin' to Enright's criticisms. 'I knows she wants it by the way she grabs my coat that time. Moreover, from the tones she speaks in, I reckons she wants it alive. Also, I don't discern no excoose for this toomult neither; which you-all is shore the most peevish bunch, Enright, an' that's whatever!'

"'Peevish or no,' retorts Enright, 'as a jedge of warjigs I figgers that we gets here jest in time. Thar you be, up ag'inst the entire tribe, an' each one with a gun. It's one of the deefects of a Colt's six-shooter that it hits as hard an' shoots as troo for a Injun or a Greaser as it does for folks. Talk about us bein' peevish! what do you-all reckon would have been results if we hadn't cut in on the *baile* at the time we does?'

"'Nothin',' says Dan, with tones of soopreme vanity, at the same time dustin' the dirt off Nell's chicken, 'nothin', except I'd hung crape on half the dobies in Chihuahua.'

"About two hours after, when things ag'in simmers to the usual, an' Nell is makin' her chicken a coop out to the r'ar of the Red Light, Enright gives a half laugh.

"'Dan,' says Enright, 'when I reflects on the hole we drug you out of, an' the way you-all gets in, you reminds me of that Thomas Benton dog I owns when I'm a yoothful child on the Cumberland. Which Thomas Benton that a-way is a mighty industrious dog an' would turn over a quarter-section of land any afternoon diggin' out a ground-hawg. But thar's this drawback to Thomas Benton which impairs his market valyoo. Some folks used to re-gyard it as a foible; but it's worse, it's a deefect. As I remarks, this Thomas Benton dog would throw his whole soul into the work, an' dig for a ground-hawg like he ain't got another dollar. But thar's this pecooliarity: After that Thomas Benton dog has done dug out the ground-hawg for a couple of hours, you-all is forced to get a spade an' dig out that Thomas Benton dog. He's dead now these yere forty years, but if he's livin' I'd shore change his name an' rebrand him " Dan'l Boggs." ' "

CHAPTER X.

The Ghost of the Bar-B-8.

"SPECTRES? Never! I refooses 'em my beliefs utter"; and with these emphatic words the Old Cattleman tasted his liquor thoughtfully on his tongue. The experiment was not satisfactory; and he despatched his dark retainer Tom for lemons and sugar. "An' you-all might better tote along some hot water, too;" he commanded. "This nosepaint feels raw an' over-fervid; a leetle dilootion won't injure it none."

"But about ghosts?" I persisted.

"Ghosts?" he retorted. "I never does hear of but one; that's a apparition which enlists the attentions of Peets and Old Man Enright a lot. It's a spectre that takes to ha'ntin' about one of Enright's Bar-B-8 sign-camps, an' scarin' up the cattle an' drivin' 'em over a precipice, an' all to Enright's disaster an' loss. Nacherally, Enright don't like this spectral play; an' him an' Peets lays for the wraith with rifles, busts its knee some, an' Peets ampytates its laig. Then they throws it loose; allowin' that now it's only got one laig, the visitations will mighty likely cease. Moreover Enright regyards ampytation that a-way, as punishment enough. Which I should shore allow the same myse'f!

"It ain't much of a tale. It turns out like all sperit stories; when you approaches plumb close an' jumps sideways at 'em an' seizes 'em by the antlers, the soopernacheral elements sort o' bogs down.

"It's over mebby fifty miles to the southeast of Wolfville, some'ers in the fringes of the Tres Hermanas that thar's a sign-camp of Enright's brand. Thar's a couple of Enright's riders holdin' down this corner of the Bar-B-8 game, an' one evenin' both of 'em comes squanderin' in,—ponies a-foam an' faces pale as milk,—an' puts it up they don't return to that camp no more.

"'Because she's ha'nted,' says one; 'Jim an' me both encounters this yere banshee an' it's got fire-eyes. Also, itse'f and pony is constructed of bloo flames. You can gamble! I don't want none of it in mine; an that's whatever!'

"Any gent can see that these yooths is mighty scared. Enright elicits their yarn only after pourin' about a quart of nosepaint into 'em.

"It looks like on two several o'casions that a handful of cattle gets run over a steep bluff from the *mesa* above. The fall is some sixty feet in the cl'ar, an' when them devoted cattle strikes the bottom it's plenty easy to guess they're sech no longer, an' thar's nothin' left of 'em but beef. These beef drives happens each time in the night; an' the cattle must have been stampeded complete to make the trip. Cattle, that a-way, ain't goin' to go chargin' over a high bluff none onless their reason is onhinged. No, the coyotes an' the mountain lions don't do it; they never chases cattle, holdin' 'em in fear an' tremblin.' These mountain lions prounces down on colts like a mink on a settin' hen, but never calves or cattle.

"It's after the second beef killin' when the two riders allows they'll do some night herdin' themse'fs an' see if they solves these pheenomenons that's cuttin' into the Bar-B-8.

"'An' it's mebby second drink time after midnight,' gasps the cow-puncher who's relatin' the adventures, 'an' me an' Jim is experimentin' along the aige of the *mesa*, when of a suddent thar comes two steers, heads down, tails up, locoed absoloote they be; an' flashin' about in the r'ar of 'em rides this flamin' cow-sperit on its flamin' cayouse. Shore! he heads 'em over the cliff; I hears 'em hit the bottom of the canyon jest as I falls off my bronco in a fit. As soon as ever I comes to an' can scramble into that Texas saddle ag'in, me an' Jim hits the high places in the scenery, in a fervid way, an' yere we-all be! An' you hear me, gents, I don't go back to that Bar-B-8 camp no more. I ain't ridin' herd on apparitions; an' whenever ghosts takes to romancin' about in the cow business, that lets me out.'

"'I reckons,' says Enright, wrinklin' up his brows, 'I'll take a look into this racket myse'f.'

"'An' if you-all don't mind none, Enright,' says Peets, 'I'll get my chips in with yours. Thar's been no one shot for a month in either Red Dog or Wolfville an' I'm reedic'lous free of patients. An' if the boys'll promise to hold themse'fs an' their guns in abeyance for a week or so, an' not go framin' up excooses for my presence abrupt, I figgers that a few days idlin' about the ranges, an' mebby a riot or two roundin' up this cow-demon, will expand me an' do me good.'

" 'You're lookin' for trouble, Doc,' says Colonel Sterett, kind o' laughin' at Peets. 'You reminds me of a onhappy sport I encounters long ago in Looeyville.'

" 'An' wherein does this Bloo Grass party resemble me?' asks Peets.

" 'It's one evenin',' says Colonel Sterett, 'an' a passel of us is settin' about in the Galt House bar, toyin' with our beverages. Thar's a smooth, goodlookin' stranger who's camped at a table near. Final, he yawns like he's shore weary of life an' looks at us sharp an' cur'ous. Then he speaks up gen'ral as though he's addressin' the ai.. "This is a mighty dull town!" he says. "Which I've been yere a fortnight an' I ain't had no fight as yet." An' he continyoos to look us over plenty mournful.

" ' " You-all needn't gaze on us that a-way," says a gent named Granger; "you can set down a stack on it, you ain't goin' to pull on no war with none of us."

" ' "Shore, no!" says the onhappy stranger. Then he goes on apol'getic: "Gents, I'm onfort'nately constitooted. Onless I has trouble at reasonable intervals it preys on me. I've been yere in your town two weeks an' so far ain't seen the sign. Gents, it's beginnin' to tell; an' if any of you-all could direct me where I might get action it would be kindly took."

" ' " If you're honin' for a muss," says Granger, " all you has to do is go a couple of blocks to the east, an' then five to the no'th, an' thar on the corner you'll note a mighty prosperous s'loon. You caper in by the side door; it says FAMILY ENTRANCE over this yere portal. Sa'nter up to the bar, call for licker, drink it; an' then you remark to the barkeep, casooal like, that you're thar to maintain that any outcast who'll sell sech whiskey ain't fit to drink with a nigger or eat with a dog. That's all; that barkeep'll relieve you of the load that's burdenin' your nerves in about thirty seconds. You'll be the happiest sport in Looeyville when he gets through."

" ' " But can't you come an' p'int out the place," coaxes the onhappy stranger of Granger. He's all wropped up in what Granger tells him. " I don't know my way about good, an' from your deescriptions I shorely wouldn't miss visitin' that resort for gold an' precious stones. Come an' show me, pard; I'll take you thar in a kerriage."

" ' At that Granger consents to guide the onhappy stranger. They drives over an' Granger stops the outfit, mebby she's fifty yards from the door. He p'ints it out to the onhappy stranger sport.

" ' Come with me," says the onhappy stranger, as he gets outen the kerriage. " Come on; you-all don't have to fight none. I jest wants you to watch me. Which I'm the dandiest warrior for the whole length of the Ohio!"

"'But Granger is firm that he won't; he's not inquis'tive, he says, an' will stay planted right thar on the r'ar seat an' await deevelopments. With that, the onhappy stranger sport goes sorrowfully for'ard alone, an gets into the gin-mill by the said FAMILY ENTRANCE. Granger' sets thar with his head out an' y'ears cocked lookin' an' listenin'.

"'Everything's plenty quiet for a minute. Then slam! bang! bing! crash! the most flagrant hubbub breaks forth! It sounds like that store's comin' down. The racket rages an' grows worse. Thar's a smashin' of glass. The lights goes out, while customers comes boundin' an' skippin' forth from the FAMILY ENTRANCE like frightened fawns. At last the uproars dies down ontil they subsides complete.

"'Granger is beginnin' to upbraid himse'f for not gettin the onhappy stranger's address, so's he could ship home the remainder. In the midst of Granger's se'f- accoosations, the lights in the gin-mill begins to burn ag'in, one by one. After awhile, she's re-illoominated an' ablaze with old-time glory. It's then the FAMILY ENTRANCE opens an' the onhappy stranger sport emerges onto the sidewalk. He's in his shirtsleeves, an' a satisfied smile wreathes his face. He shore looks plumb content!

"'"Get out of the kerriage an' come in, pard," he shouts to Granger. "Come on in a whole lot! I'd journey down thar an' get you, but I can't leave; I'm tendin' bar!"'"

"'You're shore right, Colonel,' says Peets, when Colonel Sterett ends the anecdote, 'the feelin' of that onhappy stranger sport is parallel to mine. Ghosts is new to me; an' I'm goin' pirootin' off with Enright on this demon hunt an' see if I can't fetch up in the midst of a trifle of nerve-coolin excitement.'

" The ghost tales of the stampeded cow-punchers excites Dan Boggs a heap. After Enright an' Peets has organised an' gone p'inting out for the ha'nted Bar-B-8 sign-camp to investigate the spook, Dan can't talk of nothin' else.

"'Them's mighty dead game gents, Enright an' Doc Peets is!' says Dan. 'I wouldn't go searchin' for no sperits more'n I'd write letters to rattlesnakes! I draws the line at intimacies with fiends.'

"'But mebby this yere is a angel,' says Faro Nell, from her stool alongside of Cherokee Hall.

"'Not criticisin' you none, Nell,' says Dan, 'Cherokee himse'f will tell you sech surmises is reedic'-lous. No angel is goin' to visit Arizona for obvious reasons. An' ag'in, no angel's doo to go skallyhootin' about after steers an' stampeedin' 'em over brinks. It's ag'in reason; you bet! That blazin' wraith, that a-way, is a shore-enough demon! An' as for me, personal, I wouldn't cut his trail for a bunch of ponies!'

"'Be you-all scared of ghosts, Dan?' asks Faro Nell.

"'Be I scared of ghosts?' says Dan. 'Which I wish I could see a ghost an' show you! I don't

want to brag none, Nellie, but I'll gamble four
for one, an' go as far as you likes, that if you
was to up an' show me a ghost right now, I
wouldn't stop runnin' for a month. But what ap-
pals me partic'lar,' goes on Dan, 'about Peets
an' Enright, is they takes their guns. Now a ghost
waxes onusual indignant if you takes to shootin'
him up with guns. No, it don't hurt him ; but he
regyards sech demonstrations as insults. It's like
my old pap says that time about the Yankees. My
old pap is a colonel with Gen'ral Price, an' on this
evenin' is engaged in leadin' one of the most intrepid retreats of the war. As he's prancin' along
at the head of his men where a great commander
belongs, he's shore scandalised by hearin' his r'ar
gyard firin' on the Yanks. So he rides back, my
old pap does, an' he says: "Yere you-all eediots!
Whatever do you mean by shootin' at them Yankees? Don't you know it only makes 'em madder?"
An' that,' concloods Dan, ' is how I feels about
spectres. I wouldn't go lammin' loose at 'em with
no guns ; it only makes 'em madder.'

" It's the next day, an' Peets an' Enright is organised in the ha'nted sign-camp of the Bar-B-8. Also,
they've been lookin' round. By ridin' along onder
the face of the precipice, they comes, one after
t'other, on what little is left of the dead steers.
What strikes 'em as a heap pecooliar is that thar's
no bones or horns. Two or three of the hoofs is
kickin' about, an' Enright picks up one the coyotes
overlooks. It shows it's been cut off at the fetlock
j'int by a knife.

"'This spectre,' says Enright, passin' the hoof to Peets, 'packs a bowie ; an' he likewise butchers his prey. Also, ondoubted, he freights the meat off some'ers to his camp, which is why we don't notice no big bones layin' 'round loose.' Then Enright scans the grass mighty scroopulous ; an' shore enough ! thar's plenty of pony tracks printed into the soil. 'That don't look so soopernacheral neither,' says Enright, p'intin' to the hoof-prints.

"'Them's shorely made by a flesh an' blood pony,' says Peets. 'An' from their goin' some deep into the ground, I dedooces that said cayouse is loaded down with what weight of beef an' man it can stagger onder.'

"That evenin' over their grub Enright an' Peets discusses the business. Thar's a jimcrow Mexican plaza not three miles off in the hills. Both of 'em is aware of this hamlet, an' Peets, partic'lar, is well acquainted with a old Mexican sharp who lives thar —he's a kind o' schoolmaster among 'em—who's mighty cunnin' an' learned. His name is Jose Miguel.

"'An' I'm beginnin' to figger,' says Peets, 'that this ghostly rider is the foxy little Jose Miguel. Which I've frequent talked with him ; an' he saveys enough about drugs an' chemicals to paint up with phosphorus an' go surgin' about an' stampedin' cattle over bluffs. It's a mighty good idee from his standp'int. He can argue that the cattle kills themse'fs—sort o' commits sooicide inadvertent— an' if we-all tracks up on him with the beef, he in-

sists on his innocence, an' puts it up that his cuttin
in on the play after said cattle done slays themse'f*
injures nobody but coyotes.'

"' Doc,' coincides Enright, after roominatin' in
silence, ' Doc, the longer I ponders, the more them
theeries seems sagacious. That enterprisin' Greaser
is jest about killin' my beef an' sellin' it to the
entire plaza. Not only does this ghost play op-
p'rate to stampede the cattle an' set 'em runnin'
cimmaron an' locoed so they'll chase over the cliffs
to their ends, but it serves to scare my cow-punchers off the range, which last, ondoubted, this Miguel
looks on as a deesideratum. However, it's goin' to
be good an' dark to-night, an' if we-all has half luck
I reckons that we fixes him.'

" It's full two hours after midnight an' while thar's
stars overhead thar's no moon; along the top of
the *mesa* it's as dark as the inside of a jug. Peets
an' Enright is Injunin' about on the prowl for the
ghost. They don't much reckon it'll be abroad, as
mebby the plaza has beef enough.

"' However, by to-morry night,' says Enright in a
whisper, ' or at the worst, by the night after, we're
shore to meet up with this marauder.'

"' Hesh !' whispers Peets, at the same time stoppin' Enright with his hand, ' he's out to-night !'

" An' thar for shore is something like a dim bloo
light movin' across the plains. Now an' then, two
brighter lights shows in spots like the blazes of
candles ; them's the fire eyes the locoed cowboys
tells of. Whatever it is, whether spook or Greaser,

it's quarterin' the ground like one of these huntin'
dogs. It's gait is a slow canter.

"'He's on the scout,' says Enright,' 'tryin' to
start a steer or two in the dark ; but he ain't located
none yet.'

"Enright an' Peets slides to the ground an' hobbles their broncos. They don't aim to have 'em go
swarmin' over no bluffs in any blindness of a first
surprise. When the ponies is safe, they bends low
an' begins makin' up towards the ground on which
this bloo-shimmerin' shadow 'is ha'ntin' about.
Things comes their way; they has luck. They've
done crope about forty rods when the ghost heads
for 'em. They can easy tell he's comin', for the
fire eyes shows all the time an' not by fits an'
starts as former. As the bloo shimmer draws nearer
they makes out the vague shadows of a man on a
hoss. Son, she's shore plenty ghostly as a vision,
an' Enright allows later, it's no marvel the punchers
vamoses sech scenes.

"'How about it,' whispers Peets; 'shall I do the
shootin'?'

"'Which your eyes is younger,' says Enright.
'You cut loose; an' I'll stand by to back the play.
Only aim plenty low. You can't he'p over-shootin'
in the dark. Hold as low as his stirrup.'

"Peets pulls himse'f up straight as a saplin' an'
runs his left hand along the bar'l as far as his arm'll
reach. An' he hangs long on the aim as shootin'
in the dark ain't no cinch. If this ghost is a bright
ghost it would be easy. But he ain't; he's bloo an'

dim like washed out moonlight, or when it's jest gettin' to be dawn.   Enright's twenty yards to one side so as to free himse'f of Peet's smoke in case he has to make a second shot.

"But Peets calls the turn.   With the crack of that Sharp's of his, the ghost sets up sech a screech it proves he ain't white an' also that he'll live through the evenin's events.   As the spectre yelps, the bloo cayouse goes over on its head an' neck an' then falls dead on its side.   The lead which only smashes the spectre's knee to splinters goes plumb through the pony's heart.

"As Peets foresees, the ghost ain't none other than the wise little Jose Miguel, schoolmaster, who's up on drugs an' chemicals.   The bloo glimmer is phosphorus ; an' the fire eyes is two of these little old lamps like miners packs in their caps.

"Enright an' Peets strolls up ; this Miguel is groanin' an' mournin' an' cryin' ' *Marie, Madre de Dios !* ' When he sees who downs him, he drags himse'f to Enright an' begs a heap abject for his life. With that, Enright silently lets down the hammer of his rifle.

"Peets when the sun comes up enjoys himse'f speshul with the opp'ration.   Peets is fond of ampytations, that a-way, and he lops off said limb with zest an' gusto.

" ' I shore deplores, Jose,' says Peets, ' to go shortenin' up a fellow scientist like this.   But thar's no he'pin' it ; fate has so decreed.   Also, as some comfort to your soul, I'll explain to Sam Enright

how you won't ride much when I gets you fairly
trimmed.   Leastwise, after I'm done prunin' you,
thar won't be nothin' but these yere woman's saddles that you'll fit, an' no gent, be he white or be
he Greaser, can work cattle from a side-saddle.'
An' Peets, hummin' a roundelay, cuts merrily into
the wounded member."

CHAPTER XI.

Tucson Jennie's Correction.

"Doc Peets, son," said the Old Cattleman, while his face wore the look of decent gravity it ever donned when that man of medicine was named, "Doc Peets has his several uses. Aside from him bein' a profound sharp on drugs, an' partic'lar cowboy drugs, he's plenty learned in a gen'ral way, an' knows where every kyard lays in nacher's deck, from them star-flecked heavens above to the earth beneath, an'—as Scripter puts it—to the 'waters onder the earth.' It's a good scheme to have a brace of highly eddicated gents, same as Colonel Sterett an' Doc Peets, sort o' idlin' 'round your camp. Thar's times when a scientist, or say, a lit'rary sport comes bluffin' into Wolfville; an' sech folks is a mighty sight too deep for Boggs an' me an' Tutt. If we're left plumb alone with a band of them book-read shorthorns like I deescribes, you-all sees your-se'f, they're bound to go spraddlin' East ag'in, an' report how darkened Wolfville is. But not after they locks horns with Doc Peets or Colonel Sterett. Wherefore, whenever the camp's invaded by any over-enlightened people who's gone too far in schools for the rest of us to break even with, we ups an' plays Doc Peets or Colonel Sterett onto 'em; an' the way either of them gents would turn in an'

tangle said visitors up mental don't bother 'em a
bit. That's straight; Peets an' the Colonel is our
refooge; they're our protectors; an' many a time
an' oft, have I beheld 'em lay for some vain-glor-
ious savant who's got a notion the Southwest, that
a-way, is a region of savagery where the folks can't
even read an' write none, an' they'd rope, throw, an'
hawgtie him—verbal, I means—an' brand his mem'ry
with the red-hot fact that he's wrong an' been wadin'
in error up to the saddle-girths touchin' the intel-
lectooal attainments of good old Arizona. Shore,—
Doc Peets has other uses than drugs, an' he dis-
charges 'em.

"Now that I thinks of the matter, it's Doc Peets
who restores Dave Tutt to full standin' with Tucson
Jennie, the time she begins to neglect Dave. You
see, the trouble is this a-way: It really starts—
leastwise I allers so believes— in Dave's beginnin'
wrong with Tucson Jennie. Troo, as I confesses
to you frequent yeretofore, I ain't married none
myse'f; still, I've been livin' a likely number of
years, an' has nacherally witnessed a whole lot
touchin' other gents an' their wives; an' sech experiences is bound to breed concloosions. An' while I
may be wrong, for these yere views is nothin' more
than a passel of ontested theeries with me, it's my
beliefs that thar's two attitoodes, speakin' gen'ral,
which a gent assoomes toward his bride. Either he
deals with her on what we-all will call the buck-
squaw system, or he turns the game about complete,
an' organises his play on the gentleman-lady system.

In the latter, the gent waits on his wife; he comes an' he goes, steps high or soft, exactly as she commands. She gives the orders; an' he rides a pony to death execootin' 'em, an' no reemonstrances nor queries. That wife is range an' round-up boss for her outfit.

"But the buck-squaw system is after all more hooman an' satisfactory. It's opposite to the other. The gent is reesponsible for beef on the hook an' flour in the bar'l. He's got to provide the blankets, make good ag'in the household's hunger, an' see to it thar's allers wood an' water within easy throw of every camp he pitches. Beyond that, however, the gent who's playin' the buck-squaw system don't wander. When he's in camp, he distinguishes himse'f by doin' nothin'. He wrops himse'f in his blankets, camps down by the fire, while his wife rustles his chuck an' fills his pipe for him. At first glance, this yere buck-squaw system might strike a neeophyte as a mighty brootal scheme. Jest the same, it'll eemerge winner twenty times to the gentleman-lady system's once. The women folks like it. Which they'll pretend they prefers the gentleman-lady system, where they sets still an' the gent attends on 'em; but don't you credit it, none whatever. It's the good old patriarchal, buck-squaw idee, where the gent does nothin' an' the lady goes prancin' about like the ministerin' angel which she is, that tickles her to death. I states ag'in, that it's my notion, Dave who begins with Tucson Jennie— they bein' man an' wife—on the gentleman-lady

system, tharby hatches cold neglect for himse'f. An'
if it ain't for the smooth savey of Doc Peets, thar's
no sport who could foretell the disast'rous end.
Dave, himse'f thinks he'd have had eventool to
resign his p'sition as Jennie's husband an' quit.

"Which I've onfolded to you prior of Jennie's
gettin' jealous of Dave touchin' that English towerist female ; but this yere last trouble ain't no like-
ness nor kin to that. Them gusts of jealousy don't
do no harm nohow ; nor last the day. They're like
thunder showers; brief an' black enough, but soon
over an' leavin' the world brighter.

"This last attitoode of Jennie towards Dave is
one of abandonment an' onthinkin' indifference that
a-way. It begins hard on the fetlocks of that interestin' event, thrillin' to every proud Wolfville
heart, the birth of Dave's only infant son, Enright
Peets Tutt. Which I never does cross up with no
one who deems more of her progeny than Jennie
does of the yoothful Enright Peets. A cow's solici-
toode concernin' her calf is chill regyard compared
tharwith. Jennie hangs over Enright Peets like
some dew-jewelled hollyhock over a gyarden fence ;
you'd think he's a roast apple ; an' I don't reckon
now, followin' that child's advent, she ever sees another thing in Arizona but jest Enright Peets. He's
the whole check-rack—the one bet that wins on the
layout of the possible—an' Jennie proceeds to conduct herse'f accordin'. It's a good thing mebby for
Enright Peets ; I won't set camped yere an' say it
ain't ; but it's mighty hard on Dave.

" Jennie not only neglects Dave, she turns herse'f loose frequent an' assails him. If he shows up in his wigwam walkin' some emphatic, Jennie'll be down on him like a fallin' star an' accoose him of wakin' Enright Peets.

" ' An' if you-all wakes him,' says Jennie to Dave, sort o' domineerin' at him with her forefinger, ' he'll be sick; an' if he gets sick, he'll die; an' if he dies, you'll be a murderer—the heartless deestroyer of your own he'pless offspring,—which awful deed I sometimes thinks you're p'intin' out to pull off.' An' then Jennie would put her apron over her head an' shed tears a heap; while Dave—all harrowed up an' onstrung—would come stampedin' down to the Red Light an' get consolation from Black Jack by the quart.

" That's the idee, son; it's impossible to go into painful details, 'cause I ain't in Dave's or Jennie's confidence enough to round 'em up; but you onderstands what I means. Jennie's forever hectorin' an' pesterin' Dave about Enright Peets; an' beyond that she don't pay no more heed, an' don't have him no more on her mind, than if he's one of these yere little jimcrow ground-owls you-all sees inhabitin' about dissoloote an permiscus with prairie-dogs. What's the result? Dave's sperits begins to sink; he takes to droopin' about listless an' onregyardful; an' he's that low an' onhappy his nose-paint don't bring him no more of comfort than if he's a graven image. Why, it's the saddest thing I ever sees in Wolfville!

" We-all observes how Dave's dwindlin' an' pinin,'
an' most of us has a foggy onderstandin' of the
trooth. But what can we do ? If thar's ever a ag-
gregation of sports who's powerless, utter, to come
to the rescoo of a comrade in a hole, it's Enright
an' Moore an' Boggs an' Texas Thompson an'
Cherokee an' me, doorin' them days when that neglect of Tucson Jennie's is makin' pore Dave's burdens more'n he can b'ar. Shore, we consults; but
that don't come to nothin' ontil the o'casion when
Doc Peets takes the tangle in ser'ous hand.

" Thar's a day dawns when Missis Rucker gets exasperated over Dave's ill-yoosage. Missis Rucker
is a sperited person an' she canters over an' onloads
her opinions on Tucson Jennie. Commonly, these
yere ladies can't think too much of one another;
but on this one division of the house of Tutt, Missis
Rucker goes out on Dave's angle of the game.
An' you-all should have seen the terror it inspires
when Missis Rucker declar's her hostile intentions.

" It's in the O. K. restauraw, when Missis Rucker,
who's feedin' us our mornin' flap-jacks an' salt hoss
as usual, turns to Old Man Enright, an' says :

" ' As soon as ever I've got the last drunkard fed
an' outen the house, I'm goin' to put on my shaker
an' go an' tell that Tucson Jennie Tutt what's on
my mind. I shore never sees a woman change more
than Jennie since the days when she cooks for me
in this yere very restauraw an' lays plans an' plots
to lure Dave into wedlock. I will say that Jennie,
nacheral, is a good wife; but the fashion wherein

she tromples on Dave an' his rights is a disgrace to her sex, an' I'm goin' to deevote a hour this mornin' to callin' Jennie's attention tharunto.'

" ' Missis Rucker is a mighty intrepid lady,' says Enright, when we goes over to the New York store followin' feed. ' I'd no more embrace them chances she's out to tackle than I'd go dallyin' about a wronged grizzly. But jest the same, I'd give a stack of reds if Peets is here! When did he say he'd be back from Tucson?'

" ' The Doc don't allow he'll come trailin' in ag'in,' says Dan Boggs, 'ontil day after to-morry. Which this female dooel will be plumb over by then, an' most likely the camp a wrack.'

" While we-all stands thar gazin' on each other, onable to su'gest anything to meet the emergency, Texas Thompson's pony is brought up from the corral, saddled an' bridled, an ready for the trail.

" ' Well, gents,' says Texas, when he sees his hoss is come, ' I reckons I'll say *adios* an' pull my freight. I'll be back in a week.'

" ' Wherever be you p'intin' for?' asks Cherokee Hall. 'Ain't this goin' of yours some sudden?'

" ' It is a trifle hasty,' says Texas; 'but do you cimmarons think I'm goin' to linger yere after Missis Rucker gives notice she's preparin' to burn the ground around Tucson Jennie about Dave? Gents, I don't pack the nerve! I ain't lived three years with my former wife who gets that Laredo divorce I once or twice adverts to, an' not know enough not to get caught out on no sech limb as this. No, sir; I sees enough of woman an' her ways to teach me that now ain't no time to be standin' about irresoloote an' ondecided, an' I'm goin' to dig out for Tucson, you bet, ontil this uprisin' subsides.'

"This example of Texas scares us up a whole lot; the fact is, it stampedes us; an' without a further word of argyment, the whole band makes a break for the corral, throws saddles onto the swiftest ponies, an' in two minutes we're lost in that cloud of alkali dust we kicks up down the trail toward the no'th.

"'Which I won't say that this exodus is necessary,' observes Enright, when ten miles out we slows up to a road gait to breathe our ponies, ' but I thinks on the whole it's safer. Besides, I oughter go over to Tucson anyway on business.'

"The rest of us don't make no remarks nor excooses; but every gent is feelin' like a great personal peril has blown by.

"The next day, we rounds up Doc Peets, an' he encourages us so that we concloods to return an' make a size-up of results.

"'I shore hopes we finds Dave safe,' says Dan Boggs.

"'It's even money,' says Jack Moore, 'that Dave pulls through. Dave's a mighty wary sport when worst comes to worst; an' as game as redhead ants.'

"'That's all right about Dave bein' game,' retorts Dan, 'but this yere's a time when Dave ain't got no show. I says ag'in, I trust he retains decision of

character sufficient to go hide out doorin' the storm.
It ain't no credit to us that we forgets to bring him
along.'

"'No; thar wasn't no harm done,' says Faro Nell,
who reports progress to us after we rounds up in
the Red Light followin' our return. Nell's a brave
girl an' stands a pat hand when the rest of us vamosed that time. 'Thar ain't no real trouble.
Missis Rucker merely sets fire to Jennie about the
way she maltreats Dave; an' she says Jennie's drivin' him locoed, an' no wonder. Also, she lets on she
don't see whatever Dave marries Jennie for any-
how!

"'At that, Jennie comes back an' reminds Missis
Rucker how she herse'f done treats Mister Rucker
that turrible he goes cavortin' off an' seeks safety
among the Apaches. An' so they keeps on slingin'
it back'ards an' for'ards for mebby two hours, an' me
ha'ntin' about to chunk in a word. Then, final, they
cries an' makes up; an' then they both concedes
that one way an' another they're the best two people each other ever sees. At this juncture,' concloods Nell, 'I declar's myse'f in on the play; an'
we-all three sets down an' admires Enright Peets an'
visits an' has a splendid afternoon.'

"'An' wherever doorin' this emute is Dave?'
asks Enright.

"'Oh, Dave?' says Nell. 'Why he's lurkin'
about outside som'ers in a furtive, surreptitious way;
but he don't molest us none. Which, now I remembers, Dave don't even come near us none at all.'

"'I should say not!' says Texas Thompson, plenty emphatic. 'Dave ain't quite that witless.'

"'Now, gents,' remarks Doc Peets, when Nell is done, an' his tones is confident like he's certain of his foothold, 'since things has gone thus far I'll sa'nter into the midst of these domestic difficulties an' adjust 'em some. I've thought up a s'lootion; an' it's apples to ashes that inside of twenty-four hours I has Jennie pettin' an' cossetin' Dave to beat four of a kind. Leave this yere matter to me entire.'

"We-all can't see jest how Peets is goin' to work these mir'cles; still, sech is our faith, we believes. We decides among ourse'fs, however, that if Peets does turn this pacific trick it'll ondoubted be the crownin' glory of his c'reer.

"After Peets hangs up his bluff, we goes about strainin' eyes an' y'ears for any yells or signal smokes that denotes the advent of said changes. An', son, hard as it is to credit, it comes to pass like Peets prognosticates. By next evenin' a great current of tenderness for Dave goes over Jennie all at once. She begins to call him 'Davy'—a onheard of weakness!—an' hovers about him askin' whatever he thinks he needs; in fact, she becomes that devoted, it looks like the little Enright Peets'll want he'p next to play his hand for him. That's the trooth: Jennie goes mighty clost to forgettin' Enright Peets now an' then in her wifely anxieties concernin' Dave.

"As for Dave himse'f, he don't onderstand his

sudden an' onmerited pop'larity; but wearin' a dazed grin of satisfied ignorance, that a-way, he accepts the sityooation without askin' reasons, an' proceeds to profit tharby. That household is the most reeconciled model fam'ly outfit in all broad Arizona. An' it so continyoos to the end.

"'Whatever did you do or say, Doc?' asks Enright a month later, as we-all from across the street observes how Jennie kisses Dave good-bye at the door an' then stands an' looks after him like she can't b'ar to have him leave her sight; 'what's the secret of this second honeymoon of Dave's?'"

"'Which I don't say much,' says Peets. 'I merely takes Jennie one side an' exhorts her to brace up an' show herse'f a brave lady. Then I explains that while I ain't told Dave none—as his knowin' wouldn't do no good—I regyards it as my medical dooty to inform her so's she'll be ready to meet the shock. "The trooth is, Missis Tutt," I says, "pore Dave's got heart disease, an' is booked to cash in any moment. I can't say when he'll die exactly; the only shore thing is he can't survive a year." She sheds torrents of tears; an' then I warns her she mustn't let Dave see her grief or bushwhack anything but smiles on her face, or mightly likely it'll stop his clock right thar. "Can't nothin' be done for Dave?" she asks. "Nothin'," I replies, "except be tender an' lovin' an' make Dave's last days as pleasant an' easy as you can. We must jump in an' smooth the path to his totterin' moccasins with gentleness an' love," I says, "an' be ready, when the blow does fall, to b'ar it with what fortitoode we may." That's all I tells her. However, it looks like it's becomin' a case of overplay in one partic'lar; our pore young namesake, Enright Peets, is himse'f gettin' a trifle the worst of it, an' I'm figgerin' that to-morry, mebby, I'll look that infant over, an' vouchsafe the news thar's something mighty grievous the matter with his lungs.' "

CHAPTER XII.

Bill Connors of the Osages.

"NACHERALLY, if you-all is frettin' to hear about Injuns," observed the Old Cattleman in reply to my latest request, "I better onfold how Osage Bill Connors gets his wife. Not that thar's trouble in roundin' up this squaw; none whatever. She comes easy; all the same said tale elab'rates some of them savage customs you're so cur'ous concernin'."

My companion arose and kicked together the logs in the fireplace. This fireplace was one of the great room's comforts as well as ornaments. The logs leaped into much accession of flame, and crackled into sparks, and these went gossiping up the mighty chimney, their little fiery voices making a low, soft roaring like the talk of bees.

"This chimley draws plenty successful," commented my friend. "Which it almost breaks even with a chimley I constructs once in my log camp on the Upper Red. That Red River floo is a wonder! Draw? Son, it could draw four kyards an' make a flush. But that camp of mine on the Upper Red is over eight thousand foot above the sea as I'm informed by a passel of surveyor sports who comes romancin' through the hills with a spyglass on three pegs; an' high altitoods allers proves a heap exileratin' to a fire.

"But speakin' of Bill Connors : In Wolfville—which them days is the only part of my c'reer whereof I'm proud an' reviews with onmixed satisfaction — Doc Peets is, like you, inquis'tive touchin' Injuns. Peets puts it up that some day he's doo to write books about 'em. Which in off hours, an' when we-all is more or less at leesure over our Valley Tan, Peets frequent comes explorin' 'round for details. Shore, I imparts all I saveys about Bill Connors, an' likewise sech other aborigines as lives in mem'ry ; still, it shakes my estimates of Peets to find him eager over Injuns, they bein' low an' debasin' as topics. I says as much to Peets.

"'Never you-all mind about me,' says Peets. 'I knows so much about white folks it comes mighty clost to makin' me sick. I seeks tales of Injuns as a relief an' to promote a average in favor of the species.'

"This Bill Connors is a good-lookin' young buck when I cuts his trail ; straight as a pine an' strong an' tireless as a bronco. It's about six years after the philanthrofists ropes onto Bill an' drags him off to a school. You-all onderstands about a philanthrofist—one of these sports who's allers improvin' some party's condition in a way the party who's improved don't like.

"'A philanthrofist,' says Colonel Sterett, one time when Dan Boggs demands the explanation at his hands ; 'a philanthrofist is a gent who insists on you givin' some other gent your money.'

" For myse'f, however, I regyards the Colonel's definition as too narrow. Troo philanthrofy has a heap of things to it that's jest as onreasonable an' which does not incloode the fiscal feachers men-tioned by the Colonel.

" As I'm sayin' ; these well-meanin' though darkened sports, the philanthrofists, runs Bill down—it's mebby when he's fourteen, only Injuns don't keep tab on their years none—an' immures him in one of the gov'ment schools. It's thar Bill gets his name, 'Bill Connors.' Before that he cavorts about, free an' wild an' happy onder the Injun app'lation of the ' Jack Rabbit.'

" Shore ! Bill's sire—a savage who's way up in the picture kyards, an' who's called ' Crooked Claw' because of his left hand bein' put out of line with a Ute arrow through it long ago—gives his consent to Bill j'inin' that sem'nary. Crooked Claw can't he'p himse'f ; he's powerless ; the Great Father in Wash-in'ton is backin' the play of the philanthrofists.

" ' Which the Great Father is too many for Crooked Claw,' says this parent, commentin' on his he'plessness. Bill's gone canterin' to his old gent to remonstrate, not hungerin' for learnin', an' Crooked Claw says this to Bill : ' The Great Father is too many for Crooked Claw ; an' too strong. You must go to school as the Great Father orders ; it is right. The longest spear is right.'

" Bill is re-branded, ' Bill Connors,' an" then he's done bound down to them books. After four years Bill gradyooates ; he's got the limit an' the philanthrofists takes Bill's hobbles off an' throws him loose with the idee that Bill will go back to his tribe folks an' teach 'em to read. Bill comes back, shore, an' is at once the Osage laughin'-stock for wearin' pale-face clothes. Also, the medicine men tells Bill he'll die for talkin' paleface talk an' sportin' a paleface shirt, an' these prophecies preys on Bill who's eager to live a heap an' ain't ready to cash in. Bill gets back to blankets an' feathers in about a month.

"Old Black Dog, a leadin' sharp among the Osages, is goin' about with a dab of clay in his ha'r, and wearin' his most ornery blanket. That's because Black Dog is in mournin' for a squaw who stampedes over the Big Divide, mebby it's two months prior. Black Dog's mournin' has got dealt down to the turn like ; an' windin' up his grief an' tears, Osage fashion, he out to give a war-dance. Shore ; the savages rings in a war-dance on all sorts of cer'monies. It don't allers mean that they're hostile, an' about to spraddle forth on missions of blood. Like I states, Black Dog, who's gone to the end of his mournful lariat about the departed squaw, turns himse'f on for a war-dance ; an' he nacherally invites the Osage nation to paint an' get in on the festiv'ties.

"Accordin' to the rooles, pore Bill, jest back from school, has got to cut in. Or he has his choice between bein' fined a pony or takin' a lickin' with mule whips in the hands of a brace of kettle-tenders whose delight as well as dooty

it is to mete out the punishment. Bill can't afford
to go shy a pony, an' as he's loth to accept the
larrupin's, he wistfully makes ready to shake a moccasin at the *baile.* An' as nothin' but feathers,
blankets, an' breech-clouts goes at a war-dance—the
same bein' Osage dress-clothes—Bill shucks his
paleface garments an' arrays himse'f after the
breezy fashion of his ancestors.   Bill attends the war
dance an' shines.   Also, bein' praised by the
medicine men an' older bucks for quittin' his paleface duds ; an' findin' likewise the old-time blanket
an' breech-clout healthful an' saloobrious—which
Bill forgets their feel in his four years at that sem'-
nary—he adheres to 'em.   This lapse into aboriginal
ways brews trouble for Bill ; he gets up ag'inst the
agent.

"It's the third day after Black Dog's war-dance,
an' Bill, all paint an' blankets an' feathers, is sa'n-
terin' about Pawhusky, takin' life easy an' Injun
fashion.   It's then the agent connects with Bill an'
sizes him up.   The agent asks Bill does he stand in
on this yere Black Dog war-dance.

"'Don't they have no roast dog at that warjig?'
asks Dan Boggs, when I'm relatin' these reminis-
cences in the Red Light.

"'No,' I says ; 'Osages don't eat no dogs.'

"'It's different with Utes a lot,' says Dan.
'Which Utes regyards dogs fav'rable, deemin'
'em a mighty sucyoolent an' nootritious dish.   The
time I'm with the Utes they pulls off a shindig,
"tea dance " it is, an', as what Huggins would call

"a star feacher" they ups an' roasts a white dog. That canine is mighty plethoric an' fat, an' they lays him on his broad, he'pless back an' shets off his wind with a stick cross-wise of his neck, an' two bucks pressin' on the ends. When he's good an' dead an' all without no suffoosion of blood, the Utes singes his fur off in a fire an' bakes him as he is. I partakes of that dog—some. I don't nacherally lay for said repast wide-jawed, full-toothed an' reemorseless, like it's flapjacks—I don't gorge myse'f none; but when I'm in Rome, I strings my chips with the Romans like the good book says, an' so I sort o' eats baked dog with the Utes. Otherwise, I'd hurt their sens'bilities; an' I ain't out to harrow up no entire tribe an' me playin' a lone hand.'

"That agent questions Bill as to the war-dance carryin's on of old Black Dog. Then he p'ints at Bill's blankets an' feathers an' shakes his head a heap disapprobative.

"'Shuck them blankets an' feathers,' says the agent, 'an' get back into your trousers a whole lot; an' be sudden about it, too. I puts up with the divers an' sundry rannikabooisms of old an' case-hardened Injuns who's savage an' ontaught. But you're different; you've been to school an' learned the virchoos of pants; wherefore, I looks for you to set examples.'

"It's then Bill gets high an' allows he'll wear clothes to suit himse'f. Bill denounces trousers as foolish in their construction an' fallacious in their plan. Bill declar's they're a bad scheme, trousers is ; an' so sayin' he defies the agent to do his worst.   Bill stands pat on blankets an' feathers.

"'Which you will, will you!' remarks this agent.

"Then he claps Bill in irons mighty decisive, an' plants him up ag'in the high face of a rock bluff which has been frownin' down on Bird River since Adam makes his first camp.   Havin' got Bill posed to his notion, this earnest agent, puttin' a hammer into Bill's rebellious hand, starts him to breakin' rock.

"'Which the issue is pants,' says the obdurate agent sport ; 'an' I'll keep you-all whackin' away at them boulders while the cliff lasts onless you yields.   Thar's none of you young bucks goin' to bluff me, an' that's whatever!'

"Bill breaks rocks two days.   The other Osages comes an' perches about, sympathetic, an' surveys Bill.   They exhorts him to be firm ; they gives it out in Osage he's a patriot.

"Bill's willin' to be a patriot as the game is commonly dealt, but when his love of country takes the form of poundin' rocks, the noble sentiments which yeretofore bubbles in Bill's breast commences to pall on Bill an' he becomes none too shore but what trousers is right.   By second drink time—only savages don't drink, a paternal gov'ment barrin' nose-paint on account of it makin' 'em too fitfully exyoo-berant—by second drink time the second evenin' Bill lays down his hand—pitches his hammer into

the diskyard as it were—an' when I crosses up with
him, Bill's that abject he wears a necktie. When
Bill yields, the agent meets him half way, an' him
an' Bill rigs a deal whereby Bill arrays himse'f
Osage fashion whenever his hand's crowded
by tribal customs. Other times, Bill inhabits
trousers ; an' blankets an' feathers is rooled out.

"Shore, I talks with Bill's father, old Crooked
Claw. This yere savage is the ace-kyard of Osage-
land as a fighter. No, that outfit ain't been on the
warpath for twenty years when I sees 'em ; then
it's with Boggs' old pards, the Utes. I asks Crooked
Claw if he likes war. He tells me that he dotes on
carnage like a jaybird, an' goes forth to battle as
joobilant as a drunkard to a shootin' match. That
is, Crooked Claw used to go curvin' off to war, joyful, at first. Later his glee is subdooed because of
the big chances he's takin'. Then he lugs out 'leven
skelps, all Ute, an' eloocidates.

"'This first maverick,' says Crooked Claw—of
course, I gives him in the American tongue, not
bein' equal to the reedic'lous broken Osage he talks
—'this yere first maverick,' an' he strokes the
braided ha'r of a old an' smoke-dried skelp, 'is easy.
The chances, that a-way, is even. Number two
is twice as hard ; an' when I snags onto number
three—I downs that hold-up over by the foot
of Fisher's Peak—the chances has done mounted
to be three to one ag'in me. So it goes gettin'
higher an' higher, ontil when I corrals my 'leventh, it's 'leven to one he wins onless he's got

killin's of his own to stand off mine. I don't reckon
none he has though,' says Crooked Claw, curlin' his
nose contemptuous. ' He's heap big squaw—a
coward ; an' would hide from me like a quail. He
looks big an' brave an' strong, but his heart is bad
—he is a poor knife in a good sheath. So I don't
waste a bullet on him, seein' his fear, but kills him
with my war-axe. Still, he raises the chances ag'inst
me to twelve to one, an' after that I goes careful an'
slow. I sends in my young men ; but for myse'f I
sort o' hungers about the suburbs of the racket,
takin' no resks an' on the prowl for a cinch,—some
sech pick-up as a sleeper, mebby. But my 'leventh
is my last ; the Great Father in Washin'ton gets
tired with us an' he sends his walk-a-heaps an'
buffalo soldiers'—these savages calls niggers ' buffalo soldiers,' bein' they're that woolly—' an' makes
us love peace. Which we'd a-had the Utes too
dead to skin if it ain't for the walk-a-heaps an'
buffalo soldiers.'

" An' at this Crooked Claw tosses the bunch of Ute
top-knots to one of his squaws, fills up his red-stone
pipe with kinnikinick an' begins to smoke, lookin'
as complacent as a catfish doorin' a Joone rise.

" Bill Connors has now been wanderin' through
this vale of tears for mebby she's twenty odd years,
an' accordin' to Osage tenets, Bill's doo to get
wedded. No, Bill don't make no move ; he comports himse'f lethargic ; the reesponsibilities of the
nuptials devolves on Bill's fam'ly.

" It's one of the excellentest things about a Injun

that he don't pick out no wife personal, deemin' himse'f as too locoed to beat so difficult a game.

" Or mebby, as I observes to Texas Thompson one time in the Red Light when him an' me's discussin', or mebby it's because he's that callous he don't care, or that shiftless he won't take trouble.

" ' Whatever's the reason,' says Texas, on that o'casion, heavin' a sigh, ' thar's much to be said in praise of the custom. If it only obtains among the whites thar's one sport not onknown to me who would have shore passed up some heartaches. You can bet a hoss, no fam'ly of mine would pick out the lady who beats me for that divorce back in Laredo to be the spouse of Texas Thompson. Said household's got too much savey to make sech a break.'

" While a Osage don't select that squaw of his, still I allers entertains a theery that he sort o' saveys what he's ag'inst an' no he'pmeet gets sawed off on him objectionable an' blind. I figgers, for all he don't let on, that sech is the sityooation in the marital adventures of Bill. His fam'ly picks the Saucy Willow out; but it's mighty likely he signs up the lady to some discreet member of his outfit before ever they goes in to make the play.

" Saucy Willow for a savage is pretty—pretty as a pinto hoss. Her parent, old Strike Axe, is a morose but common form of Osage, strong financial, with a big bunch of cattle an' more'n two hundred ponies. Bill gets his first glimpse, after he comes back from school, of the lovely Saucy Willow at a dance. This ain't no war-dance nor any other cer'monious splurge; it's a informal merrymakin', innocent an' free, same as is usual with us at the Wolfville dance hall. Shore, Osages, lacks guitars an' fiddles, an' thar's no barkeep nor nosepaint—none, in trooth, of the fav'rable adjuncts wherewith we makes a evenin' in Hamilton's hurdygurdy a season of social elevation, an' yet they pulls off their fandangoes with a heap of verve, an' I've no doubt they shore enjoys themse'fs.

"For two hours before sundown the kettletenders is howlin' an' callin' the dance throughout the Osage camp. Thar's to be a full moon, an' the dance—the *Ingraska* it is; a dance the Osages buys from the Poncas for eight ponies—is to come off in a big, high-board corral called the 'Round House.'

"Followin' the first yell of the kettle-tenders, the young bucks begins to paint up for the hilarity. You might see 'em all over camp, for it's August weather an' the walls of the tents an' teepees is looped up to let in the cool, daubin' the ocher on their faces an' braidin' the feathers into their ha'r. This organisin' for a *baile* ain't no bagatelle, an' two hours is the least wherein any se'f-respectin' buck who's out to make a centre shot on the admiration of the squaws an' wake the envy of rival bucks, can lay on the pigments, so he paints away at his face, careful an' acc'rate, sizin' up results meanwhile in a jimcrow lookin' glass. At last he's as radiant as a rainbow, an' after garterin' each laig with a belt of sleigh-bells jest below the knee, he regyards himse'f

with a fav'rable eye an' allows he's ondoubted the
wildest wag in his set.

"Each buck arrives at the Round House with his
blanket wropped over his head so as not to blind
the onwary with his splendours. It's mebby second
drink time after sundown an' the full moon is
swingin' above effulgent. The bucks who's doo to
dance sets about one side of the Round House on a
board bench; the squaws—not bein' in on the
proposed activities—occupies the other half,
squattin' on the ground. Some of 'em packs their
papooses tied on to a fancy-ribboned, highly beaded
boa'rd, an' this they makes a cradle of by restin' one
end on the ground an' the other on their toe,
rockin' the same meanwhile with a motion of the
foot. Thar's a half hoop over the head-end of these
papoose boards, hung with bells for the papoose to
get·infantile action on an' amoose his leesure.

"The bucks settin' about their side of the Round
House, still wrops themse'fs in their blankets so as
not to dazzle the squaws to death preematoor. At
last the music peals forth. The music confines
itse'f to a bass drum—paleface drum it is—which is
staked out hor'zontal about a foot high from the
grass over in the centre. The orchestra is a
decrepit buck with a rag-wropped stick; with this
weepon he beats the drum, chantin' at the same
time a pensive refrain.

"Mebby a half-dozen squaws, with no papooses
yet to distract 'em, camps 'round this vir-
chuoso with the rag-stick, an' yoonites their

girlish howls with his. You-all can put down a bet
it don't remind you none of nightingales or mockin'
birds; but the Injuns likes it. Which their simple
sperits wallows in said warblin's! But to my
notion they're more calc'lated to loco a henhawk
than furnish inspiration for a dance.

"'Tunk! tunk! tunk! tunk!' goes this rag-stick
buck, while the squaws chorus along with, 'Hy–yah!
hy–yah! hy–yah–yah–yah! Hy–yah! hy–yah!
hy–yah–yah–yah!' an' all grievous, an' make no
mistake!

"At the first ' tunk!' the bucks stiffen to their
feet and cast off the blankets. Feathers, paint, an'
bells! they blaze an' tinkle in the moonlight
with a subdooed but savage elegance. They
skates out onto the grass, stilt-laig, an' each buck
for himse'f. They go skootin' about, an' weave an'
turn an' twist like these yere water-bugs jiggin' it
on the surface of some pond. Sometimes a buck'll
lay his nose along the ground while he dances—
sleigh bells jinglin', feathers tossin'! Then he'll
straighten up ontil he looks like he's eight foot
tall; an' they shore throws themse'fs with a heap of
heart an' sperit.

"It's as well they does. If you looks clost you
observes a brace of bucks, and each packin' a blacksnake whip. Them's kettle-tenders,—floor mana-
gin' the *baile* they be ; an' if a buck who's dancin'
gets preeoccupied with thinkin' of something else
an' takes to prancin' an' dancin' listless, the way
the kettle-tenders pours the leather into him to

remind him his fits of abstraction is bad form, is
like a religious ceremony. An' it ain't no bad idee;
said kettle-tenders shore promotes what Colonel
Sterett calls the *elan* of the dancin' bucks no end.

"After your eyes gets used to this whirlin' an'
skatin' an' skootin' an' weavin' in an' out, you notes
two bucks, painted to a finish an' feathered to the
stars! who out-skoots an' out-whirls an' out-skates
their fellow bucks like four to one. They gets their
nose a little lower one time an' then stands higher
in the air another, than is possible to the next best
buck. Them enthoosiasts ain't Osages at all;
which they're niggers — full-blood Senegambians
they be, who's done j'ined the tribe. These Round
House festivals with the paint, the feathers, an' the
bells, fills their trop'cal hearts plumb full, an' forgettin' all about the white folks an' their gyarded
ways, they're the biggest Injuns to warm a heel
that night.

"Saucy Willow is up by the damaged rag-stick
buck lendin' a mouthful or two of cl'ar, bell-like alto
yelps to the harmony of the evenin'. Bill who's a
wonder in feathers an' bells, an' whose colour-scheme
would drive a temp'rance lecturer to drink, while
zippin' about in the moonlight gets his eye on her.
Mighty likely Bill's smitten; but he don't let on,
the fam'ly like I relates, allers ropin' up a gent's
bride. It's good bettin' this yere Saucy Willow
counts up Bill. If she does, however,—no more
than Bill,—she never tips her hand. The Saucy
Willow yelps on onconcerned, like her only dream

of bliss is to show the coyotes what vocal failures they be.

"It's a week after the *Ingraska*, an' Bill's fam'ly holds a round-up to pick Bill out a squaw. He ain't present, havin' the savey to go squanderin' off to play Injun poker with some Creek sports he hears has money over on the Polecat. Bill's fam'ly makes quite a herd, bucks an' squaws buttin' in on the discussion permiscus an' indiscrim'nate. Shore! the squaws has as much to say as the bucks among Injuns. They owns their own ponies an' backs their own play an' is as big a Injun as anybody, allowin' for that nacheral difference between squaw dooties an' buck dooties—one keeps camp while the other hunts, or doorin' war times when one protects the herds an' plunder while the other faces the foe. You hears that squaws is slaves? However is anybody goin' to be a slave where thar's as near nothin' to do in the way of work as is possible an' let a hooman live? Son, thar ain't as much hard labour done in a Injun camp in a week—ain't as much to do as gets transacted at one of them rooral oyster suppers to raise money for the preacher!

"Bill's fam'ly comes trailin' in to this powwow about pickin' out a squaw for Bill. Besides Crooked Claw, thar's Bill's widow aunt, the Wild Cat—she's plumb cunnin', the Wild Cat is, an' jest then bein' cel'brated among the Osages for smokin' ponies with Black B'ar, a old buck, an' smokin' Black B'ar out of his two best cayouses. Besides these two, thar's The-man-who-bleeds, The-man-who-sleeps,

Tom Six-killer, The-man-who-steps-high, an' a dozen
other squaws an' bucks, incloosive of Bill's mother
who's called the Silent Comanche, an' is takin' the
play a heap steady an' livin' up to her name.

"The folks sets 'round an' smokes Crooked Claw's
kinnikinick. Then the Wild Cat starts in to deal
the game. She says it's time Bill's married, as a
onmarried buck is a menace ; at this the others
grunts agreement. Then they all turns in to
overhaul the el'gible young squaws. Which they
shore shows up them belles ! One after the other
they're drug over the coals. At last the Wild
Cat mentions the Saucy Willow jest as every savage
present knows will be done soon or late from the
jump. The Saucy Willow obtains a speshul an' onusual run for her money. But it's settled final that
while the Saucy Willow ain't none too good, she's
the best they can do. The Saucy Willow belongs
to the Elk clan, while Bill belongs to the B'ar
clan, an' that at least is c'rrect. Injuns don't believe in inbreedin' so they allers marries out of
their clan.

"As soon as they settles on the Saucy Willow as
Bill's squaw, they turns in to make up the ' price.'
The Wild Cat, who's rich, donates a kettle, a side of
beef, an' the two cayouses she smokes outen the
besotted Black B'ar. The rest chucks in accordin'
to their means, Crooked Claw comin' up strong
with ten ponies ; an' Bill's mother, the Silent Comanche, showin' down with a bolt of calico, two
buffalo robes, a sack of flour an' a lookin' glass.

This plunder is to go to the Saucy Willow' s folks as a ' price ' for the squaw.   No, they don't win on the play ; the Saucy Willow's parents is out *dinero* on the nuptials when all is done.   They has to give Bill their wickeyup.

" When Bill's outfit's fully ready to deal for blood they picks out some bright afternoon.   The Saucy Willow's fam'ly is goin' about lookin' partic'lar harmless an' innocent ; but they're coony enough to be in camp that day.   A procession starts from the Crooked Claw camp.   Thar's The-man-who-steps-high at the head b'arin' a flag, union down, an' riotin' along behind is Tom Six-killer, The-man-who-sleeps, the Wild Cat and others leadin' five ponies an' packin' kettles, flour, beef, an' sim'lar pillage.   They lays it all down an' stakes out the broncos about fifty yards from Strike Axe's camp an' withdraws.

" Then some old squaw of the Strike Axe outfit issues forth an' throws the broncos loose.   That's to show that the Saucy Willow is a onusual excellent young squaw an' pop'lar with her folks, an' they don't aim to shake her social standin' by acceptin' sech niggard terms.

" But the Crooked Claw outfit ain't dismayed, an' takes this rebuff phlegmatic.   It's only so much ettyquette ; an' now it's disposed of they reorganise to lead ag'in to win.   This time they goes the limit, an' brings up fifteen ponies an' stacks in besides with blankets, robes, beef, flour, calico, kettles, skillets, and looking-glasses enough to fill eight

waggons. This trip the old Strike Axe squaw onties
the fifteen ponies an' takin' 'em by their ropes
brings 'em in clost to the Strike Axe camp, tharby
notifyin' the Crooked Claw band that their bluff
for the Saucy Willow is regyarded as feasible an'
the nuptials goes. With this sign, the Crooked
Claws comes caperin' up to the Strike Axes an' the
latter fam'ly proceeds to rustle a profoosion of grub ;
an' with that they all turns in an' eats old Strike
Axe outen house an' home. The 'price' is split up
among the Strike Axe bunch, shares goin' even to
second an' third cousins.

"Mebby she's a week later when dawns the weddin' day. Bill, who's been lookin' a heap numb
ever since these rites becomes acoote, goes projectin' off alone onto the prairie. The Saucy Willow is hid in the deepest corner of Strike Axe's
teepee ; which if she's visible, however, you'd be
shore amazed at the foolish expression she wears,
but all as shy an' artless as a yearlin' antelope.

" But it grows time to wind it up, an' one of the
Strike Axe bucks climbs into the saddle an' rides
half way towards the camp of Crooked Claw.
Strike Axe an' Crooked Claw in antic'pation of
these entanglements has done pitched their camps
about half a mile apart so as to give the pageant
spread an' distances. When he's half way, the
Strike Axe buck fronts up an' slams loose with his
Winchester ; it's a signal the *baile* is on.

" At the rifle crack, mounted on a pony that's the
flower of the Strike Axe herd, the Saucy Willow

comes chargin' for the Crooked Claws like a shootin' star. The Saucy Willow is a sunburst of Osage richness! an' is packin' about five hundred dollars' worth of blankets, feathers, beads, calicoes, ribbons, an' buckskins, not to mention six pounds of brass an' silver jewelry. Straight an' troo comes the Saucy Willow; skimmin' like a arrow an' as rapid as the wind!

"As Saucy Willow embarks on this expedition, thar starts to meet her—afoot they be but on the run—Tom Six-killer an' a brace of squaw cousins of Bill's. Nacherally, bein' he out-lopes the cousins, Tom Six-killer runs up on the Saucy Willow first an' grabs her bronco by the bridle. The two young squaw cousins ain't far behind the Six-killer, for they can run like rabbits, an' they arrives all laughter an' cries, an' with one move searches the Saucy Willow outen the saddle. In less time than it takes to get action on a drink of licker the two young squaws has done stripped the Saucy Willow of every feather, bead an' rag, an' naked as when she's foaled they wrops her up, precious an' safe in a blanket an' packs her gleefully into the camp of Crooked Claw. Here they re-dresses the Saucy Willow an' piles on the gew-gaws an' adornments, ontil if anything she's more gorgeous than former. The pony which the Saucy Willow rides goes to the Six-killer, while the two she-cousins, as to the balance of her apparel that a-way, divides the pot.

"An' now like a landslide upon the Crooked Claws comes the Strike Axe household. Which they're thar to the forty-'leventh cousin; savages keepin' exact cases on relatives a mighty sight further than white folks. The Crooked Claw fam'ly is ready. It's Crooked Claw's turn to make the feast, an' that eminent Osage goes the distance. Crooked Claw shorely does himse'f proud, while Bill's mother, the Silent Comanche, is hospitable, but dignified. It's a great weddin'. The Wild Cat is pirootin' about, makin' mean an' onfeelin' remarks, as becomes a widow lady with a knowledge of the world an' a bundle the size an' shape of a roll of blankets. The two fam'lies goes squanderin' about among each other, free an' fraternal, an' thar's never a cloud in the sky.

"At last the big feed begins. Son, you should have beheld them fool Osages throw themse'fs upon the Crooked Claw's good cheer. It's a p'int of honour to eat as much as you can; an' b'arin' that in mind the revellers mows away about twenty pounds of beef to a buck—the squaws, not bein' so ardent, quits out on mighty likely it's the thirteenth pound. Tom Six-killer comes plenty clost to sacrificin' himse'f utter.

"This last I knows, for the next day I sees the medicine men givin' some sufferer one of their aboriginal steam baths. They're on the bank of Bird River. They've bent down three or four small saplin's for the framework of a tent like, an' thar's piled on 'em blankets an' robes a foot deep so she's plumb airtight. Thar's a fire goin' an' they're heatin' rocks, same as Colonel Sterett tells about when they baptises his grandfather into the church. When the rocks is red-hot they takes 'em, one by one, an' drops 'em into a bucket of water to make her steam. Then they shoves this impromptoo cauldron inside the little robe house where as I'm aware—for I onderstands the signs from the start—thar's a sick buck quiled up awaitin' relief. This yere invalid buck stays in thar twenty minutes. The water boils an' bubbles an' the steam gets that abundant not to say urgent she half lifts the robes an' blankets at the aiges to escape. The ailin' buck in the sweat tent stays ontil he can't stay no more, an' then with a yowl, he comes burstin' forth, a reek of sweat an' goes splashin' into the coolin' waters of Bird River. It's the Six-killer; that weddin' feast comes mighty near to downin' him—gives him a ' bad heart,' an' he ondergoes the steam bath for relief.

"But we're strayed from that weddin'. Bein' now re-arrayed in fullest feather the Saucy Willow is fetched into the ring an' receives a platter with the rest. Then one of the bucks, lookin' about like he's amazed, says : ' Wherever is the Jack Rabbit ? ' that bein' Bill's Osage title. Crooked Claw shakes his head an' reckons most likely the Jack Rabbit's rummagin' about loose some'ers, not knowin' enough to come in an' eat. A brace of bucks an' a young squaw starts up an' figgers they'll search about an' see if they can't round him up. They goes out an' thar's Bill settin' off on a rock a quarter of a mile with his back to the camp an' the footure.

"The two sharps an' the squaw herds Bill into camp an' stakes him out, shoulder to shoulder, with the little Saucy Willow.   Neither Bill nor the little Saucy Willow su'gests by word, screech or glance that they saveys either the game or the stakes, an' eats on, takin' no notice of themse'fs or any of the gluttons who surrounds 'em.   Both Bill an' the little Saucy Willow looks that witless you-all would yearn to bat 'em one with the butt of a'mule whip if onfortoonately you're present to be exasperated by sech exhibitions.   At last, however, jest as the patience of the audience is plumb played, both Bill an' the little Saucy Willow gives a start of surprise.   Which they're pretendin' to be startled to find they're feedin' off the same dish.   Thar you be ; that makes 'em 'buck an' squaw'—'man an' wife ;' an' yereafter, in Osage circles they can print their kyards 'Mister an' Missis Bill Connors,' while Bill draws an' spends the little Saucy Willow's annooty on payment day instead of Strike Axe."

CHAPTER XIII.

When Tutt first saw Tucson.

"An' speakin' of dooels," remarked the Old Cattleman, apropos of an anecdote of the field of honour wherewith I regaled his fancy, "speakin' of dooels, I reckons now the encounter Dave Tutt involves himse'f with when he first sees Tucson takes onchallenged preecedence for utter bloodlessness. She's shore the most lamb's-wool form of single combat to which my notice is ever drawn. Dave enlightens us concernin' its details himse'f, bein' incited tharunto by hearin' Texas Thompson relate about the Austin shootin' match of that Deaf Smith.

"'Which this yere is 'way back yonder on the trail of time,' explains Dave, 'an' I'm hardened a heap since then. I've jest come buttin' into Tucson an' it's easy money I'm the tenderest an' most ontaught party that ever wears store-moccasins. What I misses knowin' would make as husky a library,—if it's printed down in books,—as ever lines up on shelves. Also, I'm freighted to the limit with the tenderfoot's usual outfit of misinformation. It's sad, yet troo! that as I casts my gaze r'arward I identifies myse'f as the balmiest brand of

shorthorn who ever leaves his parents' shelterin'
roof.'

"'All the same,' says Dan Boggs, plenty con-
ceited, 'I'll gamble a hoss I'm a bigger eediot when
I quits Missouri to roam the cow country than ever
you-all can boast of bein' in your most drivelin'
hour.'

"'Do they lock you up?' asks Dave.

"'No,' says Dan, 'they don't lock me up none,
but——'

"'Then you lose,' insists Dave, mighty prompt.

"'But hold on,' says Dan; 'don't get your chips
down so quick. As I starts to explain, I ain't
locked up; but it's because I'm in a camp like
Wolfville yere that ain't sunk to the level of no calaboose. But what comes to be the same, I'm
taken captive an' held as sech ontil the roodiments
of Western sense is done beat into me. It takes
the yoonited efforts of four of the soonest sharps
that ever happens; an' final, they succeeds to a
p'int that I'm deemed cap'ble of goin' about alone.'

"'Well,' retorts Dave, 'I won't dispoote with
you; an' even at that I regyards your present attitoode as one of bluff. I thinks you're shore the
cunnin'est wolf in the territory, Dan, an' allers is.
But, as I'm sayin', when I first begins to infest
Tucson, I'm so ignorant it's a stain on that meetropolis. At this yere epock, Tucson ain't spraddled to its present proud dimensions. A gent
might have thrown the loop of a lariat about the
outfit an' drug it after him with a pony. No one,

however, performs this labour, as the camp is as petyoolant as a t'rant'ler an' any onauthorised dalliance with its sensibilities would have led to vivid plays. Still, she ain't big, Tucson ain't ; an' I learns my way about from centre to suburbs in the first ten minutes.

" ' At the beginnin' I'm a heap timid. I suffers from the common eastern theery an' looks on Arizona as a region where it's murder straight an' lynchin' for a place. You-all may jedge from that how erroneous is my idees. Then, as now, the distinguishin' feacher of Tucson existence is a heavenly ca'm. Troo, thar's moments when the air nacherally fills up with bullets like they're a passel of swallow-birds, an' they hums an' sings their merry madrigals. However, these busy seasons don't set in so often nor last so long but peaceful folks has ample chance to breathe.

" ' Never does I b'ar witness to as many as seven contemporaneous remainders but once; and then thar's cause. It's in a poker game ; an' the barkeep brings the dealer a cold deck onder a tray whereon he purveys the drinks. Which the discovery of this yere solecism, as you-all well imagines, arouses interest, earnest an' widespread like I deescribes. I counts up when the smoke lifts an' finds that seven has sought eternal peace. Commonly two is the number ; three bein' quite a shipment. Shore, it's speshul sickly when as many as seven quits out together !

" ' Bein' timid an' ignorant I takes good advice.

It's in the Oriental. Thar's that old gray cimmaron hibernatin' about the bar whose name is Jeffords.

"'"Be you-all conversant with that gun you packs?" asks Jeffords.

"'I feels the hot blush mountin' in my tender cheeks, but I concedes I ain't. "Pard," I replies, "speakin' confidenshul an' between gent an' gent, this yere weepon is plumb novel to me."

"'"Which I allows as much," he says, "from the egreegious way you fidges with it. Now let me pass you-all a p'inter from the peaks of experience. You caper back to the tavern an' take that weepon off. Or what's as well, you pass it across to the barkeep. If you-all goes romancin' 'round with hardware at your belt it's even money it'll get you beefed. Allers remember while in Arizona that you'll never get plugged—onless by inadvertence—as long as you wander about in onheeled innocence. No gunless gent gets downed; sech is the onbreakable roole."

"'After that I goes guiltless of arms; I ain't hungerin' for immortality abrupt.

"'Old Jeffords is shore right; in the Southwest if you aims to b'ar a charmed life, never wear a six-shooter. This maxim goes anywhere this side of the Mississippi; east of that mighty river it's the other way.

"'Bein' nimble-blooded in them days, I'm a heap arduous about the dance-hall. I gets infatyooated with the good fellowship of that hurdygurdy; an' even after I leaves Tucson an' is camped some miles

away, I saddles up every other evenin', rides in an',
as says the poet, "shakes ontirin' laig even into the
wee small hours."

" ' Right yere, gents" an' Dave pauses like he's
prounced on by a solemn thought, · I don't reckon
I has to caution none of you-all not to go repeat-
in' these mem'ries of gay days done an' gone,
where my wife Tucson Jennie cuts their trail. I
ain't afraid of Jennie; she's a kind, troo he'pmeet;
but ever since that onfortunate entanglement with
the English towerist lady her suspicions sets up nervous in their blankets at the mere mention of frivoli-
ties wherein she hears my name. I asks you, tharfore, not to go sayin' things to feed her doubts.
With Tucson Jennie, my first business is to live
down my past.'

" ' You-all can bet,' says Texas Thompson, while
his brow clouds, ' that I learns enough while enjoyin' the advantages of livin' with my former wife to
make sech requests sooperfluous in my case. Speshully since if it ain't for what the neighbours done
tells the lady she'd never go ropin' 'round for that
divorce. No Dave; your secrets is plumb safe with
a gent who's suffered.

" ' Which I saveys I'm safe with all of you,' says
Dave, his confidence, which the thoughts of Tucson
Jennie sort o' stampedes, beginnin' to return. ' But
now an' then them gusts of apprehensions frequent
with married gents sweeps over me an' I feels weak.
But comin' back to the dance-hall: As I su'gests
thar's many a serene hour I whiles away tharin.

Your days an' your *dinero* shore flows plenty swift
in that temple of merriment; an' chilled though I
be with the stiff dignity of a wedded middle age, if
it ain't for my infant son, Enright Peets Tutt, to
whom I'm strivin' to set examples, I'd admire to
prance out an' live ag'in them halcyon hours; that's
whatever!

"'Thar's quite a sprinklin' of the *elite* of Tucson
in the dance-hall the evenin' I has in mind. The
bar is busy; while up an' down each side sech refreshin' pastimes as farobank, monte an' roulette
holds prosperous sway. Thar's no quadrille goin'
at the moment, an' a lady to the r'ar is carollin'
" Rosalie, the Prairie Flower."

> " Fair as a lily bloomin' in May,
> Sweeter than roses, bright as the day!
> Everyone who knows her feels her gentle power,
> Rosalie the Prairie Flower."

"'On this yere o'casion I'm so far fortunate as to
be five drinks ahead an' tharfore would sooner listen
to myse'f talk than to the warblin' of the cantatrice.
As it is, I'm conversin' with a gent who's standin'
hard by.

"'At my elbow is posted a shaggy an' forbiddin'
outlaw whose name is Yuba Tom, an' who's more
harmonious than me. He wants to listen to
"Rosalie the Prairie Flower." Of a sudden, he
w'irls about, plenty peevish.

"'Stick a period to that pow-wow," observes
Yuba; " I wants to hear this prima donna sing."

"'Bein' gala with the five libations, I turns on

Yuba haughty. " If you're sobbin' to hear this songstress," I says, "go for'ard an' camp down at her feet. But don't come pawin' your way into no conversations with me. An' don't hang up no bluff."

" 'Which if you disturbs me further," retorts Yuba, " Ill turn loose for shore an' crawl your hump a lot."

" ' Them foolhardy sports," I replies, "who has yeretofore attempted that enterprise sleeps in on-known graves ; so don't you-all pester me, for the outlook's dark."

" ' It's now that Yuba,—who's a mighty cautious sport, forethoughtful an' prone to look ahead,— regyards the talk as down to cases an' makes a flash for his gun. It's concealed by his surtoot an' I ain't noticed it none before. If I had, most likely I'd pitched the conversation in a lower key. How- ever, by this time, I'm quarrelsome as a badger ; an' a willin'ness for trouble subdooes an' sets it's feet on my nacheral cowardice an' holds her down.'

" ' Dave, you-all makes me nervous,' says Boggs, with a flash of heat, ' settin' thar lyin' about your timidity that a-way. You're about as reluctant for trouble as a grizzly bar, an' you couldn't fool no gent yere on that p'int for so much as one white chip.'

" ' Jest the same,' says Dave, mighty dogmatic, ' I still asserts that in a concealed, inborn fashion, I'm timid absoloote. If you has ever beheld me stand up ag'in the iron it's because I'm 'shamed to quit. I'd wilt out like a jack-rabbit if I ain't held by pride.

" ' " You're plenty ready with that Colt's," I says to Yuba, an' my tones is severe. " That's because you sees me weeponless. If I has a gun now, I'd make you yell like a coyote."

" ' " S'pose you ain't heeled," reemonstrates Yuba, " that don't give you no license to stand thar aboosin' me. Be I to blame because your toilet ain't complete? You go frame yourse'f up, an' I'll wait ; " an' with that, this Yuba takes his hand from his artillery.

" ' Thar's a footile party who keeps the dance-hall an' who signs the books as Colonel Boone. He's called the " King of the Cowboys"; most likely in a sperit of facetiousness since he's more like a deuce than a king. This Boone's packin' a most excellent six-shooter loose in the waistband of his laiggin's. Boon's passin' by as Yuba lets fly his taunts an' this piece of ordnance is in easy reach. With one motion I secures it an' the moment fol-lowin' the muzzle is pressin' ag'inst a white pearl button on Yuba's bloo shirt.

" ' " Bein' now equipped," I says, " this war-dance may proceed."

" ' I'm that scared I fairly hankers for the privilege of howlin', but I realises acootely that havin' come this far towards homicide I must needs go through if Yuba crowds my hand. But he don't; he's for-bearin' an' stands silent an' still. Likewise, I sees his nose, yeretofore the colour of a over-ripe violin, begin to turn sear an' gray. I recovers sperit at this as I saveys I'm saved. Still I keeps the artillery on him. It's the inflooence of the gun that holds Yuba spellbound an' affects his nose, an' I feels shore if I relaxes he'll be all over me like a baggage waggon.'

"'Which I should say so!' says Jack Moore, drawin' a deep breath. 'You takes every chance, Dave, when you don't cut loose that time!'

"'When Boone beholds me,' says Dave, 'annex his gun he almost c'lapses into a fit. He makes a backward leap that shows he ain't lived among rattlesnakes in vain. Then he stretches his hand towards me an' Yuba, an' says, "Don't shoot! Let's take a drink; it's on the house!"

"'Yuba, with his nose still a peaceful gray, turns from the gun an' sidles for the bar; I follows along, thirsty, but alert. When we-all is assembled, Boone makes a wailin' request for his six-shooter.

"'"Get his," I says, at the same time, animadvertin' at Yuba with the muzzle.

"'Yuba passes his weepons over the bar an' I follows suit with Boone's. Then we drinks with our eyes on each other in silent scorn.

"'"Which we-all will see about this later," growls Yuba, as he leaves the bar.

"'"Go as far as you like, old sport," I retorts, for this last edition, as Colonel Sterett would term it, of Valley Tan makes me that brave I'm miseratin' for a riot.

"'It's the next day before ever I'm firm enough

to come ag'in to Tucson.   This stage-wait in the
tragedy is doo to fear excloosive. I hears how
Yuba is plumb bad ; how he's got two notches on
his stick ; how he's filed the sights off his gun ; an'
how in all reespects he's a murderer of merit an' re-
nown.   Sech news makes me timid two ways : I'm
afraid Yuba'll down me some ; an' then ag'in I'm
afraid he's so pop'lar I'll be lynched if I downs him.
Shore, that felon Yuba begins to assoome in my
apprehensions the stern feachers of a whipsaw.
At last I'm preyed on to that degree I'm desperate ;
an' I makes up my mind to invade Tucson, cross up
with Yuba an' let him come a runnin'.   The ner-
vousness of extreme yooth doubtless is what goads
me to this decision.

    " ' It's about second drink time in the afternoon
when, havin' donned my weepons, I rides into Tucson.   After leavin' my pony at the corral, I turns
into the main street.   It's scorchin' hot an' barrin'
a dead burro thar's hardly anybody in sight.   Up in
front of the Oriental, as luck has it, stands Yuba
and a party of doobious morals who slays hay for
the gov'ment, an' is addressed as Lon Gilette.   As I
swings into the causeway, Gilette gets his eye on
me an' straightway fades into the Oriental leavin'
Yuba alone in the street.   This yere strikes me as
mighty ominous ; I feels the beads of water come
onder my hatband, an' begins to crowd my gun a
leetle for'ard on the belt.   I'm walkin' up on the
opp'site side from Yuba who stands watchin' my
approach with a serene mien.

" ' " It's the ca'mness of the tiger crouchin' for a spring," thinks I.

" ' As I arrives opp'site, Yuba stretches out his hand. " Come on over," he sings out.

" ' " Which he's assoomin' airs of friendship," I roominates, " to get me off my gyard."

" ' I starts across to Yuba. I'm watchin' like a lynx ; an' I'm that harrowed, if Yuba so much as sneezes or drops his hat or makes a r'arward move of his hand, I'm doo to open on him. But he stands still as a hill an' nothin' more menacin' than grins. As I comes clost he offers his hand. It's prior to my shootin' quick an' ackerate with my left hand, so I don't give Yuba my right, holdin' the same in reserve for emergencies an' in case thar's a change of weather. But Yuba, who can see it's fear that a-way, is too p'lite to make comments. He shakes my left hand with well-bred enthoosiasm an' turns an' heads the way into the Oriental.

" ' As we fronts the bar an' demands nosepaint Yuba gives up his arms ; an' full of a jocund light-heartedness as I realises that I ain't marked for instant slaughter I likewise yields up mine. We then has four drinks in happy an' successful alternation, an' next we seeks a table an' subsides into seven-up.

" ' " Then thar ain't goin' to be no dooel between us ? " I says to Yuba. It's at a moment when he's turned jack an' I figgers he'll be more soft an' leenient. " It's to be a evenin' of friendly peace ? "

" ' " An' why not ? " says Yuba. " I've shore took

all the skelps that's comin' to me ; an' as for you-all, you're young an' my counsel is to never begin. That pooerile spat we has don't count. I'm drink-in' at the time, an' I don't reckon now you attaches importance to what a gent says when he's in lick-er ? "

" ' " Not to what he says," I replies ; " but I does to what he shoots. I looks with gravity on the gun-plays of any gent, an' the drunker he is the more ser'ous I regyards the eepisode."

" ' " Well, she's a thing of the past now," ex-plains Yuba, " an' this evenin' you're as pop'lar with me as a demijohn at a camp-meetin'."

" ' Both our bosoms so wells with joy, settin' thar as we do in a atmosphere of onexpected yet perfect fraternalism an' complete peace, that Yuba an' me drinks a whole lot. It gets so, final, I refooses to return to my own camp ; I won't be sep'rated from Yuba. When we can no longer drink, we turns in at Yuba's wickeyup an' sleeps. The next mornin' we picks up the work of reeconciliation where it slips from our tired hands the evenin' before. I does intend to reepair to my camp when we rolls out ; but after the third conj'int drink both me an' Yuba sees so many reasons why it's a fool play I gives up the idee utter.

" ' Gents, it's no avail to pursoo me an' Yuba throughout them four feverish days. We drifts from one drink-shop to the other, arm in arm, as peaceful an' pleased a pair of sots as ever disturbs the better element. Which we're the scandal of

Tucson; we-all is that thickly amiable it's a insult to other men. Thus ends my first dooel; a conflict as bloodless as she is victorious. How long it would have took me an' Yuba to thoroughly cement our friendships will never be known. At the finish, we-all is torn asunder by the Tucson marshal an' I'm returned to my camp onder gyard. Me an' Yuba before nor since never does wax that friendly with any other gent; we'd be like brothers yet, only the Stranglers over to Shakespear seizes on pore Yuba one mornin' about a hoss an' heads him for his home on high.' "

CHAPTER XIV.

The Troubles of Dan Boggs.

'THIS yere," remarked the Old Cattleman, at the heel of a half-hour lecture on life and its philosophy, " this yere is a evenin' when they gets to discussin' about luck. It's doorin' the progress of this dispoote when Cherokee Hall allows that luck don't alternate none, first good an' then bad, but travels in bunches like cattle or in flocks like birds. ' Whichever way she comes,' says Cherokee, ' good or bad, luck avalanches itse'f on a gent. That's straight!' goes on Cherokee. ' You bet! I speaks from a voloominous experience an' a life that, whether up or down, white or black, ain't been nothin' but luck. Which nacherally, bein' a kyard sharp that a-way, I studies luck the same as Peets yere studies drugs; an' my discov'ries teaches that luck is plumb gregar'ous. Like misery in that proverb, luck loves company; it shore despises to be lonesome.'

"'Cherokee, I delights to hear you talk,' says Old Man Enright, as he signs up Black Jack for the Valley Tan. ' Them eloocidations is meant to stiffen a gent's nerve an' do him good. Shore; no one needs encouragement nor has to train for a conflict with good luck; but it's when he's out

ag'inst the iron an' the bad luck's swoopin' an'
stoopin' at him, beak an'claw like forty hawks, that
your remarks is doo to come to his aid an' uplift
his sperits some. An' as you says a moment back,
thar's bound in the long run to be a equilibr'um.
The lower your bad luck, the taller your good
luck when it strikes camp. It's the same with the
old Rockies, an' wherever you goes it's ever a
never-failin' case of the deeper the valley, the
higher the hill!

"'As is frequent with me,' says Dan Boggs, after
we sets quiet a moment, meanwhiles tastin' our
nosepaint thoughtful—for these outbursts of Cherokee's an' Enright's calls for consid'rations,—'as is
frequent with me,' says Dan, ' I reckons I'll string
my chips with Cherokee. The more ready since
throughout my own checkered c'reer—an' I've done
most everything 'cept sing in the choir,—luck has
ever happened bunched like he asserts. Which I
gets notice of these pecooliarities of fortune early.
While I'm simply doin' nothin' to provoke it, a
gust of bad luck prounces on me an' thwarts me
in a noble ambition, rooins' my social standin' an'
busts two of my nigh ribs all in one week.

"' I'm a colt at the time, an' jest about big enough
to break. My folks is livin' in Missouri over back
of the Sni-a-bar Hills. By nacher I'm a heap
moosical; so I ups—givin' that genius for harmony
expression—an' yoonites myse'f with the " Sni-a-bar
Silver Cornet Band." Old Hickey is leader, an' he
puts me in to play the snare drum, the same bein'

the second rung on the ladder of moosical fame, an'
one rung above the big drum. Old Hickey su'gests
that I start with the snare drum an' work up.
Gents, you-all should have heard me with that
instrooment! I'd shore light into her like a storm
of hail!

"'For a spell the "Sni-a-bar Silver Cornet Band"
used to play in the woods. This yere Sni-a-bar commoonity is a mighty nervous neighbourhood, an'
thar's folks whose word is above reproach who
sends us notice they'll shoot us up if we don't; so at
first we practises in the woods. But as time goes
on we improves an' plays well enough so we
don't scare children; an' then the Sni-a-bar people
consents to let us play now an' then along the road.
All of us virchewosoes is locoed to do good work, so
that Sni-a-bar would get reeconciled, an' recognise
us as a commoonal factor.

"'Well do I recall the day of our first public
appearance. It's at a political meetin' an' everything, so far as we're concerned at least, depends on
the impression we-all makes. If we goes to a balk
or a break-down, the "Sni-a-bar Silver Cornet
Band's" got to go back an' play in the woods.

"'It's not needed that I tells you gents, how we-all
is on aige. Old Hickey gets so perturbed he shifts
me onto the big drum; an' Catfish Edwards, yeretofore custodian of that instrooment, is given the
snare. This play comes mighty clost to breakin'
my heart; for I'm ambitious, an' it galls my soul to
see myse'f goin' back'ards that a–way. It's the

beginnin' of my bad luck, too. Thar's no chance to duck the play, however, as old Hickey's word is law, so I sadly buckles on the giant drum.

" ' We're jest turnin' into the picnic ground where this meetin's bein' held an' I've got thoughts of nothin' but my art—as we moosicians says—an' elevatin' the local opinion of an' concernin' the meelodious merits of the band. We're playin' "Number Eighteen" at the time, an' I've got my eagle eye on the paper that tells me when to welt her ; an' I'm shorely leatherin' away to beat a ace-flush.

" ' Bein' I'm new to the big drum, an' onduly eager to succeed, I've got all my eyes picketed on the notes. It would have been as well if I'd reeserved at least one for scenery. But I don't ; an' so it befalls that when we-all is in the very heart of the toone, an' at what it's no exaggeration to call a crisis in our destinies, I walks straddle of a stump. An' sech is my fatal momentum that the drum rolls up on the stump, an' I rolls up on the drum. That's the finish ; next day the Silver Cornet Band by edict of the Sni-a-bar pop'lace is re-exiled to them woods. But I don't go ; old Hickey excloodes me, an' my hopes of moosical eminence rots down right thar.

" ' It's mebby two days later when I'm over by the postoffice gettin' the weekly paper for my old gent. Thar's goin' to be a Gander-Pullin' by torch-light that evenin' over to Hickman's Mills with a dance at the heel of the hunt. But I ain't allowin' to be present none. I'm too deeply chagrined about my failure with that big drum ; an' then ag'in, I'm scared to ask a girl to go. You-all most likely has missed noticin' it a heap—for I frequent forces myse'f to be gala an' festive in company—but jest the same, deep down onder my belt, I'm bashful. An' when I'm younger I'm worse. I'm bashful speshul of girls ; for I soon discovers that it's easier to face a gun than a girl, an' the glance of her eye is more terrifyin' than the glimmer of a bowie. That's the way I feels. It's a fact ; I remembers a time when my mother, gettin' plumb desp'rate over my hoomility, offers me a runnin' hoss if I'd go co't a girl ; on which o'casion I feebly urges that I'd rather walk.

"'On the evenin' of this yer dance an' Gander-Pullin' I'm pirootin' about the Center when I meets up with Jule James ;—Jule bein' the village belle. "Goin' to the dance?" says Jule. "No," says I. "Why ever don't you go ?" asks Jule. "Thar, ain't no girl weak-minded enough to go with me," I replies ; "I makes a bid for two or three but gets the mitten." This yere last is a bluff. "Which I reckons now," says Jule, givin' me a look, "if you'd asked me, I'd been fool enough to go." Of course, with that I'm treed ; I couldn't flicker, so I allows that if Jule'll caper back to the house with me I'll take her yet.

"'We-all gets back to my old gent's an' I proceeds to hitch up a Dobbin hoss we has to a side bar buggy. It's dark by now, an' we don't go to the house nor indulge in any ranikaboo uproar about it, as I figgers it's better not to notify the folks. Not that they'd be out to put the kybosh on this enter-prize; but they're powerful fond of talk my folks is, an' their long suit is never wantin' you to do what-ever you're out to execoote. Wherefore, as I ain't got no time for a j'int debate with my fam'ly over technicalities I puts Jule into the side-bar where it's standin' in the dark onder a shed; an' then, hook-in' up old Dobbin a heap surreptitious, I gathers the reins an' we goes softly p'intin' forth for Hick-man's.

"'As we-all is sailin' thoughtlessly along the trail, Dobbin ups an' bolts. Sech flights is onpree-ceedented in the case of Dobbin—who's that sedate he's jest alive—an' I'm shore amazed; but I yanks him up an' starts anew. It's twenty rods when Dob-bin bolts ag'in. This time I hears a flutter, an' reaches 'round Jule some to see if her petticoats is whippin' the wheel. They ain't; but Jule—who esteems said gesture in the nacher of a caress—seemin' to favour the idee, I lets my arm stay 'round. A moment later an' this yere villain Dobbin bolts the third time, an' as I've sort o' got my one arm tangled up with Jule, he lams into a oak tree.

"'It's then, when we're plumb to a halt, I does hear a flutter. At that I gets down to investigate. Gents, you-all may onderstand my horror when I finds 'leven of my shawl-neck game chickens roost-in' on that side-bar's reach! They're thar when we pulls out. They've retired from the world an' its cares for the night an', in our ignorance of them chicken's domestic arrangements, we blindly takes 'em with us. Now an' then, as we goes rackin' along, one of 'em gets jolted off. Then he'd hang by his chin an' beat his wings ; an' it's these frenzied efforts he makes to stay with the game that evolves them alarmin' flutterin's.

" ' Jule—who don't own chickens an' who ain't no patron of cockfights neither—is for settin' the shawl-necks on the fence an' pickin' 'em up as we trails back from the Gander-Pullin'.

" ' " As long as it's dark," says Jule, " they'll stay planted ; an' we rounds 'em up on our return."

" ' But I ain't that optimistic. I knows these chickens an' they ain't so somnolent as all that. Besides it's a cinch that a mink or a fox comes squanderin' 'round an' takes 'em in like gooseberries. 'Leven shawl-necks ! Why, it would be a pick-up for a fox !

" ' " You're a fine Injun to take a girl to a dance ! " says Jule at last, an' she's full of scorn.

" ' " Injun or no Injun," I retorts a heap sullen, " thar ain't no Gander-Pullin' goin' to jestify me in abandonin' my 'leven shawl-necks an' me with a main to fight next month over on the Little Bloo ! "

" ' At that I corrals the chickens an' imprisons 'em in the r'ar of the side-bar an' goes a-weavin' back for camp, an' I picks up three more shawl-necks where they sets battin' their he'pless eyes in the road.

" ' But I shore hears Jule's views of me as a beau !

They're hot enough to fry meat! Moreover, Jule tells all Sni-a-bar an' I'm at once a scoff an' jeer from the Kaw to the Gasconade. Jule's old pap washes out his rifle an' signs a pledge to plug me if ever ag'in I puts my hand on his front gate. As I su'gests, it rooins my social c'reer in Sni-a-bar.

"'While I'm ground like a toad that a-way beneath the harrow of this double setback of the drum an' Jule, thar's a circus shows up an' pitches its merry tent in Sni-a-bar. I knows this caravan of yore—for I'm a master-hand for shows in my yooth an' allers goes—an' bein' by virchoo of my troubles ready to plunge into dissipation's mad an' swirlin' midst, I sa'nters down the moment the waggons shows up; an' after that, while that circus stays, folks who wants to see me, day or night, has to come to the show.

"'The outfit is one of them little old jim-crow shows that charges two-bits an' stays a month; an' by the end of the first day, me an' the clown gets wropped up like brothers; which I'm like one of the fam'ly! I fetches water an' he'ps rub hosses an', speakin' gen'ral, does more nigger work than I ever crosses up with prior endoorin' my entire life. But knowin' the clown pays for all; sech trivial considerations as pullin' on tent ropes an' spreadin' sawdust disappears before the honour of his a'quaintance. It's my knowin' the clown that leads to disaster.

"'This merrymaker, who's a "jocund wight" as Colonel Sterett says, gets a heap drunk one evenin' an' sleeps out in the rain, an' he awakes as hoarse as bull-frogs. He ain't able to sing his song in the ring. It's jest before they begins.

"'"Dan," he croaks, plenty dejected, "I wish you'd clown up an' go in an' sing that song."

"'This cantata he alloodes to, is easy; it's "Roll Jurdan, Roll," an' I hears it so much at nigger camp meetin's an' sim'lar distractions, that I carols it in my sleep. As the clown throws out his bluff I considers awhile some ser'ous. I feels like mebby I've cut the trail of a cunnin' idee. When Jule an' old Hickey an' the balance of them Sni-a-bar outcasts sees me in a clown's yooniform, tyrannisin' about, singin' songs an' leadin' up the war-jig gen'-ral, they'll regret the opinions they so freely expresses an' take to standin' about, hopin' I'll bow. They'll regyard knowin' me as a boon. With that, I tells the clown to be of good cheer. I'll prance in an' render that lay an' his hoarseness won't prove no setback to the gaiety of nations.

"'But I don't sing after all; an' I don't pile up Jule an' old Hickey an' the sports of Sni-a-bar neither in any all 'round jumble of amazement at my genius.

"'"Dan," says the ring master when we're in the dressin' room, "when the leapin' begins, you-all go on with the others an' do a somersault or two?"

"'"Shore!" I says.

"'I feels as confidant as a kangaroo! Which I never does try it none; but I supposes that all you has to do is hit the springboard an' let the springboard do the rest. That's where I'm barkin' at a knot!

"'This yere leapin' comes first on the bill. I ain't been in the ring yet; the tumblin' business is where I makes my deeboo. I've got on a white clown soote with big red spots, an' my face is all flour. I'm as certain of my comin' pop'larity as a wet dog. I shore allows that when Jule an' old Hickey observes my graceful agility an' then hears me warble "Roll Jurdan, Roll," I'll make 'em hang their heads.

"'The tumblin' is about to begin; the band's playin', an' all us athletes is ranged Injun file along a plank down which we're to run. I'm the last chicken on the roost.

"'Even unto this day it's a subject of contention in circus cirkles as to where I hits that springboard. Some claims I hits her too high up; an' some says too low; for myse'f, I concedes I'm ignorant on the p'int. I flies down the plank like a antelope! I hears the snarl of the drums! I jumps an' strikes the springboard!

"'It's at this juncture things goes queer. To my wonder I don't turn no flip-flap, but performs like a draw-shot in billiards. I plants my moccasins on the springboard; an' then instead of goin' on an' over a cayouse who's standin' thar awaitin' sech events, I shoots back'ard about fifteen foot an' lands in a ondistinguishable heap. An' as I strikes a plank it smashes a brace of my ribs.

"'For a second I'm blurred in my intellects,

Then I recovers; an' as I'm bein' herded back into the dressin' room by the fosterin' hands of the ring master an' my pard, the clown, over in the audience I hears Jule's silvery laugh an' her old pap allowin' he'd give a hoss if I'd only broke my neck. Also, I catches a remark of old Hickey: "Which that Boggs boy allers was a ediot!" says old Hickey.'"

CHAPTER XV.

Bowlegs and Major Ben.

"WHICH this yere Major Ben," remarked the Old Cattleman, "taken in conjunction with his bosom pard, Billy Bowlaigs, frames up the only casooalty which gets inaug'rated in Wolfville."

"What!" I interjected; "don't you consider the divers killings,—the death of the Stinging Lizard and the Dismissal of Silver Phil, to say nothing of the taking off of the Man from Red Dog—don't you, I say, consider such bloody matters casualties?"

"No, sir," retorted my friend, emitting the while sundry stubborn puffs of smoke, "no, sir; I regyards them as results. Tharfore, I reiterates that this yere Major Ben an' Bowlaigs accomplishes between 'em the only troo casooalty whereof Wolfville has a record."

At this he paused and surveyed me with an eye of challenge; after a bit, perceiving that I proposed no further contradiction, he went on:

"This Billy Bowlaigs at first is a cub b'ar—a black cub b'ar: an' when he grows up to manhood, so to speak, he's as big, an' mighty near as strong physical, as Dan Boggs. Nacherally, however, Dan lays over Bowlaigs mental like a ace-full.

" It's Dave Tutt who makes Bowlaigs captive ;
Dave rounds Bowlaigs up in his infancy one time
when he's pesterin' about over in the foothills of
the Floridas lookin' for blacktail deer. Dave meets
up with Bowlaigs an' the latter's mother who's out,
evident, on a scout for grub. Bowlaig's mother has
jest upturned a rotten pine-log to give little Bowlaigs
a chance to rustle some of these yere egreegious white
worms which looks like bald catapillars, that a-way,
when all at once around a p'int of rocks Dave
heaves in view. This parent of Bowlaigs is as besotted about her son as many hooman mothers ; for
while Bowlaigs stands almost as high as she does
an' weighs clost onto two hundred pounds, the
mother b'ar still has the idee tangled up in her intel-
ligence that Bowlaigs is that small an' he'pless, day-
old kittens is se'f-sustainin' citizens by compar'son
to him. Actin' on these yere errors, Bowlaig's
mother the moment she glimpses Dave grabs young
Bowlaigs by the scruff of the neck an' goes caperin'
off up hill with him. An' to give that parent b'ar
full credit, she's gettin' along all right an' conductin'
herse'f as though Bowlaigs don't heft no more than
one of them gooseha'r pillows, when, accidental, she
bats pore Bowlaigs ag'in the bole of a tree—him
hangin' outen her mouth about three foot—an' while
the collision shakes that monarch of the forest some,
Bowlaigs gets knocked free of her grip an' goes rollin' down the mountain-side ag'in like a sack of bran.
It puts quite a crimp in Bowlaigs. The mother b'ar,
full of s'licitoode to save her offspring turns an'

charges Dave ; tharupon Dave downs her, an' young
Bowlaigs becomes a orphan an' a pris'ner on the
spot.

"Followin' the demise of Bowlaig's mother, Dave
sort o' feels reesponsible for the cub's bringin' up an'
he ties him hand an' foot, an' after peelin' the pelt
from the old mother b'ar, packs the entire outfit
into camp. Dave's pony protests with green eyes
ag'in carryin' sech a freight, but Dave has his way
as he usually does with everything except Tucson
Jennie.

"At first Dave allows he'll let Bowlaigs live with
him a whole lot an' keep him ontil he grows up, an'
construct a pet of him. But as I more than once
makes plain, Dave proposes but Tucson Jennie disposes ; an' so it befalls that on the third day after
the cub takes up his residence with her an' Dave,
Jennie arms herse'f with a broom an' harasses the
onfortunate Bowlaigs from her wickeyup. Jennie
declar's that she discovers Bowlaigs organisin' to
devour her child Enright Peets Tutt, who's at that
epock comin' three the next spring round-up.

"'I could read it in that Bowlaigs b'ar's eyes,'
says Jennie, 'an' it's mighty lucky a parent's facul-
ties is plumb keen. If I hadn't got in on the play
with my broom, you can bet that inordinate Bowlaigs would have done eat little Enright Peets all
up.

"Shore, no one credits these yere apprehensions
of Jennie's ; Bowlaigs would no more have chewed
up Enright Peets than he'd played table-stakes with

him; but a fond mother's fears once stampeded is
not to be headed off or ca'med, an' Bowlaigs has to
shift his camp a heap.

"Bowlaigs takes up his abode on the heels of him
bein' run out by Tucson Jennie, over to the corral;
that is, he bunks in thar temp'rary at least. An' he
shore grows amazin', an' enlarges doorin' the next
three months to sech a degree that when he stands
up to the counter in the Red Light, acceptin' of
some proffered drink, Bowlaigs comes clost to bein'
as tall as folks. He early learns throughout his
wakeful moments—what I'd deescribe as his business
hours—to make the Red Light a hang-out; it's the
nosepaint he's hankerin' after, for in no time at all
Bowlaigs accoomulates a appetite for rum that's a
fa'r match for that of either Huggins or Old Monte,
an' them two sots is for long known as far west as
the Colorado an' as far no'th as the Needles as the
offishul drunkards of Arizona. No; Bowlaigs ain't
equal to pourin' down the raw nosepaint; but Black
Jack humours his weakness an' Bowlaigs is wont
to take off his libations about two parts water to
one of whiskey an' a lump of sugar in the bottom,
outen one of these big tumbler glasses; meanwhiles
standin' at the bar an' holdin' the glass between
his two paws an' all as ackerate an' steady as the
most talented inebriate.

"'An' Bowlaigs has this distinction,' says Black
Jack, alloodin' to the sugar an' water; 'he's shore
the only gent for whom I so far onbends from reg'-
lar rools as to mix drinks.'

" Existence goes flowin' onward like some glad sweet song for Bowlaigs for mighty likely it's two months an' nothin' remarkable eventuates. He camps in over to the corral, an' except that new ponies, who ain't onto Bowlaigs, commonly has heart-failure at the sight of him, he don't found no disturbances nor get in anybody's way. Throughout his wakin' hours, as I su'gests former, Bowlaigs ha'nts about the Red Light, layin' guileful an' cunnin' for invites to drink; an' he execootes besides small excursions to the O. K. Restauraw for chuck, with now an' then a brief journey to the Post Office or the New York store. These visits of Bowlaigs to the last two places, both because he don't get no letters at the post office an' don't demand no clothes at the store, I attribootes to motives of morbid cur'osity, that a-way.

" The first real trouble that meets up with Bowlaigs—who's got to be a y'ar old by now—since Jennie fights the dooel with him with that broom, overtakes him at the O. K. Restauraw. Missis Rucker for one thing ain't over fond of Bowlaigs, allegin' as he grows older day by day he looks more an' more like Rucker. Of course, sech views is figments as much as the alarms of Tucson Jennie about Bowlaigs meditatin' gettin' away with little Enright Peets ; but Missis Rucker, in spite of whatever we gent folks can say in Bowlaigs's behalf, believes firm in her own slanders. She asserts that Bowlaigs as he onfolds looks like Rucker; an' for her at least that settles the subject an' she assoomes towards Bowlaigs attitoodes which would perhaps have been proper had her charge been troo.

"Still, I'll say for that most esteemable lady, that Missis Rucker never lays for Bowlaigs or assaults him ontil one afternoon when he catches the dinin'-room deserted an' off its gyard an' goes romancin' over, cat-foot an' surreptitious, an' cleans up the tables of what chuck has been placed thar in antic'pation of supper. The first news Missis Rucker has of the raid is when Bowlaigs gets a half-hitch on the tablecloth an' winds up his play by yankin' the entire outfit of spoons, tin plates an' crockery off onto the floor. It's then Missis Rucker sallies from the kitchen an' puts Bowlaigs to flight.

"Bowlaigs, who's plumb scared, comes lumberin' over to the Red Light an' puts himse'f onder our protection. Enright squar's it for him; for when Missis Rucker appears subsequent with a Winchester an' a knife an' gives it out cold she's goin' to get Bowlaig's hide an' tallow an' sell 'em to pay even for that dinin'-room desolation of which he's the architect, Enright counts up the damage an' pays over twenty-three dollars in full settlement. Does Bowlaigs know it? You can gamble the limit he knows it; for all the time Missis Rucker is prancin' about the Red Light denouncin' him, he secretes himse'f, shiverin', behind the bar; an' when that lady withdraws, mollified an' subdooed by the money, he creeps out, Bowlaigs does, an' cries an' licks Enright's hand Oh, he's a mighty

appreciative b'ar, pore Bowlaigs is; but his nerves
is that onstrung by the perils he passes through
with Missis Rucker it takes two big drinks to
recover his sperits an' make him feel like the same
b'ar.   It's Texas Thompson who buys the drinks:

"'For I, of all gents, Bowlaigs,' says Texas, as
he invites the foogitive to the bar, 'onderstands
what you-all's been through.   It may be imagination, but jest the same thar's them times when Missis Rucker goes on the warpath when she reminds
me a lot of my divorced Laredo wife.'   With that
Texas pours a couple of hookers of Willow Run
into Bowlaigs, an' the latter is a heap cheered an'
his pulse declines to normal.

"It's rum, however, which final is the deestruction of Bowlaigs, same as it is of plenty of other
good people who would have else lived in honour an'
died respected an' been tearfully planted in manner
an' form to do 'em proud.

"Excloosive of that casooalty which marks his
wind-up, an' which he combines with Major Ben to
commit, thar's but one action of Bowlaigs a enemy
might call a crime.   He does prounce on a mail bag
one evenin' when the post-master ain't lookin', an'
shore rends an' worrits them letters scand'lous.

"Yes, Bowlaigs gets arrested, an' the Stranglers
sort o' convenes informal to consider it.   I allers
remembers that session of the Stranglers on account
of Doc Peets, an' Colonel William Greene Sterett
entertain' opp'site views an' the awful language
they indulges in as they expresses an' sets 'em forth

" ' Which I claims that this Bowlaigs b'ar,' says Peets, combatin' a su'gestion of Dan Boggs who's sympathisin' with an' urges that Bowlaigs is 'ignorant of law an' tharfore innocent of offence,' ' which I claims that this Bowlaig b'ar is guilty of rustlin' the mails an' must an' should be hanged. His ignorance is no defences, for don't each gent present know of that aphorism of the law, *Ignoratis legia non excusat !* '

" Dan, nacherally, is onable to combat sech profound bluffs as this, an' I'm free to confess if it ain't for Colonel Sterett buttin' in with more Latin, the same bein' of equal cogency with that of Peet's, the footure would have turned plenty dark an' doobious for Bowlaigs. As Dan sinks back speechless an' played from Peet's shot, the Colonel, who bein' eddicated like Peets to a feather aige is ondismayed an' cool, comes to the rescoo.

" ' That law proverb you quotes, Doc,' says the Colonel, ' is dead c'rrect, an' if argyment was to pitch its last camp thar, your deductions that this benighted Bowlaigs must swing, would be ondeniable. But thar's a element lackin' in this affair without which no offence is feasible. The question is, —an' I slams it at you, Doc, as a thoughtful eddicated sharp—does this yere Bowlaigs open them letters an' bust into that mail bag *causa lucræ?* I puts this query up to you-all, Doc, for answer. It's obv'ous that Bowlaigs ain't got no notion of money bein' in them missives an' tharfore he couldn't have been moved by no thoughts of gain. Wherefore I

asserts that the deed is not done *causa lucræ*, an'
that the case ag'in this he'pless Bowlaigs falls to the
ground.'

"Followin' this yere collision of the classics between two sech scientists as Peets an' the Colonel,
we-all can be considered as hangin' mighty anxious
on what reply Doc Peets is goin' to make. But
after some thought, Peets agrees with the Colonel.
He admits that this *causa lucræ* is a bet he overlooks,
an' that now the Colonel draws his attention to it,
he's bound to say he believes the Colonel to be
right, an' that Bowlaigs should be made a free on-
fettered b'ar ag'in. We breathes easier at this, for
the tension has been great, an' Dan himse'f is that
relieved he comes a heap clost to sheddin' tears.
The trial closes with the customary drinks; Bowlaigs gettin' his forty drops with the rest, on the
hocks of which he signalises his reestoration to his
rights an' freedom as a citizen by quilin' up in his
corner an' goin' to sleep.

"But the end is on its lowerin' way for Bowlaigs.
Thar's a senile party who's packed his blankets into
camp an' who's called ' Major Ben.' The Major, so
the whisper goes, used to be quartermaster over to
Fort Craig or Fort Apache, or mebby now it's Fort
Cummings or some'ers; an' he gets himse'f dis-
missed for makin' away with the bank-roll. Be that
as it may, the Major's plenty drunk an' military
while he lasts among us; an' he likewise has *dinero*
for whatever nosepaint an' food an' farobank he sees
fit to go ag'inst. From the jump the Major makes

up to Bowlaigs an' the two become pards. The Major allows he likes Bowlaigs because he can't talk.

"'Which if all my friends,' says the Major, no doubt alloodin' to them witnesses ag'in him when he's cashiered, 'couldn't have talked no more than Bowlaigs, I'd been happy yet.'

"The Major's got a diminyootive wickeyup out to the r'ar of the corral, an' him an' Bowlaigs resides tharin. This habitat of the Major an' Bowlaigs ain't much bigger than a seegyar box; it's only eight foot by ten, is made of barn-boards an' has a canvas roof. That's the kind of ranch Bowlaigs an' the Major calls 'home'; the latter spreadin' his blankets on one side while Bowlaigs sleeps on t'other on the board floor, needin' no blankets, havin' advantage over the Major seein' he's got fur.

"The dispoote between Bowlaigs an' the Major which results in both of 'em cashin' in, gets started erroneous. The Major—who's sometimes too indolent an' sometimes too drunk to make the play himse'f—instructs Bowlaig how to go over to the Red Light an' fetch a bottle of rum. The Major would chuck a silver dollar in a little basket, an' Bowlaigs would take it in his mouth same as you-all has seen dogs, an' report with the layout to Black Jack. That gent would make the shift, bottle for dollar, an' Bowlaigs would reepair back ag'in to the Major, when they'd both tank up ecstatic.

"One mornin' after Bowlaigs an' the Major's been campin' together about four months, they wakes up mighty jaded. They've had a onusual spree the

evenin' prior an' they feels like a couple of sore-
head dogs. The Major who needs a drink to line
up for the day, gropes about in his blankets, gets a
dollar, pitches it into the basket an' requests Bowlaigs to caper over for the Willow Run. Bowlaigs is
nothin' loth ; but as he's about to pick up the basket,
he observes that the dollar has done bounced out
an' fell through a crack in the floor. Bowlaigs
sees it through the same crack where it's layin'
shinin' onder the house.

"Now this yere Bowlaigs is a mighty sagacious
b'ar, also froogal, an' so he goes wallowin' forth
plenty prompt to recover the dollar. The Major,
who's ignorant of what's happened, still lays thar
groanin' in his blankets, feelin' like a loser an' nursin'
his remorse.

"The first p'inter the Major gets of a new deal in
his destinies is a grand crash as the entire teepee
upheaves an' goes over, kerwallop! on its side,
hurlin' the Major out through the canvas. It's the
thoughtless Bowlaigs does it.

When Bowlaigs gets outside, he finds he can't
crawl onder the teepee none, seein' it's settin' too
clost to the ground ; an' tharupon, bein' a one-
ideed b'ar, he sort o' runs his right arm in beneath
that edifice an' up-ends the entire shebang, same as
his old mother would a log when she's grub-huntin'
in the hills. Bowlaigs is pickin' up the dollar
when the Major comes swarmin' 'round the ruins
of his outfit, a bowie in his hand, an' him fairly
locoed with rage.

"Shore, thar's a fight, an' the Major gets the knife plumb to Bowlaigs's honest heart with the first motion. But Bowlaigs quits game; he turns with a warwhoop an' confers on the Major a swat that would have broke the back of a bronco; an' then he dies with his teeth in the Major's neck.

"The Major only lives a half hour after we gets thar. An' it's to his credit that he makes a statement exoneratin' Bowlaigs. 'I don't want you-all gents,' says the Major, 'to go deemin' hard of this innocent b'ar, for whatever fault thar is, is mine. Since Texas Thompson picks up that dollar, this thing is made plain. What I takes for gratooitous wickedness on Bowlaigs' part is nothin' but his efforts to execoote my desires. Pore Bowlaigs! it embitters my last moments as I pictures what must have been his opinions of me when I lams loose at him with that knife! Bury us in one grave, gents; it'll save trouble an' show besides that thar's no hard feelin's between me an' Bowlaigs over what—an' give it the worst name—ain't nothin' but a onfortunate mistake.'"

CHAPTER XVI.

Toad Allen's Elopement.

"FOUR days after that pinfeather person," remarked the Old Cattleman, while refilling his pipe, "four days after that pinfeather person gains Old Man Enright's consent to make use of Wolfville as a pivotal p'int in a elopement, him an' his loved one comes bulgin' into camp. They floats over in one of these yere mountain waggons, what some folks calls a 'buckboard'; the pinfeather person's drivin'. Between him an' his intended—all three settin' on the one seat—perches a preacher gent, who it's plain from the look in his eyes is held in a sort o' captivity that a-way. What nacherally bolsters up this theery is that the maiden's got a six-shooter in her lap.

"'Which if thar's a wearied hectored gent in Arizona,' observes the pinfeather party, as he descends outen the buckboard at the corral an' tosses the reins to a hoss-hustler, 'you-all can come weavin' up an' chance a yellow stack that I'm shore that gent.'

"The preacher sharp, who's about as young an' new as the pinfeather party, looks like he yoonites with him in them views. As they onload themse'fs, the pinfeather person waves his hand to where we-all's gathered to welcome 'em, an' says by way of introduction :

" 'Gents, yere's Abby ; or as this Bible sport will say later in the cer'mony, Abigail Glegg.'

" Of course, we, who represents the Wolfville public, comports ourse'fs as becomes gents of dig-nity, an' after takin' off our sombreros, plumb p'lite, Enright su'gests the O. K. Restauraw as a base of op'rations.

" ' Don't you-all reckon,' says Enright to the pin-feather party, ' that pendin' hostilities, Abby had better go over to Missis Rucker's ? Thar she gets combs an' breshes an' goes over her make-up an' straightens out her game.'

" The pinfeather party allows this yere is a excel-lent notion, only him an' Abby don't seem cl'ar as to what oughter be done about the preacher sharp.

" 'You see, he don't want to come,' explains the pinfeather party, ' an' it's cost me an' Abby a heap of trouble to round him up.   I ain't none shore but he seizes on the first chance to go stampedin' ; an' without him these rites we-all is bankin' on would cripple down.'

" ' No, friends,' says the preacher sharp ; ' I will promise to abide by you an' embrace no openin' to escape. Since I'm here I will yoonite you-all as you wish ; the more readily because I trusts that as man an' wife you'll prove a mootual restraint one upon the other ; an' also for that I deems you both in your single-footed capac'ty as a threat to the commoonity. Fear not; prepare yourse'fs an' I'll bring you together in the happy bonds of matrimony at the drop of the hat.'

" 'You notes, Dan,' says Texas Thompson, who's off to one side with Dan Boggs, 'you notes he talks like his heart's resentful. Them culprits has r'iled him up; an' now he allows that the short cut to play even is to marry 'em as they deserves. Which if you-all knows that former wife of mine, Dan, you'll appreciate what I says.'

" Even after the preacher sharp gives his p'role, Abby acts plenty doobious. She ain't shore it's wise to throw him loose. It's Doc Peets who reasshores her.

" 'My dear young lady,' says Peets, at the same time bowin' to the ground, 'you may trust this maverick with me. I'll pledge my word to prodooce him at the moment when he's called for to make these nuptials win.'

" 'Which I'm a heap obleeged to you, Mister,' says Abby to Peets, sizing him up approvin'; 'an' now that I'm convinced thar's no chance of my footure sufferin' from any absenteeism on the part of this pastor, I reckons I better go over, like you-all hints, an' take a look or two in the glass. It ain't goin' to consoome a moment, however,—this yere titivation I plans; an' followin' said improvements we-all better pull off this play some prompt. My paw,—old Ben Glegg,—is on our trail not five miles behind; he'll land yere in half a hour an' I ain't none convinced he won't land shootin'.' An' with

this bluff, an' confidin' the preacher sharp to Peets,
Abby goes curvin' over to the O. K. Restauraw.

"However does this yere virgin look? Son, I
hes'tates to deescribe a lady onless the facts flows
fav'rable for her. Which I'll take chances an' lie a
lot to say that any lady's beautiful, if you-all will
only give me so much as one good feacher to go on.
But I'm powerless in the instance of Abby. Thar's
a blizzard effect to her face ; an' the best you can
say is that if she don't look lovely, at least she
looks convincin'. The gnurliest pineknot burns
frequent the hottest, an' you can take my word for
it, this Abby girl has sperit. Speakin' of her
appearance, personal, Missis Rucker—who's a fair
jedge—allows later to Enright that if Abby's a
kyard in a faro game, she'd play her to lose.

"'Which she looks like a sick cat in the face, an'
a greyhoun' in the waist,' says Missis Rucker ;' an'
I ain't got mortal use for no sech spindlin' trollops
as this yere Abby girl is, nohow.'

"'I don't know,' says Enright, shakin' his head ;
'I ain't been enriched with much practical experience with women, but I reckons now it's love that
does it. Whoever is that gent, Peets, who says,
"love is blind"? He knows his business, that
sport does, an' about calls the turn.'

"'I ain't none so shore neither,' says Peets.
'Love may be blind, but somehow, I don't sign up
the play that way. Thar's plenty of people, same
as this pinfeather party, who discerns beauties in
their sweethearts that's veiled to you an' me.'

"Of course, these yere discussions concernin' Abby's charms takes place weeks later. On the weddin' day, Wolfville's too busy trackin' 'round an' backin' Abby's game to go makin' remarks. In this connection, however, it's only right to Abby to say that her pinfeather beau don't share Missis Rucker's views. Although Abby done threatens him with a gun-play to make him lead her to the altar that time her old paw creases him, an' he begins to wax low-sperited about wedlock, still, the pinfeather party's enamoured of Abby an' wropped up in her.

"'Shore! says this pinfeather party to Texas Thompson, who, outen pity for him, takes the bridegroom over to the Red Light, to be refreshed; 'shore! while thar's no one egreegious to go claimin' that my Abby's doo to grade as "cornfed," all the same she's one of the most fascinatin' ladies, —that is, an' give her a gun,—in all the len'th an' breadth of Arizona. I knows; for I've seen my Abby shoot.'

"'Excoose me, pard,' says Texas, after surveyin' the pinfeather party plenty sympathetic; 'pardon my seemin' roodness, if I confers with the barkeep aside. On the level! now,' goes on Texas to Black Jack as he pulls him off to a corner an' whispers so the pinfeather party don't hear; 'on the level, Jack! ain't it my dooty—me who saveys what he's ag'inst—to go warn this victim ag'in matrimony in all its horrors?'

"'Don't you do it!' remonstrates Black Jack,

an' his voice trembles with the emphasis he feels;
'don't you do it none! You-all stand paws off!
Which you don't know what you'll be answerable
for! If this yere marriage gets broke off, who knows
what new line of conduct this Abby maiden will
put out. She may rope onto Boggs, or Peets, or
mebby even me. As long as Abby ain't marryin'
none of us, Wolfville's attitoode oughter be one of
dignified nootrality.'

" Texas sighs deep an' sad as he turns ag'in to the
pinfeather party ; but he sees the force of Black
Jack's argyments an' yields without a effort to
combat 'em.

" ' After all,' says Texas bitterly to himse'f, ' others
has suffered ; wherefore, then, should this jaybird
gent escape ? ' An' with that, Texas hardens his heart
an' gives up any notion of the pinfeather person's
rescoo.

" Which Abby now issues forth of the O. K.
Restauraw an' j'ines the pinfeather party when he
emerges from the Red Light.

" ' This sky pilot,' says Dan Boggs, approachin'
the happy couple, ' sends word by me that he's
over in the New York store. In deefault of a shore-
enough sanchooary, he allows he yootilises that
depot of trade as a headquarters ; an' he's now
waitin', all keyed up an' ready to turn his little
game. Likewise, he's been complainin' 'round
some querulous that you folks is harsh with him,
an' abducts him an' threatens his skelp.'

" ' Now, see thar ! ' ejac'lates Abby, liftin' up her

hands. 'Does mortal y'ears ever before listen to
sech folly! I suppose he takes that gun I has as
threats! I'm a onprotected young female, an' nacherally, when I embarks on this yere elopement, I
packs one of paw's guns. Besides, this sweetheart
of mine might get cold feet, an' try to jump the
game, an' then I'd need said weepon to make good
my p'sition. But it's never meant for that pastor!
When I'm talkin' to him to prevail on him to come
along, an' that gun in my hand at the time, I does
sort o' make references to him with the muzzle.
But he needn't go gettin' birdheaded over it; thar's
nothin' hostile meant!'

"'Enright explains to him satisfact'ry,' says
Boggs. 'An' as you urges, it don't mean nothin'.
Folks on the brink of bein' married that a-way gets
so joyfully bewildered it comes mighty near the
same as bein' locoed.'

"'Well,' says the pinfeather party, who's been
stackin' up a dust-cloud where some one's gallopin'
along about three miles over on the trail, 'if I'm
any dab at a guess that's your infuriated paw pirootin' along over yonder, an' we better get these
matrimonial hobbles on without further onreasonable delays. That old murderer would plug me;
an' no more hes'tation than if I'm a coyote! But
once I'm moved up into p'sition as his son-in-law, a
feelin' of nearness an' kinship mighty likely op'rates
to stay his hand. Blood's thicker than water, an'
I'm in a hurry to get reelated to your paw.'

" But Enright has his notions of what's proper,

an' he su'gests the services be delayed ontil old Glegg gets in. Meanwhile he despatches Jack Moore an' Dan Boggs as a gyard of honor to lead old Glegg to our trystin' place in the New York store.

" ' An' the first thing you-all do, Jack,' says En-right, as Jack an' Dan rides away, ' you get that outcast's guns.'

" It ain't no more'n time for one drink when Jack an' Dan returns in company of this Glegg. He's a fierce, gray old gent with a eye like a wolf. Jest before he arrives, Enright advises the pinfeather person an' the bride Abby, to go camp in the r'ar room so the sudden sight of 'em won't exasp'rate this parent Glegg to madness.

" 'Whatever's the meanin' of this yere con-course?' demands old Glegg, as he comes into the New York store, an' p'intin' to where Peets an' Texas an' Cherokee Hall, along with Enright, is standin' about; ' an' why does these hold-ups '—yere he indicates Dan an' Jack,—' denoode me of my hardware, I'd like to know?'

" 'These gents,' says Enright, ' is a quorum of that respectable body known as the Wolfville Stranglers, otherwise a Vig'lance Committee; an' your guns was took so as to redooce the chances of hangin' you—the same bein' some abundant, nach-eral,—to minimum. Now who be you? also, what's your little game?'

" ' My name's Benjamin Glegg,' responds old Glegg. ' I owns the Sunflower brand an' ranch.

As for my game : thar's a member of my fam'ly es-
capes this mornin'—comes streamin' over yere, I
onderstands—an' I'm in the saddle tryin' to round
her up. Gents,' concloods old Glegg, an' he displays emotion, ' I'm simply a harassed parent on the
trail of his errant offspring.'

"Then Enright makes old Glegg a long, soft talk,
an' seeks to imboo him with ca'mness. He relates
how Abby an' the pinfeather sport dotes on each
other; an' counsels old Glegg not to come pesterin'
about with roode objections to the weddin'.

" ' Which I says this as your friend,' remarks Enright.

" ' It's as the scripter says,' replies old Glegg,
who's mollified a lot, ' it's as the good book says : A
soft answer turneth away wrath ; but more speshully
when the opp'sition's got your guns. I begins to
see things different. Still, I hates to lose my Abby
that a-way. Since my old woman dies, Abby, gents,
has been the world an' all to me.'

" ' Is your wife dead ? " asks Enright, like he
sympathises.

" ' Shore ! ' says old Glegg ; ' been out an' gone
these two years. She's with them cherubim in
glory. But folks, you oughter seen her to onderstand my loss. Five years ago we has a ranch over
back of the Tres Hermanas by the Mexico line.
The Injuns used to go lopin' by our ranch, no'th
an' south, all the time. You-all recalls when they
pays twenty-five dollars for skelps in Tucson ? My
wife's that thrifty them days that she buys all her

own an' my child Abby's clothes with the Injuns she pots. Little Abby used to scout for her maw. "Yere comes another!" little Abby would cry, as she stampedes up all breathless, her childish face aglow. With that, my wife would take her hands outen the wash-tub, snag onto that savage with her little old Winchester, and quit winner twenty-five right thar.'

" ' Which I don't marvel you-all mourns her loss,' says Enright consolin'ly.

" ' She's shorely—Missis Glegg is—' says old Glegg, shakin' his grizzly head; ' she's shore the most meteoric married lady of which hist'ry says a word. My girl Abby's like her.'

" ' But whatever's your objection,' argues Enright, ' to this young an' trusty sport who's so eager to wed Abby ? '

" ' I objects to him because he gambles,' says old Glegg. ' I can see he gambles by him pickin' up the salt cellar between his thumb an' middle finger with the forefinger over the top like it's a stack of chips, one evenin' when he stays to supper an' I asks him to "pass the salt." Then ag'in, he don't drink; he tells me so himse'f when I invites him to libate. I ain't goin' to have no teetotal son-in-law around, over-powerin' me in a moral way; I'd feel criticised an' I couldn't stand it, gents. Lastly, I don't like this yere felon's name none.'

" ' Whatever is his name, then ? ' asks Enright. ' So far he don't confide no title to us.''

" ' An' I don't wonder none!' says old Glegg.

'It shows he's decent enough to be ashamed. Thar's hopes of him yet. Gents, his name's Toad Allen. "Allen" goes, but, gents, I flies in the air at "Toad." Do you-all blame me? I asks you, as onbiased sports, would you set ca'mly down while a party named "Toad" puts himse'f in nom'nation to be your son-in-law?'

"'None whatever!' says Jack Moore; an' Dan an' Cherokee an' Texas echoes the remark.

"'You-all camp down yere with a tumbler of Valley Tan,' says Enright, 'an' make yourse'f comfortable with my colleagues, while I goes an' consults with our Gretna Green outfit in the r'ar room.'

"Enright returns after a bit, an' his face has that air of se'f-satisfaction that goes with a gent who's playin' on velvet.

"'Your comin' son-in-law,' says Enright to old Glegg, 'defends himse'f from them charges as follows: He agrees to quit gamblin'; he says he lies a whole lot when he tells you-all he don't drink none; an' lastly, deplorin' "Toad" as a cognomen, an' explainin' that he don't assoome it of free choice but sort o' has it sawed off on him in he'pless infancy, he offers—you consentin' to the weddin'—to reorganise onder the name of "Benjamin Glegg Allen."'

"Son, this yere last proposal wins over old Glegg in a body. He not only withdraws all objections to the nuptials, but allows he'll make the pinfeather sport an' Abby full partners in the Sunflower. At this p'int, Enright notifies the preacher sharp that all depends on him; an' that excellent teacher at once acquits himse'f so that in two minutes Wolfville adds another successful weddin' to her list of triumphs.

"'It 'lustrates too,' says Enright, when two days later the weddin' party has returned to Tucson, an' Wolfville ag'in sinks to a normal state of slumbrous ease, 'it sort o' 'lustrates how open to argyments a gent is when once he's lost his weepons. Now if he isn't disarmed that time, my eloquence wouldn't have had no more effect on old Glegg than throwin' water on a drowned rat.'"

CHAPTER XVII.

The Clients of Aaron Green.

"AND so there were no lawyers in Wolfville?" I said. The Old Cattleman filled his everlasting pipe, lighted it, and puffed experimentally. There was a handful of wordless moments devoted to pipe. Then, as one satisfied of a smoky success, he turned attention to me and my remark.

"Lawyers in Wolfville?" he repeated. "Not in my day; none whatever! It's mighty likely though that some of 'em's done come knockin' along by now. Them jurists is a heap persistent, not to say diffoosive, an' soon or late they shore trails into every camp. Which we'd have had 'em among us long ago, but nacherally, an' as far as argyments goes, we turns 'em off. Se'f-preservation is a law of nacher, an' these maxims applies to commoonities as much as ever they does to gents personal. Wherefore, whenever we notices a law wolf scoutin' about an' tryin' to get the wind on us, we employs our talents for lyin', fills him up with fallacies, an' teaches him that to come to Wolfville is to put down his destinies on a dead kyard; an' he tharupon abandons whatever of plans he's harbourin' ag'in us, seein' nothin' tharin.

"It's jest before I leaves for the East when one of these coyotes crosses up with Old Man Enright in Tucson, an' submits the idee of his professional invasion of our camp.

"'Which I'm in the Oriental at the time,' says Enright, when he relates about his adventure, 'an' this maverick goes to jumpin' sideways at me in a friendly mood. Bein' I'm a easy-mannered sport with strangers, he has no trouble gettin' acquainted. At last he allows that he aims to pitch his teepee in Wolfville, hang out a shingle, an' plunge into joorisprudence. "I was thinkin'," says he, "of openin' a joint for the practice of law. As a condition prior advised by the barkeep, an' one which also recommends itse'f to me as dictated of the commonest proodence, I figgers on gainin' your views of these steps."

" " "You does well," I replies, "to consult me on them p'ints. I sees you're shore a jo-darter of a lawyer; for you handles the language like a mule-skinner does a blacksnake whip. But jest the same, don't for one moment think of breakin' in on Wolf-ville. That outfit don't practice law none; she practices facts. It offers no openin' for your game. Comin' to Wolfville onder any conditions is ever a movement of gravity, an onless a gent is out to chase cattle or dandle kyards or proposes to array himse'f in the ranks of commerce by foundin' a s'loon, Wolfville would not guarantee his footure any positive reward."

" " "Then I jest won't come a whole lot," says this law sharp. Whereupon we engages in mootual drinks an' disperses to our destinies.'

" 'What you tells this sport,' says Texas Thomp-

son, who's listenin' to Enright, 'echoes my sentiments exact. Anything to keep out law! It ain't
alone the jedgments for divorce which my wife
grabs off over in Laredo, but it comes to me as the
frootes of a experience which has been as wide as
it has been plenty soon, that law is only another
word for trouble in egreegious forms.'

"'So I decides,' retorts Enright. 'Still, I'm proud
to be endorsed by as good a jedge of public disorder
an' its preventives as Texas Thompson. Sech
approvals ever tends to stiffen a gent's play. As I
states, I reeverses this practitioner an' heads him
t'other way. Wolfville is the home of friendly confidence; the throne of yoonity an' fraternal peace.
It must not be jeopardised. We-all don't want to
incur no resks by abandonin' ourse'fs to real shore-
enough law. It would debauch us: we'd get plumb
locoed an' take to racin' wild an' cimarron up an'
down the range, an' no gent could foresee results.
It's better than even money, that with the advent
of a law sharp into our midst, historians of this
hamlet would begin their last chapter. They would
head her: " Wolfville's Last Days."

"'It's twenty years ago,' goes on Enright, 'while
I'm that season in Texas, that a sharp packs his
blankets into Yellow City an' puts it up he'll practice some law. No; he ain't wanted, but he never
does give no gent a chance to say so. He comes
trackin' in onannounced, an' the first we-all saveys,
thar's his sign a-swingin', an' ashoorin' the sports of
Yellow City of the presence of

AARON GREEN, Esq. ATTORNEY-AT-LAW.

"'Nobody gets excited; for while we agrees to prevail on him ultimately to shift his camp a heap, the sityooation don't call for nothin' preecipitate. In fact, the idee of him or any other besotted person turnin' loose that a-way in Yellow City, strikes us as loodicrous. Thar's nothing for a law-gent to do. I've met up with a heap of camps in my day; an' I've witnessed the work of many a vig'lance committee; but I'm yere to state that for painstakin' ardour an' a energy that never sleeps, the Stranglers of Yellow City is a even break with the best. They uses up a bale of half-inch rope a year; an' as for law an' order an' a scene of fragrant peace, that outfit is compar'ble only with flower gyardens on a quiet hazy August afternoon.

"'This Aaron Green who prounces thus on Yellow City, intendin' to foment litigations an' go ropin' 'round for fees, is plenty young; but he's that grave an' dignified that owls is hilarious to him. One after the other, he tackles us in a severe onmitigated way, an' shoves his professional kyard onto each an' tells him that whenever he feels ill-used to come a-runnin' an' have his rights preserved. Shore! the boys meets this law person half way. They drinks with him an' fills him up with licker an' fictions alternate, an' altogether regyards him as a mighty yoomerous prop'sition.

"'Also, observin' how tender he is, an' him takin' in their various lies like texts of holy writ, they names him "Easy Aaron." Which he don't look on "Easy Aaron" none too well as a title, an' insists

on bein' called "Jedge Green" or even "Squar'
Green." But Yellow City won't have it; she sticks
to "Easy Aaron"; an' as callin' down the entire
camp offers prospects full of fever an' oncertainty,
he at last passes up the insult an' while he stays
among us, pays no further heed.

"'Doorin' the weeks he harbours with us, a gen'ral
taste deevelops to hear this Easy Aaron's eloquence.
Thar's a delegation waits on him an' requests Easy
Aaron to come forth an' make a speech. We su'-
gests that he can yootilise the Burnt Boot Saloon as
a auditorium, an' offers as a subject "Texas: her
Glorious Past, her Glitterin' Present, an' her Trans-
cendent Footure!"

"'"Thar's a topic!" says Shoestring Griffith to
Easy Aaron—Shoestring is the cha'rman of the committee,—"thar's a burnin' topic for you! An'
if you-all will only come surgin' over to the Burnt
Boot right now while you're warm for the event, I
offers two to one you makes Cicero look like seven
cents."

"'But Easy Aaron waves 'em arrogantly away.
He declines to go barkin' at a knot. He says it'll
be soon enough to onbuckle an' swamp Yellow City
with a flood of eloquence when proper legal o'casion
onfolds.

"'In the room to the r'ar of the apartments where
this Easy Aaron holds forth as a practitioner, thar's
a farobank as is nacheral enough. It's about second
drink time in the afternoon, bein' a time of day
when the faro game is dead. A passel of con-

spirators, with Shoestring Griffith in the lead, goes to this room an' reelaxes into a game of draw. Easy Aaron can hear the flutter of the chips through the partition—the same bein' plenty thin—where he's camped like a spider in its web an' waitin' for some sport who needs law to show up. Easy Aaron listens careless an' indifferent to Shoestring an' his fellow blacklaigs as they deals an' antes an' raises an' rakes in pots, an' everybody mighty joobilant as is frequent over poker.

"'Of a suddent, roars an' yells an' reecriminations yoosurps the place of merriment. Then the guns! An' half the lead comes spittin' an' splittin' through that intervenin' partition like she's kyardboard. The bullets flies high enough to miss Easy Aaron, but low enough to invoke a gloomy frame of mind.

"' This yere artillery practice don't continyoo long before Yellow City descends on Shoestring an' his band of homicides ; an' when they've got 'em sorted out, thar's Billy Goodnight too defunct to skin, an' Shoestring Griffith does it.

"'Thar's no time lost; the Stranglers convenes in the Burnt Boot, an' exact jestice stands on expectant tiptoe for its prey. But Shoestring raises objections.

"" ' Which before ever you-all reptiles takes my innocent life," says Shoestring, " I wants a lawyer. I swings off in style or I don't swing. You hear me! send across for Easy Aaron. You can gamble, I'm going to interpose a defense."

" ' " That's but right," says Waco Anderson who's
the chief of the Stranglers. " Assembled as we be
to revenge the ontimely pluggin' of the late Billy
Goodnight, still this Shoestring may demand a even
deal. If some gent will ramble over an' round up
Easy Aaron, as Shoestring desires, it will be regyarded by the committee, an' this lynchin' can then
proceed."

" ' Easy Aaron is onearthed from onder his desk
where he's still quiled up, pale an' pantin', by virchoo of the bullets. Jim Wise, who goes for him,
explains that the shower is over ; an' also that he's
in enormous demand to save Shoestring for beefin'
Billy Goodnight. At this, Easy Aaron gets up an'
coughs 'round for a moment or two, recoverin' his
nerve ; then he buttons his surtoot, assoomes airs of
sagacity, tucks the Texas Statootes onder his arm,
reepairs to the Burnt Boot an' allows he's ready to
defend Shoestring from said charges.

" ' " But not onless my fees is paid in advance,"
says this Easy Aaron.

" ' At that, we-all passes the hat an' each chucks
in a white chip or two, an' when Waco Anderson
counts up results it shows wellnigh eighty-five
dollars. Easy Aaron shakes his head like it's
mighty small ; but he takes it an' casts himse'f
loose. An', gents, he's shore verbose ! He pelts
an' pounds that committee with a hailstorm of observations, ontil all they can do is set thar an' wag
their y'ears an' bat their eyes. Waco Anderson
himse'f allows, when discussin' said oration later,

that he ain't beheld nothin' so muddy an' so much since the last big flood on the Brazos.

"'After Easy Aaron holds forth for two hours, Waco preevails on him with a six-shooter to pause for breath. Waco's tried twenty times to get Easy Aaron to stop long enough to let the Stranglers get down a verbal bet, but that advocate declines to be restrained. He treats Waco's efforts with scorn an' rides him down like he, Easy Aaron, is a bunch of cattle on a stampede. Thar's no headin' or holdin' him ontil Waco, in desperation, takes to tyrannisin' at him with his gun.

"'"It's this," says Waco, when Easy Aaron's subdooed. "If the eminent gent will quit howlin' right yere an' never another yelp, the committee is willin' to throw this villain Shoestring loose. Every one of us is a slave to dooty, but we pauses before personal deestruction in a awful form. Billy Goodnight is gone; ondoubted his murderer should win the doom meted out for sech atrocities; but dooty or no dooty, this committee ain't called on to be talked to death in its discharge. Yellow City makes no sech demands of its servants; wherefore, I repeats, that if this Easy Aaron sits mute where he is, we agrees to cut Shoestring's bonds an' restore him to that freedom whereof he makes sech florid use."'

"'At this, Easy Aaron stands up, puffs out his chest, bows to Waco an' the others, an' evolves 'em a patronisin' gesture signifyin' that their bluff is called. Shoestring Griffith is saved.

" 'Doorin' the subsequent line-up at the bar which concloods the ceremonies, Easy Aaron waxes indignant an' is harrowed to observe Billy Goodnight imbibin' with the rest.

" ' "I thought you-all dead!" says Easy Aaron, in tones of wrathful reproach.

" ' "Which I was dead," says Billy, sort o' apol'getic, "but them words of fire brings me to."

" 'Easy Aaron don't make no answer, but as he jingles the fee the sour look relaxes.

" 'As I remarks, Easy Aaron ain't with us over long. Yellow City is that much worsé off than Wolfville that she has a little old 'doby calaboose that's been built since the old Mexico days. Thar's no shore-enough jedge an' jury ever comes to Yellow City ; an' if the kyards was so run that we has a captive which the Stranglers deems beneath 'em, he would be drug 'way over yonder to some county seat. It's but fair to say that no sech contretemps presents itse'f up to the advent of Easy Aaron ; an' while thar's now an' then a small accoomulation of felons doorin' sech seasons as the boys is off on the ranges or busy with the round-ups, thar never fails to come a clean-up in plenty of time. The Stranglers comes back ; jestice resoomes her sway, an' the calaboose is ag'in as empty as a church.

" 'It befalls, however, that doorin' the four or five weeks to follow the acquittal of that homicide Shoestring, an' while Waco Anderson an' a quorum of the committee is away teeterin' about in their own affairs, the calaboose gets filled up with two white men and either four or five Mexicans—I can't say the last for shore, as I ain't got a good mem'ry for Mexicans. These parties is held for divers malefactions from shootin' up a Greaser dance-hall to stealin' a cow over on the Honeymoon.

"'To his joy, Easy Aaron is reetained to defend this crim'nal herd. It's shore pleasant to watch him! I never sees the sport who's that proudly content. Easy Aaron visits these yere clients of his every day; an' when he has time, he walks out onto the plains so far that you-all can't hear his tones, an' rehearses the speeches he's aimin' to make when he gets them cut-throats before a jury. We-all could see him prancin' up an' down, tossin' his hands' an' all in the most locoed way. As I states, he's too far off to be heard none; but he's in plain view from the front windows of the Burnt Boot, an' we-all finds them antics plumb divertin.'

"'"These cases," says Easy Aaron to me, for he's that happy an' enthoosiastic he's got to open up on some gent; "these cases is bound to fix my fame as the modern Demosthenes. You knows how eloquent I am about Shoestring? That won't be a marker to the oration I'll frame up for these mis-creants in the calaboose. For why? Shorestring's time I ain't organised; also, I'm more or less shook by the late bullets buzzin'an' hummin' like a passel of bloo-bottle flies about my office. But now will be different. I'll be ready; an' I'll be in a cool frenzy,

the same bein' a mood which is excellent, partic'lar
if a gent is out to break records for rhetoric.
I shore regyards them malefactors as so many
rungs for my clamberin' up the ladder of fame."
An' with that this Easy Aaron goes pirootin' forth
upon the plains ag'in to resoome his talkin' at a
mark.

"'It's mebby a week after this exultation of
Easy Aaron's, an' Waco Anderson an' the others
is in from the ranges. Yellow City is onusual
vivacious an' lively. You-all may jedge of the
happy prosperity of local feelin' when I assoores
you that the average changed in at farobank each
evenin' ain't less than twenty thousand dollars.
As for Easy Aaron, he's goin' about in clouds of
personal an' speshul delight. It's now crowdin'
along towards the time when him an' his clients will
adjourn over to that county seat an' give Easy
Aaron the opportoonity to write his name on the
deathless calendars of fame.

"'But black disapp'intment gets Easy Aaron
squar' in the door. One morning he reepairs to
the calaboose to consult with the felons on whose
interests he's ridin' herd. Horror seizes him ; he
finds the cells as vacant as a echo.

"'"Where's these clients?" asks Easy Aaron,
while his face grows white.

"'"Vamosed !" says the Mexican who carries
the calaboose keys; an' with that he turns in mighty
composed, to roll a cigarette.

"'"Vamoosed, where at?" pursoos Easy Aaron.

"'"*Por el inferno !*" says the Mexican; he's got his cigarette lighted, an' is puffin' as contented as hoss-thieves. "See thar, *Amigo !*" goes on the Greaser, indicatin' down the street.

"'Easy Aaron gazes where the Mexican p'ints, an' his heart turns to water. Thar swayin' an' swingin' like tassels in the mornin' breeze, an' each as dead as Gen'ral Taylor, he beholds his entire docket hangin' to the windmill. Easy Aaron approaches an' counts 'em up. Which they're all thar! The Stranglers shorely makes a house cleanin'. As Easy Aaron looks upon them late clients, he wrings his hands.

"'"Thar hangs fame!" says Easy Aaron; "thar hangs my chance of eminence! That eloquence, wherewith my heart is freighted, an' which would have else declar'd me the Erskine of the Brazos, is lynched with my clients." Then wheelin' on Waco Anderson who strolls over, Easy Aaron demands plenty f'rocious: "Whoever does this dastard deed?"

"'"Which this agitated sport," observes Waco coldly to Shoestring Griffith, who comes loungin' up likewise, "asks whoever does these yere dastard deeds! Does you-all recall the fate, Shoestring, of the last misguided shorthorn who gives way to sech a query? My mem'ry is never ackerate as to trifles, an' I'm confoosed about whether he's shot or hung or simply burned alive."

"'"That prairie dog is hanged a lot," says Shoestring. "Which the boys was goin' to burn him, but on its appearin' that he puts the question more in ignorance than malice, they softens on second thought to that degree they merely gets a rope, adds him to the windmill with the others, an' lets the matter drop."

" ' Easy Aaron don't crowd his explorations further. He can see thar's what you-all might call a substratum of seriousness to the observations of Waco an' Shoestring, an' his efforts to solve the mystery that disposes of every law case he has, an' leaves him to begin life anew, comes to a halt!

" ' But it lets pore Easy Aaron out. He borrys a hoss from the corral, packs the Texas Statootes an' his extra shirt in the war-bags, an' with that the only real law wolf who ever makes his lair in Yellow City, p'ints sadly no'thward an' is seen no more. As he's about to ride away, Easy Aaron turns to me. He's sort o' got the notion I ain't so bad as Waco, Shoestring, an' the rest. " I shall never return," says Easy Aaron, an' he shakes his head plenty disconsolate. " Genius has no show in Yellow City. This outfit hangs a gent's clients as fast as ever he's retained an' offers no indoocements— opens no opportoonities, to a ambitious barrister." ' "

CHAPTER XVIII.

Colonel Sterett Relates Marvels.

"As I asserts frequent," observed the Old Cattle-man, the while delicately pruning a bit of wood he'd picked up on his walk, "the funds of information, gen'ral an' speshul, which Colonel William Greene Sterett packs about would freight a eight-mule team. It's even money which of 'em saveys the most, him or Doc Peets. For myself, after careful study, I inclines to the theery that Colonel Sterett's knowledge is the widest, while Peets's is the most exact. Both is college gents; an' yet they differs as to the valyoo of sech sem'naries. The Colonel coppers colleges, while Peets plays 'em to win.

"'Them temples of learnin',' says the Colonel, 'is a heap ornate; but they don't make good.' This is doubted by Peets.

"One evenin' Dan Boggs, who's allers tantalisin' 'round askin' questions—it looks like a sleepless cur'osity is proned into Dan—ropes at Peets concernin' this topic :

"'Whatever do they teach in colleges, Doc?' asks Dan.

"'They teaches all of the branches,'' retorts Peets.

"'An' none of the roots,' adds Colonel Sterett,

'as a cunnin' Yank once remarks on a o'casion sim'lar.'

" No, the Colonel an' Peets don't go lockin' horns in these differences. Both is a mighty sight too well brought up for that; moreover, they don't allow to set the camp no sech examples. They entertains too high a regyard for each other to take to pawin' about pugnacious, verbal or otherwise.

" The Colonel's information is as wide flung as a buzzard's wing. Thar's mighty few mysteries he ain't authorised to eloocidate. An' from time to time, accordin' as the Colonel's more or less in licker, he enlightens Wolfville on a multitoode of topics. Which the Colonel is a profound eddicational inflooence; that's whatever!

" It's one evenin' an' the moon is swingin' high in the bloo-black heavens an' looks like a gold doorknob to the portals of the eternal beyond. Texas Thompson fixes his eyes tharon, meditative an' pensive, an' then he wonders:

"' Do you-all reckon, now, that folks is livin' up thar?'

"' Whatever do you think yourse'f, Colonel?' says Enright, passin' the conundrum over to the editor of the *Coyote*. 'Do you think thar's folks on the moon?'

"' Do I think thar's folks on the moon?' repeats the Colonel as ca'mly confident as a club flush. ' I don't think,—I knows.'

"' Whichever is it then?' asks Dan Boggs, whose ha'r already begins to bristle, he's that inquisitive.

'Simply takin' a ignorant shot in the dark that away, I says, " No." That moon looks like a mighty lonesome loominary to me.'

" ' Jest the same,' retorts the Colonel, an' he's a lot dogmatic, ' that planet's fairly speckled with people. An' if some gent will recall the errant fancies of Black Jack to a sense of dooty, I'll onfold how I knows.

" ' It's when I'm crowdin' twenty,' goes on the Colonel, followin' the ministrations of Black Jack, ' an' I'm visitin' about the meetropolis of Looeyville. I've been sellin' a passel of runnin' hosses ; an' as I rounds up a full peck of doubloons for the fourteen I disposes of, I'm feelin' too contentedly cunnin' to live. It's evenin' an' the moon is shinin' same as now. I jest pays six bits for my supper at the Galt House, an' lights a ten cent seegyar—Oh! I has the bridle off all right !—an' I'm romancin' leesurly along the street, when I encounters a party who's ridin' herd on one of these yere telescopes, the same bein' p'inted at the effulgent moon. Gents, she's shorely a giant spy-glass, that instroment is ; bigger an' longer than the smokestack of any steamboat between Looeyville an' Noo Orleans. She's swung on a pa'r of shears ; each stick a cl'ar ninety foot of Norway pine. As I goes pirootin' by, this gent with the telescope pipes briskly up.

" ' " Take a look at the moon ? "

" ' " No," I replies, wavin' him off some haughty, for that bag of doubloons has done puffed me up. " No, I don't take no interest in the moon."

" 'As I'm comin' back, mebby it's a hour later, this astronomer is still swingin' an' rattlin' with the queen of night. He pitches his lariat ag'in an' now he fastens.

" ' " You-all better take a look ; they're havin' the time of their c'reers up thar."

" ' "Whatever be they doin' ? "

" ' " Tellin' wouldn't do no good," says the savant ; " it's one of them rackets a gent has to see to savey."

" ' " What's the ante ? " I asks, for the fires of my cur'osity begins to burn.

" ' " Four bits! An' considerin' the onusual doin's goin' for'ard, it's cheaper than corn whiskey."

" 'No ; I don't stand dallyin' 'round, tryin' to beat this philosopher down in his price. That ain't my style. When I'm ready to commit myse'f to a enterprise, I butts my way in, makes good the tariff, an' no delays. Tharfore, when this gent names four bits, I onpouches the *dinero* an' prepares to take a astronomic peek.

" ' " How long do I gaze for four bits ? " I asks, battin' my right eye to get it into piercin' shape.

" ' " Go as far as you likes," retorts the philoso•pher ; " thar's no limit."

" 'Gents,' says the Colonel, pausin' to renoo his Valley Tan, while Dan an' Texas an' even Old Man Enright hitches their cha'rs a bit nearer, the interest is that intense ; 'gents, you-all should have took a squint with me through them lenses. Which if you enjoys said privilege, you can gamble Dan an'

Texas wouldn't be camped 'round yere none to-
night, exposin' their ignorance an' lettin' fly croode
views concernin' astronomy. That telescope actooally brings the moon plumb into Kaintucky ;—
brings her within the reach of all. You could
stretch to her with your hand, she's that clost.'

" ' But is thar folks thar ? ' says Dan, who's excited by the Colonel's disclosures. 'Board the
kyard, Colonel, an' don't hold us in suspense.'

" ' Folks ! ' returns the Colonel. ' I wishes I has
two-bit pieces for every one of 'em ! The face of
that orb is simply festered with folks ! She teems
with life ; ant-hills on election day means desertion
by compar'son. Thar's thousands an' thousands of
people, mobbin' about indiscrim'nate; I sees 'em as
near an' plain as I sees Dan.'

" ' An' whatever be they doin' ? ' asks Dan.

" ' They're pullin' off a hoss race,' says the Colonel, lookin' steady in Dan's eye. ' An' you hears
me ! I never sees sech bettin' in my life.'

" Nacherally we-all feels refreshed with these experiences of Colonel Sterett's, for as Enright observes, it's by virchoo of sech casooal chunks of
information that a party rounds out a eddication.

" ' It ain't what a gent learns in schools,' says
Enright, ' that broadens him an' stiffens his mental
grip ; it's knowledge like this yere moon story from
trustworthy sources that augments him an' fills him
full. Go on, Colonel, an' onload another marvel
or two. You-all must shore have witnessed a
heap ! '

" ' Them few sparse facts touchin' the moon,' returns Colonel Sterett, ' cannot be deemed wonders
in any proper sense. They're merely interestin'
details which any gent gets onto who brings science
to his aid. But usin' the word " wonders," I does
once blunder upon a mir'cle which still waits to be
explained. That's a shore-enough marvel! An' to
this day, all I can state is that I sees it with these
yere eyes.'

" ' Let her roll ! ' says Texas Thompson. ' That
moon story prepares us for anything.'

" ' Texas,' observes the Colonel, a heap severe,
' I'd hate to feel that your observations is the jeerin'
offspring of distrust.'

" ' Me distrust ! ' replies Texas, hasty to squar'
himse'f. ' I'd as soon think of distrustin' that
Laredo divorce of my former he'pmeet ! An' as
the sheriff drives off two hundred head of my cattle by way of alimony, I deems the fact of that
sep'ration as fixed beyond cavil. No, Colonel, you
has my fullest confidence. I'd go doubtin' the
evenhanded jestice of Cherokee's faro game quicker
than distrustin' you.'

" ' An' I'm present to say,' returns the Colonel
mighty complacent, ' that I looks on sech assoor-
ances as complimentary. To show which I onhesitatin'ly reels off that eepisode to which I
adverts.

" ' I'm only a child ; but I retains my impressions
as sharp cut an' cl'ar as though she happens yester-
day. It's a time when one of these legerdemain

sharps pastes up his bills in our village an' lets on
he'll give a show in Liberty Hall on the comin'
Saturday evenin'. An' gents, to simply read of the
feats he threatens to perform would loco you!
Besides, thar's a picture of Satan, black an' fiery an'
frightful, where he's he'pin' this gifted person to
foist said mir'cles upon the age. I don't exagger-
ate none when I asserts that the moment our
village gets its eye on these three-sheets it comes to
a dead halt.

" 'Old Squar' Alexanders is the war chief of the
hamlet, an' him an' the two other selectmen c'llects
themse'fs over their toddies an' canvasses whether
they permits this wizard to give his fiendish exhibitions in our midst. They has it pro an' con ontil the thirteenth drink, when Squar' Alexanders
who's ag'in the wizard brings the others to his
views; an' as they staggers forth from the tavern
it's the yoonanimous decision to bar that Satan-aided
show.

" " " Witches, wizards, elves, gnomes, bull-beg-
gars, fiends, an' devils is debarred the Bloo Grass
Country," says Squar' Alexanders, speakin' for
himse'f an' his fellow selectmen, " an' they're not
goin' to be allowed to hold their black an' sulphur-
ous mass meetin's yere."

" ' It comes Saturday evenin' an' the necromancer
is in the tavern eatin' his supper. Shore ! he looks
like common folks at that! Squar' Alexanders is
waitin' for him in the bar. When he shows up,
carelessly pickin' his teeth, it's mebby half a hour

before the show, Squar' Alexanders don't fritter away no time, but rounds up the wizard.

"'"Thar's no show which has Satan for a silent partner goin' to cut itse'f loose in this village," says Squar' Alexanders.

"'"What's this talk about Satan?" responds the wizard. "I don't savey no more about Satan than I does about you."

"'"Look at them bills," says Squar' Alexanders, an' he p'ints to where one is hangin' on the bar-room wall. It gives a picture of the foul fiend, with pitchfork, spear-head tail an' all. "Whatever do you call that?"

"'"That's a bluff," says the wizard. "If Kaintucky don't get tangled up with Satan ontil I imports him to her fertile shores, you cimmarons may regyard yourse'fs as saved."

"'"Be you-all goin' to do the sundry deeds you sets forth in the programmes?" asks Squar' Alexanders after a pause.

"'"Which I shorely be!" says the wizard, "an' if I falls down or fails you can call me a ab'litionist."

"'"Then all I has to say is this," returns Squar' Alexanders; "no gent could do them feats an' do 'em on the level. You'd have to have the he'p of demons to pull em off. An' that brings us back to my first announcement; an' stranger, your show don't go."

"'At this the wizard lets on he's lost patience with Squar' Alexanders an' declares he won't discuss with him no more.　Also, he gives it out that, Satan, or no Satan, he'll begin to deal his game at eight o'clock.

"'"Very well!" rejoins Squar' Alexanders. "Since you refooses to be warned I shall shore instruct the constable to collar you on the steps of Liberty Hall." As he says this, Squar' Alexanders p'ints across to Chet Kishler, who's the constable, where he's restin' himse'f in front of Baxter's store.

"'This yere Chet is a giant an' clost onto eight foot high. It's a warm evenin', an' as the wizard glances over at Chet, he notices how that offishul is lazily fannin' himse'f with a barn-door which he's done lifted off the hinges for that coolin' purpose. The wizard don't say nothin', but he does turn a mite pale; he sees with half a eye that Satan himse'f would be he'pless once Chet gets his two paws on him.　However, he assoomes that he's out to give the show as per schedoole.

"'It's makin' toward eight when the wizard lights a seegyar, drinks four fingers of Willow Run, an' goes p'intin' out for Liberty Hall.　Chet gets up, hangs the barn door back on its hinges, an' sa'nters after.　Squar' Alexanders has posted Chet as to his dooties an' his orders is to prounce on the necro-mancer if he offers to enter the hall.　That's how the cavalcade lines up: first, the wizard; twenty foot behind is Chet; an' twenty foot behind our constable comes the public in a body.

"'About half way to Liberty Hall the wizard begins to show nervous an' oncertain.　He keeps

lookin' back at Chet; an' even in my childish simplicity I sees that he ain't pleased with the outlook.
At last he weakens an' abandons his idee of a show.
Gents, as I fills my glass, I asks you-all however now
do you reckon that wizard beats a retreat?'

"Thar's no reply. Dan, Texas, an' the others,
while Colonel Sterett acquires his licker, shakes
their heads dumbly as showin' they gives it up.

"'Which you'd shorely never guess!' retorts the
Colonel, wipin' his lips. 'Of a sudden, this wizard
tugs somethin' outen his pocket that looks like a
ball of kyarpet-rags. Holdin' one end, quick as
thought he tosses the ball of kyarpet-rags into the
air. It goes straight up ontil lost to view, onwindin'
itse'f in its flight because of the wizard holdin' on.

"'Gents, that ball of kyarpet-rags never does
come down no more! An' it's all done as easy as
a set-lock rifle! The wizard climbs the danglin'
string of kyarpet-rags, hand over hand; then he
drifts off an' up'ards ontil he don't look bigger
than a bumble-bee; an' then he's lost in the gatherin' shadows of the Jooly night.

"'Squar' Alexanders, Chet, an' the village stands
strainin' their eyes for twenty minutes. But the
wizard's vamosed; an' at last, when each is convinced tharof, the grown folks led by Squar'
Alexanders reepairs back into the tavern an' takes
another drink.'

"'That's a mighty marvellous feat your necro-
mancer performs, Colonel,' remarks Enright, an' the
old chief is grave as becomes the Colonel's revela-

tions; 'he's a shore-enough wonder-worker, that wizard is!'

"But I ain't got to the wonders none as yet,' ree-monstrates the Colonel, who spunks up a bit peevish for him. 'An' from the frequent way wherein I'm interrupted, it don't look much like I will. Goin' sailin' away into darklin' space with that ball of enchanted kyarpet-rags,—that ain't the sooper-nacheral part at all! Shore! ondoubted it's some hard to do as a feat, but still thar's other feachers which from the standp'int of the marvellous overpowers it like four kings an' a ace. That wonder is this: It's quarter to eight when the wizard takes his flight by means of the kyarpet-rags. Gents, at eight o'clock sharp the same evenin' he walks on the stage an' gives a show at St. Looey, hundreds of miles away.' "

CHAPTER XIX.

The Luck of Hardrobe.

"WHICH I tells this yere narrative first, back in one of them good old Red Light evenin's when it's my turn to talk."

The Old Cattleman following this remark, considered me for a moment in silence. I had myself been holding the floor of discussion in a way both rambling and pointless for some time. I had spoken of the national fortune of Indians, their superstitions, their ill-luck, and other savage subjects various and sundry. My discourse had been remarkable perhaps for emphasis rather than accuracy; and this too held a purpose. It was calculated to rouse my raconteur and draw him to a story. Did what I say lack energy, he might go to sleep in his chair; he had done this more than once when I failed of interest. Also, if what I told were wholly true and wanting in ripple of romantic error, even though my friend did me the compliment of wakefulness, he would make no comment. Neither was he likely to be provoked to any recital of counter experiences. At last, however, he gave forth the observation which I quote above and I saw that I had brought him out. I became at once wordless and, lighting a cigar, leaned back to listen.

"As I observes," he resumed, following a con-
siderable pause which I was jealous to guard against
word or question of my own; "I tells this tale to
Colonel Sterett, Old Man Enright, an' the others
one time when we're restin' from them Wolfville
labours of ours an' renooin' our strength with nosepaint in the Red Light bar. Jest as you does now,
Dan Boggs takes up this question of luck where
Cherokee Hall abandons it, an' likewise the subject
of savages where Texas Thompson lays 'em down,
an' after conj'inin' the two in fashions I deems a
heap weak, allows that luck is confined strictly to
the paleface; aborigines not knowin' sufficient to
become the target of vicissitoodes, excellent or
otherwise.

"'Injuns is too ignorant to have what you-all
calls "luck,"' says Dan. 'That gent who's to be
affected either up or down by "luck" has got to
have some mental cap'bilities. An' as Injuns don't
answer sech deescriptions, they ain't no more open
to "luck" than to enlight'ment. "Luck" an' Injuns when took together, is preepost'rous! It's like
talkin' of a sycamore tree havin' luck. Gents, it
ain't in the deck!' An' tharupon Dan seals his
views by demandin' of Black Jack the bottle with
glasses all 'round.

"'When it comes to that, Boggs,' says Colonel
Sterett, as he does Dan honour in four fingers of
Valley Tan, 'an' talkin' of luck, I'm yere to offer
odds that the most poignant hard-luck story on
the list is the story of Injuns as a race. An' I

won't back-track their game none further than Co-
lumbus at that. The savages may have found life
a summer's dream prior to the arrival of that Eytal-
ian mariner an' the ornery Spainiards he surrounds
himse'f with. Bnt from the looks of the tabs, the
deal since then has gone ag'inst 'em. The Injuns
don't win once. White folks, that a-way, is of
themse'fs bad luck incarnate to Injuns. The savage never so much as touches 'em or listens to 'em
or imitates 'em, but he rots down right thar. Which
the pale-face shorely kills said Injuns on the nest!
as my old grand-dad used to say.'

"'When I recalls the finish of Hardrobe,' I remarks, sort o' cuttin' into the argyment, the same
bein' free an' open to all, ' an' I might add by way
of a gratootity in lines of proof, the finish of his
boy, Bloojacket, I inclines to string my chips with
Colonel Sterett.'

"'Give us the details concernin' this Hardrobe,' says Doc Peets. 'For myse'f, I'm prone
an' eager to add to my information touchin' Injuns
at every openin'.'

"As Enright an' the rest makes expression sim'-
lar, I proceeds to onbuckle. I don't claim much
for the tale neither. Still, I wouldn't copper it
none for it's the trooth, an' the trooth should allers
be played ' open ' every time. I'll tell you-all this
Hardrobe story as I onfolds it to them."

It was here my friend began looking about with
a vaguely anxious eye. I saw his need and pressed
the button.

"I was aimin' to summon my black boy, Tom," he said.

When a moment later his favourite decanter appeared in the hands of one of the bar-boys of the hostelry, who placed it on a little table at his elbow and withdrew, the necessity for "Tom" seemed to disappear, and recurring to Hardrobe, he went on.

"Hardrobe is a Injun—a Osage buck an' belongs to the war clan of his tribe. He's been eddicated East an' can read in books, an' pow-wows American mighty near as flooent as I does myse'f. An' on that last p'int I'll take a chance that I ain't tongue-tied neither.

"Which this yere is a long time ago. Them is days when I'm young an' lithe an' strong. I can heft a pony an' I'm six foot two in my moccasins. No, I ain't so tall by three inches now; old age shortens a gent up a whole lot.

"My range is on the south bank of Red River—over on the Texas side. Across on the no'th is the Nation—what map folks call the 'Injun Territory.' In them epocks we experiences Injuns free an' frequent, as our drives takes us across the Nation from south to no'th the widest way. We works over the old Jones an' Plummer trail, which thoroughfare I alloodes to once or twice before. I drives cattle over it an' I freights over it,—me an' my eight-mule team. An' I shorely knows where all the grass an' wood an' water is from the Red River to the Flint Hills.

"Speakin' of the Jones an' Plummer trail, I once

hears a dance-hall girl who volunteers some songs over in a Tucson hurdygurdy, an' that maiden sort o' dims my sights some. First, she gives us *The Dying Ranger*, the same bein' enough of itse'f to start a sob or two; speshul when folks is, as Colonel Sterett says, 'a leetle drinkin'.' Then when the public clamours for more she sings something which begins:

" ' Thar's many a boy who once follows the herds,
　On the Jones an' Plummer trail ;
　Some dies of drink an' some of lead,
　An' some over kyards, an' none in bed ;
　But they're dead game sports, so with naught but good words,
　We gives 'em " Farewell an' hail." ' "

" Son, this sonnet brings down mem'ries ; and they so stirs me I has to *vamos* that hurdygurdy to keep my emotions from stampedin' into tears. Shore, thar's soft spots in me the same as in other gents ; an' that melody a-makin' of references to the old Jones an' Plummer days comes mighty clost to meltin' everything about me but my guns an' spurs.

" This yere cattle business ain't what it used to be ; no more is cow-punchers. Things is gettin' effete. These day it's a case of chutes an' brandin' pens an' wire fences an' ten-mile pastures, an' thar's so little ropin' that a boy don't have practice enough to know how to catch his pony.

" In the times I'm dreamin' of all this is different. I recalls how we frequent works a month with a beef herd, say of four thousand head, out on the stark an' open plains, ropin' an' throwin' an' runnin' a road-brand onto 'em. Thar's a dozen different range brands in the bunch, mebby, and we needs a road-brand common to 'em all, so in case of stampedes on our trip to the no'th we knows our cattle ag'in an' can pick 'em out from among the local cattle which they takes to minglin' with. It's shorely work, markin' big strong steers that–away! Throwin' a thousand-pound longhorn with a six hundred-pound cayouse is tellin' on all involved an' a gent who's pitchin' his rope industrious will wear down five broncos by sundown.

"It's a sharp winter an' cattle dies that fast they simply defies the best efforts of ravens an' coyotes to get away with the supply. It's been blowin' a blizzard of snow for weeks. The gales is from the no'th an' they lashes the plains from the Bad Lands to the Rio Grande. When the storm first prounces on the cattle up yonder in the Yellowstone country, the he'pless beasts turns their onprotestin' tails and begins to drift. For weeks, as I remarks, that tempest throws itse'f loose, an' night an' day, what cattle keeps their feet an' lives, comes driftin' on.

"Nacherally the boys comes with 'em. Their winter sign-camps breaks up an' the riders turns south with the cattle. No, they can't do nothin'; you-all couldn't turn 'em or hold 'em or drive 'em back while the storm lasts. But it's the dooty of the punchers to keep abreast of their brands an' be thar the moment the blizzard abates.

"It's shore a spectacle! For a wild an' tossin'

front of five hundred miles, from west to east, the storm-beat herds comes driftin'. An' ridin' an' sw'arin' an' plungin' about comes with 'em the boys on their broncos. They don't have nothin' more'n the duds on their backs, an' mebby their saddle blankets an' slickers. But they kills beef to eat as they needs it, an' the ponies paws through the snow for grass, an' they exists along all right. For all those snow-filled, wind-swept weeks they're ridin' an' cussin'. They comes spatterin' through the rivers, an' swoopin' 'an' whoopin' over the divides that lays between. They crosses the Heart an' the Cannon Ball an' the Cheyenne an' the White an' the Niobrara an' the Platte an' the Republican an' the Solomon an' the Smoky an' the Arkansaw, to say nothin' of the hundreds of forks an' branches which flows an' twines an' twists between; an' final, you runs up on boys along the Canadian who's come from the Upper Missouri. An' as for cattle! it looks like it's one onbroken herd from Fort Elliot to where the Canadian opens into the Arkansaw!

"The chuck waggons of a thousand brands ain't two days behind the boys, an' by no time after that blizzard simmers, thar's camp-fires burnin' an' blinkin' between the Canadian an' the Red all along from the Choctaw country as far west as the Panhandle. Shore, every cow-puncher makes for the nearest smoke, feeds up an' recooperates; and then he with the others begins the gatherin' of the cattle an' the slow northern drive of the return. Which the spring overtakes 'em an' passes 'em on it's way

to the no'th, an' the grass is green an' deep before
ever they're back on their ranges ag'in.

"It's a great ride, says you? Son, I once attends
where a lecture sharp holds forth as to Napoleon's
retreat from Moscow. As was the proper thing I
sets silent through them hardships. But I could, if
I'm disposed to become a disturbin' element or
goes out to cut loose cantankerous an' dispootatious
in another gent's game, have showed him the French
experiences that Moscow time is Sunday school excursions compared with these trips the boys makes
when on the breath of that blizzard they swings
south with their herds. Them yooths, some of
'em, is over eight hundred miles from their home-
ranch; an' she s the first an only time I ever meets
up with a Yellowstone brand on the Canadian.

"You-all can put down a bet I'm no idle an' listless looker-on that blizzard time; an' I grows speshul active at the close. It behooves us Red River
gents of cattle to stir about. The wild hard-ridin'
knight-errants of the rope an' spur who cataracts
themse'fs upon us with their driftin' cattle doorin'
said tempest looks like they're plenty cap'ble of
drivin' our steers no'th with their own, sort o'
makin' up the deeficiencies ⁻{ the storm.

"I brands over four tho sand calves the spring
before, which means I has at least twenty thousand
head,—or five times what I brands—skallihootin'
an' hybernatin' about the ranges. An' bein' as you-
all notes some strong on cattle, an' not allowin'
none for them Yellowstone adventurers to drive any

of 'em no'th, I've got about 'leven outfits at work,
overhaulin' the herds an' round-ups, an' ridin' 'round
an' through 'em, weedin' out my brand an' throwin'
'em back on my Red River range. I has to do it,
or our visitin' Yellowstone guests would have stole
me pore as Job's turkey.

"Whatever is a ' outfit' you asks? It's a range
boss, a chuck waggon with four mules an' a range
cook, two hoss hustlers to hold the ponies, .eight
riders an' a bunch of about seventy ponies—say
seven to a boy. These yere 'leven outfits I speaks
of is scattered east an' west mebby she's a hundred
miles along the no'th fringe of my range, a-combin'
an' a-searchin' of the bunches an' cuttin' out all
specimens of my brand when found. For myse'f,
personal, I'm cavortin' about on the loose like,
stoppin' some nights at one camp an' some nights
at another, keepin' cases on the deal.

"It's at one of my camps one evenin' when I
crosses up first with this yere Hardrobe. His boy,
Bloojacket, is with him. Hardrobe himse'f is mebby
goin' on fifty, while Bloojacket ain't more'n say
twenty-one. Shore, they're out for cattle, too ;
them savages has a heap of cattle, an' since they
finds their brands an' bunches same as the rest of us
all tangled up with the Yellowstone aliens doorin'
the blizzard, Hardrobe an' his boy Bloojacket rides
up an' asks can they work partners with a outfit of
mine.

"As I explains previous I'm averse to Injuns,
but this Hardrobe is a onusual Injun ; an' as he's

settin' in ag'inst a stiff game the way things is
mixed up, an' bein' only him an' his boy he's too
weak to protect himse'f, I yields consent, I yields
the more pleasant for fear,—since I drives through
the Osage country now an' then—this Hardrobe an'
his heir plays even by stampedin' my cattle some
evenin' if I don't.   Thar's nothin'like a dash of se'f-
interest to make a gent urbane, an' so I invites
Hardrobe an' Bloojacket to make my camp their
headquarters like I'd been yearnin' for the chance.

"As you-all must have long ago tracked up on the
information, it's sooperfluous for me to su'gest that
a gent gets used to things.   Moreover he gets used
frequent to things that he's born with notions
ag'inst; an' them aversions will simmer an' subside
ontil he's friendly with folks he once honed to shoot
on sight.   It turns out that a-way about me an' this
Hardrobe an' his boy Bloojacket.   What he'ps, no
doubt, is they're capar'soned like folks, with big hats,
bloo shirts, trousers, cow-laiggin's, boots an' spurs,
fit an' ready to enter a civilised parlour at the
drop of the handkerchief.   Ceasin' to rope for
reasons, however, it's enough to say these savages
an' me waxes as thick as m'lasses.   Both of 'em's
been eddicated at some Injun school which the gov'-
ment—allers buckin' the impossible, the gov'ment
is,—upholds in it's vain endeavours to turn red into
white an' make folks of a savage.

"Bloojacket is down from the Bad Land country
himself not long prior, bein' he's been servin' his
Great Father as one of Gen'ral Crook's scouts in the

Sittin' Bull campaign. This young Bloojacket,—
who's bubblin' over with sperits—has a heap of interestin' stories about the 'Grey Fox.' It's doo to
Bloojacket to say he performs them dooties of his
as a scout like a clean-strain sport, an' quits an'
p'ints back for the paternal camp of Hardrobe in high
repoote. Thar's one feat of fast hard ridin' that
Injun performs, which I hears from others, an' which
you-all might not find oninterestin' if I saws it onto
you.

"Merritt with three hundred cavalry marches
twenty-five miles one mornin'. Thar's forty Injun
scouts along, among 'em this Bloojacket; said
copper-hued auxiliaries bein' onder the command
of Gen'ral Stanton, as game an' good a gent as ever
packs a gun. It's at noon; Merritt an' his outfit
camps at the Rawhide Buttes. Thar's a courier
from Crook overtakes 'em. He says that word
comes trailin' in that the Cheyennes at the Red
Cloud agency is makin' war medicine an' about to
go swarmin' off to hook up with Sittin' Bull an'
Crazy Hoss in the Sioux croosades. Crook tells
Merritt to detach a band of his scouts to go flutterin' over to Red Cloud an' take a look at the
Cheyennes's hand.

"Stanton tells off four of his savages an' lines
out with them for the Red Cloud agency; Bloo
jacket bein' one. From the Rawhide Buttes to
the Red Cloud agency is one hundred even
miles as a bullet travels. What makes it more
impressive, them one hundred miles is across a

trailless country, the same bein' as rocky as Red Dog whiskey an' rough as the life story of a mule. Which Stanton, Bloojacket an' the others makes her in twelve hours even, an' comes up, a crust of dust an' sweat, to the Red Cloud agency at midnight sharp. The Cheyennes has already been gone eight hours over the Great Northern trail.

"Stanton, who's a big body of a man an' nacherally tharfore some road-weary, camps down the moment he's free of the stirrups an' writes a letter on the agency steps by the light of a lantern. He tells Merritt to push on to the War Bonnet an' he'll head the Cheyennes off. Then he sends the Red Cloud interpreter an' four local Injuns with lead hosses to pack this information back to Merritt who's waitin' the word at the Rawhide Buttes. Bloojacket, for all he's done a hundred miles, declar's himse'f in on this second excursion to show the interpreter the way.

"'But you-all won't last through,' says Stanton, where he sets on the steps, quaffin' whiskey an' reinvig'ratin' himse'f.

"'Which if I don't, I'll turn squaw!' says Bloojacket, an' gettin' fresh hosses with the others he goes squanderin' off into the midnight.

"Son, them savages, havin' lead hosses, rides in on Merritt by fifth drink time or say, 'leven o'clock that mornin';—one hundred miles in 'leven hours! An' Bloojacket some wan an' weary for a savage is a-leadin' up the dance. Mighty fair ridin' that boy Bloojacket does! Two hundred miles in twenty-

three hours over a clost country ain't bad ! Which
it's me who says so: an' one time an' another I
shore shoves plenty of scenery onder the hoofs
of a cayouse myse'f.

"About the foogitive Cheyennes? Merritt moves
up to the War Bonnet like Stanton su'gests, corrals
'em, kills their ponies an' drives 'em back to the
agency on foot. Thar's nothin' so lets the whey
outen a hoss-back Injun like puttin' him a-foot: an
the Cheyennes settles down in sorrow an' peace
immediate.

"While Hardrobe an' his boy Bloojacket is with
me, I'm impressed partic'lar by the love they b'ars
each other. I never does cut the trail of a father
an' son who gives themse'fs up to one another like
this Hardrobe an' his Bloojacket boy. I can see
that Bloojacket regyards old Hardrobe like he's the
No'th Star ; an' as for Hardrobe himse'f, he can't
keep his eyes off that child of his. You'd have had
his life long before he'd let you touch a braid of
Bloojacket's long ha'r. Both of 'em's plenty handsome for Injuns ; tall an' lean an' quick as coyotes,
with hands an' feet as little as a woman's.

"While I don't go pryin' 'round this Hardrobe's
private affairs—savages is mighty sensitive of sech
matters—I learns, incidental, that Hardrobe is fair
rich. He's rich even for Osages ; an' they're as
opulent savages as ever makes a dance or dons
a feather. Later, I finds out that Hardrobe's
squaw—Bloojacket's mother—is dead.

"'See thar?' says Hardrobe one day. We're in

the southern border of the Osage country on the Grayhoss at the time, an' he p'ints to a heap of stones piled up like a oven an' chimley, an' about four foot high. I saveys thar's a defunct Osage inside. You-all will behold these little piles of burial stones on every knoll an' hill in the Osage country. 'See thar,' says this Hardrobe, p'intin'. 'That's my squaw. Mighty good squaw once; but heap dead now.'

"Then Hardrobe an' Bloojacket rides over an' fixes a little flag they've got in their war-bags to a pole which sticks up'ards outen this tomb, flyin' the ensign as Injuns allers does, upside down.

"It's six months later, mebby—an' it's now the hard luck begins—when I hears how Hardrobe weds a dance-hall girl over to Caldwell. This maiden's white; an' as beautiful as a flower an' as wicked as a trant'-ler. Hardrobe brings her to his ranch in the Osage country.

"The next tale I gets is that Bloojacket, likewise, becomes a victim to the p'isenous fasc'nations of this Caldwell dance-hall damsel, an' that him an' Hardrobe falls out; Hardrobe goin' on the warpath an' shootin' Bloojacket up a lot with a Winchester. He don't land the boy at that; Bloojacket gets away with a shattered arm. Also, the word goes that Hardrobe is still gunnin' for Bloojacket, the latter havin' gone onder cover some'ers by virchoo of the injured pinion.

"As Colonel Sterett says, these pore aborigines experiences bad luck the moment ever they takes to braidin' in their personal destinies with a pale-face. I don't blame 'em none neither. I sees this Caldwell seraph on one o'casion myse'f; she's shore a beauty! an' whenever she throws the lariat of her loveliness that a-way at a gent, she's due to fasten.

"It's a month followin' this division of the house of Hardrobe when I runs up on him in person. I encounters him in one of the little jim-crow restau-raws you-all finds now an' then in the Injun country. Hardrobe an' me shakes, an' then he camps down ag'in at a table where he's feedin' on fried antelope an' bakin' powder biscuit.

"I'm standin' at the counter across the room. Jest as I turns my back, thar's the *crack!* of a rifle to the r'ar of the j'int, an' Hardrobe pitches onto the floor as dead as ever transpires in that tribe. In the back door, with one arm in a sling, an' a gun that still smokes, ca'm an' onmoved like Injuns allers is, stands Bloojacket.

"'My hand is forced,' he says, as he passes me his gun; 'it's him or me! One of us wore the death-mark an' had to go.'

"'Couldn't you-all have gone with Crook ag'in?' I says. 'Which you don't have to infest this yere stretch of country. Thar's no hobbles or sidelines on you; none whatever!'

"Bloojacket makes no reply, an' his copper face gets expressionless an' inscrootable. I can see through, however; an' it's the hobbles of that Caldwell beauty's inflooence that's holdin' him.

"Bloojacket walks over to where Hardrobe's layin' dead an' straightens him round—laigs an' arms—an' places his big white cow hat over his face. Thar's no more sign of feelin', whether love or hate, in the eyes of Bloojacket while he performs these ceremonies than if Hardrobe's a roll of blankets. But thar's no disrespects neither; jest a great steadiness. When he has composed him out straight, Bloojacket looks at the remainder for mebby a minnte. Then he shakes his head.

"'He was a great man,' says Bloojacket, p'intin' at his dead father, with his good hand; 'thar's no more like him among the Osages.'

"Tharupon Bloojacket wheels on the half-breed who runs the deadfall an' who's standin' still an' scared, an' says:

"'How much does he owe?' Then he pays Hardrobe's charges for antelope steaks an' what chuck goes with it, an' at the close of these fiscal op'rations, remarks to the half-breed—who ain't sayin' no more'n he can he'p,—'Don't touch belt nor buckle on him; you-all knows me!' An' I can see that half-breed restauraw party is out to obey Bloojacket's mandates.

"Bloojacket gives himse'f up to the Osages an' is thrown loose on p'role. But Bloojacket never gets tried.

"A week rides by, an' he's standin' in front of the agency, sort o' makin' up some views concernin' his destinies. He's all alone; though forty foot off four Osage bucks is settin' together onder a cottonwood playin' Injun poker—the table bein' a red blanket spread on the grass,—for two bits a corner. These yere sports in their blankets an' feathers, an' rifflin' their greasy deck, ain't sayin' nothin to Bloojacket an' he ain't sayin' nothin' to them. Which jest the same these children of nacher don't like the idee of downin' your parent none, an' it's apparent Bloojacket's already half exiled.

" As he stands thar roominatin,' with the hot August sun beatin' down, thar's a atmosphere of sadness to go with Bloojacket. But you-all would have to guess at it ; his countenance is as ca'm as on that murderin' evenin' in the half-breed's restauraw.

" Bloojacket is still thar, an' the sports onder the cottonwood is still gruntin' joyously over their poker, when thar comes the patter of a bronco's hoofs. Thar's a small dust cloud, an' then up sweeps the Caldwell beauty. She comes to a pullup in front of Bloojacket. That savage glances up with a inquirin' eye an' the glance is as steady as the hills about him. The Caldwell beauty—it seems she disdains mournin'—is robed like a rainbow ; an' she an' Bloojacket, him standin', she on her bronco, looks each other over plenty intent.

" Which five minutes goes by if one goes by, an' thar the two stares into each other's eyes ; an' never a word. The poker bucks keeps on with their gamble over onder the cottonwood, an' no one looks at the two or seems like they heeds their existence. The poker savages is onto every move ; but they're

troo to the Injun idee of p'liteness an' won't inter-
fere with even so much as the treemor of a eyelash
with other folks's plays.

"Bloojacket an' the Caldwell beauty is still gazin'.
At last the Caldwell beauty's hand goes back, an'
slow an' shore, brings to the front a eight-inch six-
shooter. Bloojacket, with his eye still on her an'
never a flicker of feelin', don't speak or move.

"The Caldwell beauty smiles an' shows her white
teeth. Then she lays the gun across her left arm, an'
all as solid as a church. Her pony's gone to sleep
with his nose between his knees; an' the Caldwell
beauty settles herse'f in the saddle so's to be ready
for the plunge she knows is comin'. The Caldwell
beauty lays out her game as slow an' delib'rate as
trees; Bloojacket lookin' on with onwinkin' eye,
while the red-blanket bucks plays along an' never a
whisper of interest.

"'Which this yere pistol overshoots a bit, !' says
the Caldwell beauty, as she runs her eye along the
sights. 'I must aim low or I'll shore make ragged
work.'

"Bloojacket hears her, but offers no retort; he
stands moveless as a stachoo. Thar's a flash an'
a crash an' a cloud of bloo smoke; the aroused
bronco makes a standin' jump of twenty foot. The
Caldwell beauty keeps her saddle, an' with never
a swerve or curve goes whirlin' away up the brown,
burnt August trail. Bloojacket lays thar on his face;
an' thar's a bullet as squar' between the eyes as you-
all could set your finger-tip. Which he's dead—

dead without a motion, while the poker bucks
plays ca'mly on."

My venerable friend came to a full stop.   After a
respectful pause, I ventured an inquiry.

" And the Caldwell beauty ? " I said.

" It ain't a week when she's ag'in the star of that
Caldwell hurdygurdy where she ropes up Hardrobe
first.   Her laugh is as loud an' as' free, her beauty
as profoundly dazzlin' as before ; she swings through
twenty quadrilles in a evenin' from ' Bow-to-your-
partners '   to   ' All-take-a-drink-at-the-bar ' ;   an'   if
she's preyed on by them Osage tragedies you shore
can't tell it for whiskey, nor see it for powder an'
paint."

CHAPTER XX.

Colonel Coyote Clubbs,

"WHICH as a roole," said the Old Cattleman, " I speaks with deference an' yields respects to whatever finds its source in nacher, but this yere weather simply makes sech attitoode reedic'lous, an' any encomiums passed tharon would sound sarkastic." Here my friend waved a disgusted hand towards the rain-whipped panes and shook his head. "Thar's but one way to meet an' cope successful with a day like this," he ran on, " an' that is to put yourse'f in the hands of a joodicious barkeep—put yourse'f in his hands an' let him pull you through. Actin' on this idee I jest despatches my black boy Tom for a pitcher of peach an' honey, an', unless youall has better plans afoot, you might as well camp an' wait deevelopments, same as old man Wasson does when he's treed by the b'ar."

Promptly came the peach and honey, and with its appearance the pelting storm outside lost power to annoy. My companion beamingly did me honour in a full glass. After a moment fraught of silence and peach and honey, and possibly, too, from some notion of pleasing my host with a compliment, I said : "That gentleman with whom you were in converse last evening told me he never passed a more delightful hour than he spent listening to you. You recall whom I mean ? "

" Recall him ? Shore," retorted my friend as he recurrred to the pitcher for a second comforter. " You-all alloodes to the little gent who's lame in the nigh hind laig. He appeals to me, speshul, as he puts me in mind of old Colonel Coyote Clubbs who scares up Doc Peets that time. Old Coyote is lame same as this yere person."

" Frighten Peets !" I exclaimed, with a great air ; " you amaze me ! Give me the particulars."

" Why, of course," he replied, " I wouldn't be onderstood that Peets is terrorised outright. Still, old Colonel Coyote shore stampedes him an' forces Peets to fly. It's either *vamos* or shoot up pore Coyote ; an' as Peets couldn't do the latter, his only alternative is to go scatterin' as I states.

" This yere Coyote has a camp some ten miles to the no'th an' off to one side of the trail to Tucson. Old Coyote lives alone an' has built himse'f a dugout—a sort o' log hut that's half in an' half outen the ground. His mission on earth is to slay coyotes—' Wolfin' ' he calls it—for their pelts ; which Coyote gets a dollar each for the furs, an' the New York store which buys 'em tells Coyote to go as far as he likes. They stands eager to purchase all he can peel offen them anamiles.

" No ; Coyote don't shoot these yere little wolves; he p'isens 'em. Coyote would take about twelve foot, say, of a pine tree he's cut down—this yere timber is mebby eight inches through—an' he'll

bore in it a two-inch auger hole every two foot.
These holes is some deep ; about four inches it's
likely.   Old Coyote mixes his p'isen with beef tallow, biles them ingredients up together a lot, an' then,
while she's melted that a-way, he pours it into these
yere auger holes an' lets it cool.   It gets good an'
hard, this arsenic-tallow does, an' then Coyote
drags the timber thus reg'lated out onto the plains
to what he regyards as a elegible local'ty an' leaves
it for the wolves to come an' batten on.   Old Coyote will have as many as a dozen of these sticks of
timber, all bored an' framed up with arsenic-tallow,
scattered about.   Each mornin' while he's wolfin',
Coyote makes a round-up an' skins an' counts up
his prey.   An' son, you hear me ! he does a flour-
ishin' trade.

"Why don't Coyote p'isen hunks of meat you
asks ?   For obvious reasons.   In sech events the
victim bolts the piece of beef an' lopes off mebby
five miles before ever he succumbs.   With this
yere augur hole play it's different.   The wolf has
to lick the arsenic-tallow out with his tongue an' the
p'isen has time an' gets in its work.   That wolf sort o'
withers right thar in his tracks.   At the most he ain't
further away than the nearest water ; arsenic makin'
'em plenty thirsty, as you-all most likely knows.

" Old Coyote shows up in Wolfville about once
a month, packin' in his pelts an' freightin' over to
his wickeyup whatever in the way of grub he
reckons he needs.   Which, if you was ever to see
Coyote once, you would remember him.   He's shore

the most egreegious person, an' in appearance is a cross between a joke, a disaster an' a cur'osity. I don't reckon now pore Coyote ever sees the time when he weighs a hundred pound ; an' he's grizzled an' dried an' lame of one laig, while his face is like a squinch owl's face—kind o' wide-eyed an' with a expression of ignorant wonder, as if life is a never-endin' surprise party.

"Most likely now what fixes him firmest in your mind is, he don't drink none. He declines nosepaint in every form ; an' this yere abstinence, the same bein' yoonique in Wolfville, together with Coyote conductin' himse'f as the p'litest an' best-mannered gent to be met with in all of Arizona, is apt to introode on your attention. Colonel Sterett once mentions Coyote's manners.

"'Which he could give Chesterfield, Coyote could, kyards an' spades,' observes the Colonel. I don't, myse'f, know this Chesterfield none, but I can see by the fashion in which Colonel Sterett alloodes to him that he's a Kaintuckian an' a jo-darter on' manners an' etiquette.

"As I says, a pecooliar trait of Coyote is that he won't drink nothin' but water. Despite this blemish, however, when the camp gets so it knows him it can't he'p but like him a heap. He's so quiet an' honest an' ignorant an' little an' lame, an' so plumb p'lite besides, he grows on you. I can almost see the weasened old outlaw now as he comes rockin' into town with his six or seven burros packed to their y'ears with pelts !

"This time when Coyote puts Doc Peets in a toomult is when he's first pitched his dug-out camp an' begins to honour Wolfville with his visits. As yet none of us appreciates pore Coyote at his troo worth, an' on account of them guileless looks of his sech humourists as Dan Boggs an' Texas Thompson seizes on him as a source of merriment.

"It's Coyote's third expedition into town, an' he's hoverin' about the New York store waitin' for 'em to figger up his wolf pelts an' cut out his plunder so he freights it back to his dug-out. Dan an' Texas is also procrastinatin' 'round, an' they sidles up allowin' to have their little jest. Old Coyote don't know none of 'em—quiet an' sober an' p'lite like I relates, he's slow gettin' acquainted—an' Dan an' Texas, as well as Doc Peets, is like so many on-opened books to him. For that matter, while none of them pards of mine knows Coyote, they manages to gain a sidelight on some of his characteristics before ever they gets through. Doc Peets later grows ashamed of the part he plays, an' two months afterwards when Coyote is chewed an' clawed to a standstill by a infooriated badger which he mixes himse'f up with, Peets binds him up an' straightens out his game, an' declines all talk of recompense complete.

"'It's merely payin' for that outrage I attempts on your feelin's when you rebookes me so handsome,' says Peets, as he turns aside Coyote's *dinero* an' tells him to replace the same in his war-bags.

"However does Coyote get wrastled by that

badger? It's another yarn, but at least she's brief
an' so I'll let you have it. Badgers, you saveys, is
sour, sullen, an' lonesome. An' a badger's feelin's is
allers hurt about something; you never meets up
with him when he ain't hostile an' half-way bent for
war. Which it's the habit of these yere morose
badgers to spend a heap of their time settin' half in
an' half outen their holes, considerin' the scenery in
a dissatisfied way like they has some grudge ag'inst
it. An' if you approaches a badger while thus em-
ployed he tries to run a blazer on you; he'll show
his teeth an' stand pat like he meditates trouble.
When you've come up within thirty feet he changes
his mind an' disappears back'ard into his hole; but
all malignant an' reluctant.

"Now, while Coyote saveys wolves, he's a heap
dark on badgers that a-way. An' also thar's a
badger who lives clost to Coyote's dug-out. One
day while this yere ill-tempered anamile is cocked
up in the mouth of his hole, a blinkin' hatefully at
surroundin' objects, Coyote cuts down on him with
a Sharp's rifle he's got kickin' about his camp an'
turns that weepon loose.

"He misses the badger utter, but he don't know
it none. Comin' to the hole, Coyote sees the
badger kind o' quiled up at the first bend in the
burrow, an' he exultin'ly allows he's plugged him an'
tharupon reaches in to retrieve his game. That's
where Coyote makes the mistake of his c'reer;
that's where he drops his watermelon!

"That badger's alive an' onhurt an' as hot as a

lady who's lost money. Which he's simply retired
a few foot into his house to reconsider Coyote an'
that Sharp's rifle of his. Nacherally when the ontaught Coyote lays down on his face an' goes to
gropin' about to fetch that badger forth the latter
never hes'tates. He grabs Coyote's hand with tooth
and claw, braces his back ag'in the ceilin' of his
burrow an' stands pat.

"Badgers is big people an' strong as ponies too.
An' obdurate! Son, a badger is that decided an'
set in his way that sech feather-blown things as
hills is excitable an' vacillatin' by comparison. This
yere partic'lar badger has the fam'ly weaknesses
fully deeveloped, an' the moment he cinches onto
Coyote, he shore makes up his mind never to let go
ag'in in this world nor the next.

"As I tells you, Coyote is little an' weak, an' he
can no more move that hardened badger, nor yet
fetch himse'f loose, than he can sprout wings an'
soar. That badger's got Coyote; thar he holds him
prone an' flat ag'in the ground for hours. An' at
last Coyote swoons away.

"Which he'd shore petered right thar, a prey to
badgers, if it ain't for a cowpuncher—he's one of
Old Man Enright's riders—who comes romancin'
along an' is attracted to the spot by some cattle
who's prancin' an' waltzin' about, sizin' Coyote up
as he's layin' thar, an' snortin' an' curvin' their tails
in wonder at the spectacle. Which the visitin' cow
sharp, seein' how matters is headed, shoves his six-
shooter in alongside of Coyote's arm, drills this be-

sotted badger, an' Coyote is saved. It's a case of touch an' go at that. But to caper back to where we leaves Dan an' Texas on the verge of them jocyoolarities.

" ' No, gentlemen,' Coyote is sayin', in response to some queries of Dan an' Texas ; ' I've wandered hither an' yon a heap in my time, an' now I has my dug-out done, an' seein' wolves is oncommon plenty, I allows I puts in what few declinin' days remains to me right where I be. I must say, too, I'm pleased with Wolfville an' regyards myse'f as fortunate an' proud to be a neighbour to sech excellent folks as you-all."

" 'Which I'm shore sorry a lot,' says Dan, 'to hear you speak as you does. Thar's a rapacious sport about yere who the instant he finds how you makes them dug-out improvements sends on an' wins out a gov'ment patent an' takes title to that identical quarter-section which embraces your camp. Now he's allowin' to go squanderin' over to Tucson an' get a docyment or two from the jedge an' run you out.'

" Son, this pore innocent Coyote takes in Dan's fictions like so much spring water ; he believes 'em utter. But the wonder is to see how he changes. He don't say nothin', but his eyes sort o' sparks up an' his face gets as gray as his ha'r. It's now that Doc Peets comes along.

" 'Yere is this devourin' scoundrel now,' says Texas Thompson, p'intin' to Peets. 'You-all had better talk to him some about it.' Then turnin' to

Peets with a wink, Texas goes on : 'Me an' Mister
Boggs is tellin' our friend how you gets a title to
that land he's camped on, an' that you allows you'll
take possession mebby next week.'

"'Why, shore,' says Peets, enterin' into the
sperit of the hoax, an' deemin' it a splendid joke;
'be you-all the maverick who's on that quarter-
section of mine ? '

"'Which I'm Colonel Coyote Clubbs,' says
Coyote, bowin' low while his lips trembles, 'an' I'm
at your service.'

"'Well,' says Peets, 'it don't make much difference about your name, all you has to do is hit the
trail. I needs that location you've done squatted
on because of the water.'

"'An' do I onderstand, sir,' says Coyote some
agitated, 'that you'll come with off'cers to put me
outen my dug-out ? '

"'Shore,' says Peets, in a case-hardened, pitiless
tone, 'an' why not? Am I to be debarred of my
rights by some coyote-slaughterin' invader an' on-
murmurin'ly accede tharto ? Which I should shore
say otherwise.'

"'Then I yereby warns you, sir,' says Coyote,
gettin' pale as paper. 'I advises you to bring your
coffin when you comes for that land, for I'll down
you the moment you're in range.'

"'In which case,' says Peets, assoomin' airs of
blood-thirsty trucyoolence, 'thar's scant use to wait.
If thar's goin' to be any powder burnin' we might
better burn it now.'

"'I've no weepon, sir,' says Coyote, limpin' about in a circle, 'but if ary of these gentlemen will favour me with a gun I'll admire to put myse'f in your way.'

"Which the appearance of Coyote when he utters this, an' him showin' on the surface about as war-like as a prairie-dog, convulses Dan an' Texas. It's all they can do to keep a grave front while pore Coyote in his ignorance calls the bluff of one of the most deadly an' gamest gents who ever crosses the Missouri—one who for nerve an' finish is a even break with Cherokee Hall.

"'Follow-me,' says Peets, frownin' on Coyote like a thunder cloud; 'I'll equip you with a weepon myse'f. I reckons now that your death an' deestruction that a-way is after all the best trail out.

"Peets moves off a heap haughty, an' Coyote limps after him. Peets goes over where his rooms is at. 'Take a cha'r,' says Peets, as they walks in, an' Coyote camps down stiffly in a seat. Peets crosses to a rack an' searches down a 8-inch Colt's. Then he turns towards Coyote. 'This yere dis-covery annoys me,' says Peets, an' his words comes cold as ice, 'but now we're assembled, I finds that I've only got one gun.'

"'Well, sir,' says Coyote, gettin' up an' limpin' about in his nervous way, his face workin' an' the sparks in his eyes beginnin' to leap into flames; 'well, sir, may I ask what you aims to propose?'

"'I proposes to beef you right yere,' says Peets, as f'rocious as a grizzly. 'Die, you miscreant!' An'

Peets throws the gun on Coyote, the big muzzle not a foot from his heart.

"Peets, as well as Dan an' Texas, who's enjoyin' the comedy through a window, ondoubted looks for Coyote to wilt without a sigh. An' if he had done so, the joke would have been both excellent an' complete. But Coyote never wilts. He moves so quick no one ever does locate the darkened recess of his garments from which he lugs out that knife; the first p'inter any of 'em gets is that with the same breath wherein Peets puts the six-shooter on him, Coyote's organised in full with a bowie.

" ' Make a centre shot, you villyun ! ' roars Coyote, an' straight as adders he la'nches himse'f at Peets's neck.

"Son, it's the first an' last time that Doc Peets ever runs. An' he don't run now, he flies. Peets comes pourin' through the door an' into the street, with Coyote frothin' after him not a yard to spar'. The best thing about the whole play is that Coyote's a cripple; it's this yere element of lameness that lets Peets out. He can run thirty foot to Coyote's one, an' the result occurs in safety by the breadth of a ha'r.

"It takes two hours to explain to Coyote that this eepisode is humour, an' to ca'm him an' get his emotions bedded down. At last, yoonited Wolfville succeeds in beatin' the trooth into him, an' he permits Peets to approach an' apol'gise.

" ' An' you can gamble all the wolves you'll ever kill an' skin,' says Doc Peets, as he asks Coyote to forgive an' forget, ' that this yere is the last time I embarks in jests of a practical character or gives way to humour other than the strickly oral kind. Barkeep, my venerated friend, yere will have a glass of water; but you give me Valley Tan.' "

CHAPTER XXI.

Long Ago on the Rio Grande.

"WHICH books that a-way," observed the Old Cattleman, "that is, story-books, is onfrequent in Wolfville." He was curiously examining Stevenson's "Treasure Island," that he had taken from my hand. "The nearest approach to a Wolfville cirk'latin' library I recalls is a copy of 'Robinson Crusoe,' an' that don't last long, as one time when Texas Thompson leaves it layin' on a cha'r outside while he enters the Red Light for the usual purpose, a burro who's loafin' loose about the street, smells it, tastes it, approoves of it, an' tharupon devours it a heap. After that I don't notice no volumes in the outfit, onless it's some drug books that Doc Peets has hived over where he camps. It's jest as well, for seein' a gent perusin' a book that a-way, operates frequent to make Dan Boggs gloomy; him bein' oneddicated like I imparts to you-all yeretofore.

"Whatever do we do for amoosements? We visits the Dance Hall; not to dance, sech frivol'ties bein' for younger an' less dignified sports. We goes over thar more to give our countenance an' endorsements to Hamilton who runs the hurdy-gurdy, an' who's a mighty proper citizen. We says

' How!' to Hamilton, libates, an' mebby watches
'em 'balance all,' or 'swing your partners,' a minute
or two an' then proceeds.   Then thar's Huggins's
Bird Cage Op'ry House, an' now an' then we-all
floats over thar an' takes in the dramy.   But mostly
we camps about the Red Light; the same bein'
a common stampin'-ground.   It's thar we find each
other; an' when thar's nothin' doin', we upholds
the hours tellin' tales an' gossipin' about cattle an'
killin's, an' other topics common to a cow country.
Now an' then, thar's a visitin' gent in town who
can onfold a story.   In sech event he's made a
lot of, an' becomes promptly the star of the
evenin'.

"Thar's a Major Sayres we meets up with once
in Wolfville,—he's thar on cattle matters with old
man Enright—an' I recalls how he grows absorbin'
touchin' some of his adventures in that War.

"Thar's a passel of us, consistin' of Boggs, Tutt,
Cherokee, an' Texas Thompson, an' me, who's
projectin' 'round the Red Light when Enright
introdooces this Major Sayres.   Him an' Enright's
been chargin' about over by the Cow Springs an'
has jest rode in.   This Major is easy an' friendly,
an' it ain't longer than the third drink before he
shows symptoms of bein' willin' to talk.

" ' Which I ain't been in the saddle so long,' says
the Major, while him an' Enright is considerin' how
far they goes since sunup, ' since Mister Lee surrenders.'

" ' You takes your part, Major,' says Enright,

who's ropin' for a reminiscence that a-way, 'in the battles of the late war, I believes.'

" 'I should shorely say so,' says the Major. 'I'm twenty-two years old, come next grass, when Texas asserts herse'f as part of the confed'racy, an' I picks up a hand an' plays it in common with the other patriotic yooths of my region. Yes, I enters the artillery, but bein' as we don't have no cannon none at the jump I gets detailed as a aide ontil something resemblin' a battery comes pokin' along. I goes through that carnage from soup to nuts, an' while I'm shot up some as days go by, it's allers been a source of felic'tation to me, personal, that I never slays no man myse'f. Shore, I orders my battery to fire, later when I gets a battery; an' ondoubted the bombardments I inaug'rates adds to an' swells the ghost census right aloug. But of my own hand it's ever been a matter of congratoolations to me that I don't down nobody an' never takes a skelp.

" 'As I turns the leaves of days that's gone I don't now remember but one individyooal openin' for blood that ever presents itse'f. An' after con- siderin' the case in all its b'arin's, I refooses the opportunity an' the chance goes glidin' by. As a result thar's probably one more Yank than other- wise; an' now that peace is yere an' we-all is earn- estly settlin' to be brothers No'th and South, I regyards that extra Yank as a advantage. Shore, he's a commoonal asset.'

" 'Tell us how you fails to c'llect this Yankee, Major,' says Faro Nell : ' which I'm plumb interested every time that some one don't get killed.'

"'I reecounts that exploit with pleasure,' says the Major, bowin' p'lite as Noo Orleans first circles an' touchin' his hat to Nell.' 'It's one day when we're in a fight. The line of battle is mebby stretched out half a mile. As I su'gests, I'm spraddlin' 'round permiscus with no stated arena of effort, carryin' despatches an' turnin' in at anything that offers, as handy as I can. I'm sent final with a dispatch from the left to the extreme right of our lines.

"'When we goes into this skrimmage we jumps the Lincoln people somewhat onexpected. They has their blankets an' knapsacks on, an' as they frames themse'fs up for the struggle they casts off this yere baggage, an' thar it lays, a windrow of knapsacks, blankets an' haversacks, mighty near a half mile in length across the plain. As we-all rebs has been pushin' the Yankees back a lot, this windrow is now to our r'ar, an' I goes canterin' along it on my mission to the far right.

"'Without a word of warnin' a Yank leaps up from where he's been burrowin' down among this plunder an' snaps a Enfield rifle in my face. I pulls my hoss back so he's almost settin' on his hocks; an' between us, gents, that onexpected sortie comes mighty near surprisin' me plumb out of the saddle. But the Enfield don't go off none; an' with that the Yank throws her down an' starts to run. He shorely does *vamos* with the velocity of jackrabbits!

"'As soon as me an' my hoss recovers our composure we gives chase. Bein' the pore Yank is afoot, I runs onto him in the first two hundred yards. As I comes up, I've got my six-shooter in my hand. I puts the muzzle on him, sort o' p'intin' between the shoulders for gen'ral results ; but when it comes to onhookin' my weepon I jest can't turn the trick. It's too much like murder. Meanwhile, the flyin' Yank is stampedin' along like he ain't got a thing on his mind an' never turnin' his head.

" 'I calls on him to surrender. He makes a roode remark over his shoulder at this military manoover an' pelts ahead all onabated. Then I evolves a scheme to whack him on the head with my gun. I pushes my hoss up ontil his nose is right by that No'thern party's y'ear. Steadyin' myse'f, I makes a wallop at him an' misses. I invests so much soul in the blow that missin' that a-way, I comes within' a ace of clubs of goin' off my hoss an' onto my head. An' still that exasperatin' Yank goes rackin' along, an' if anything some faster than before. At that I begins to lose my temper ag'in.

" ' I reorganises,—for at the time I nearly makes the dive outen the stirrups, I pulls the hoss to a stop,—an' once more takes up the pursoot of my locoed prey. He's a pris'ner fair enough, only he's too obstinate to admit it. As I closes on him ag'in, I starts for the second time to drill him, but I can't make the landin'. I'm too young ; my heart ain't hard enough ; I rides along by him for a bit an' for the second time su'gests that he surrender. The Yank ignores me ; he keeps on runnin'.

"'Which sech conduct baffles me! It's absolootely ag'in military law. By every roole of the
game that Yank's my captive; but defyin' restraint
he goes caperin' on like he's free.

"'As I gallops along about four foot to his r'ar
I confess I begins to feel a heap he'pless about him.
I'm too tender to shoot, an' he won't stop, an' thar
we be.

"'While I'm keepin' him company on this retreat, I reflects that even if I downs him, the war
would go on jest the same; it wouldn't stop the
rebellion none, nor gain the South her independence.
The more I considers, too, the war looks bigger an'
the life of this flyin' Yank looks smaller, Likewise,
it occurs to me that he's headed no'th. If he keeps
up his gait an' don't turn or twist he'll have quitted
Southern territory by the end of the week.

"'After makin' a complete round-up of the sityooation I begins to lose interest in this Yank; an'
at last I leaves him, racin' along alone. By way of
stim'lant, as I pauses I cracks off a couple of loads
outen my six-shooter into the air. They has a excellent effect; from the jump the Yank makes at
the sound I can see the shots puts ten miles more
run into him shore. He keeps up his gallop ontil
he's out of sight, an' I never after feasts my eyes on
him.

"'Which I regyards your conduct, Major, as
mighty hoomane,' says Dan Boggs, raisin' his glass
p'litely. 'I approves of it, partic'lar.'

"The Major meets Dan's attentions in the sperit

they're proposed. After a moment Enright speaks
of them cannons.

"But you-all got a battery final, Major?' says
Enright.

"'Six brass guns,' says the Major, an' his gray
eyes beams an' he speaks of 'em like they was six
beautiful women. 'Six brass guns, they be,' he
says. 'We captured 'em from the enemy an' I'm
put in command. Gents, I've witnessed some suc-
cesses personal, but I never sees the day when I'm
as satisfied an' as contentedly proud as when I finds
myse'f in command of them six brass guns. I was
like a lover to every one of 'em.

"' I'm that headlong to get action—we're in
middle Loosiana at the time—that I hauls a couple
of 'em over by the Mississippi an' goes prowlin'
'round ontil I pulls on trouble with a little Yankee
gun boat. It lasts two hours, an' I shore sinks that
naval outfit an' piles the old Mississippi on top of
'em. I'm so puffed up with this yere exploit that
a pigeon looks all sunk in an' consumptif beside me.

"' Thar's one feacher of this dooel with the little
gun boat which displeases me, however. Old Butler's got Noo Orleans at the time, an' among other
things he's editin' the papers. I reads in one of 'em
a month later about me sinkin' that scow. It says
I'm a barb'rous villain, the story does, an' shoots
up the boat after it surrenders, an' old Butler allows
he'll hang me a whole lot the moment ever he gets
them remarkable eyes onto me. I don't care none
at the time much, only I resents this yere charge.

I shore never fires a shot at that gunboat after it gives up; I ain't so opulent of amm'nition as all that. As time goes on, howevej, thar's a day when I'm goin' to take the determination of old Butler more to heart.

"'Followin' the gun-boat eepisode I'm more locoed than ever to get my battery into a fight. An' at last I has my hopes entirely fulfilled. It's about four o'clock one evenin' when we caroms on about three brigades of Yanks. Thar's mebby twelve thousand of us rebs an' all of fourteen thousand of the Lincoln people. My battery is all the big guns we-all has, while said Yanks is strong with six full batteries.

"'The battle opens up; we're on a old sugar plantation, an' after manooverin' about a while we settles down to work. It's that day I has my dreams of carnage realised in full. I turns loose my six guns with verve an' fervour, an' it ain't time for a second drink before I attracts the warmest attention from 'every one of the Yankee batteries. She's shore a scandal the way them gents in bloo does shoot me up! Jest to give you-all a idee: the Yankees slams away at me for twenty minutes; they dismounts two of my guns; they kills or creases forty of my sixty-six men; an' when they gets through you-all could plant cotton where my battery stands, it's that ploughed up.

"'It's in the midst of the *baile*, an' I'm standin' near my number-one gun. Thar's a man comes up with a cartridge. A piece of a shell t'ars him

open, an' he falls across the gun, limp as a towel,
an' then onto the ground. I orders a party named
Williams to the place. Something comes flyin'
down outen the heavens above an' smites Williams
on top the head ; an' he's gone. I orders up another. He assoomes the responsibilities of this
p'sition jest in time to get a rifle bullet through
the jaw. He lives though; I sees him after
the war.

" ' As thar's no more men for the place, I steps
for'ard myse'f. I'm not thar a minute when I sinks
down to the ground. I don't feel nothin' an' can't
make it out.

" ' While I'm revolvin' this yere phenomenon of
me wiltin' that a-way' an' tryin to form some opinions about it, thar's a explosion like forty battles
all in one. For a moment, I reckons that somehow
we-all has opened up a volcano inadvertent, an' that
from now on Loosiana can boast a Hecla of her own
But it ain't no volcano. It's my ammunition waggons
which with two thousund rounds is standin' about
one hundred yards to my r'ar. The Yanks done
blows up the whole outfit with one of their shells.

" ' It's strictly the thing, however, which lets my
battery out. The thick smoke of the two thousand
cartridges drifts down an' blankets what's left of us
like a fog. The Yanks quits us; they allows most
likely they've lifted me an' my six brass guns plumb
off the earth. Thar's some roodiments of trooth
in the theery for that matter.

" ' These last interestin' details sort o' all happens

at once. I've jest dropped at the time when my
ammunition waggons enters into the sperit of the
o'casion like I describes. As I lays thar one of my
men comes gropin' along down to me in the
smoke.

"'" Be you hurt, Major? " he says.

"'" I don't know," I replies: " my idee is that
you better investigate an' see."

"' He t'ars open my coat; thar's no blood on my
shirt. He lifts one arm an' then the other; they're
sound as gold pieces. Then I lifts up my left laig ;
I've got on high hoss-man boots.

"'" Pull off this moccasin," I says.

"' He pulls her off an' thar's nothin' the matter
thar. I breaks out into a profoose sweat ; gents,
I'm scared speechless. I begins to fear I ain't
plugged at all ; that I've fainted away on a field of
battle an' doo to become the scandal of two armies.
I never feels so weak an' sick !

"' I've got one chance left an' trembles as I plays
it ; I lifts up my right boot. I win ; about a quart
of blood runs out. Talk of reprievin' folks who's
sentenced to death ! Gents, their emotions is only
imitations of what I feels when I finds that the
Yanks done got me an' nary doubt. It's all right—
a rifle bullet through my ankle !

"' That night I'm mowed away, with twenty other
wounded folks, in a little cabin off to one side, an'
thar's a couple of doctors sizin' up my laig.

"'" Joe," says one, that a-way, " we've got to cut
it off."

" 'But I votes " no" emphatic ; I'm too young to talk about goin shy a laig. With that they ties it up as well as ever they can, warnin' me meanwhile that I've got about one chance in a score to beat the game. Then they imparts a piece of news that's a mighty sight worse than my laig.

" ' " Joe," says this doctor, when he's got me bandaged, " our army's got to rustle out of yere a whole lot, She's on the retreat right now. Them Yanks outheld us an' out-played us an' we've got to go stampedin'. The worst is, thar's no way to take you along, an' we'll have to leave you behind."

" ' " Then the Yanks will corral me ? " I asks.

" ' " Shore," he replies, " but thar's nothin' else for it."

" ' It's then it comes on me about that gunboat an' the promises old Butler makes himse'f about hangin' me when caught. Which these yere reflections infooses new life into me. I makes the doctor who's talkin' go rummagin' about ontil he rounds up a old nigger daddy, a mule an' a twowheel sugar kyart. It's rainin' by now so's you-all could stand an' wash your face an' hands in it. As that medical sharp loads me in, he gives me a bottle of this yere morphine, an' between jolts an' groans I feeds on said drug until mornin'.'

" ' That old black daddy is dead game, He drives me all night an' all day an' all night ag'n, an' I'm in Shreveport ; my ankle's about the size of a bale of cotton. Thar's one ray through it all, however; I

misses meetin' old man Butler an' I looks on that
as a triumph which shore borders on relief.'

"'An' I reckons now,' says Dan Boggs, 'you
severs your relations with the war?'

"'No,' goes on the Major; 'I keeps up my voylence to the close. When I grows robust enough
to ride ag'in I'm in Texas. Thar's a expedition
fittin' out to invade an' subdoo Noo Mexico, an' I
j'ines dogs with it as chief of the big guns. Thar's
thirty-eight hundred bold and buoyant sperits rides
outen Austin on these military experiments we
plans, an' as evincin' the luck we has, I need only
to p'int out that nine months later we returns with
a scant eight hundred. Three thousand of 'em
killed, wounded an' missin' shows that efforts to
list the trip onder the head of "picnics" would be
irony.

"'Comin', as we-all does, from one thousand miles
away, thar ain't one of us who saveys, practical, as
much about the sand-blown desert regions we invades as we does of what goes on in the moon.
That Gen'ral Canby, who later gets downed by the
Modocs, is on the Rio Grande at Fort Craig. While
we're pirootin' about in a blind sort o' fashion we
ropes up one of Canby's couriers who's p'intin'
no'th for Fort Union with despatches. This Gen'ral
Canby makes the followin' facetious alloosion: After mentionin' our oninvited presence in the territory, he says:

"'"But let 'em alone. We'll dig the potatoes
when they're ripe."

"'Gents, we was the toobers!' An' yere the Major pauses for a drink. 'We was the potatoes which Canby's exultin' over! We don't onder-stand it at the time, but it gets cl'arer as the days drifts by.

"'I'm never in a more desolate stretch of what would be timber only thar ain't no trees. Thar's nothin' for the mules an' hosses; half the time thar ain't even water. An' then it's alkali. An' our days teems an' staggers with disgustin' experiences. Once we're shy water two days. It's the third day about fourth drink time in the evenin'. The sun has two hours yet to go. My battery is toilin' along, sand to the hubs of gun-carriages an' caissons, when I sees the mules p'int their y'ears for'ard with looks of happy surprise. Then the intelligent ana-miles begins a song of praise; an' next while we-all is marvellin' thereat an' before ever a gent can stretch hand to bridle to stop 'em, the mules begins to fly. They yanks my field pieces over the desert as busy an' full of patriotic ardour as a drunkard on 'lection day. The whole battery runs away. Gents, the mules smells water. It's two miles away,—a big pond she is,—an' that locoed battery never stops, but rushes plumb in over its y'ears; an' I lose sixteen mules an' two guns before ever I'm safe ag'in on terry firmy.

"'It's shore remarkable,' exclaims the Major, settin' down his glass, 'how time softens the view an' changes bitter to sweet that a-way. As I brings before me in review said details thar's nothin' more

harassin' from soda to hock than that campaign on
the Rio Grande. Thar's not one ray of sunshine to
paint a streak of gold in the picture from frame to
frame; all is dark an' gloom an' death. An' yet,
lookin' back'ard through the years, the mem'ry of
it is pleasant an' refreshin', a heap more so than
enterprises of greater ease with success instead of
failure for the finish.

"'Thar's one partic'lar incident of this explorin'
expeditions into Noo Mexico which never recurs to
my mind without leavin' my eyes some dim. I
don't claim to be no expert on pathos an' I'm far
from regyardin' myse'f as a sharp on tears, but
thar's folks who sort o' makes sadness a speshulty,
women folks lots of 'em, who allows that what I'm
about to recount possesses pecooliar elements of
sorrow.

"'Thar's a young captain—he ain't more'n a boy
—who's brought a troop of lancers along with us.
This boy Captain hails from some'ers up 'round
Waco, an' thar ain't a handsomer or braver in all
Pres'dent Davis's army. This Captain—whose
name is Edson,— an' me, bein' we-all is both young,
works ourse'fs into a clost friendship for each other;
I feels about him like he's my brother. Nacherally,
over a camp fire an' mebby a stray bottle an' a
piece of roast antelope, him an' me confides about
ourse'fs. This Captain Edson back in Waco has
got a old widow mother who's some rich for Texas,
an' also thar's a sweetheart he aims to marry when
the war's over an' done. I reckons him an' me

talks of that mother an' sweetheart of his a hundred times.

"'It falls out that where we fords the Pecos we
runs up on a Mexican Plaza—the "Plaza Chico"
they-all calls it—an' we camps thar by the river a
week, givin' our cattle a chance to roll an' recooper-
ate up on the grass an' water.

"'Then we goes p'intin' out for the settin' sun
ag'in, allowin' to strike the Rio Grande some'ers
below Albuquerque. Captain Edson, while we're
pesterin' 'round at the Plaza Chico, attaches to his
retinoo a Mexican boy; an' as our boogles begins
to sing an' we lines out for that west'ard push, this
yere boy rides along with Edson an' the lancers.

"'Our old war chief who has charge of our wanderin's is strictly stern an' hard. An' I reckons
now he's the last gent to go makin' soft allowances
for any warmth of yooth, or puttin' up with any
'primrose paths of gentle dalliance,' of any an' all
who ever buckles on a set of side arms. It thus
befalls that when he discovers on the mornin' of
the second day that this Mexican boy is a Mexican
girl, he goes ragin' into the ambient air like a eagle.

"'The Old Man claps Edson onder arrest an'
commands the girl to saddle up an' go streakin' for
the Plaza Chico. As it's only a slow day's march
an' as these Mexicans knows the country like a
coyote, it's a cinch the girl meets no harm an' runs
no resks. But it serves to plant the thorns of
wrath in the heart of Captain Edson.

"'The Old Man makes him loose an' gives him

back his lancers before ever we rides half a day,
but it don't work no mollifications with the young
Captain. He offers no remarks, bein' too good a
soldier ; but he never speaks to the Old Man no
more, except it's business.

"'"Joe," he says to me, as we rides along, or
mebby after we're in camp at night, " I'll never go
back to Texas. I've been disgraced at the head of
my troop an' I'll take no sech record home."

"'"You oughter not talk that a-way, Ed," I'd
say, tryin' to get his sensibilities smoothed down.
"If you don't care none for yourse'f or for your
footure, you-all should remember thar's something
comin' to the loved ones at home. Moreover, it's
weak sayin' you-all ain't goin' back to Texas. How
be you goin' to he'p it, onless you piles up shore-
enough disgrace by desertin' them lancers of
yours? "

"'"Which if we has the luck," says this Captain
Edson, "to cross up with any Yanks who's capable
of aimin' low an' shootin' half way troo, I'll find a
way to dodge that goin' back without desertin'.' "

"' No, I don't make no argyments with him ; it's
hopeless talkin' to a gent who's melancholly an'
who's pride's been jarred ; thar's nothing but time
can fix things up for him. An' I allers allows that
this boy Captain would have emerged from the
clouds eventooal, only it happens he don't get the
time. His chance comes too soon ; an' he shore
plays it desperate.

"' Our first offishul act after reachin' the Rio

Grande is to lay for a passel of Yank cavalry—
thar's two thousand of 'em I reckons. We rides
up on these yere lively persons as we sounds a halt
for the evenin'. It looks like our boogles is a
summons, for they comes buttin' into view through
a dry arroya an' out onto the wide green bottoms of
the Rio Grande at the first call. They're about a
mile away, an' at sight of us they begins in a
fashion of idle indifference to throw out a line of
battle. They fights on foot, them bloo folks do;
dismountin', with every fourth man to hold the
hosses. They displays a heap of insolence for
nothin' but cavalry an' no big guns; but as they
fights like infantry an' is armed with Spencer seven-
shooters besides, the play ain't so owdacious
neither.

"'Thar's mebby a hour of sun an' I'm feelin'
mighty surly as I gets my battery into line. I'm
disgusted to think we've got to fight for our night's
camp, an' swearin' to myse'f in a low tone, so's
not to set profane examples to my men, at the idee
that these yere Yanks is that preecip'tate they can't
wait till mornin' for their war-jig. But I can't he'p
myse'f. That proverb about it takin' two to make
a fight is all a bluff. It only takes one to make a
fight. As far as we-all rebs is concerned that evenin' we ain't honin' for trouble, leastwise, not ontil
mornin'; but them inordinate Yanks will have it,
an' thar you be. The fight can't be postponed.

"'Thar's no tumblin' hurry about how any of us
goes to work. Both sides has got old at the game

an' war ain't the novelty she is once. The Yanks
is takin' their p'sition, an' we're locatin' our lines
an' all as ca'mly an' with no more excitement than
if it's dress p'rade. The Yanks is from Colorado.
My sergeant speaks of 'em to me the next day an'
gives his opinion touchin' their merits.

" ' " Where did you say them Yankees comes from,
Major? " says my serjeant.

" ' " Colorado," I replies.

" ' " Which thar's about thirty minutes last evenin'," says my serjeant, " when I shorely thinks they're
recrooted in hell," an' my serjeant shakes his head.

" ' While I'm linin' up my battery mighty discon-
tented an' disgruntled, an orderly pulls my sleeve.

" ' " Look thar, Major ! " he says.

" ' I turns, an' thar over on our right, all alone,
goes Captain Edson an' his lancers. Without
waitin', an' without commands, Captain Edson has
his boogler sound a charge ; an' thar goes the
lancers stampedin' along like they're a army corps
an' cap'ble of sweepin' the two thousand cool an'
c'llected Yankees off the Rio Grande.

" ' For a moment all we does is stand an' look ;
the surprise of it leaves no idee of action. The
lancers swings across the grassy levels. Thar's not a
shot fired ; Edson's people ain't got nothin' but them
reedic'lous spears, an' the Yanks, who seems to
know it, stands like the rest of us without firin' an'
watches 'em come. It's like a picture, with the thin
bright air an' the settin' sun shinin' sideways over
the gray line of mountains fifty miles to the west.

"'I never sees folks more placid than the Yanks an' at the same time so plumb alert. Mountain lions is lethargic to 'em. When Captain Edson an' his lancers charges into 'em the Yanks opens right an' left, each sharp of 'em gettin' outen the way of that partic'lar lancer who's tryin' to spear him; but all in a steady, onruffled fashion that's as threatenin' as it is excellent. The lancers, with Captain Edson, goes through, full charge, twenty rods to the r'ar of the Yankee line. An', gents, never a man comes back.

"'As Edson an' his troop goes through, the Yanks turns an' opens on 'em. The voices of the Spencers sounds like the longroll of a drum. Hoss an' man goes down, dead an' wounded; never a gent of 'em all rides back through that awful Yankee line. Pore Edson shore has his wish; he's cut the trail of folks who's cap'ble of aimin' low an' shootin' half way troo.

"'These sperited moves I've been relatin' don't take no time in the doin'. The hairbrain play of Captain Edson forces our hands. The Old Man orders a charge, an' we pushes the Yanks back onto their hosses an' rescoos what's left of Edson an' his lancers. After skirmishin' a little the Yanks draws away an' leaves us alone on the field. They earns the encomiums of my serjeant, though, before ever they decides to *vamos*.

"'Edson's been shot hard and frequent; thar's no chance for him. He looks up at me, when we're bringin' him off, an' says:

"'"Joe," an' he smiles an' squeezes my hand, while his tones is plenty feeble, "Joe, you notes don't you that while I ain't goin' back to Texas, I don't have to desert."

"'That night we beds down our boy Captain in a sol'tary Mexican 'doby. He's layin' on a pile of blankets clost by the door while the moon shines down an' makes things light as noonday. He's been talkin' to me an' givin' me messages for his mother an' the rest of his outfit at Waco, an' I promises to carry 'em safe an' deliver 'em when I rides in ag'in on good old Texas. Then he wants his mare brought up where he can pet her muzzle an' say *Adios* to her.

"'"For, Joe," he says, "I'm doo to go at once now, an' my days is down to minutes."

"'"The medicine man, Ed," I says, "tells me that you-all has hours to live."

"'"But, Joe," he replies, "I knows. I'm a mighty good prophet you recalls about my not goin' back, an' you can gamble I'm not makin' any mistakes now. It's down to minutes, I tells you, an' I wants to see my mare."

"'Which the mare is brought up an' stands thar with her velvet nose in his face; her name's "Ruth," after Edson's sweetheart. The mare is as splendid as a picture; pure blood, an' her speed an' bottom is the wonder of the army. Usual a hoss is locoed by the smell of blood, but it don't stampede this Ruth; an' she stays thar with him as still an' tender as a woman, an' with all the sorrow in her heart of folks. As Edson rubs her nose with his weak hand an' pets her, he asks me to take this Ruth back to his sweetheart with all his love.

"'"Which now I'm goin'," he whispers, "no one's to mention that eepisode of the Pecos an' the little Mexican girl of Plaza Chico!"

"'Edson is still a moment; an' then after sayin' "Good-by," he lets on that he desires me to leave him alone with the mare.

"'"I'll give Ruth yere a kiss an' a extra message for my sweetheart," he says, "an' then I'll sleep some."

"'I camps down outside the 'doby an' looks up at the moon an' begins to let my own thoughts go grazin' off towards Texas. It's perhaps a minute when thar's the quick *crack!* of a six-shooter, an' the mare Ruth r'ars up an' back'ard ontil she's almost down. But she recovers herse'f an' stands sweatin' an' shiverin' an' her eyes burnin' like she sees a ghost. Shore, it's over; pore Edson won't wait; he's got to his guns, an' thar's a bullet through his head.'"

THE END.